**Completely Caroline**

Virginia is for Lovers Series, Book 2

By K.C. O'Neill

Completely Caroline

First Printing, 2017

ISBN 978-1-943010-04-2

Cover design by Indie Solutions

This one is for anyone who's ever dared to dream.

In the immortal words of Shia LaBeouf:
"Don't let your dreams be dreams.  Just DO IT!

Chapter One

# Caroline

THERE ARE MOMENTS IN LIFE when you realize that everything that comes next will be different from what came before. That *everything* is about to change. And then there are moments when you suddenly realize that, for all of life's many changes, some things will always stay the same.

You could see this from a grand perspective — a circle-of-life type of point-of-view: We are born, we grow up, we die. The End. Or, you can look at the little things.

There will always be liars. There will always be cheaters. There will always be thieves. Addicts will always be addicts. And sorority bitches will *always* be bitches.

I was not unfamiliar in the least with the shittier aspects of life. That said, occasionally its bluntness still managed to catch me off guard.

Take, for instance, my start at this esteemed university. I had been thrilled...elated...*ecstatic* about leaving everyone I knew behind (with the exception of Nate, my very best friend in the world) to head halfway across the country to the East Coast.

It wasn't that home sucked, because really, it could have been worse. I had a perfectly normal twenty-first century suburban family, with the two-car garage and the two-point-five kids. My mom worried too much—a habit she'd formed and fine-tuned over the past two years. I couldn't blame her, and I didn't love her any less for it. My step-dad was great, and while my step-sister and I had never been close, my half-brother and I were, so leaving them was definitely a bummer.

I was also at least a little upset to be leaving behind my boyfriend. Dan was great, and I loved him, but I had my reasons for not following him to the University of Michigan like we had originally planned. That said, knowing he was much more than a short drive away was kind of...sad.

Despite all the people I was sorry to leave behind, I needed a change of scenery like an addict needs cigarettes in rehab.

I was thrilled to finally be enrolling in college, period. But, beyond that, being in Virginia meant that I was just a nineteen-year-old freshman who could finally figure out what she wanted to do. I was ready to branch out—I wanted new experiences, and I wanted to know who the *new* Caroline Delia Olsen was going to be.

That was two weeks ago. As of today, the New Caroline Delia Olsen was starting to piss me off, mostly because she was going to get me into a shit-ton of trouble.

I couldn't really blame Nate, at least not as much as I may have wanted to. My roommate Jen

had insisted on attending the party as well, and since she and Nate got along like Bonnie and Clyde (minus all the really hot sex I assume Bonnie and Clyde must have had during their wild-and-free crime spree,) I stood a snowball's chance in hell at talking them out of it. Not that I had really tried all that hard. This was decidedly an "if-I-knew-then" scenario.

Because somehow, among the dozens, maybe *hundreds* of parties that were surely happening across campus during move-in week, we somehow managed to find the one house in Charlottesville containing the single person from my entire home state of Michigan who absolutely hated me.

Mother-effing Sammi Preston.

What happened would be almost funny if it wasn't so very sad. Because, really, at this point it wasn't about what she could take from me; it was more a matter of, *What did I have left to lose?*

Apparently, Sammi thought the answer to that was something because we weren't in that house five minutes before she made her presence known.

"Oh my God! *Caroline Olsen*?!"

Seeing as, at this point, I lived in a bright, happy world of, *No one at this party knows me! Hoorah!*, I couldn't immediately figure out why the shrilly incredulous, whining shout sounded so familiar. The slight turn of my head that brought her petite frame into view was all it took to answer that question.

She had the same hair, so blonde it practically disappeared in bright light, hanging in pin-straight layers down to her collarbone. The same eyes— bright, crystalline blue, slanted into angry dashes that

punctuated her pinched face with disbelief. The same pursed mouth—thin lips that almost withered away entirely under the completely unconcealed loathing that coated her face every single time she looked in my direction. A face she'd been sending my way for the past fifteen years.

This girl seriously needed a hobby—or at least a new one—because she was taking hating me to strange new levels of dedication. Scratch that. *Obsession.*

I hadn't seen Sammi since she graduated with Dan a year-and-a-fucking-half ago. I admit, she definitely caught me off guard. We had pre-gamed for about two hours before heading to the party, so I also wasn't really in the best frame of mind to make full sense of the situation. That said, by the time Nate had tensed up at my side, I realized that, for reasons completely unknown to me, Fate was still looking to fuck with me.

Because, really, how was it remotely fair that one person should have to suffer *this* much?

Fortunately for me—or maybe unfortunately, depending on how you looked at it—New Caroline decided to handle the situation in a way that Old Caro never would have. And since New Caroline had been drinking for, I repeat, *two hours,* she did this quickly, thoughtlessly, and without mercy.

"Wow, Sammi. Long time, no see."

"I figured you would have followed your boyfriend to UMich once you finally got out of high school." She said it like I failed a year for smoking too much weed or getting knocked up—like it was

*dirty*—and I couldn't stop the humorless chuckle that escaped my lips.

"Funny, I figured the same. My delayed graduation could have been your big chance. Didn't your high school to-do list begin and end with fucking my boyfriend?"

She didn't react visibly, but it took her a moment to find her words.

"You're not that special, Caro. My life doesn't revolve around you or your boyfriend. Even if you are broken."

The thing is, under normal circumstances that would have probably hurt. At least a little. I mean, I'd come a long way toward getting back to a normal life—accepting what I'd been given as well as what I lost and all that jazz. I'd talked to therapists—lots of therapists—and after countless months of both physical and psychological healing, I could confidently say that I was much less "broken" than I had been before. I could definitely find some solace in that, but...

It still kind of sucked to be different. While I would never call myself insecure, I was not completely immune to someone pointing out my, quote-unquote, flaws.

Even if that person was Sammi Preston.

But New, Drunk Caroline completely laughed off the b-word. And, for a moment, I couldn't help but be a little impressed.

"That's what kills you, isn't it? That even broken, scarred from head to toe, with a fake fucking leg, he still wanted me over you. You just couldn't compete with the girl with the broken body, no matter how many times you offered to suck his dick or let him stick it in your ass. No matter how many pictures you sent to his phone, no matter how many times you messaged him online. He didn't even want you drunk, when you told him that you could 'pretend to be me.'"

Now, I should point out that at this moment, in this house—and yet far away from where I was standing at that moment, on a stage in the great play of *Life*— a lot was happening that I failed to notice or comprehend. The music had faded, turned down to a low thrum instead of the head-throbbing intensity it had been blaring at since our arrival. I also failed to notice the swarming crowd that had formed a tight circle around us, many of whom had smart phones of every shape and size clenched between their fingers, little black eyes pointed toward us, avidly watching our interaction.

Most significant of the things that I completely didn't comprehend was the heaviness of fate and the feel of the moment. Because this was one of those life-defining instances. Not that I had any idea. Everything after this would be completely different from what had come before, and yet I just didn't stop—*couldn't* stop. New, Drunk Caroline was on a roll, and she was *not* going to back down.

"It didn't matter how many guys you fucked at parties to make him jealous because, let's face it, there's no way he 'accidentally' walked in on you six separate times with six separate people. And it didn't matter how many times you changed your hair, your clothes, your body... How many times you threw up your lunch in the bathroom to get just a little bit skinnier, just a little bit more like the broken girl. You shoulda just chopped a leg off. Maybe he would have fucked you then."

And just like that, the moment was gone, taking Old Caro with it, once and for all.

Nate grabbed my arm hard, which managed to tamp down my smug grin a bit, as Sammi's face turned a bright, utterly enraged shade of red. Just as I felt his heavy hand give a strong tug to pull me backwards—an attempt that I shrugged out of, not without a decent amount of pain—Sammi sprang into motion. Her fists tightened into tiny balls, and her elbows pulled back as she charged, barreling in my direction and shrieking, "You cyborg *bitch*!"

Seriously, though? It might have been the stupidest thing she'd ever done.

I didn't even move, just planted myself and let her cross the four feet between us in the crowded living room. Once she was within striking distance, I dropped my shoulder into her pelvis and lifted, flipping her onto her back before dropping her directly onto the floor behind me, where partygoers scrambled to get out of the way of the flailing, falling sorority bitch.

The noise broke through then, a collection of mixed reactions ranging from loudly muttered, "Holy shits" to a few drunken cheers, as well as plenty of gossipy muttering. I didn't get a chance to take any of it in because next thing I knew I was being pulled away from the stage, away from the crowd, and outside into the cool night air.

## Chapter Two

*Jimmy*

WHEN NATE BAKER BLEW THROUGH the front door of the Theta Sig house, I was standing on the wide, wooden porch in the furthest, darkest corner, listening to Maddie bitch on the phone about... Actually, I have no fucking *clue* what she was bitching about.

He was tugging on the arm of a slender girl who stood just a few inches shorter than him, dark hair flowing over her shoulder and into her face as he pulled her across the porch. Just as my eyes began to drift back to him, the girl, who appeared to be struggling to get back in the house, looked up and met my gaze. In half a second, her jaw went slack, and the fight left her posture, shoulders hunching forward as she wrapped her arms around herself subconsciously before finally shrugging off his hand.

Her eyes left mine and shot to his, and I saw her lips move to mutter, "I'm fine" before she walked forward to head down the stairs. When she got to the first step, she paused for just a moment to look back my way, sparing me one more glance that lasted barely a second before she shook her head and descended the stairs.

I looked back at Baker to find him peering in my direction with a smile and a wave. Covering the mouthpiece of the cell phone, I met his eyes and mouthed, "You alright?"

His eyes slanted, confusion suffusing his face before we both heard, "Nate, where's Jen?" from the front yard. I saw him mouth the word "Shit" before turning to talk—or shout, rather—to the girl. At that moment, Maddie snagged my attention.

"...even listening to me, James?!"

*Fuck. "James." She sounds like my fucking Mom.*

"Yeah, Mads, I'm listening."

"No, fuck it. Just go. Get back to your party or whatever. I have to go anyway."

"Maddie," I began, but she had already disconnected.

I slipped the phone into my pocket and looked up to find Baker staring me in the face while the girl stood, hip propped against the railing to my left, angrily tapping the screen of her phone like she wanted to punish it.

"Hey, man," he started with a reluctant tone. "Any chance you can do me a quick favor?"

I eyed him for a moment before slowly nodding once. To be honest, I didn't know the kid all that well. In fact, the sum of my knowledge was that he was a nineteen-year-old freshman from Michigan who'd deferred his start at UVA for a year after he'd graduated. We'd only met twice so far: once at the pre-season meeting and then again at tryouts, where he'd literally skated onto the team with ease. We'd talked a bit, and he seemed pretty cool, but right now I was beginning to have my doubts.

"What's up?"

"Please just watch my drunk friend for a minute while I go find her drunk roommate, who we somehow managed to lose."

My eyebrows raised, almost of their own volition, prompting him to curse quietly under his breath before he aimed a hard look at his friend. She didn't notice the look that only lasted a second before he focused on me again. "I know, and I'm sorry, but after the shit she just pulled in there, she cannot go back into that house. I'll just be a second."

Curiosity overtook my lack of desire to babysit a drunk teenager. I had no clue what she could have possibly done in the house that made it so she couldn't go back in, but I found myself wondering. Taking a moment to study her, I nodded as Baker muttered, "Thanks" before heading back for the crush of bodies past the door. While she was only a few inches shorter than Baker, I practically towered over her lithe frame. In the darkness, I just barely caught a flash of blue in her eyes as they moved over the lit phone screen she held in her hand.

Even cast in shadows and defined by the glow of the device in her hand, she was gorgeous. My eyes scanned her features as well as they could in the darkness, just barely able to make out the gentle slope of her straight nose and the curve of her cheekbone. The soft arc of her jaw and the wide bow of her bottom lip, which glistened faintly in the low light. Mindlessly I continued my appraisal, gliding down over curves that somehow managed to be both toned and generous. She looked soft but strong, the exact opposite of the stick-figure girls who usually populated these parties, and I couldn't help but wonder if she was an athlete. The slender, yet muscular legs she displayed under her tight denim had me guessing track. I could easily picture her running in Lycra or Spandex, maybe showing off tanned skin under nothing but a sweat-soaked sports bra.

My subconscious hijacked the innocent thought almost immediately, sweeping it away with images of her laid out across my bed, sweat coating her flushed, bare skin. Those long legs wrapped around my back, and her long fingers gripping-

*What the fuck are you doing, Jimmy?*

I rubbed a shaking hand across my face and forced the inappropriate thoughts from my mind. What *was* I doing?

Before I could find the answer to that loaded question, I watched her slide the phone into her back pocket. One delicate finger tapped her lips twice before she lifted her eyes from the ground and narrowed them on the door. As she launched off the railing to make for the house, I moved to intervene, nudging in front of her just in time to put my hands out as a human barrier.

"You can't go in there."

Her eyes stayed narrowed as they shifted up to focus on me.

"*Excuse* me? Why the fuck not?"

I couldn't hold back my sigh. "You should probably be telling me that. What the hell did you do in there?"

Blatant anger suffused her face as one finger came up to poke my chest hard. "What did I do? Let's talk about what that bitch did! I mean, how the fuck-"

After listening to Maddie bitch on the phone for the past hour, I was honestly relieved when Baker's reappearance at the door abruptly cut off her growing tirade. He was towing a second drunk girl across the porch, this one also dark haired and slightly shorter than Drunk Girl Number One.

His eyes dropped to my hands, hands which were, for some reason, resting on Drunk Girl Number One's hips. Even worse, my thumbs had started drawing small circles on the indents that resided next to her sharp hipbones. The girl was definitely in shape; she couldn't hide it, even under a loose t-shirt and jeans.

*You're still fucking touching her, asshole!*

My hands jumped off her skin like they were on fire, and I took a quick step back, dislodging her hand from where it had been resting against my chest. I felt only marginally better when I realized she looked as surprised as I felt.

As I stepped aside, she crossed her arms over her chest and moved straight to Drunk Girl Number Two, grabbing her arm and dragging her toward the steps.

"Holy shit, Caro!" I heard Girl Number Two shout as they made their way down the front steps, followed slowly by Baker, who nodded once in my direction before meeting them where they stood on the lawn. I pulled my phone back out of my pocket and pretended to stare at it while I listened in to the conversation.

"Where the fuck did you go, Jen?"

Girl Number Two, the roommate Jen, answered, "I went to thank the girl who invited us, and then I stopped to talk to this guy for, like, a *second*! By the time I got back upstairs, you had somehow become the only thing that anyone was willing to talk about. What the fuck happened in there, Caroline?" Her voice broke at the end before segueing into quiet but uncontrolled laughter.

"This isn't funny. Tell her this isn't funny, Nate."

"Yeah..." he finally joined the conversation, sounding almost reluctant. "I'm actually gonna go with Caro on this one and say that that was really not funny."

"What did you... Oh, shit." That was Jen, and her voice had lost all its humor.

"What, Jen?" Caroline pestered when Jen failed to continue. Next, I heard an almost indecipherable noise. I guessed it was a video once I glanced up to see the three of them crowded around Jen's phone, which was emitting both noise and light.

"...even broken, scarred from head to toe, with a fake fucking leg, he still wanted me over you..."

The sound cut out, and Jen dropped her hand to her side as Caroline nervously began to pace away from the other two.

"This is... This is not good."

"Caro..." Baker called gently, speaking so quietly I almost couldn't hear him. "This isn't that big of a deal. It's not like anyone cares."

All attempts at subtle eavesdropping demolished, I was now blatantly staring at the scene taking place on the lawn. I saw the graceful way that Caroline stopped and faced him, tilting her head to the side for a moment before she shook her head dazedly. "I just want to go home."

Jen nodded almost frantically. "Come on. Homeward bound."

Without another word, the three of them headed for the sidewalk and out of sight. I felt a strong urge to follow them, to creep behind in the shadows just to hear her talk some more. But before I could step off the porch, I convinced myself that I wasn't a fucking stalker and that that would just be fucking weird. Instead, I shoved my phone back into my pocket and headed inside.

There was a reason I avoided sorority-house parties—I just usually forgot about it until I walked through the door.

So many bitches.

They fucking thrived here. Clustered together in groups of threes and fours, seeking out the next target for their next game. Everything was always a fucking game.

It used to be, in moments like these, I'd feel thankful for having Maddie in my life. So glad to have found someone who hated games as much as I did. Someone who got me. Someone who really cared where I was and how I was doing. How I was feeling.

But I'd started to feel like a pawn in our relationship a long fucking time ago. I just didn't have the time, energy, or inclination to do a damn thing about it.

I liked to think that our relationship was mutually beneficial. She got a sounding board for her daily list of complaints and problems, and I got a nice suit of armor against the bitches.

If I thought about it too hard, it hurt that this was what our relationship had become. Maddie had been my entire world once upon a time. Now she felt like just another responsibility on my daily checklist of duties and obligations. Did I love her? Sure. Did I see us managing to stick to the plan of graduating this year and moving in together in just eight months? Every day it seemed less and less likely.

My thoughts remained dark through my visit to the kitchen; my trek to the basement; and the first five minutes of my conversation with Soto, Brooks, and Collins. Every minute that passed just reminded me how much I didn't want to be here. The only reason I had shown was because the guys on the team had decided against throwing a party at the hockey house. Theta Sig was already doing the work, anyway. Two of the guys on the team were dating sisters, and, apparently, that meant the entire men's hockey team was welcome to gatecrash. The bitches alone would have been bad enough, but since almost the whole team had turned out, the groupies had shown up as well. Bitches were bullshit, but there was really nothing worse than a hockey groupie.

It was Soto who managed to drag me from my completely shitty thoughts.

"What the fuck is up with you, McCarthy?"

I shook my head to clear my mind before responding. "Nothing. Fucking exhausted."

"Too much phone sex last night?" Brooks laughed as he delivered the joke, but it hit closer to home than I'm sure he'd intended.

*When was the last time I got laid?*

I honestly couldn't fucking remember. *No, wait, last Spring Break?* It had to be. That was the last time Maddie had come to visit, since she'd chosen to stay in Williamsburg over the summer for an internship instead of coming home to see family. To see me.

And phone sex? Yeah-fucking-right.

"You know it," I told him, tacking on my best attempt at a cocky grin to make the despondent words feel lighthearted. I needed to move. Needed to get out of this basement.

Hopping off the couch I had settled on, Solo cup in hand, I started for the stairs that would take me straight to the kitchen. Once there, I refilled my cup from the keg without meeting the eyes of anyone in the small, overly lit space, focusing instead on the dirty linoleum flooring and the dark cabinets that lined the wall. My cup was full when I heard a high-pitched voice mention Caroline's name, and it locked me in place. I stood at the counter, back to the room, and listened to a familiar female voice whine about "that fucking cyborg bitch" who had apparently "ruined her life."

I leaned a hip against the counter and took a sip of beer before glancing back quickly to scan the room over my shoulder. I knew the girl talking, at least vaguely. Sarah... Sheila... No clue, but she'd tried to fuck me during Rush Week last year. I'd told her about Maddie, which she'd seemed to see as a non-issue, and I had promptly made my exit. Even without Mads, I would never have gone for her. It took exactly one look to know that she *loves* to play the game.

I felt a strong urge to say something. Correction: I felt a strong urge to tell her to shut her fucking mouth because she didn't know the first thing about Caroline. But the truth of the matter was that *I* didn't know the first thing about Caroline. I had no clue what had happened—and I had no *desire* to know—but from what I'd picked up, the two had a history. Despite what my gut told me about the bitch whose name I couldn't remember, for all I knew she could very well be the injured party.

I derailed that entire train of thought. None of this should matter to me at all. What did I care if she was talking shit?

I knew I *shouldn't* care, and the fact that I *did* frustrated me more than I could comprehend. Too tired to deal with my head or this house or these people that I didn't want to be around, I left my full cup of beer on the kitchen counter and walked straight down the hall and out the front door. When I reached my car, parked just a few houses down Greek Row, I paused at the door to stare up at the sky.

So many stars. So many more than I could see, stretched out across an endless sky. And yet I'd only ever looked up at these ones. Sure, they changed, spun, cycled. But that was more us spinning inside them than them spinning around us. We're not that important. In the grand scheme of things, I wasn't that important, either.

But I wasn't unimportant enough to leave. And I never would be. It would always be *these* same stars, *this* same sky.

And even though I'd accepted my life and the role I'd been given years ago, it was starting to feel like it wasn't enough.

Chapter Three

# CaroLine

THE DAWN AFTER MY SCENE at the Theta Sig house broke bright and early, and I woke to Nate's heavy-handed knocking on my front door. It was the last day before classes started, and the absolute last thing I wanted to do was work out, but I knew he wouldn't let me sleep in.

That's not to say I didn't try because I sure as fuck did. I lay in bed and completely ignored the pounding on the front door of the two-bedroom suite I shared with Jen. I was prepared to ignore him forever, but not long after the cacophony began, I heard angry footsteps cross the living room, and then the pounding abruptly stopped. My bleary eyes aimed a quick, squinty-eyed glance across the room to see if I had locked my bedroom door and...*fuck*.

The door swung inward, and almost immediately my body flew several inches straight into the air as Nate landed on my mattress with a grunt. Worst of all, he was singing. Loudly and out of key.

"Sweet Caroline. DUN, DUN, DUNNNNN..."

I didn't bother pulling my head out of the pillows before I cursed a muffled, "Fuck yourself, Nathaniel Baker. We're not friends anymore."

"Okay. I'll just take the coffee I got you with me as I go."

I rolled over to face him and heaved an exasperated sigh. "Your petty attempts at bribery won't work."

"Then I guess you don't want any of this either."

I watched him reach a hand down to the floor by the bed before it was returning with...*holy fucking...*

"Krispy Kremes? Oh my God, give me one now." I was halfway across the bed, kneeling on one leg to tackle the donuts out of his hand before he could threaten to take them away. Nate dropped the box onto the bed, laughing at me while I settled back on the mattress.

Once I was sitting safely, I wasted no time in ripping the box open. I'd just gotten three quarters of a donut squeezed into my mouth when Jen's voice burst across the suite. "Do you have Krispy Kremes?"

I glanced at Nate, and a grin spread across my frantically chewing mouth. Offering no assistance, he simply shook his head and smiled as he handed me my coffee and leaned back to readjust his legs across the mattress. I returned Jen's shout with a "No!" that was less than convincing when you factored in the laughter in my voice and the half-chewed donut in my mouth. By the time she made it into my room, I was working on donut number two, stuffing the glazed dough between my lips with gusto, not the least bit embarrassed by the moans coming out of my mouth every few perfectly sweet bites.

Seriously, these things were my weakness. And, as luck had it, my roommate understood the sheer heavenly delight that was a Krispy Kreme donut.

We had made it halfway through the box, and I'd already swallowed half of my coffee before anyone even spoke. Finally, in between bites, Jen looked at Nate and I sitting together on the bed and shook her head before announcing, "You guys are disgusting."

I eyed her, seated in my desk chair in a pair of black yoga pants and a tank top, working through donuts almost as quickly as I was, and one of my eyebrows rose with a question that she read and answered.

"Who eats an entire box of donuts before going to the gym?"

I looked straight at Nate, and his face broke into a smile when he saw the smirk that her words elicited.

"The gym sucks. Donuts make it better."

My words triggered the flashback, but, then again, they weren't really my words. After months of being confined to a bed, then a wheelchair, there wasn't a single thing I had wanted to do less than put on my newly fit prosthesis and start the physical therapy that it would take to get me to walk again. Back then, walking seemed like a long shot. Almost too long of a shot to get my hopes up.

Out of all the people who tried to urge me out of the depressed slump I had fallen into, it had taken Nate showing up, a dozen glazed donuts in hand, to get me out the door. His exact words had been, "I get it: It sucks. Donuts will make it better. And you'll need to go to work them all off." He had fought, tooth and nail, to keep me going to PT, and he had been my biggest supporter.

I loved Dan, but there were times I wished I felt even the slightest bit of attraction toward Nate.

Nope. Over the course of our entire sixteen-year friendship, there had never been even a tiny non-platonic feeling between us. He was the best friend I'd ever had and the best teammate I'd ever skated with, but as much as I might have wished otherwise, there had never been anything more.

It's not that Nate wasn't good-looking; he definitely was. Just shy of six feet (which drove him crazy), with dark hair, dark eyes, and just enough muscle, he was empirically attractive. There was just nothing there for me.

Shaking my head, I focused back on my roommate and cleared my sleep- and dough-clogged throat.

"Back, after the accident, donuts were what got me out of bed for PT."

Jen nodded, her face expressionlessly chewing. Honestly, that non-reaction as one of the things I'd grown to love about the girl since we'd both moved into this space a week ago.

Jen was a sophomore Communications major from Philadelphia. I had been a little nervous moving into the apartment with a roommate that I knew very little about...for a few reasons. Primarily because, since my mother protested my original housing assignment on the basis of my "disability," I had been reassigned to a first-floor room in a building that was typically off-limits to freshmen. Jen hadn't cared.

We clicked instantly. There was no awkwardness and no weird, space-sharing quirks. I got along with Jen better than I got along with the step-sister I had known for thirteen years.

"So, what are you guys doing after you've finished torturing yourselves into peak levels of physical fitness?"

I smiled at her question and took a minute to swallow the mouthful I was currently chewing as I looked at Nate.

"I was planning on using your TV to watch Netflix instead of sitting in my dorm room with the Yogi."

Swallowing the last bite of donut number four, I opened my mouth but Jen got there first.

"Who's the Yogi?"

Nate sighed before he answered the question. "My roommate. Spends every evening playing soothing soundscapes during an hour of both yoga and meditation. He refuses to accept the fact that he is never going to get me into it. He's also a firm believer in crystal healing, and he actually gave me..." He trailed off as he stuck a hand into a pocket of the green-and-yellow Hornets Hockey shorts he was wearing, feeling around a bit before pulling out a small, green crystal. "...this before I left this morning. Says it's an energy crystal, and I should have it on me anytime I do physical activity."

Jen and I both burst out laughing just as Nate chucked the crystal directly at my head. I managed to swat it, and it landed on the bedspread where we all let it lie.

"What are you doing to celebrate the last day of zero responsibilities?" I asked her, grabbing donut number five. I normally didn't let myself eat this many, but I figured with the amount of alcohol I had imbibed the evening before, I should flush my body with sugar and fat. It felt like a recovery plan based on some sort of science.

"I'm not sure. That guy from last night texted me. I was thinking about hooking up with him later."

"Ooh," I grinned. "A hot date?"

"Not quite," she answered with a smirk. "I told you—I've sworn off relationships. I just like sex too much to quit men entirely."

"Ah, yes. The prick ex-boyfriend who convinced you that men can't be trusted."

Nate chuckled before hitting her with his most charming smile. "Jen, I told you: Cole was a dick, but that doesn't mean we're all bad."

She rolled her eyes and swallowed her last bite before rising from the chair. "And I told you, Nathanial: Even if I was looking for a relationship, I don't date hockey players."

I glanced at him as she headed out the door, but he didn't show any sign of disappointment at her shut-down. He'd been trying to get in with Jen since he'd met her, the very same day I had, and she'd repeatedly, and quite humorously, turned him down each and every time

"Never gonna happen," I told him with a smile.

"I don't like to listen when people tell me the odds are against me. Funny, but I thought you'd feel the same."

I gave him a slight, seated bow for that. "Touché, Mr. Baker. Now get out of my room, so I can get dressed."

Once we were out the door and headed for the student fitness center, I decided to bring up his crush on Jen again. The day was already gearing up to be gorgeous, but, as early as it was, there was hardly anyone out and about as we made our way across campus.

"Dude, seriously though, do you really, like, like Jen?"

He shot me a quick glance that I couldn't decipher before looking back down at the sidewalk. "I don't know. I mean, I think she's cool." He shrugged. "I think I mostly like screwing with her. She's fun to get a rise out of." He looked at me with an adorable grin, and although I had a feeling he was downplaying the situation, I let him get away with it because, really, what did it matter?

We were both quiet for a few minutes before he spoke.

"What's up with Dan? Did you talk to him last night?"

I bit the corner of my lip as I considered the two texts that I'd sent to my boyfriend last night. There was first a simple, **Hey, on my way home. You**

**still out?** When that went unanswered, I sent another: **Going to bed, love you.**

I still hadn't heard from him this morning.

"No. I texted him, no answer. And normally I'd be worried, but I'm sure he's just still pissed about Thanksgiving."

At that, Nate sent a guilty glance my way. "Are you sure you don't want to fly home? I'll be fine here."

"I already told you no. And I already told my mom no. If she could get over it, which she totally has, then Dan can too."

"Yeah, because it really seems like he's getting over it."

"Whatever. It didn't help that I sprung it on him, and..." I let out a tired sigh because I really just didn't have the energy to discuss my relationship at the moment.

"It's alright, Caro. I get it," he ceded, and I gave him a weak but appreciative smile. Nate read me better than anyone, and in moments like this, there was no one in the world I'd rather have for a best friend.

"So," he started, "what was up with you and Jimmy?"

I quirked a brow and stared at him. "Who?"

"McCarthy," he answered, as if a last name would help me any more, before continuing with, "The guy on the porch last night?"

Images rushed through my mind like a stop-motion film: me deciding to walk back in, him keeping me detained on the porch, his hands resting on my hips like they fucking belonged there, and my hand...

"I was drunk. That was nothing."

Nate nodded. "Uh huh. Sure."

"Stop it, Nate."

"I'm not doing anything, Caroline."

"You have that look."

"I don't have a look," he scoffed with a shake of his head.

"You absolutely do, and you can put whatever thoughts you have in your head to rest."

That prompted an eye roll in my direction. "Whatever, Caro."

I eyed him suspiciously, but he didn't say anything more, and I let myself relax. Nate had a fairly one-track mind, and I just needed to let him forget about whatever he thought he saw.

Because, really, it had been nothing.

It wasn't until we left the gym that I realized how severely I, the fearless, new, part-alcoholic Caroline Olsen had fucked up the night before.

More specifically, it was the moment I walked back into my building and was greeted by a group of polo-shirt-wearing twenty-somethings who took one look at me and gaped.

"Holy shit," the tallest of the four men, who all looked like they belonged on a water polo team, said in my direction. "It's the cyborg."

This led to explosive laughter, which I ignored by pointing my eyes at the floor and turning left to head down the hall toward my room. As I left them behind, I heard at least two of them shout out different versions of, "You're awesome, broken girl," which I ignored as well, unlocking the door as quickly as humanly possible with shaky hands.

Once I had escaped into the suite and slammed out the sound of their laughter, I checked Jen's room to find it empty. I headed across to mine to grab clothes before walking to our private (*thank God*) bathroom.

Once I'd turned the water on as hot as I could get it, I let the small room fill with steam before stripping. After dropping my clothes to the floor, I sat on the first of two tiny plastic chairs I had bought for the bathroom and pressed the small silver button that would release the suction holding the prosthesis onto what was left of my thigh. Once I had the leg off, I rolled the liner and sock off my skin before setting them on the bathroom counter.

I'm really not shallow, but it kind of sucked to stare at the stump of ragged flesh, torn from both the accident and the operation—operations, really, because it had taken a lot of work to get my body back into a usable, functional state. The scars continued up the skin of my left leg to my hip, branching to my lower stomach before finally ending, and, while I'd take a body of patchwork scars over being dead any day, I'd also take no scars over the unattractive collection of raised, jagged lines that I currently sported.

Finally ready, I stood on my remaining leg and grabbed the first of two suction bars I had installed into the tiled, walk-in shower. With three ungraceful hops, I was safely behind the glass door and able to drop onto the second seat, one with convenient suction cups attached to the legs that kept it stable. That chair I used to keep from splitting my head open by attempting to balance on one leg on the shower's wet floor.

Once I was safely seated, I let the water work its way across my skin, breathing in the warm steam with slow, deep breaths. For five minutes I didn't move, only focused on the feel of the water running over my skin, the way it washed everything else away.

Once I decided that I'd spent enough time moping, I quickly washed off, taking special care with my thigh. Working out in a prosthesis was a bitch for a few reasons, but the most obnoxious of those was the sweat. By the time I was finished, I felt better. More ready to face whatever I had done last night.

I hopped back out, re-attached my leg, and got dressed before heading out the door for my room. When I spotted Jen sitting on the couch watching Vampire Diaries, I gave her a quick wave before tossing my gym clothes into my hamper and heading back to the living room. I dropped my body down on the couch and propped my good foot on the coffee table to get comfortable.

"Hey. Where'd you go earlier?" I asked, eyes drifting to the screen where a seriously sexy vampire was being tortured by a bunch of bad-guy humans. Jen paused the show and turned to face me before answering.

"I had to get a book before tomorrow. How was the gym?" Her question came out strange, the tone too high. That meant that she knew something, and I had a feeling I knew what it was.

"Fine, actually. I didn't hear the word 'cyborg' at all until I got back here."

She winced. "And, I'm guessing since you're not completely freaking out, you haven't checked Facebook yet?"

*Fuck.* Pressing my head into the cushion behind me, I closed my eyes as an exasperated groan escaped my lips.

"How bad is it?"

"It's..." When she trailed off, I slid one eye open in her direction to catch her at a loss for words.

"Shit. It's bad."

"It's not bad, Caroline. Okay, so the titles of most of the videos I've seen start with the words 'Cyborg Bitch,' but, to be honest, you just look super bad-ass. Plus, it's not like anyone likes that whore anyway. So you're a little famous? You just need to make it work for you."

"I don't want to be famous! Especially not because I went on a rant about Sammi-fucking-Preston and announced to the world that I'm broken!"

"That's what I don't get," she announced in response to my hissy fit. "Who is this bitch?"

I twisted on the couch until my back was against the arm and my leg was comfortably bent across the cushion. Once I was facing her, I considered the best way to answer the question.

"When I was five, I skated into her at our local rink. She's hated me ever since. When we were younger, it was mostly from a distance, but high school forced us into close contact. We were both popular, moved in a lot of the same circles, and," I shrugged, "something about that pissed her off. Plus, I'm pretty sure she's been in love with Dan half her life, so there's that."

She nodded before pulling her bottom lip into her mouth for just a second. "Just give it a couple days. It'll blow over. I'm sure it'll all be fine, Caro."

"Yeah," I responded into the quiet room a moment later. "I'm sure, too."

Jen switched the show back on, but I wasn't in the mood for blood and death. Instead, I angled off the couch and headed straight for my desk to face the music. I grabbed my cell phone from where I'd left it after plugging it in last night.

Before I could even press a key to light the screen, it was going off in my hand with a new text message. That made...five. Lovely. As well as two missed calls and one voicemail.

Unsurprisingly, it was all from Dan.

I ignored the messages and tapped the screen until the call started ringing. While I waited for him to answer, I brought the computer to life and clicked around to pull up my browser. It took a ring-and-a-half before his voice was in my ear.

"Someone had an interesting night last night, I take it?"

His relaxed tone instantly put me at ease, and I felt my lips curl into a slight smile. "Yeah, you'd be right. I take it you've seen the video?"

"Videos, you mean? And yeah. I'm not exactly sure how, but it was all over my Facebook this morning. Everyone from home had seen it."

"Fantastic. I'm sure that was a great way to wake up."

He laughed at that. "Eh, it wasn't too terrible. Caro, you have to admit, it was kind of hilarious."

"Maybe I just need to gain a little distance, but I have yet to see the humor in this situation. I'll let you know when that changes." Even so, I smiled as I said the words. I was just preparing to ask him about last night when his voice grew uneasy.

"Care Bear, I wanted to apologize. I was a dick, and I'm sorry. I was just upset that I'm not going to see you, that's all. I didn't mean to..."

"It's okay," I cut him off quickly, letting him off the hook, but he refused to give it up.

"No, it's not. I trust you. Completely. And I love you. And, yes, I worry about you being there by yourself, but I'm sorry for taking that out on you. It wasn't cool."

"Thanks," I said quietly, trying to clear the emotion from my throat. There was a moment of silence before he broke it again.

"Are we okay?"

I nodded until I realized he couldn't see me.

"Yeah, we're okay."

"Good. And are *you* okay?"

That question wasn't as easy to answer, but I had gotten good practice in the months after the accident.

"I will be."

There was really nothing else to say.

Chapter Four

Jimmy

THE FIRST WEEK OF CLASSES flew by, as it has a habit of doing. Between work, school, and brother-sitting duties, I barely had enough time to shave, shower, and sleep, and that was *before* the season kicked off and practice started.

Here's the thing. Hockey had been a part of my life since I was five years old. That's sixteen years devoted to a hobby that, if I'm honest, I was never really that talented at. I started playing hockey for two reasons. One, my dad, a lifelong ice hockey player and fan, was our youth coach. And two, my best friend played. That was it.

That best friend? He was talented. Even at six years old, it was obvious that Ash was going to go somewhere. Going to do something big. And somehow, sixteen years later, he refused to play, and I was the one busting my ass to stay important to the team.

When I was younger, I played because it made my dad proud. And because, let's face it, Ash thought hockey was cool, and I wanted him to think I was cool too. But mostly, it was for the look in Chris McCarthy's eyes when I skated onto the ice in my first tournament game and when my high school team took first in our division.

Once I got to college, though, something changed. Hockey became the one thing I really loved to do. On my nearly endless list of responsibilities, hockey was the only one that felt purely rewarding. Sure, I knew my dad appreciated the work I did at the rink—I'd been helping him run it for years—but that didn't mean it gave me a whole lot of fulfillment.

When it came to my brother, well, being around Jack was definitely rewarding, at times. Other times it was incredibly difficult. Don't get me wrong, I love my little brother more than anyone on the planet, but there were moments when being his brother was the hardest job in the world.

That didn't matter, though, because it wasn't a job I would ever give up. It was one I was prepared to do for the rest of my life. I knew I'd be living here in ten, twenty, thirty years—running the rink, taking care of Jack, doing what I was supposed to be doing—and I was fine with that.

But the thing was, this was my last year of school. I'd be graduating in just nine months, so even though I knew I would most likely end up exhausting myself, I was determined to make as many memories as I could possibly make.

It was sort of a relief when practices started. Everything melted away on the ice. It was just me, the stick, and the puck. The best kind of therapy.

Our first practice was an exhausting four hours of drills to welcome the newbies and punish the returning players who hadn't kept in shape during the off-season. I was so beat by the end of the night that I completely ignored all the guys who tried to convince me to go to the bar. I headed straight home for bed, and I'd be willing to bet I was asleep before they'd been served their first pitcher of lukewarm beer.

Our second practice later that week wasn't as rough. After spending some time talking plays and formations, we at least got to scrimmage a bit before going back to drills. When Coach called it quits, I shuffled into the locker room to shower and change before heading home, listening to the guys plan another night out that I wanted nothing to do with. I took my time at my locker and in the shower, waiting until almost everyone else had already left before getting out and dressed. Once I'd thrown my clothes on, I grabbed my shit and headed out the door.

Stepping out into the warm night air, I heard a loud shout that I ignored to soak up the weather. September was my favorite month in Virginia for nights exactly like this one. Temperatures high enough for shorts and a t-shirt with none of the shitty daytime humidity. It was perfect.

It wasn't until I turned toward my car that I caught sight of Brooks, Soto, both Collins brothers, and Nate Baker standing on the sidewalk, waiting for me.

"Come on, McCarthy!" Brooks shouted. "We're getting a beer, and you're coming."

I moved closer with the intention of letting them know that I really wasn't in the mood, and that's when I spotted Baker's friend Caroline heading toward the group of guys. I watched her until she had reached Baker's side, where she leaned in to give him a quick hug and a bright smile.

Before I could process my decision (not that I even wanted to), I was nodding and following behind as everyone began to shuffle down the sidewalk. I couldn't help but overhear Baker as he spoke to Caroline just a few feet in front of my spot at the back of the herd of hockey players.

"Fuck. I know that face. Tell me."

"I don't have a face."

"Don't be stupid. Just tell me, Obi Wan."

I surreptitiously glanced to my left to catch her lick her lips before they curved into a small smile.

"I thought your feet looked slow and your stick looked heavy. Also," she added, "we're doubling your cardio."

The look I angled at her this time wasn't surreptitious at all. It was pure *curious as fuck*.

"Did you sit in on practice?"

I heard myself ask the question as if I was standing outside my body. Caroline spun toward me so fast I was worried she'd hurt herself, and Baker jumped like he'd had no idea I was right behind them. I honestly wasn't sure which of the three of us was most surprised by the sound of my voice. Baker's shock faded the fastest, so he jumped to fill the suddenly awkward-as-hell silence.

"Jimmy McCarthy, Caroline Olsen. Caroline, Jimmy. There, now you've officially met." I caught the tail end of the glare that Caroline aimed in Baker's direction before she gave me an apologetic smile.

"Yeah, I was there."

I nodded and fell silent, at a loss for what to say next. "Why?" seemed like a really stupid question, and I wasn't sure why I even cared. I mean, okay, maybe I had thought of her a few times since the night of the party, but I didn't want to get to know her. Didn't want anything to do with her life.

*Don't you, though?* The question my mind posed was quiet and heavy, and I didn't bother searching for an answer. Instead, I forced myself to tune out Baker and Caroline's quiet conversation, falling back to spend the last minutes of the short walk in silence.

A mere half hour after we had arrived at the bar, I was starting to lose my mind. In the process of us grabbing a table, I'd managed to seat myself next to the girl that I'd decided I needed to stay away from. And for thirty minutes straight, I'd been nothing but completely distracted by her.

The way her hair kept falling over her shoulder, despite her attempts to hold it back, had my fingers itching to weave between the silken strands. The way she laughed, low and throaty—God, it was the sexiest fucking sound I'd ever heard. The fact that every time she moved I smelled the barest trace of... I don't even know what, but she smelled like summer. Like beaches and sand and sun and hot skin. It was absolutely intoxicating. Everything about her called out to me on the most basic, physical level.

I tried to focus on the people speaking around me, but every time I heard her voice it was like my body was obligated to listen. To learn. To soak up every bit of information I could find in her words. Despite my determination to keep my distance, there was just something about her that drew me in.

She radiated potential. She felt limitless.

I was so tuned in to her energy, I felt the exact second she started to withdraw. It was like the light that she constantly gave off just evaporated, bit by bit, until she wasn't even speaking. Eyes downcast, she mindlessly played with the soggy paper coaster on the wooden table in front of her. It took me a minute, but then I heard the voices from the bar behind us. The cutting words. And I knew exactly who they were directed at.

I didn't fucking think, and I didn't fucking hesitate. I shot out of my seat and was across the floor in seconds.

"Is something funny?" I directed my question at the cockiest of the four assholes with their backs to the bar, seated facing our table. I could just tell by the look in his eyes that he was the ringleader of the group of frat-boy dickheads.

"Well, shit," he said, rising slowly from his barstool, "are you the cyborg's boyfriend?"

"Say that word again, and I'll make sure you can't speak by the end of the night."

Refusing to break eye contact, I watched from the corner of my eye as his friends all turned to him for guidance. I'd obviously picked the right guy; I just needed to wait to see if he had enough sense—of both the common and self-preservation varieties—to back down. I had five inches and probably forty pounds of solid muscle on him. Still, I was guessing he wouldn't make the smart decision.

"I just have one question," he started, face growing serious for a moment. "Does she or doesn't she wear the leg when you fuck her? Because I think that could be-"

My fist cut across his cheekbone faster than he or any of his friends could react. As I pulled back to swing again, I felt an arm hook violently around mine, and then I was being tugged backwards, strong fingers gripping the forearm above my tightly clenched fist. I fought the pull for only a moment before giving in, just as Dickhead's friends finally began to jump in my direction. The guys from the team were already there, pushing them back as an invisible force pulled me out the door.

As soon as the fresh air hit my face, I felt like the world's biggest idiot. *What the fuck are you doing, McCarthy?*

I had no fucking clue.

I moved toward the exterior wall and turned around to lean against it, which is when I finally caught sight of Baker a few feet away, hands on his head, breathing deep. The look on his face was pure concern, and I watched his mouth open and close a few times as he searched for something to say.

"I'm not going to pretend to know you, man. Still, that was...weird. Are you...?" Dropping both hands, he paused, shook his head. "Do you...?" Shook it again.

I surged out a breath in relief when he didn't finish either question.

"I'm sorry," I finally offered lamely. "I just... I didn't want them to make her uncomfortable." I had no other explanation.

He shook his head quickly. "No, no apology necessary. I was getting ready to say something myself; you just beat me to it." His lips curved up at the pun, but nothing was funny in my world right now, so I simply nodded and kept my mouth shut. I needed to stay silent before I dug this hole so deep I couldn't climb back out.

"I'm...ah...I'm heading back inside. You sure you're alright?" Keeping my eyes locked to the ground, back pressed firmly to the brick, I nodded to reassure him.

"Yeah, I'm fine. Thanks, man."

One more nod, then he headed back inside and left me alone.

*What the fuck am I even doing?* I still didn't have a single answer. I had no idea why I had jumped up—actually *hit* somebody—just because they said shit about a girl that I literally knew nothing about. She was absolutely *no one* to me, and yet I felt her distress, and I just fucking *reacted*.

I needed to get my shit together. What I *really* needed to do was go home, but I didn't want to just up and leave after that stupidly ridiculous show without letting the guys know I was going. That would only make everything look a thousand times worse.

I was still trying to prepare myself to walk back inside when the door opened again. I didn't even need to look up to know who it was.

I fucking *felt* her.

"Hey."

So quiet. Her voice was timid, maybe even afraid. And I probably would be too, if I was her, after watching me do...whatever the fuck I had just done.

"I just wanted to thank you." I snapped my eyes up to hers in time to see her go on. "Honestly, that was kind of awesome and..." Her eyes shifted nervously, Toward the ground, to the wall next to my head. Finally, back to me. "Just... Thanks."

I was stuck recovering, partly from her words and partly from the way it felt to have her eyes locked onto mine. It was like I was invincible. Like I could do anything in the world. Whatever I wanted. The sensation was heady and disarming, so much so that she had already started back toward the door by the time I could force my mouth to move. "You ever going to tell me what happened at this party?"

When her eyes came back to mine, they were clouded with confusion. She took one step closer before asking, "You haven't seen the video?"

I shook my head. She took another step closer.

"Huh. I figured, especially after that..."

For a moment, I wished I'd lied about seeing the video. I mean, sure, I'd overheard a few people talking, so I had an idea of what went down, but I felt even stupider for defending her over something that I hadn't even witnessed. When she settled her arm against the wall just a few inches away from me, I was so caught off guard, so wrapped up in being in her space, that I said the first thing that came to mind.

"I could feel that it was bothering you. I just wanted it to stop."

My gaze had dropped to her throat while I spoke, but I forced it back up to her eyes by the time I was done. When it became clear I had managed to catch her off guard, I used my advantage to press the issue.

"So, spill. What exactly did you do the night we met?"

Chapter Five

# Caroline

WITH MY SHOULDER PRESSED AGAINST the warm, scratchy brick, I tried to find the words to answer his question, despite how much I *really* didn't want to. It felt like the least he deserved after going all white-knight in the bar.

Which was something I was desperately trying to avoid thinking about.

"It seems that just about everyone on campus has seen a video of me from the night we met where I may have verbally attacked a sorority bitch before announcing that not only is she a bulimic hoe, but I'm an amputee, so, naturally, it's caused some waves."

I resolutely pointed my eyes at the ground, at his shoes, at the cigarette butts that littered the cement under our feet. All three of them. *Ha. That's funny.*

Three cigarette butts. Three feet.

I tried to hold out against the heat of his stare as it burned into my forehead. He just wasn't *saying* anything.

The second I lifted my eyes to his, his mouth opened. "I heard you also laid her out." I caught the tilt of his lips, and that tiny movement hit me like the engine of a 747. I felt *shredded*. When he lifted a hand to run it through his slightly-too-long, dark-blond hair, almost nervously, I had to force moisture back into my bone-dry mouth. Once my tongue worked again, I ran it across my lips before I allowed them to tip up.

"Yeah, that might have happened too."

If I had been torn apart by just a lip tilt, the force of his full smile was utterly tectonic. If I hadn't been leaning against the wall, I would have been looking up at him as a pile of mush on the ground.

I felt a quick flash of guilt over the fact that I had never reacted so viscerally, so primitively, to my own boyfriend, but I rationalized it by acknowledging that, no offense to Dan, Jimmy was possibly the most attractive guy I had ever met. I was used to the bulky build of a hockey player, but it was like he had been sculpted solely to play the game; the look worked better for him than anyone I'd ever known. Even the slightly crooked nose, clearly broken a time or two, worked in his favor. He was real and rough, and yet, when he smiled, his face became positively ethereal.

"I'm sorry about those assholes, Caroline."

Recovering from his smile and the thrill I felt when he said my name, his deep voice wrapping around the consonants and vowels in a way that made it feel absolutely explicit, hindered my attempt to regain an acceptable train of thought.

"Don't," I finally said. Shaking my head, I managed to string a few words together that would hopefully convince him I wasn't insane. "Don't apologize for them. It's not even worth it. I just haven't really gotten used to it yet. I mean, don't get me wrong, at home I was a novelty too. I guess I was just enjoying this place being different and all. I kind of fucked that, so I just need to deal with it." I added a defensive shrug at the end, as if he was to blame for my word vomit.

"You shouldn't have to deal with anything. People suck sometimes."

That made me smile, despite the fact that this was quickly becoming one of the strangest conversations I'd ever had.

"Yeah, they do. Still, I'm learning that every so often, people can surprise you in good ways too."

That brought his smile back again, and I wanted to capture the moment on film to keep it until I was old and looking to remember the 'good old days.' I got the distinct impression that the guy standing in front of me didn't smile nearly enough, and the fact that I had gotten two out of him felt like an accomplishment.

I can picture exactly how we looked in that moment, as if I were standing just down the street, watching from a distance. Me, shoulder against the wall, stupid smile on my face, eyes pointed straight up into his as he looked down from what had to have been a mere six inches away but what felt like a mile. It felt like *way too far*.

I can picture it perfectly, so I know exactly what Nate saw when he walked out the door and found us locked in the world's most incriminating staring match. Making it even worse was the fact that neither Jimmy nor I noticed the sound of the door opening, and we were both completely unaware of him until he had walked close enough to grab my arm.

"Caroline."

*Shit. Shit. Shit.*

I felt my cheeks heat, and I dropped my eyes to the ground for a second before turning to face my clearly pissed-off best friend.

"You ready to go?"

I nodded quickly. "Yeah. Let's go."

I took a step toward him, then reconsidered, turning to say goodbye to Jimmy. At the last second, though, I froze, suddenly very conscious of Nate standing three feet behind me, radiating tension, and my own slightly inappropriate reaction to the man standing in front of me.

"Goodbye, Caroline."

At his words, which reeked of finality, I managed to drag my eyes up to his. I saw the regret before he turned away and headed back into the bar.

I forced myself back around but refused to meet Nate's eyes as we headed toward the dorms. I got that he was angry. I could get that he was suspicious. But I hadn't actually done anything wrong. It was kind of bullshit for him to get mad at me when Jimmy was the one who punched some rando in a bar.

I mean, *come on*.

"Caro, what's going on?"

I rolled my eyes because New Caroline was all about sarcasm and attitude when she got pissed. And I was most definitely *pissed*.

"Nothing is 'going on,' Nate."

"Really? Because that's not what it looked like."

"Dude, I fucking get what it looked like." The words burst out, hot and angry, and I think we were both surprised by their force because, suddenly, we were squared off on the sidewalk, about to have it out. "But once again, it was nothing. I don't fucking appreciate you getting pissed at me when nothing happened, and nothing would have happened. But I'm glad you have so much confidence in my ability to commit to relationships."

"Jesus Christ," he groaned. "Caroline, that's not... Look, I'm sorry for acting like a prick. It just kind of freaked me out. Dude, Jimmy has a girlfriend. Like, long-term, serious-as-fuck girlfriend. According to the guys on the team, in the three years he's been here, he's never shown any interest in anyone. Now...this. And you, I know you like him, Caro. At the very least, you're attracted to him. I can see it, so don't lie to me. I just don't want you to get hurt, and this feels like a dangerous situation."

I kept up my glare for another ten seconds before I sighed and hooked my arm through his. With a quick tug, I managed to get him moving back over the concrete before I found the words to reassure him.

"I appreciate your concern, but, I promise, you don't need to be worried. Sure, the guy's cool, but nothing is or will ever happen there."

The slight pout to his lips told me he wasn't completely convinced, but after a long look at my completely neutral expression, his face relaxed.

"Okay."

"Okay?" I asked, with a single raised eyebrow.

"Yeah. Okay."

With a less annoyed eye roll, I tightened my arm around his and said a silent word of thanks that the conversation was over.

Once I got into my room, I changed out of my clothes and into a baggy pair of sweatpants and an old t-shirt of Dan's before heading out to plop onto the couch next to Jen. She was lounging in Yankees yoga pants and a tank top, hands wrapped around a game controller.

"Aren't you supposed to be a Phillies fan?"

She didn't take her eyes off the screen to answer. "Fuck the Phillies."

"Have you even done anything else tonight but play this game? This is exactly where I left you almost five hours ago."

"Don't judge me when you and Nate did the same thing just last night. How is loverboy, by the way?"

Jen was convinced that Nate was secretly in love with me. I'd almost laughed myself to death when she'd shared that.

"He's fine."

"And the other loverboy?"

"Dan's fine too. I talked to him while I was waiting for the guys to wrap up after practice."

"Oh yeah? What'd you guys do?"

I shrugged. "Went to the bar. Hung out." *Caused a fight between two strangers. You know, typical Thursday night...*

She nodded, thankfully more focused on killing digital people than hearing about my night. Sitting restlessly on the couch, I still felt remnants of guilt that had my frustration growing by the second. I hadn't actually done anything wrong, but I couldn't move past it so, instead of sitting and stewing, I said goodnight and headed to my room.

Once I'd gotten ready for bed, I crawled under the covers and held my phone in my hand. I considered it for a few minutes before tapping out a text to Dan.

Me: **Love you**

It took a moment, but then he replied.

Dan: **You okay?**
Me: **Yeah, just miss you.**

I waited for an answer, but in seconds the phone was ringing in my hand. I answered quickly, lips curving up as I pressed it to my ear.

"Hey."

"Hey. I miss you too."

"How was your night?"

"Pretty quiet. Just hung out at the apartment."

I knew that he had moved off-campus, renting a place with three guys he'd met last year. Besides

their first names, I didn't know a thing about them—
or his place. I knew nothing about his life in Ann
Arbor, aside from the bits and pieces he told me
about classes or what he did on the weekends.

And it had never seemed like a big deal
before, but, suddenly, it felt massive.

"How about you?"

I thought about it. Thought about Jimmy
jumping up without even a word from me and
getting in that guy's face because, as he'd said, he'd
felt it bother me. Thought about the moment when
time had slowed down as I watched him swing. I
knew I should probably feel disgusted at the
violence—at the very least turned off by his caveman-
style brutality. I should feel indignant at the fact that
a total stranger rushed to defend me, when I neither
asked for nor needed it.

But I'd sure as hell wanted it, and I'd enjoyed
it. I loved watching him hit that guy, as fucked up as
that might sound.

And even though it was something I could
never hold against him, I couldn't imagine Dan ever
coming to my defense like that. Couldn't even picture
him getting into a fight. Sure, he might have said
something. Maybe. It was more likely that he would
have pulled me up and out the door. The path of least
resistance. Dan wasn't a fighter; in fact, he got along
with just about everyone. That's why we had always
been great together.

Because this was the heart of the matter and
the problem with New Caroline. Old Caroline, the
Caroline I had been in Michigan, she chose the path

of least resistance too. She smiled at everyone, made sure to ask them how they were doing. She was kind and courteous, and even after the accident, when she wanted to tell all the well-wishers to go to hell, she kept her cool, calmly holding their hands and reassuring them. *No, really, I'm okay. I know, it is such a shame that I'll never play again. Yes, I was scared, but I'm getting past it. One day at a time.*

The fucking insanity of it all. Me, lying in a hospital bed, reassuring *them*.

But that was me. That was Caroline. And that was why we'd always been perfect. Everyone had said it: the perfect couple.

I suddenly felt like an impostor.

"Care Bear?"

A *lying* impostor.

"Sorry. It was fine. We just hung at the bar for a bit and then headed home."

"You sure you're okay?"

*No.*

"Yeah. Just tired."

"Alright. Well, I'll let you go. I love you."

"Love you too."

"Goodnight."

Before I could return the sentiment, he was gone. I spent the rest of my night trying to figure out what the fuck I was going to do. Who I was going to be. Because I may not have been Old Caroline anymore, but New Caroline was still practically a stranger to me. New Caroline was whomever and whatever I wanted her to be.

Now I just needed to figure out exactly what and who that was.

## Chapter Six

*Jimmy*

BY THE TIME THE WEEKEND rolled around, I was looking forward to spending two days in my apartment, avoiding every single person outside my front door.

Friday night though, I still ended up at Marco's. It was supposed to be chill. He had promised me it would be, but Marco's place was hardly ever chill anymore, unless it was just us and Ash hanging out to play video games. I tried not to give Marco a hard time—Ash did that enough for the both of us—but I'd slowly grown more and more concerned.

Marco had been part of our group for years, almost as long as Ash and I had been friends, but since we'd started school, it was like he'd become an entirely different person. Sure, I'd smoke some weed every once in a while, and I liked to drink as much as your average twenty-one-year-old college kid, but Marco was a pro when it came to getting fucked up. And I'd been able to handle that, but recently, it seemed like partying was all he really cared about.

I ended up leaving his place early. Despite mine and Marco's best attempts to keep him there, Ash had taken off pretty quickly, muttering something about his new maybe-girlfriend, which was something I still couldn't wrap my head around. After he was gone, when Marco had hordes of people trying to get his attention for one reason or another, I felt awkward and uncomfortable. After giving him a half-assed excuse and apology, I headed out the door.

I called Maddie on the way home, but she was busy and didn't have time to talk. Her unavailability left me alone with my self-deprecation and a wired mind, and by the time I was home and in bed, I was wide awake and feeling especially sorry for myself.

My mind tripped over Caroline's name, and once she was there, she stayed there. I couldn't help but wonder what she was doing, if she was home or out at a party getting herself into trouble. So far, my few encounters with her had given me the impression that she was a magnet for trouble.

There was so much that I wanted to know—so many questions that needed answers. Beyond the fact that she was hands-down one of the most beautiful girls I'd ever seen, there was something about her that felt familiar, something that called out to me in a way that had nothing to do with sex or attraction.

I was officially over keeping my distance.

Sure, Thursday night I'd been convinced that I needed to stay far away from this girl who played with my sanity like it was a fucking chew toy. When I said goodbye, I had meant it. And then I spent the next twelve hours contemplating every word I'd heard her say, every moment we shared outside, and my decisions and conclusions seemed like all the wrong ones.

I just wanted to be her friend.

I'd never experienced such an intense need to learn more about someone, and I figured I could totally be her friend. An absolutely platonic friendship.

Completely doable.

Definitely.

The next morning, I was more than ready to spend the day watching TV in my boxers, but it wasn't even ten when Dad texted.

Dad: **You busy today?**

*Would it really be that horrible to just say yes?*

Me: **Not at all. What's up?**

Dad: **I need to head to the rink, and your mom needs to run some errands.**

Dad: **Think you could hang out with Jack for a bit?**

Me: **No problem.**

It took me two minutes to throw on sweatpants and a t-shirt, and I was headed down the stairs and out the door, straight across the driveway to the back door of my childhood home. It was unlocked, so I let myself into the kitchen, where my mom was standing at the counter, writing a grocery list.

"Hey, Ma." I dropped a quick kiss onto her cheek and then turned toward the dining room before her voice called me back.

"Need anything while I'm at the store, James? When was the last time you went grocery shopping?"

I stifled my sigh. "I'm fine. I went last weekend."

"Okay."

I headed through the dining room and around the corner that led to the living room. There I found Jack sitting on the couch, game controller in hand, staring at the black TV screen.

"Hey, Jackie." I got the typical Jack greeting: a wide smile and eyes that wouldn't meet mine.

"Wanna play."

"Did you check with Dad?"

He shook his head roughly.

"Wanna play." Another rough head jerk. "Wanna play with you."

"Okay, dude. Let me just check with Dad first."

I heard him sigh but ignored it to head up the stairs to the second floor. Passing my old room, and then Jack's, I knocked on my parents' closed bedroom door.

"Hey, Dad."

The door swung open a second later, and I got a small smile before he turned back around to walk toward his dresser.

"What's up, Jim?"

"Jack wants to play PlayStation. Is that ok?"

He glanced at the watch that he was busy strapping to his left wrist before he nodded. "Sure, that's fine. Just a half an hour or so, though. I was hoping you could help him with a school project."

I was less than thrilled with the idea, but I nodded. "Sure. What is it?"

"He needs to make a family tree. He can tell you about it."

I backed away from the door as he headed my way, and we both descended into the living room, where Jack was still staring at the screen like he could set up the game and turn on the TV through sheer force of will.

"Jack," Dad called out as he lumbered toward the dining room, only to stop in the doorway, "Jim's gonna hang out until Mom and I get back, alright? You guys can play for a bit, but when Jim says it's time to turn it off, you need to listen. You told me you'd do your project today, remember?"

Jack rolled his eyes, and I couldn't stop the smile that curved across my lips.

"Jack." Dad refused to let him off the hook. "Game now. Project later."

"Okay, Dad." His words slid out, slow and sullen. I managed to catch a glimpse of Dad's slight smile before he shook his head and walked toward the kitchen. I was still setting up the game two minutes later when we heard both Mom and Dad shout goodbye. Then the door opened and closed, leaving us alone.

"I don't know why you want to play this game," I said into the now-quiet house. "You know that I'm just going to kick your ass."

I turned in time to catch his slow smile and the way his eyes darted from the corner of the TV screen to my chin before falling away again. Once the TV was on, I grabbed a second controller and settled onto the couch, leaving a foot of space between us, before maneuvering through the menu to bring up the game. The *only* game my brother liked to play.

My brother had wanted to play hockey really badly when he was younger. He actually had, for a couple of years, but then he'd become a lot more hypersensitive to touch, and eventually he had to quit when he couldn't make it through a game without a breakdown. I had the brilliant idea of getting a video game, so we could play hockey together without having to step onto ice, and, well, Jack had been hooked ever since.

"You ready, kid?" My question knocked the grin off his face and planted one on mine.

"Not a kid."

I laughed quietly. "Right. I forgot; you're thirteen now. Big, bad teenager. You got a girlfriend yet?"

He smirked, and his eyes landed on my cheekbone this time. Getting closer.

"Girls are stupid." He shuddered with the force of his declaration, and I had to laugh.

"You think that, but it just means you haven't found the right one yet. Don't worry, little bro. It'll happen."

His face went serious then, tuning me out completely as the game began. And even though I could usually block out my thoughts during our gaming sessions, today they seemed too insistent. Too loud to be ignored.

I wanted my brother to grow up to live as normal a life as possible. I wanted him to be happy and fulfilled because, if he was, then maybe there was a chance I could find that too. But, in a place deep down, one that I wouldn't allow myself to talk about, a part of me was afraid that him living "normally" wouldn't ever be possible. I didn't know if he'd be able to live on his own. I didn't know if he'd ever fall in love, or even have a relationship. Even though I told him all the time that he could do whatever he wanted, this world was going to be a really hard place for him. That fucking terrified me.

Jack was the bravest person I knew. He was almost always happy—blissful even—and completely un-fucking-deterred by the hand he'd been dealt. It was one of my favorite things about him. Most of the time, he was just so fucking excited to be alive. Sure, it might not be obvious to everyone, but I always noticed the way his eyes lit at the smallest, simplest things, and I loved trying to see the world from his point of view almost as much as I hated it.

Because it felt like such a lie.

I spent Sunday in my apartment. More specifically, I spent it sitting on the couch in a pair of sweatpants, marathoning some ridiculous show about vampires that I had overheard Caroline mention at the bar on Thursday.

*That's* how pathetic I was.

Although, not that I was planning on ever admitting this out loud, it actually wasn't completely terrible. At least the vampires in this one didn't sparkle. And the evil brother was kind of hilarious.

Still... I was a sad, sad man.

At around eight, I glanced up and realized that it was dark on the other side of the windows. I forced myself off the couch to eat something. Once I'd made and swallowed a peanut butter sandwich, I headed toward the bathroom and undressed to climb in the shower.

It was while I was under the hot water that my brain started pelting me with all the shit I didn't want to think about.

Jack's future.

My future.

Maddie.

*Caroline.*

The last one floated through my mind like a whisper, a nearly silent suggestion. And it—she—was the thing I most wanted to avoid thinking about. At least while I was in the shower. I wasn't a complete prick.

I turned the water to ice cold and finished as quickly as possible. Once I'd toweled off, I headed toward my room to get dressed but wasn't halfway there before I heard the knock at my door.

I had no clue who it could possibly be at eight-thirty on a Sunday, but, whoever it was, I didn't think they'd appreciate me opening the door buck-ass naked.

"Just a sec," I shouted, then ducked into my room to throw on a pair of basketball shorts and a t-shirt. Once I was decent, I headed to the stairs and down to the door. I pulled it open and stopped short at the sight of Maddie standing on the other side of the threshold.

"Hey." Her voice was soft but steady, filled with a quiet determination that matched the light in her amber eyes. I was so surprised to see her that it took me a second to respond. I used that second to really look her over, noting the way her naturally auburn hair looked lighter, as if it had been bleached by days spent in the sun. It was also shorter than I was used to, hitting her just at the collarbone. She looked tan, and she looked tired, but she looked good, and I felt something settle into my chest. Something that felt a little like relief and a lot like comfort.

"Hey," I finally managed and stepped back out of the way so she could follow me inside. I reached around her to shut the door and leaned in to lightly press my mouth to hers. I tried to relax into the kiss, but she ended it almost immediately, pulling back to move around me and up the stairs.

I followed her up and over to the couch, where we both sat on the cushions with an uncomfortably large amount of space between us.

"So, what are you doing here?" I asked when she made no move to speak. She flinched as if she had forgotten there was anyone else in the room, and I moved closer to her. "Hey, what's wrong?"

She shook her head and then looked up at me. "Sorry. I was at my parents' house. I came home for the weekend, and I'm headed back to school tonight, but I wanted to stop by before I hit the road."

I tensed, and she must have seen it because she leaned back. "Seriously?" I asked quietly. She narrowed her eyes, but I didn't give her a chance to talk. "You've been fifteen minutes away for the past two days and just didn't feel like letting me know?"

She huffed and rolled her eyes. "It's not a big deal, James. I just had to talk to my parents about some stuff."

"Okay, but that doesn't explain why you didn't tell me. Because," I continued, sliding away to get the space I needed, "I can't understand why, when I texted you repeatedly and we talked on the phone last night, you didn't find a way to mention that you were at your fucking parent's house!"

"I didn't come here to argue with you, you know."

"So why did you come? Because I'm honestly getting the feeling that you didn't want to."

She was quiet for a moment then, and I felt bad for losing my temper, but that didn't mean I wasn't hurt. I hadn't seen her in months. I'd fucking missed her. And she'd been practically walking distance from my house and just didn't feel like mentioning it.

Really, though, what the fuck *was* that?

"Look, I just... I needed to talk to my parents, and then..." She stopped for a moment to tug on one earlobe, and years of shared history told me that the gesture was a sign of nerves. Suddenly, her visit felt like a bad omen. "I kind of just ended up here."

I took one deep breath to calm myself, but it wasn't enough. Two wasn't either. After three, my hands felt steadier.

"What's going on, Mads?"

"I'm thinking about moving to Italy."

It took me a moment to process the words—to actually convince myself that I had heard her right. Even so, I decided to double-check.

"What did you just say?"

"It's not... Nothing's been settled yet. I'm still just considering the idea."

My hands were shaking again, and all I wanted to do was get up and walk the fuck out. Or tell her to get out. Or something. I couldn't just sit here and listen to this.

"Okay." That was all I could manage. I couldn't breathe. I couldn't think about anything but every plan I'd ever made falling apart in the span of one conversation.

She sighed loudly, which, unfortunately, brought me back into the moment. "You can't just say, 'Okay' when I tell you that I'm debating moving to Italy."

I was too raw, way too vulnerable to censor my reaction to her words. "Do me a favor, Mads: Don't fucking tell me what to say after you tell me that you're up and leaving the goddamn country."

"I'm not 'up and leaving!' I mean, I'm not even sure if... I just felt like you should know."

I laughed, but it was hollow. "Well, thanks for that, I guess. I appreciate the heads-up."

Another heavily annoyed sigh had my hands tightening at my sides. "James, it's not-"

"What do you want me to say?!" I cut her off, and she leaned back for a second, shocked by the force of my outburst. Then she got right back into my face.

"I don't know, okay?!" I saw the tears starting to build in her eyes, but I didn't—I wouldn't—back down. I wasn't the one who was backing out of the future we had been working toward and the plans we'd made together. "I'm sorry," she finally managed. "I just wanted to talk it over with you. I mean, it's a great opportunity for me, and I just..."

I leaned back against the soft couch and allowed my eyes to close heavily, forcing the anger to fade. As much as I might have hated it, I could understand if my future wasn't enough for her. It didn't feel like enough for me. And, really, if I was honest, I was fucking jealous as hell. Not necessarily over Italy, but over the fact that I'd never get to even consider moving somewhere new. Exciting. Different.

I reached out a hand and, cracking one eye, wrapped it around her knee before giving a soft tug that had her falling against my side. She was stiff for a second before she settled against me, resting her hand on my chest and then laying her head on top. I pressed my lips into her hair and inhaled.

If Caroline smelled like summer, Maddie smelled like spring—fresh and new, with just a hint of something flowery that reminded me of being at church on Easter as a child. Not necessarily my favorite association, but one I'd come to know as pure Maddie and appreciate as such.

"I'm sorry. I didn't mean to be a dick."

I felt her nod against my mouth, which was still pressed to her hair, and I pulled back to rest my head back against the couch. "So... tell me about it."

Her hand pressed against my chest as she moved until she was sitting, straddling my lap. Just as I started to lift my head, her fingers slid into my hair, and I felt her lips trace my Adam's apple before her tongue darted out to taste the skin along my jawbone.

"Later." Her voice was quiet and breathy, and despite the fact that I was still angry—not to mention a good bit terrified of where my life was suddenly headed—it had me shifting underneath her, uncomfortably hard in a matter of seconds.

Her lips slid back to my throat, kissing and biting as she worked her hand down my chest until she reached the waistband of my shorts. Pushing the white cotton of my shirt up, she slid one finger across the skin there before moving down to palm me through the thin mesh. *Oh, fuck...*

My hands wrapped around her jean-clad hips, and I pulled her down against me, dislodging her hand and pressing myself against the heat between her denim-covered legs.

"Fuck, Jimmy."

I brought my mouth to hers as she began to work her hips, creating the friction we both needed. Her lips parted, and my tongue swept in, desperate for a taste of her.

It had been entirely too fucking long since we'd done this.

She pulled her mouth from mine to breathlessly whisper, "I need you." The words had my skin tightening, and I felt myself jerk against her. It was possibly the most erotic thing I'd ever heard her say, considering her severe aversion to dirty talk, and my blood pressure spiked viciously as the need to bury myself inside her intensified to the point of pain.

I didn't last long. With anyone else, in any other situation, I would have been embarrassed at just how quickly I came once I'd finally gotten inside her. But after months of coming in my hand, I didn't stand a chance. Thankfully, Maddie seemed to react the same way, coming around me practically the second I entered her, and within minutes we had both collapsed together, the only sound the frantic panting of our breath.

My life had become a train wreck, but lying in a sweaty pile of limbs on the couch and feeling truly satisfied for the first time in a long time, I found that I just didn't give a shit about anything.

It was fucking bliss, and I was going to ride it for as long as I could.

Chapter Seven

# Caroline

I SPENT THE WEEKEND HIDING out in the dorm, leaving only once to go to the gym. Nate tried to drag me out both Friday and Saturday nights, but I refused, wanting nothing to do with the world at large. My wonderfully boring weekend became an awfully crappy one on Sunday night, though. Not only did I wake up shortly after midnight from a nightmare about the accident, but I spent the rest of the night trying to ignore phantom-limb pains long enough to fall back asleep. It didn't work, and I finally caved around 3 a.m., taking one of the pills that was supposed to calm the sensations. I hated taking them because they always made me foggy, but it had gotten so bad that I had no choice.

I laid back down and got about three hours of sleep before Jen's blaring alarm woke me up through two closed doors and across the living room. From then on, I'd been up, my mind in a weird state of being both wide awake and still half asleep.

Even after two cups of coffee, the daze hadn't lifted, and my morning classes were torture. I couldn't focus on a word anyone said, and to make matters worse, halfway through my last class before my break for lunch, I felt someone pinch my left pinky toe hard.

The pinky toe I didn't have anymore.

I couldn't stop the groan that burst from my lips, a noise that made heads turn toward me all across the lecture hall. I ignored every one of them and dropped my head against the desk, gritting my teeth through pain that wouldn't let up.

I spent half an hour like that, refusing to move until I heard people shuffling around me, heading toward the door. After filling my bag, I ducked into the hall and grabbed my phone from my back pocket to text Jen, who got out of class ten minutes before me.

Me: **Lunch?**

I headed out of the building and into the bright September day. The air was warm, but there was a breeze that felt a bit too chilly for my short-sleeved t-shirt. I wrapped my arms around myself as I settled onto a bench outside the building to wait for her reply.

Jen: **Yes, please. Student Center?**

I sent her a message to confirm, picked myself up, and started the trek to the student center. Inside, I made my way through the busy building and straight toward the back, where the caf was. I had been hungry, but standing surrounded by competing smells in the small, food-filled space, I suddenly wanted nothing to do with eating. So I headed for the coffee shop next to the seating area.

I paid for my drink and a cookie I planned on eating later and then navigated around the crowd into the seating area to search for Jen. It didn't take long to spot her, and I shuffled over to the table to pour myself into a seat.

"Hey," I muttered once I had propped my head between my hands, elbows against the cool table.

"Wow," she returned with a wince. "Are you okay? You look..."

I forced a tired smile and shook my head. "I'm fine. Just exhausted. I didn't get a lot of sleep last night."

"How many more classes do you have today?"

"Just one, thank God."

She nodded and took a bite of the giant burrito sitting in front of her. Still chewing, she looked up to say, "Good. You can go get some sleep."

I nodded before lifting my head to take a sip of coffee. Before the cup could make it to my mouth, I spotted the hips stopped right next to our table and froze. I scanned the body I'd already identified much more slowly than I probably should have, but at that point I was existing in a weird state of semi-consciousness that meant I didn't fully realize he was actually standing two feet away until he spoke.

"Hey."

It was the smile that threw me—the wide, relaxed grin that seemed so at odds with the Jimmy I was coming to know. It put every other smile he'd given me so far to shame and left me utterly speechless. Jen finally came to my rescue when it seemed I wasn't ever going to figure out how to talk again.

"Hey. I'm Jen. Who are you?"

I watched him divert his caramel gaze from me to my roommate across the table, and while his smile faded a bit, it was no less genuine.

"James McCarthy. Nice to meet you, Jen."

"You too, James," she said gently, sneaking me a wide-eyed look as he turned his head back to me.

"How was your weekend?"

I nodded stupidly and forced my mouth open. "Pretty boring, but definitely could have been worse." He smiled, and I licked my lips nervously before continuing. "How was yours?"

"Pretty boring, but definitely could have been worse."

*Fuck, now I'm smiling too. Why does this keep happening?*

I shook my head, trying to clear it, which was nearly impossible when faced with my pill-induced stupor and an overabundance of female hormones.

"Do you want to sit, or...?"

"No," he said quickly, shaking his head. "I've gotta run, but I saw you, and I wanted to say hi." He grinned and dropped his eyes almost bashfully before bringing them right back with a small shrug. "So... Hi."

I laughed, and my voice was low when I responded, "Hi." His caramel-colored eyes dropped to half-mast, and he took a half-step backwards before pausing.

"So, there's a party. Next weekend at my friend's apartment. You should come." He looked quickly at Jen, who was watching our exchange like it was a fucking tennis match, a slight smile on her face. "You too. Or," he added back at me, "Nate. Bring whoever you want. But...you should come."

I knew I should just say no, but when I looked to Jen and saw her widened eyes and urgent nod, that's not what happened.

"Okay," I said with a shrug. "We'll come."

"Cool." The bright smile had returned, and as much as I wanted to just stare at it, I also really needed it—him—to go away, so I could manage to string two coherent thoughts together. "Why don't you give me your number, and I can text you the address?"

Without thinking, I rattled off my cell number and then watched him wave goodbye to first Jen and then me before he was walking away after a parting promise to talk to me soon.

Once he was out of earshot, my inquisitive roommate turned her eyes on me. "So..." she started, with fake nonchalance. "Who was that?"

I dropped my head right back into my hands.

"James McCarthy, apparently."

Her eyes narrowed at my response. "What does that mean?"

"I've only met him twice. He's on the hockey team, and he went to the bar with us the other night."

"Okay..." she said slowly before, "So what aren't you telling me?"

I started to deny the omission but stopped and sighed. "While we were at the bar, this guy started saying shit that was bothering me, and, literally out of nowhere, Jimmy got up and told him to knock it off. When he didn't, Jimmy decked him. It was kind of insane. After Nate pulled him outside, we talked for a little while, but I didn't think it meant we were friends."

"Caroline, I can guarantee that boy didn't come over here with 'friendship' on his mind."

"He has a girlfriend, Jen."

"So? That just means he's an asshole."

I groaned and dropped my head to the table with a bang just as my leg sent another stabbing jolt through my nervous system. Letting out a long stream of curses under my breath, I counted to three and waited for the pain to fade. When it didn't, I tried again. One, two, three.

Nope. Still hurt like a bitch.

I pushed off the table and to my feet awkwardly, swaying a bit on the way up before gaining my balance.

"Whatever. I'll tell him we can't go."

"No, we're definitely going."

"You just said he's an asshole."

"I know, but he's sexy as fuck."

"Jennifer, he has a *girlfriend*."

"I know, but sexy guys move in herds. We're going. Tell Nate. And where are you headed? I thought you still had half an hour before class?"

I grabbed my coffee and the rest of my cookie while shaking my head. "I'm going home. Fuck this day. I'm going to take something to sleep, so if you get home and I seem dead, I'm probably fine."

She nodded with a sympathetic frown. "Okay. Text me if you need anything. I can stop somewhere on my way."

"Thanks."

She really was the best.

I did exactly what I'd said I was going to do, and, thankfully, it worked—perhaps a little too well. I slept until nine-thirty and woke up to three missed calls and two texts.

*Yikes.*

The first call was from my mom, as was one of the texts, which simply said **CALL ME!!!!!!**

Not exactly subtle.

Another call was from my step-dad, Steve, who I figured had been instructed by Mom to track me down.

The last call was from Dan.

The last text message, however, was from my roommate.

Jen: **I really hope you're still breathing. Please let me know once you've risen from your coma.**

That had me smiling as I dialed my mom's cell. She answered after half a ring.

"Caroline?"

"Hey, Mom." I stifled a yawn as I stretched and sat up in bed. "Sorry, I was asleep when you called."

"Why were you sleeping? Did you go to classes? Are you depressed?"

I half-heartedly rolled my eyes as she panicked, but I understood where the panic came from, so I refused to let my annoyance bleed into my tone.

"I'm fine, Mom. I didn't get a lot of sleep last night, so after my classes I came back here to take a nap." It was only one-third a lie.

"Are you sure?" She was obviously unconvinced.

"Yes, Mom. I am not depressed."

She sighed and was quiet for a moment before finally moving on. "Okay. Well, I just wanted to check in with you. See how everything was going..."

"Everything's good. Classes are good so far. I'm really liking it here."

"Good, sweetie. I'm glad." She might have been glad, but I knew part of her was hoping I would change my mind and run back to Michigan. I wasn't going to let her know it, but even if I had hated Virginia, I wasn't going home for anything more than the occasional visit anytime soon.

"Alright," she finally continued, "Well, I'll let you go. I miss you, Cary."

"Miss you too, Mom. I love you."

"Love you too, sweetheart."

After hanging up, I texted Steve to let him know I was fine and that I had talked to Mom. Then I called Dan. That call was sent straight to voicemail, and I disconnected before leaving a message. Dropping my phone, I angled myself toward the edge of the bed and grabbed the crutches I always kept close by. Once I'd positioned them under my arms, I heaved myself up and through my bedroom door.

Jen was sitting in the living room, which didn't bother me, but the decently attractive dude sitting on our couch left me feeling just a bit self-conscious about the thigh that ended somewhere under the left pant leg of my mesh shorts.

"Hey! You're alive!"

I cracked a small smile and nodded. "I'm alive."

I stood there for another moment and glanced awkwardly from Jen to mystery dude before nodding my head toward the bathroom. "I just need to..."

"Oh, yeah! Sorry," she muttered sheepishly, and I laughed softly and gimped my way into the bathroom. Once I'd finished up, I made my way back into the living room to find that her friend had mysteriously vanished.

"You feeling any better?"

I found her in the kitchen grabbing two bottles of water from the fridge. She used her hip to close the refrigerator door before handing a bottle to me.

"Thanks. And yeah. Loads."

"Good."

"Where's your friend?"

She grinned and pointed toward her closed bedroom door.

"Ah, well, I'll let you get back to...whoever he is."

She smirked as I turned back toward my room. "Night, Caro."

"Night, Jen."

Once I was back in my room, I sat myself at my desk and tried Dan's cell again with no luck. This time I left a message after the beep.

"Hey, it's me. I just wanted to talk to you. I took a nap earlier, so I'll probably be up for a while if you want to call me back. If not, I'll talk to you tomorrow. Love you."

Once I'd plugged in my phone to charge, I spent some time on my computer before the sounds of Jen and Cute Guy having sex filtered through the walls. I tried to ignore it, but they got louder, and no matter how hard I tried, I couldn't tune them out.

I finally rolled the chair across the floor, so I could crawl into bed. Once there, I grabbed my iPod from my nightstand and stuck the earbuds in, turning it on and up as quickly as possible. I was assaulted by the last song I'd listened to, a screamy rock tune that nearly blew my eardrums out as it started blaring. I turned it down before flipping to something mellower, an Ed Sheeran song that had always reminded me of Dan.

Except it wasn't Dan I thought about while I lay in bed and listened to soft love songs. And I didn't know what that said about me, but I also kind of didn't care anymore.

It was Wednesday night before Jimmy finally texted me. Not that I was impatiently waiting or anything. That would have been weird.

It came in while I was watching some horrible, foreign slasher movie with Nate. Thankfully, he was way more into it than I was.

Unknown: **Hey Caroline**
Unknown: **Its Jimmy**

I forced my face to remain completely blank and saved his number into my phone before sending a message back.

Me: **Hey there**
Jimmy: **What are you up to?**

I snuck a glance at Nate before quickly typing back.

Me: **Watching a really shitty movie. Hbu?**
Jimmy: **Sitting at work. Bored out of my mind.**
Me: **I'd probably take that over sitting here. This movie really sucks ass.**

"Who are you talking to?"

I jumped at Nate's quiet question. For a brief moment, I considered lying. With a reluctant sigh, I decided against it.

"Uh, Jimmy. I ran into him Monday, and he invited Jen and me—and you too—to this party on

Friday, so I gave him my number, so we could work out the details." *And I need to shut the fuck up because I'm rambling.*

Nate noticed and rolled his eyes at me before turning them back toward the TV. "I'm not going to say a word, although I can't believe you're actually considering going."

I shrugged as my phone vibrated in my hand. "It could be fun. Besides, Jen's determined. She wants to fuck one of his friends."

He smirked at that and turned his head back to me. "Did she have a particular one in mind, or...?"

"Not that I know of," I said with a small grin. "But she said something about hot guys in herds so I think she's just generally optimistic."

He chuckled before focusing on the movie. "Whatever. If you guys want to go, we'll go."

With his dismissal, I looked back down at the screen in my hand.

Jimmy: **What's it about?**

Me: **Japanese slasher flick. There's an evil biddy who keeps seducing people in a really creepy way before cutting them to pieces.**

Jimmy: **Sounds awesome ;)**

I smiled, but my hands hesitated over the screen before tapping out a response. I still wasn't sure what Jimmy thought was going on here, and I didn't want to send the wrong signals. Instead, I decided to get the conversation on the right track.

Me: **So I think the three of us are definitely going to come Friday**

Each of his messages after that maintained a subtle air of formality, a detached friendliness that managed to both relieve and disappoint me at the same time. I didn't know how to handle either of those feelings, so I sauntered blindly past them and thanked him for the invite once he had sent me the address and told us to come any time after seven.

Through the rest of the movie, and even after Nate left, when I was lying in bed, I forced myself to avoid analyzing the conversation and worrying about Friday night. I was just going to go to a party with my friends, and in the process I'd make it clear to Jimmy that we were just going to be friends. No biggie.

New Caroline was in charge, and she could handle anything.

## Chapter Eight

*Jimmy*

I WANTED TO BAIL. My week had been so shitty that, by Friday, I was equal parts exhausted and annoyed, and I really didn't want to go to Marco's. That said, I didn't want to text Caroline last minute, and I really didn't want to just not show up. Once I finished hanging with Jack, I forced myself to shower and change before heading out the door.

I'd told Caroline 7 p.m., but as I parked down the block from Marco's apartment building at 7:30, I desperately hoped she hadn't shown up yet. For a moment, I regretted the entire situation. It was stressing me the fuck out, and I wasn't even sure what I was trying to do here anyway.

*Be her friend. You just want to be her friend.*

The door had been propped open with a brick, and I yanked on the handle to let myself in. I jogged up the three flights of stairs, and once I got to his door—one of only two on his floor—I headed straight inside.

Marco's place was massive. I think my entire apartment could fit in his living room—it was that huge. It was also gorgeous, not that he had anything to do with that. The apartment had been a fully furnished gift from his dad, who worked with Ash's dad. Translation: the guy was *loaded*.

The place was also already fucking filled with people, most of whom I didn't know.

I moved straight to the kitchen to grab a beer from the fridge and then headed toward the living room, where I found Marco on the couch with a blonde on his lap and a brunette at his side.

"Jimmy!" He grinned and gestured for me to sit, but there wasn't a chance in hell I was getting on that couch.

"I'm cool."

Somehow, his grin got wider. "You seen Ash?"

I shook my head and scanned the room with the pretense of looking for him, coming across neither Ash nor Caroline. My gaze made it back to Marco in time to catch the tail end of his shrug, and then the brunette was whispering in his ear, dragging his attention away from me.

Pulling my phone from my pocket, I lit the screen to check for a message I may have missed, but there was nothing waiting for me except the realization that I was fucking pathetic.

I polished off my first beer quickly, and then the second. I was on the third before Ash walked in the door, ever-present, cocky-as-fuck grin on his face. Skipping the kitchen, he headed straight in my direction and nodded in greeting once he was a few feet away.

"Hey, man. How you been?"

He shrugged and rubbed a hand across his chin before answering. "Alright, I guess."

I smirked at that. "Girl problems?"

"Fuck you, dude. We can't all find our soulmates in high school."

I ignored the comment about Maddie and focused on the implication in his words. "Damn, 'soulmate?' That's some heavy shit."

He mumbled something under his breath but didn't respond otherwise. I just shook my head and let it go.

I should have been pacing myself. I did the opposite. As one hour passed, and then two, without any sign of Caroline, I poured back beer after beer. I got more drunk with each consecutive game of flip cup I played, and the urge to text her grew to near overwhelming proportions. I resisted, but just barely.

Parker, Ash's girl, ended up showing. I wanted to talk to her, wanted to get a feel for their situation, but because I was tense and pissed, I avoided her, Ash, and Marco as they all made nice and got to know one another. I was on edge, and I figured it'd be easier to make up for my standoffishness later than to try and avoid being a dick now.

The night only got shittier. When a dick from high school showed up and tried to start shit with Ash, I was all too eager to put my fist through his face, but Marco got there first and threw the asshole out. All my adrenaline had nowhere to go, leaving me even more amped. Ash and his girl disappeared, and, not long after, Marco came to find me, holding a bowl much smaller than the massive bong he'd been sending around the room earlier. I took it from his outstretched hand gratefully, taking two hits in quick succession. They were enough to take the edge off the angry, frustrated anxiety that made my hands shake as I tried to use the lighter. I took another hit for good measure before handing the piece back to him.

"Thanks, dude."

He shrugged. "You alright?"

I jerked my head up once. "Yeah. I'm good."

He looked like he wanted to press the issue, so I dodged him by turning to head for the kitchen and another beer. As soon as I passed through the hallway and into the living room, my skin prickled with awareness, and I looked up directly into her eyes.

I was drunk and pretty high at this point, but I swear to fucking God, it was like everything around us—every person in that apartment—froze. The only things that existed were Caroline and me. I took in the tight, gray v-neck t-shirt that dipped dangerously low on her chest and the black jeans that sat low on her hips, the tiniest strip of golden skin on display between the fabrics. *Fuck, she's gorgeous*. Her hair was pulled back tonight, and, more than anything, I wanted it down, falling around her face and over her shoulders like water. I wanted my hands in it, and I wanted...

"Hey!"

The word snapped me out of my daze. Her blue eyes caught mine from less than two feet away. They were dark, but shining, and when I watched her wobble once on her feet before reaching out for Jen, I realized that she was possibly as drunk as I was.

*Thank fuck.*

She laughed at herself and then calmed down enough to focus back on me.

"Sorry. We kind of started drinking, like, three hours ago."

I smiled and shrugged. "So did I."

I heard a throat being cleared, and then Caroline took a step back quickly. "Uh, you remember Jen?"

I found her and nodded, mumbling a "Hey," but I couldn't keep my eyes off the girl in front of me.

"Hey, man," Nate suddenly said a bit too enthusiastically, and I turned quickly to find him staring at me, looking less than thrilled.

"Hey. Glad you could make it." I forced my eyes to stay still while I gave him what I hoped passed for a genuine smile, then I let them drift back to Caroline.

"So, uh, kitchen's right over that way." I gestured with my thumb toward the room off to our side. "You guys can help yourselves."

That was all it took for Jen. She was darting through the crowd toward the kitchen before I had even finished getting the words out. Once it was just the three of us, Nate pulled Caroline to his side to whisper something in her ear before he was interrupted by someone shouting, "Baker!" across the room. He turned and waved before focusing back on Caroline to give her a look that I didn't fully understand before he, too, walked away.

When he was gone, I caught myself staring again, only this time she returned it, slowly moving her eyes first down and then back up my body. I felt it. Inch by burning inch, her scorching hot gaze blazed against my skin.

Her appreciative appraisal made it back to my face, and once again, for just a second, the world faded. This time, though, I didn't let it catch me off guard.

"Do you want a drink?"

She ran her tongue across her bottom lip in a way that I was starting to guess meant she was nervous. Whether because of me or just from being here, I wasn't sure. Still, she nodded and then turned to head toward the kitchen.

Jen was standing at the counter as we made our way over, chatting up some guy I'd never met. She didn't spare us even a glance as I leaned a hip against the counter.

"What's your poison?"

"Got tequila?"

I grinned and turned from scanning the bottles to wink at her. "A girl after my heart. Wanna do a shot?"

"Sure."

I poured the amber liquid into two shot glasses I'd grabbed from a cabinet and passed one to Caroline. As she reached out to take it, our fingers brushed. It felt like taking a two-second hit with a stun gun. I hoped she didn't notice my jaw go slack and my eyes glaze over. Thankfully, she was just drunk enough that I figured I'd gotten away with it.

Picking up my own shot, I looked down to find her eyes. "What are we going to toast to?"

She stared at the tiny glass in her hand for a moment before looking back up at me. "To new friends."

I shrugged. "Works for me."

We clinked and tossed back the shots. I breathed through the burn as Caroline coughed twice. The sound made me smile again.

"Another?"

She nodded and set the glass down. Once it had been filled, and we'd both picked our glasses up, I looked to her for another toast, but she shook her head. "Your turn."

I took a second to think it over before raising my glass.

"To feeling limitless."

Her brow wrinkled, and her lips puckered like she was trying to work that out, but I didn't give her a chance to question it before I tapped my glass to hers lightly and threw back the shot. By her cough, I'd guessed she'd done the same.

"Okay, I need a break from the liquor."

I smiled and took the shot glass from her, placing it with mine in the sink before I turned and grabbed her hand. "Come on. I'll show you around."

I took her around the apartment, completely ignoring everyone who tried to talk to me. We finally made it to Marco's storage room, which I unlocked with the key he kept hidden on top of the door frame.

"This is probably my favorite room."

She snorted. "Not the one with the seventy-inch projection screen and every game console known to mankind? 'Cause that's probably mine."

I smiled but ignored her to flip on the lights before pulling her in behind me and shutting the door. I gave her a moment to take in the room on her own.

"Holy shit."

Holy shit was right. Marcos's dad collected movie memorabilia, and he'd gotten Marco into to the hobby early on, so the entire space, excepting one wall lined with bookshelves and cardboard boxes, was filled with iconic set pieces and costumes hanging on mannequins.

I followed Caroline around the room, pointing out the ones I liked the most—the animatronic Gremlin, the whip that Indy used in Raiders of the Lost Ark, and a few others—before leading her toward the case for my favorite item. She stood in front of the wooden box, and I leaned in behind her, leaving just an inch between our bodies.

It felt way too close.

It felt way too far.

"This is my favorite," I said quietly into her ear, watching the tiny hairs that had escaped her ponytail move with my breath.

"What is it?" Her voice was just as quiet, but laced with something I couldn't identify.

"Inigo Montoya's sword from The Princess Bride."

She turned to face me, and we were so close, her cheek brushed against mine in the process. I forced myself to lean back and took in her clueless expression.

"Seriously? You've never seen The Princess Bride?"

She shook her head, and her lips twisted into a small smile. "Nate's been trying to get me to watch it for years."

At the mention of the guy who seemed to never leave her side, I had to force myself not to question her about her relationship (or possible lack of one), since it wasn't like it mattered. At least not to me.

We were just friends.

"So, why haven't you?" I steered myself back on track. "It's a great movie."

"I believe you. I'll get around to it, one day."

"I have it. We should watch it sometime."

Her brow furrowed again, and I wanted to lift a finger to smooth away the wrinkle that formed, but her next words completely killed the urge.

"I have a boyfriend."

I forced a nonchalant shrug that was much harder than it should have been. "Okay. I have a girlfriend." It might have been wishful thinking, but I could have sworn that she deflated the smallest bit.

"I know, actually. I just..." That tongue peeked out to wet her lips, and the sight mesmerized me so much that I almost didn't hear the rest of her words. "I don't really know what's happening here."

*Casual. Act fucking casual.*

"New friends, remember? There's no rule that says two people who are both in relationships can't be friends, right?"

She smiled, but it didn't reach her eyes. "Yeah, of course. I just... I'm not sure that being your friend is a good idea."

I forced a playful eye roll, even as my palms started to sweat. "It's a fucking great idea. I'm an awesome friend."

That time I got a full smile, eyes and all. "Oh, yeah?"

"Yeah. I'm going to blow your mind with how good of a friend I am. You'll be ruined for any other friends once I'm done with you."

I noticed the slight blush that stained her cheeks with my words, and I forced myself to stop making non-platonic innuendos. Instead, I wiped my hand against my jeans before pushing it into the empty space between us.

"Friends?"

She hesitated, but then slowly wrapped her cool fingers around mine and shook my hand gently, once.

"Friends."

# Chapter Nine

# Caroline

AFTER OUR CONVERSATION IN THE spare room, Jimmy led me back out to the kitchen to grab another drink. One drink turned into two, which turned into three, and before I knew it, I was trashed.

No, not trashed.

*Wasted.*

Jen and I spent some time on the makeshift dance floor in the dining room, making complete fools of ourselves while Nate watched from a distance. I tried not to notice, but it was hard to miss Jimmy watching too, from a corner of the room where he stood by himself. I thought about trying to pull him onto the dance floor, just to loosen him up a bit. He seemed so on edge all the time, like he was carrying the weight of the world between his shoulder blades. I wanted to get rid of the tension that lined his face whenever he forgot to hide it.

By the time the party started to die down, I was exhausted, sweaty, and drunk, but I really wasn't ready for the night to end. It had been the most fun I'd had in months.

"Come on, Caro," Nate said, as I took my time finishing the final beer I'd convinced him to let me drink. "Just chug it. I want to get home."

I took a quick sip before glancing around the room. "Where did Jen go?"

"Bathroom. When she comes back, we're leaving."

I took another drink. "I'm going to walk home."

"Uh, no, you're not. You're drunk. I'm not letting you walk by yourself."

I speared him with my best glare, but I'm not sure how effective it was with my blood alcohol level hovering well above the legal limit. "I can take care of myself, Nathanial."

"Jesus Christ," he muttered, rolling his eyes up to the ceiling in what looked like a silent prayer. "Please just finish your beer, so we can go."

Part of me wanted to take my time just to spite him, but I really did want to drink it, so I chugged the rest of the alcohol as Jen made her way back to my side.

"Awesome," Nate said sarcastically, once I had set the empty can on a table in the living room. "Let's go."

He turned and headed for the door as Jen linked her arm through mine and tugged me along beside her. "What's his problem?"

"He gets pissy when it's his turn to be DD."

Her drunken giggle lasted longer than my statement really deserved, but it had me smiling all the same. "No, that's not it."

"You guys know I can hear you, right?" Nate called from a few steps below us on the stairwell, but Jen ignored him to continue.

"His problem is that he needs to get laid."

I laughed outright as Nate hit the first-floor landing and turned to face us. "You offering to do the job, Jen?"

"In your dreams, Baker."

"Then shut your mouth, and let's go."

We pushed out the door into the cool air, and I took a deep breath. It was a gorgeous night, chilly but not cold, and the alcohol was doing a fantastic job of keeping me plenty warm. I snuck my arm out of Jens hold and, instead of following toward the car, headed for the sidewalk. I only made it about four feet before Nate realized I wasn't with them.

"Caroline, I'm not doing this tonight. Just get in the car."

I waved an arm back in his direction, which quickly proved to be a bad idea. For some reason, as I moved, gravity got a whole lot stronger, and I listed starboard, heading straight toward the ground.

"Whoa," I heard in my ear, just as two arms wrapped around my torso and kept me standing. "You alright?"

I didn't even need to look to know that it was Jimmy coming to my rescue once again. Even if he hadn't whispered in my ear with his gruff voice that seriously messed with my need-to-get-laid hormones, I *knew* it was him.

I nodded, and he stepped away as Nate got Jen settled into the passenger seat and headed back in my direction.

"Caro, please, just come on."

"I'm walking, Nate."

"You almost just cracked your head open on the sidewalk."

"I don't care. I'm walking."

Somewhere in the back of my alcohol-fuzzed brain, I knew I was acting like a child. I also knew Nate was right—I probably shouldn't be walking home at 2 a.m. by myself, but I was damn sure going to do it. To prove that point, I turned away from the guys and started heading home. This time, I didn't hear Nate calling after me, which was a relief, but after a minute or so, I heard footsteps and turned back to find Jimmy jogging down the sidewalk toward me. Once he'd reached my side, he matched my pace, and we walked along together in silence for a minute until I broke it.

"What are you doing?"

"Walking you home."

It was what I'd been expecting him to say, but I sighed nonetheless. "You really don't need to do that."

"I know."

We made it to the end of the street and turned toward campus before he spoke again. "Can I ask you a question?"

I turned to him with a wry grin. "You just did." He rolled his eyes but smirked, and I nodded to encourage him.

"You're from Michigan, right?" It took me a moment to realize that Nate must have mentioned it at some point.

"Yep."

"So, why Virginia?"

I'd been expecting pretty much any other question, so that took me by surprise. I had to consider it for a moment to find the best way to dodge it.

"That's a really long story."

He held both his hands up to gesture at our surroundings before rubbing one along his jaw against the stubble that grew there. I found myself so fascinated watching him that I barely avoided tripping over a hole in the concrete. Forcing my eyes forward, I stared at the ground to keep myself upright.

"We have some time. Where do you even live?"

"Copeley."

He laughed quietly. "Yeah, we have time. You realize that we're about four miles, give or take, from your place, right?"

I laughed too, but mine wasn't quiet. "Really? The big, bad hockey captain is complaining about a four-mile walk?"

"For starters, I'm an alternate. And it's four for you, then another ten for me to get home once I drop you off, but no, actually, I'm not complaining at all. Just making sure you're up for it."

I rolled my eyes at that. "I'm pretty sure I can handle it."

I hadn't meant for the words to come out as caustically as they had, but I'd had about two years' worth of people doubting what I was capable of, and I was *really* over it.

"Fuck." The word was a quiet groan, and then his hand was on my arm, squeezing tightly enough to get my attention while he stopped us both in the middle of the sidewalk. I tried to ignore how warm his hand felt and the way his touch electrified my skin; I tried but only half succeeded. "Caroline, I didn't mean... I wasn't even thinking about that. Seriously, I was just making a bad joke."

He seemed more tense than he really should have been. Soft brown eyes nervously scanned my expression, and the vulnerability on his face took my breath away. Immediately, I felt bad for assuming the worst about his meaningless statement.

"It's fine," I assured him with a gentle shake of my head. "I'm sorry. I'm a little sensitive sometimes. It's... Well, it's something I'm working on." I shrugged, and the motion finally knocked his hand from its perch just above my elbow.

"You don't need to apologize. I get it."

I raised an eyebrow at that and gave him a small smile, but I turned and started moving back down the sidewalk before I responded. "No offense—I'm not sure I believe you. Still, I appreciate the sentiment." Peeking my eyes to the side, I glanced at him to see if I'd gotten a reaction. I found him looking my way with a heavy expression.

"I might not know what it's like to be an amputee, but I understand being sensitive to something."

There was something about the weighty way he said those words that convinced me he was telling the truth. "Okay. Sorry."

"You apologize too much."

"What does that mean?"

"Exactly that," he said, like it was so obvious. "You apologize all the time. For shit that's not even your fault."

"I do not."

"You do."

I sighed and gave up the fight. "It's a habit."

"A bad one."

I dropped a shoulder in deference to that. "I'll add it to the list." We came to an intersection and stopped to wait for a car to pass, which gave me the chance to look at him in time for his query.

"The list?"

"Of stuff that I'm working on."

I caught the full tilt of his lips as I turned away to cross the street, and then we walked in silence for a few minutes before he brought us full circle. "So? The long story. What are you doing in Virginia?"

"Right," I said with a sigh, "the long story." If he really wanted to know, I was just going to lay it out there. "So, about two years ago I was in a car accident. I lost my left leg from just above my knee. I spent a while in the hospital and ended up having to repeat my senior year. I had applied early admission to the University of Michigan with Dan right before the accident, but I just... I didn't really want to do the whole high-school-part-two thing, you know? Especially since I would have been a year behind everyone I knew. Nate had deferred for a year to stay in Michigan with me, and I knew he was coming here, so I applied, and..." I shrugged. "Here I am."

"That's it?"

I heaved a breath at his disbelieving tone. "I mean, no. It's a little bit more complicated than that. That's the watered-down version."

"Okay..." He stretched the word out, and I knew he was working something over in his mind. "Nate put off college for you?"

I nodded, and his jaw tightened for barely a second. Quickly enough that I shouldn't have noticed, but I had, and I wasn't about to let it go. "What?"

"What what?"

"That pissed you off."

Shaking his head, he grabbed my arm gently to pull me around a corner before muttering, "Shortcut. And it didn't piss me off. I just hadn't decided whether he was gay or in love with you. Now I know it's the latter."

"No, it's neither."

He laughed quietly. "If you say so."

His dismissive tone seriously pissed me off, almost as much as his know-it-all attitude. Because, really, who was he to tell me how Nate felt about me?

"I do say so. You have no fucking clue what you're talking about."

"I'm not trying to piss you off," he fired back. "I'm just telling you what I know. Admittedly, it isn't a whole lot, but seriously, Caroline? You're fucking gorgeous. Sexy as hell, hilariously funny, you know hockey, and you shoot tequila like you were raised to do it. Nothing there is a turn off. And a guy would need to be really fucking stupid to get a good look at everything you are and not want to do whatever it takes to make you his. Nate Baker is not that stupid."

I was having a really hard time trying to block out the effect those words insisted upon having on me. But, as nice as it sounded, he was wrong.

"Nate is the brother I never wanted but always needed, and I promise you, he feels the same. And when it comes to everything else you just said, trust me, it might seem kind of cool at first, but no one wants the one-legged chick."

"Says the one-legged chick in a relationship."

I laughed then, and when I spoke, I could only blame my lingering drunkenness for what came out. "Trust me, he's not that into it either."

Jimmy didn't find it nearly as amusing as I had. I figured that out by the scowl he leveled at me. "What does that mean?"

I chuckled again, somewhat unable to believe that we were actually having this conversation. My cheeks heated with a mixture of embarrassment and sudden nerves, and I licked my lips before answering. "I mean, it's not something we've really talked about, but sex with Dan was definitely better before the accident. It's not like our sex life was all that great before, but now... It's just not really the same."

I steadfastly avoided looking in his direction by focusing on the buildings and houses we were surrounded by, but I couldn't tune him out enough to miss his next words.

"He sounds like a fucking tool."

I very briefly considered ignoring that statement, but once again I opened my mouth when it was better left closed.

"He's not. Dan's great, and I know he loves me. I can't blame him for being turned off by my wreck of a body. Trust me, you can't see it, but it's pretty bad."

I saw him shake his head out of the corner of my eye, but, thankfully, he didn't respond. I waited a moment so my abrupt conversational shift wasn't as noticeable before I asked, "So, what's the deal with your girlfriend?"

He let out a soft sigh. "Maddie's family moved to Charlottesville the summer before our senior year. It sounds kind of stupid, but when I saw her, I just knew. She was the most gorgeous…" He stopped and cleared his throat before going on. "We hit it off, and from there...I fell in love with her."

He went quiet then, but it was a heavy silence, uncomfortable and filled with something I couldn't put a name to. It lasted for a few minutes before he continued like he'd never stopped.

"Then high school was over, and even though I was staying here and she wanted to go to William and Mary, I didn't care. I loved her, and I figured it wouldn't be a big deal. We'd make it work, you know?" I nodded. "She was supposed to move back home after school. We were going to get a place nearby and start a life together, and now..." He lifted the shoulder closest to me, then dropped it before sighing heavily. "I'm just not sure why I tried for three years to make something work for her to suddenly decide that it's not good enough."

My eyebrows slanted, and I turned to watch his face while I asked, "What do you mean? What's not good enough?"

"Maddie's an Art History major. There's not a whole lot to do with that around here. And between my family and the rink..." I was totally lost, but he must have guessed that because he explained, "My dad owns a hockey rink that's going to be mine one day, which is cool and all, but my future honestly doesn't look that exciting. She has this opportunity to move to Italy for work after graduation, and...part of me wants her to go. I want her to get everything she wants out of life, and this would be an incredible thing for her."

I waited a moment to see if he would continue, but he didn't. "And the other part of you?"

"The other part..." One shoulder lifted slightly, and when he looked up at me, his face revealed a sheen of exhaustion. The sudden change was drastic and disarming. "The other part hates her for wanting to leave me behind."

He sounded so hopeless then, so desperate for something, though I wasn't entirely sure what. I guessed absolution—someone to tell him that the way he felt was totally natural. And it was. It definitely was. Still, I was stuck on something else he'd said, so I wasn't really focused on providing any comfort.

"So... What? You're just giving up?"

He stopped walking and looked at me, annoyance sliding across his features as I came to a wobbly halt in front of him. "I'm not giving up. But I can't exactly keep her here if she doesn't want to be here."

"Okay, but if she means that much to you, wouldn't your dad understand if you said, 'Sorry, but I love this girl, and I'm going to follow her to Italy?' I'm getting the feeling that you don't want to stay here a whole lot, either."

He shook his head roughly and then abruptly started walking again. I hurried to follow just as he said, "It's not... The rink isn't what's keeping me here."

"Okay," I said slowly. "So, what's keeping you here?"

He took so long to respond that I didn't think he was going to at all. We'd made it another two blocks before he finally said one word. "Jack."

"Who's Jack?"

"My brother."

Now I was really confused.

"Why...?" I started, before abruptly stopping. I had a sudden—almost alarming—moment of clarity. Or maybe it was sobriety. Either way, I forced my mouth shut the second my brain realized that this conversation was almost certainly a minefield.

I was prepared to just let the subject go, but a minute later Jimmy spoke again. "Jack's autistic. I help my parents out, taking care of him and stuff. I'm not going to leave him behind."

I had no idea what to say to that, so I licked my lips and managed, "Oh."

He huffed out an unamused chuckle. "Yeah."

I took a deep breath and let it out slowly before venturing into the suddenly uncomfortable-as-hell silence. "I'm sorry."

"Don't fucking apologize, Caroline. Especially not for this."

"I just mean-"

"No," he interrupted. "I'm serious. Jack is... I love my brother, and I'd do anything...give up anything to make him happy. Maddie included. I'm not sorry about that—at all—so don't you dare apologize."

"Okay." One word, and then I shut my mouth for good. It really was the safest option.

It didn't take much longer to get to my building, thank God, because with us not talking, my mind spent every second analyzing Jimmy's apparently failing relationship and his commitment to his brother. I thought the way he spoke about Jack was beautiful, and, somehow, I just knew he meant every word he said. He really would give up anything to see his brother happy.

I had to wonder what Maddie was looking for if she'd already found Jimmy and decided he wasn't enough. Also, I thought she might be just a little bit crazy. Because, really, James McCarthy was seemingly closer to perfect than any other guy I'd ever met, barroom brawls notwithstanding.

I checked my phone when we started up the walk to the front door of my building and was shocked to see that it was already after three.

"How much longer of a walk do you have?"

"A couple miles. It's no big deal."

"Why don't you just crash here?"

One side of his mouth tilted up, and his eyes darkened in a way that made my nipples tighten under my shirt.

*Oh, my god. That was so not a friendly look.*

"I think that's an incredibly bad idea."

I licked my lips reflexively and noticed his eyes drop to watch. "It's a two-bedroom, and we have a couch. You'll have the living room all to yourself."

He reached up to squeeze the back of his neck, and I could tell he was about to argue the point when he let out a massive yawn that had me smiling. "Come on. I'll feel really crappy if you walk home, tired and alone, after getting me here safely."

He gave me a small grin that I took as his agreement, and then I was letting us both through the door and leading him down the hall. Once I'd unlocked the door to the suite, I flicked the lights and headed past the kitchen into the living room.

"Nice place." At the sound of his voice, I turned to find him scanning the small space. It wasn't anything swanky, nothing like Marco's posh apartment, but Jen and I had put some effort into decorating, so it at least looked nicer than a typical college dorm.

"Thanks. I'm going to grab you a pillow and a blanket. Just give me a sec." He nodded, and I headed toward my room. I snatched one of my two pillows from my bed before grabbing the spare blanket I had stashed in the closet. It was from my bed at home—

bright purple with large daisies all over it—and I smiled at the thought of muscled and manly Jimmy stretched out under it.

Once I had what I needed, I headed back out to find him standing next to the couch, phone in hand. His face was hard, and he didn't notice me until I spoke from a mere two feet away. "Everything okay?"

He jumped and shot me a tight smile that I didn't buy for a second before nodding. "Yeah. Thanks," he added, taking the blanket and pillow from my hands and dropping them onto the couch. Once my hands were empty, I headed for the fridge and grabbed two bottles of water. I walked back to where he was still standing by the couch and handed him one, which he took with a grateful smile. It was slightly more genuine than his first attempt.

"Do you need anything else?"

"No. Thanks, though."

I nodded and gestured to the door behind me. "I'm right there if you need anything, and the bathroom is right over there." I pointed.

"I'll be fine. Thanks, again." I gave him one last smile and turned toward my room, just reaching the door before I heard him quietly add, "Goodnight, Caroline." I turned to take him in and had to fight back a smile at the simple sight of him standing in my living room, earnestly wishing me a good night.

"Goodnight, James."

I watched him grin before I turned the knob and escaped into my room.

## Chapter Ten

Jimmy

I AWOKE TO A PAIR of unfamiliar eyes staring into mine from beside the couch, less than a foot away. Freaked the fuck out, I bolted up to sitting and narrowly avoided slamming my head into the stranger's. *Not a stranger*, I realized as my eyes and my brain worked to play catch-up. *Caroline's roommate.* After a frantic glance around the room and a quick recap of the night before, I quickly remembered where I was and was able to start calming my racing heartbeat.

"What the fuck?" I groaned, throwing myself backward onto the couch, one arm slung over my eyes.

"'What the fuck' yourself, dude? You're on my couch."

"What time is it?"

"Seven-thirty."

I peeled my arm from my face to glare in her direction. "Seriously? Why are you even up?"

"Seriously?" she echoed, voice rising by the second. "Why are you on my couch?!"

"Shit," I muttered, pushing up to swing my legs down to the floor. "You're fucking loud. And

Caroline invited me to stay," I told her before rubbing both hands down my face.

"She did *what*?!"

Right on cue, Caroline's bedroom door inched open, and she poked just her head through the crack. "Jen, can I borrow you for a sec?"

Jen gave me one last scathing look before backing away from the couch and into Caroline's room. Once they were both behind the door, I grabbed my phone and car keys from where I'd stashed them on the floor and shoved myself up and into the bathroom.

When I finished, up, I headed back out to gather the pillow and blanket. I was in the process of folding the latter when Jen reemerged alone, shutting the door behind her. This time, she ignored me completely to walk to her room before retracing her steps and placing a set of keys on the kitchen counter. I'd finished folding the blanket and had gathered up the pillow when I turned to find her standing right beside me.

"Listen up, McCarthy. I'm onto you. And if you do *anything* that in any way hurts that girl, I'll hunt you down and demolish your testicles with a set of needle nose pliers and a hand saw." I raised my eyebrows and opened my mouth to argue, but she cut me off by lifting a hand, palm out in my direction. "Serious ball torture. Just keep your hands and your endearing qualities to yourself, and we'll be fine."

Once again, Caroline had perfect fucking timing because suddenly I heard her door opening, and Jen was walking back to her room without even giving me a chance to respond, which, really, I was completely okay with.

"Hey."

At the softly spoken word, I turned and took her in. Her hair was down around her face, and she was wearing loose, gray sweatpants along with a light yellow t-shirt that stretched tightly across her chest. Not that I paid attention to that.

At least, not much.

"Morning," I managed to get out around my suddenly clogged throat. I cleared it before continuing. "I, uh, have your stuff..."

"Oh, great. Thanks..."

*Fuck, this is awkward.* I decided to make a swift exit and moved to her quickly, pushing the bedding into her hands.

"So, I'm gonna head out. I'll see you around, okay?"

I had started to turn toward the door when she blurted, "No, wait! I'll drive you." She took a step around me and dropped her hands, letting the pile of fabric fall to the couch cushions. "I already got Jen's keys, so we're good to go. I just need coffee, so we have to stop on the way."

"Don't worry about it. I can walk."

"It's really not a big deal. I have to head out anyway."

"I'm just walking back to Marco's for my car. I'm fine, Caroline."

She huffed out a breath and rolled her eyes. "Has anyone ever told you that you're stubborn as shit?"

One half of my mouth lifted at that. "Maybe not in those exact words, but yeah, you're definitely not the first."

"Good," she replied, moving around me to grab Jen's keys from the counter. "Just wanted to make sure you knew. Let's go."

Caroline led the way out of the building to a small, red sedan parked directly out front. Once we were both inside the car, she strapped herself in and started the engine before turning to face me.

"Buckle up."

Only once I had securely buckled my seatbelt did she put the car in gear and then we were backing out of the spot and driving off toward the center of campus with the early-morning traffic.

No more than four minutes later, albeit a silent four minutes, Caroline had pulled the car into a small shopping center, parking directly in front of a tiny coffee shop I'd never noticed before. I slowly climbed out for lack of anything better to do as she practically ran from the driver's side, slamming the door shut as she darted away to push through the entrance to the coffee shop without a word back toward me.

By the time I got inside, she was standing at the counter, looking back at me impatiently. "Do you want anything?"

I couldn't stop the chuckle that rumbled from my chest. I shook my head, and she snapped her torso around to hand over the credit card between her fingers. She'd gotten it back by the time I reached her, and it wasn't a minute later that she was holding a large paper cup in her hands. I watched her bring the cup to her mouth before I looked away, grabbing the back of my neck in the process. I didn't need to see her throat working as she swallowed the hot coffee or her pursed lips as she pulled the cup away. I'd watched her drink enough beer last night that the image was soldered into my brain, despite my best efforts to keep it out. She'd lowered the cup by the time I glanced back up to meet her apologetic eyes.

"Sorry. I really needed that."

I smirked, following behind again as she headed toward the door and led us both back outside.

"Not a morning person?"

"I can usually handle mornings. I mean, I like my coffee, but I'm not totally addicted. I just..." Her eyes darted to me almost shyly before focusing in front of us again. "I didn't get a lot of sleep last night."

Just like that, my brain couldn't focus on anything other than her lying in that bed alone. I didn't know what the room looked like, what color her sheets were, or what she slept in, but my mind was making every attempt to fill in the blanks. As we climbed back into the car, I desperately tried to will my thoughts away from her with visions of grandmas and dead puppies, but it wasn't working, and I seriously needed a distraction. Unfortunately, she was more focused on taking small sips of coffee for the first few minutes of the drive, and I suffered along in silence.

The car was stopped at a red light a few minutes later when I noticed her tapping her fingers on the steering wheel nervously. I had just opened my mouth to question it when she spoke. "I wanted to thank you again for inviting us last night." She glanced at me quickly before the light turned green and she turned through the intersection. As the car picked up speed, I watched her tongue dart out to wet her lips before she continued. For the second time in less than ten minutes, I was losing the fight against getting hard. "I had more fun than I've had in a while."

"Good," I told the windshield, a small smile curving across my lips. "I'm glad. You're welcome anytime."

"I also..." She hesitated then, and against my better judgment I turned my head, just in time to see her teeth release her bottom lip.

*Fuck. That lip is going to be the death of me.*

"I wanted to apologize." I started to argue, but she cut me off. "Really, I didn't mean to get all...up in your business. It wasn't fair, so I'm sorry."

I thought about that, and, really, she was right; it probably wasn't cool of her to call me out. We were still in the early stages of getting to know one another. It had pissed me off in the moment, but that was before the three hours I'd spent lying awake on her couch, thinking about what she'd said. Maybe it was because I just felt so fucking lonely that some days I wanted to scream, but I couldn't answer her with anything but the truth.

"You're the only person I've really talked to in months. I know I was kind of a dick, but, really... I just appreciated feeling like someone cared."

I forced my eyes to stay locked on the road in front of us throughout my confession, but I couldn't miss the look she sent my way—an even mixture of surprise and sympathy. I could feel her working herself up to a response, so I cleared my throat and spoke before she had the chance. "I think I'm going to have to get involved with kicking this apologizing habit of yours."

She was quiet for a few seconds before she let out what I guessed was a relieved sigh.

"Oh yeah?"

I finally let my eyes slide to her to see a small smile playing on her lips. I was so distracted, I completely forgot to respond until she prompted me with, "How are you planning to do that?"

I directed my gaze out the window as she made the last turn onto Marco's street. "I'm the black Volkswagen." I pointed, directing her to an open spot on the street behind where I'd left my car overnight. As she slid the car to the curb, I turned back to face her and continued, "I'm not sure yet. I'll think of something."

I grabbed the handle of the door and gave her one last grin. "Thanks for the ride, Caroline."

She smiled. "I'll see you around, Jimmy."

I nodded, then opened the door and stepped onto the sidewalk. As I grabbed my keys out of my pocket, I watched her navigate her way away from the curb and into the street, waving over her shoulder at me as she pulled away. Once she was out of sight, I took one deep, slow breath. Then I climbed into my car and headed home.

I spent the rest of Saturday with Jack while Dad went to work and Mom did...whatever Mom does. By the time I'd gotten back to my apartment Saturday night, I was seriously feeling the effect of my sleep deprivation, and I ended up collapsing in bed almost immediately. I hit the sheets face-first and was asleep in seconds.

It was great Saturday night, but at 6 a.m. Sunday morning, wide awake with absolutely nothing to do, I was less than thrilled with myself. I tried to get some reading done for school but by six-thirty, I was restless. When I realized I had read the same sentence three times without understanding or absorbing it, I decided to call it quits. Pushing my books aside, I threw on a pair of jeans and a t-shirt and brushed my teeth before I pushed my way out the door, keys in hand. Ten minutes later I was headed East on I-64 toward the College of William and Mary.

I had made this trip at least once a month—if not twice—freshman year. Back then, Maddie and I had been almost desperate to see each other as much as possible. We'd both put a lot of miles on our cars, traveling the four-hour round-trip. After that first year, the visits had slowly become more and more sporadic, the trips fewer and further between. Maddie had started canceling weekends because of work or school stuff, and I ended up spending more and more time with Jack than I ever had before. Our lives grew in separate directions and changed so much that a part of me was honestly amazed we'd managed to hold on to each other through all of it.

That said, I still didn't want to give up. I wasn't ready to let go of what we'd had or the future we were so close to. I just wanted to get back to the good. I wanted to put in the effort to get us back to the Jimmy and Maddie that we used to be.

I needed that.

I hit some traffic around Richmond but otherwise made good time, pulling into a parking spot near Maddie's place just before nine. As I stopped outside the front door of her building, I pulled my phone from my pocket and dialed her number. It rang and rang before switching to voicemail. I ended the call and was about to dial her again when the door swung open from the inside. I grabbed it and held it open for a tiny redhead on her way out, letting her dart though before ducking in.

Once inside, I headed for the stairs, taking them two at a time up to the second floor, where I took a left down the hall. I was stepping in front of her door when my phone vibrated with an incoming call.

"Hey," I said as I answered. "Come to your front door."

"Wh-" The word was cut in half by a massive yawn. "-at?"

"Just come open your door, and let me in."

I heard shuffling across the line and then soft footsteps closed in from the other side of the wall. I ended the call as I heard the locks, and then the door was opening, and she was there.

Silhouetted in the soft morning light streaming through the windows behind her, she looked gorgeous. Dark curls fell haphazardly around her face, and her pale skin contrasted starkly with the tiny, black tank top and shorts that she had slept in. I smiled at her confused expression as she took a step back to let me inside.

"What are you doing here?" The quiet question came once she had shut the door and taken three steps to stand in front of me. I lifted one shoulder and grabbed her hand with mine.

"I woke up early this morning and just... I wanted to see you."

One half of her mouth twisted up in a shy smile. I took that moment to lean in and softly press my lips against hers. I felt her hands come to rest on my waist, and I deepened the kiss until the sound of a door opening and a male voice behind me jolted steel into my spine.

"Shit, sorry guys."

Maddie took a quick step backwards, giving me space to turn and spot the tall, male stranger, wearing only a pair of unbuttoned jeans, striding out of the bathroom and across the common room. He grabbed a wrinkled t-shirt from the floor by the couch and pulled it on before stuffing a wallet, cell phone, and set of keys from the coffee table into his pants pockets.

"I'm outta here. Maddie, you're a lifesaver, as always. I'll see you tomorrow, yeah?"

She nodded in his direction, and I think she even said something back, but I was too busy trying to figure out who the fuck this guy was and what the hell he was doing here to pay any attention to the details.

It was the slamming of the front door that snapped me back to reality. Maddie had reclaimed the distance between us, but I shuffled backwards until I had enough space to breathe.

"Jimmy?" Her eyes were trained on my face and obviously concerned.

And I tried. I really fucking tried to calm myself down enough to think about the situation rationally. Because, sure, it didn't look great, but what the fuck did I know? After all, I'd slept at Caroline's place just two nights ago.

It was that thought that helped me keep my voice level and low as I asked, "Who was that?"

Since we were kids, I'd always been able to read Maddie. I could almost always tell what she was thinking, just based on her expression or the look in her eyes. But something in the way that her face shut down at my question, the way her eyes went completely blank, put me even more on edge.

"My friend, Sean. We have a few classes together."

I took a breath and waited for her to go on. She didn't.

"Okay," I said slowly, drawing the word out while I looked for a way to phrase my next question. The words I chose probably weren't the best, but they were all I had. "Did you guys have a fun sleepover?"

The blank expression disappeared as if it had never been there. A second later, her eyes had turned cold, and she twisted away from me to storm toward the kitchen. "Seriously, James?"

I followed her slowly, watching as she grabbed a glass from the counter and filled it with tap water. While I did this, I tried to stop myself. I really did. I had done almost the exact same thing, and I knew it was bullshit. I just couldn't do it.

"Really, Madeline? You don't understand why I would be curious about a guy walking around half naked in your dorm room at 9 a.m. when you've clearly just woken up? Sorry if that seems like a dick move to you, but I think it's probably pretty fucking normal."

"Nothing happened. He's been having problems with his roommate, and he needed a place to crash last night."

"And, what? You're the first name in his speed dial? Who is this guy, Maddie?"

"He's a friend," she forced out through clenched teeth. "Like I said, we have classes together, and we've hung out. He's helped me out a lot this year."

I sucked in a deep breath and turned around just as one of the four closed doors in the suite flew open.

"Madeline Rose Campbell! I swear to God, if you don't tell Sean to stop fucking with my Netflix list- Oh!"

The threat cut off abruptly when a tall blonde wearing only a long t-shirt passed through the open door and made eye contact with me. I forced myself to ignore the sight of her bare legs, training my gaze on her confused expression as she scanned me first and then found Maddie behind me.

"Shit. I'm sorry."

"Susi, this is Jimmy. Jimmy, Susi."

The confusion faded, and Susi smiled huge. "No fucking way, dude! I didn't even think you really existed! I mean, Maddie talks about you all the time, but, still... You're like a ghost, you know? Never here, and she's never there. Me and Trish just kinda figured you were made up."

I barely followed her mile-a-minute words, but Maddie must have been used to it because while I was playing catch-up, she responded. "Fantastic, Susi."

"What?"

"It's just great to know that my roommates thought I was making up a fake boyfriend!"

I shook my head and wormed my way into the conversation before Susi could reopen her mouth. "It's nice to meet you."

She nodded as Maddie interjected, "Can you please put clothes on?"

Susi glanced down quickly and then rolled her eyes back up with a bored expression. "I'm totally decent."

I heard a soft sigh behind me, and then Maddie was grabbing my hand and pulling me out of the kitchen, past the tiny couch, toward the room next to Susi's. Once we were inside, she shut the door and headed for her closet to start picking through clothes.

"She seems..." I started and then paused, searching for the right word.

"Insane?" Maddie supplied helpfully.

"I was going to go with fun, but insane works too."

"Yeah," she sighed, finally pulling away from her wardrobe with a shirt and a pair of jeans, both neatly draped across hangers. Despite the tension still strung tightly though my body, I smiled at the sight, remembering the first time I'd seen her putting clothes away in her room at home. It was back when things had been good between us, great even, and I fell out of the room and into the memory, so distracted I missed half of what she said next.

"-you wanna go?"

I jolted back to the present as her hand came to my forearm. Shaking off my daze, I looked up to find her staring at me expectantly.

"Sorry, what?"

"I said I have tons of stuff to do today, but I think I have time for breakfast. Do you wanna go?"

I tried not to let my disappointment show through the tightening of my chest. "Seriously? You don't even have a few hours to spend with me after I just drove two hours to see you?"

She let out an annoyed sigh and turned back to the closet before she started speaking. "I'm sorry, but, honestly, I don't. And if you had called to ask before you drove those two hours, I could have told you that beforehand."

"Yeah," I muttered, "well, sorry for trying to give you a nice surprise."

I saw her shoulders fall, and she twisted back toward me. "Hey, I'm sorry, okay? It was a nice surprise. I just really do have a lot to do today."

I nodded but dropped my eyes from hers to stare at my hands as I rubbed them together. "It's okay. I get it. Let's do breakfast, and then I'll head back home."

There was a moment of silence before, "I really am sorry, Jimmy."

Her apology didn't make me feel any better, but I nodded again all the same. "It's okay." It might have been a lie, but these days, it took too much energy to be honest all the time. Even to myself.

The trip to the diner was quiet and uncomfortable. Maddie stared out the window once she'd finished giving me directions, apparently lost in thought. I was too preoccupied trying to come up with literally *anything* to say that would get us back on the right track. I knew if we didn't fix shit between us soon, we were headed for a quick and catastrophic derailment.

I parked my car, and Maddie led us both into the small restaurant. It was nothing special to look at, but the air inside was saturated with amazing smells that reminded me just how hungry I was. We seated ourselves at a booth and had gotten coffee and ordered breakfast by the time I reached across the table and pulled one of her hands into both of mine.

"I wanted to talk to you about something," I began hesitantly, slowly raising my eyes to hers. Her expression had taken on it's earlier emptiness, and it was so unsettling that my heart started beating a little bit faster. I didn't know when she'd started feeling like she needed to hide her emotions from me, and I had no idea why, but it was just more proof that somewhere along the line, this 'relationship' had become epically fucked up.

"Oookay," she finally acknowledged, dragging the word out like she wasn't ready to completely part with it. I sucked in a deep breath and let it out slowly, twining our fingers together above the laminate table top.

"I know that things have been kind of weird between us. I'm not really sure why, but, honestly, Maddie? I don't care. I just want to fix it." She tried to interrupt, but I gave her fingers a soft squeeze and continued. "I'm going to fix it." I stopped and swiped my tongue across my bottom lip before I took a bracing breath.

"I also know a lot of things are up in the air right now, and I know you're still thinking about Italy. If you want to go, go. Go and live the life you want to live. But I won't let you leave without telling you that I don't want you to go. I want to be selfish and keep you here, at least somewhat nearby, where I know there's still a chance for us. So, I'm telling you now, up until the day you get on that plane, I'm going to work my ass off to make you realize what you'd be leaving behind. And it might not seem like much at first, but I think you're going to be surprised by what you'll lose if you decide to go."

She glanced down at the table, at our linked hands, and ran her thumb across my knuckles, back and forth twice. The action would have been soothing if I wasn't waiting with literal bated breath for her to do or say anything in response to my declaration.

When she finally spoke, the solitary word was immensely underwhelming.

"Okay."

I eyed her tentatively and repeated, "Okay?"

She nodded. "I'm still not sure what I'm going to do, but...I'll take what you said under consideration."

The half-smile she shot me as the waitress arrived with our food calmed me enough that my hands didn't shake too badly when I pulled them away to grab my fork. It wasn't really the response I had been looking for, but I would take it for now. As long as she knew where I stood, I was willing to work as hard as I needed to. I would put in the time and the effort, and if she still wanted to walk away, at least I'd know that I gave her everything I had to give.

And if that didn't work, I'd figure out how to pull my life together without her.

## Chapter Eleven

# Caroline

I HAD KNOWN BEFORE CLASSES even started that Monday mornings were seriously going to suck for me. I already hated Mondays purely on principle, but that hatred was quickly compounded by the brutal lineup of Intro Business classes I had managed to schedule for the morning hours. It's not that the classes were that terrible; it just seemed that no matter how I spent the night before, I always had problems staying focused on Monday mornings.

Since I'd woken up late and skipped breakfast to make it to my first class on time, as soon as the last class wrapped up, I raced out of the building to grab some food. I texted Jen about meeting for lunch, but she answered quickly to let me know she needed to talk to one of her TAs and to just go without her. Since it was just me, I didn't feel like walking all the way to the eternally busy student center. Instead, I headed in the opposite direction toward a small sandwich shop a block away.

I'd only taken a few steps when my phone rang from my back pocket. Fishing it out, I tapped the screen once I saw Nate's face.

"Hey."

"So, I'm calling to ask for a favor."

"I know better than to agree to anything before I know the details." Because I *really* did. I'd learned that lesson more than once, unfortunately.

"I just need you to come out with me one night next week."

I chewed on the corner of my lip and considered his request. "What's the catch?"

He sighed loudly into the phone, resulting in an almost painfully loud crackle across the line. "Can you please just say yes?"

"What's the catch, Nate?"

A pause, and then, "I need you to pretend to be my girlfriend for like, two hours tops."

I stopped dead on the crowded sidewalk, forcing the flow of coeds to spread around me like a rock dropped into a river. "Excuse me?"

"Please, Caro?"

"You're serious?" I asked as I started walking again, only a few feet from my destination now, which was good because even over the noise of the bustling sidewalk and Nate in my ear, I could hear my stomach begging for food. More like demanding, based on the insistent, completely feral noises coming from my belly.

"Yes," he groaned exasperatedly. "It won't be that bad, I promise."

I pushed through the door of the restaurant and took a spot at the end of the short line. Lowering my voice, I asked, "What possible reason could you have for needing me to pretend to be your girlfriend?"

"I plead the fifth."

I snorted. "Fine, then I'm not helping."

"Seriously, Caro?"

"Just tell me why, Nate..."

"You're so annoying."

I smirked. "You love me anyway."

He let out another pained sigh. "There's this girl-"

I let out a bark of laughter and interrupted him right there. "Seriously?"

"Know what? Forget I asked."

I calmed my lingering giggles and tried to sound as genuine as possible for my next words. "No, stop. I'm sorry, Nathanial. Please tell me how me pretending to be your girlfriend is going to get you a girl?"

"No way," he retorted. "I know what you're doing right now."

I rolled my eyes even though he couldn't see and took a step closer to the counter with the line. "I'm not doing anything."

"Bullshit. You're doing your whole, 'I-don't-really-care-but-I'll-pretend-I-care-and-then-laugh-about-it-later' thing. Forget it. I'm asking Jen."

At the thought of him making his asinine request to Jen, I dissolved into peals of laughter that I was only able to calm once I'd noticed more than a few customers giving me odd glances. "Oh my God, please ask her while I'm there. I really want to see that."

"Screw you, Caroline."

"Love you too, Nate."

He started to speak, but at the same moment the last person in front of me stepped aside, and I was able to make my way to the counter. "Hold on a sec," I said quickly into the phone before pulling it from my ear to place my order. I paid and took my receipt and bottle of water to a small table near the pick-up counter before lifting the phone and dropping my bag to the floor and my butt in a seat.

"Sorry, I'm getting lunch."

"It's fine. Are you coming to practice tonight?"

"I have a bunch of homework, so I don't think so."

"Okay. Well, can I come by afterwards?"

I started to tell him, "Sure," but before the word left my lips, a body was falling into the only other seat at the bistro table. Nope, not falling, because that would imply it was accidental. He was *sitting*. I felt goosebumps rise over my arms at the sudden charge in the air, and, as was becoming the norm, I didn't even need to see his face to know who it was. Still, I looked up to meet his eyes, and the restaurant flickered out of existence. For a tiny moment, it was just Jimmy and I in a place where absolutely nothing was wrong, or complicated, or broken.

"...oline?"

I dropped my eyes to the table at the sound of Nate's voice, shaking my head twice to clear the lingering, hot-guy haze.

"I gotta run. I'll call you later." Ignoring the sound of his mildly concerned curiosity, I ended the call and set the phone on the table. I sucked in a breath that didn't do nearly enough to fortify me before I allowed my eyes to slide back up to his. "Are you stalking me or something?"

Half of his mouth bent up, and I had to fight against the current of that smile. It pulled and tugged at my sanity and my resolve.

"No, I come here all the time. Are you stalking me?"

I laughed softly, nervously, and lifted a hand to push my hair back where it'd fallen over my shoulder. "No, Jimmy. I promise I'm not stalking you."

"Do you mind if I join you?"

I shook my head, perhaps a tad too quickly. "No, not at all."

He nodded, and then we were both silent for a moment until we broke into matching uncomfortable smiles. To escape the moment, I took another breath before speaking.

"How was your weekend?"

One of his hands traveled up to scratch at his ear, and he seemed to be considering the question carefully. "I went to see Maddie," he finally said, mouth falling to rest in a straight line. I waited for him to go on but realized he wasn't going to after a heavy silence.

"And how was that?"

He opened his mouth, but before a word could escape, my order number was being shouted from the counter. I held up a quick finger and slid to standing. Once I got my food and sat back down, I waved a hand to gesture him on.

"Honestly? I don't even know."

My eyes slid from the sandwich I'd been lifting toward my mouth to meet his as he continued.

"I couldn't stop thinking about what you said to me the night of the party. About giving up. And I don't want to give up on her. I'm not ready to yet. I went there to tell her that, but..."

I swallowed the bite I'd been chewing and watched his eyes as they absentmindedly scanned something over my shoulder.

"What happened?"

He shrugged. "Things are weird now, between her and I. It's like we can't be honest with each other, but I don't know why. I don't know if it's her that's changed, or me, or what, but it all just seems so much harder than it used to."

"I think that's normal, though," I said slowly, taking comfort in the fact that his eyes were still off me. "As we get older, life gets harder. It makes sense that our relationships would, too."

"I know that, I just..." He stopped and shrugged again before finally bringing his gaze back to mine. "Maddie and I... It was never hard before. That's one of the things I loved about it. And we sure as hell never had to lie to each other, or keep secrets."

I chewed my lip and considered his words, barely eaten sandwich forgotten on the table between us. Maybe it was the way he spoke about Maddie, or maybe it was the look on his face, but something didn't sit right with me.

"Can I ask you a question?" Propping my chin between my fists, I focused on his face through his nod. "What is it about Maddie?" At his narrow-eyed confusion, I clarified. "What makes you so sure that she's it for you? Because what you're describing sounds like a pretty typical reason to end a relationship. You just seem so certain..." I trailed off, suddenly unsure. I mean, maybe he had opened the door by sharing about his weekend, but I definitely didn't need to be... God, what was I even *doing*? Trying to convince him that he needed to dump his girlfriend?

*Quit while you're ahead, Caro.*

"I'm sorry. That was... Just forget I said anything."

"No," he shook his head gently, "it's okay. Ask your question."

Talking to him felt like running a marathon—I ended up exhausted just trying to understand him a little bit more. And if understanding him was the finish line, I hadn't even hit the 5k mark yet.

"I guess what I'm trying to say is, I think most guys in your position would have called it quits by now. So, what makes her so special? What about her tells you that you want to spend the rest of your life with her?"

He was quiet for a moment, his heavy gaze sinking to the table where my leftover lunch sat. Then one shoulder lifted up the barest bit. "I could ask you the same thing. How do you know that Dan is the one?"

I saw the deflection for what it was, which only made me that much more curious about his near-desperate need to save his relationship. Still, I let it go for now to focus on answering his question. It might have been because I was still more focused on him and Maddie than Dan and I, or maybe because he'd been nothing but honest with me, but either way, I found myself speaking the words that I hadn't yet been able to say to anyone else.

"I'm not sure that he is."

I could tell he was surprised. His eyes widened a bit and slid back up to mine. For a moment I could have sworn by the set of his jaw that he was frustrated, but that fast it was gone, and I didn't have the time to press it before he asked, "So why are you still with him?"

I shrugged. "Because I don't know that he isn't. In Michigan... Everything was so different when we started dating. Being here, leaving home, none of this was even a thought in my mind before the accident. Back there, we made sense. Dan and I were good together. And now... I didn't think it was fair to break up with him just because I don't know how realistic our future looks."

"Isn't it more unfair to lead him on?"

"I'm not leading him on."

"Really? So, after school, you're moving back home?" I knew the answer to that question, and by the look on my face, he must have known it too. "Then he's moving here?"

I rolled my eyes. "I get your point."

He leaned forward then, resting both arms along the table as he met my eyes. "I'm just saying, if you don't see a future with him..."

"It's not that easy," I retorted. "You should know that better than anyone. Can you honestly say that you still see a future with Maddie?"

"That's all I see, Caroline." His voice had grown hard, almost cold. Detached. "That's all I've seen for years. Even when we were in high school, I knew what my life would look like five, ten, fifteen years down the road. I knew what our lives would be and how they would play out. That's the one thing I've always seen."

For a moment, neither of us spoke, and it took a few more before I had the courage to open my mouth. "Maybe that's not all there is though." I could tell he wanted to argue that point, so I hurried on. "Life isn't just about the plans we make. In fact, my experience would suggest that it's not about our plans at all. Our lives are defined by the things that knock us off our paths, the things that force us to reevaluate and react." I took a breath before finishing with, "I just think that sometimes, when we focus so hard on one thing, we can miss out on something even better."

His gaze never left me, and for some reason the air felt heavier than it had just a minute ago. My breaths became short, and I slid my hands along my pants under the table to wipe away the moisture they had gathered.

When he finally spoke, his voice was low, warm, and filled with something I couldn't quite name. "And do you think I'm missing out on something better?"

My first insane reaction was to shout, "Yes, ME!" I shook that asinine thought away and mumbled incoherently for half a second while his lips curled into a tiny grin.

"I don't know. It's possible. I think...everything happens for a reason, right? Maybe this is all part of the plan."

"Do you really believe that? That everything happens for a reason?" His smile was gone. In its place was a small frown accompanied by an intense stare. Based on the way he had leaned forward another inch and tightened his fists against the table, I knew my answer mattered to him. I just wished I had a better one because my truth was less than inspiring, at best.

"I kind of have to. Maybe I'm wrong. Maybe there is no purpose—no meaning to life or the things that happen to us. But if I didn't force myself to believe that there's a reason for everything, I don't know how I'd get out of bed every day. What would be the point?"

He offered a nod, but nothing else. The silence stretched on, and my eyes fell to the sandwich in front of me. Our conversation had managed to kill my appetite, so I started to wrap the leftovers. The sound of crunching paper was the only noise between us until my phone suddenly starting buzzing against the table. At the sight of Dan's face flashing on the screen, I dropped the food to snatch up my phone, feeling both guilty and embarrassed. Neither one of those was an explainable or welcome sensation.

"I can call him later."

"It's alright," he murmured, rising to his feet quickly. "I have to run anyway."

I followed him up, grabbing my bag on the way and sliding my sandwich inside before hooking the strap over my shoulder. "I'll walk out with you."

I watched from the corner of my eye, so I saw his smile as we headed out of the restaurant to the busy sidewalk. Once there, he stopped me with a gentle hand on my arm. "Thank you."

"For what?"

"For listening." He sounded so sincere, but I couldn't imagine he was as alone as those two words implied. Sure, he kind of had a crappy girlfriend (in my totally non-biased opinion...), but he had friends. Family. He had to have someone to talk to besides me.

*Didn't he?*

I ignored that thought and shrugged. "That's what friends are for, right?"

His chuckle was completely devoid of humor. "By that definition, you're the best friend I have."

Before I could come up with anything to say, he shook his head. "I'll see you around, Caroline." Then he was gone.

I stood on the sidewalk for a few minutes after he left, drained and out of breath. Trying to understand him just a little bit more. Feeling like I was just running in place.

After my last class, I headed straight home to get some work done. Which I did, mostly successfully. The non-successful parts were the minutes I caught myself distracted by thoughts of Jimmy and our lunchtime conversation. Still, those were mostly few and far between, and I was proud of that.

Since I worked through dinner, when Nate texted to say that he was on his way over, I begged him to bring food. He showed up at the door, pizza in hand, and he, Jen, and I all crowded around the counter, shoving cheesy goodness into our mouths.

I waited until I'd inhaled my first slice and cleared my mouth with a sip of water before I spoke. "Nate, didn't you need to talk to Jen about something?"

I hid my smile behind another mouthful of pizza as Nate sent a glare my way. Jen, meanwhile, was looking at Nate with an expectant expression, and when he saw it, he sighed heavily. "Any chance you'd be willing to pretend to be my girlfriend for two hours?"

She swallowed and shrugged. "Sure."

Nate's grin was wide as he turned to face my disappointed expression.

"Seriously?" I asked her. "Just like that, no questions asked?"

She considered that and turned back to Nate. "Will I be compensated?"

"With food and drinks at the bar."

"Sounds good to me." She grabbed one last slice and backed away from the counter toward her bedroom. "When are we doing this?"

"Next week sometime. I'll let you know."

She nodded at him and disappeared behind her door. Once she was gone, Nate's triumphant grin turned to me. "How's about them apples, *Care Bear*?"

I twitched at the nickname and glared at him. "Don't call me that. And I have no clue what just happened."

"It's all right, Caro. You don't have to know everything, all the time."

"Ha ha, Mr. Baker." Finishing my last bite, I grabbed my water and shuffled to the couch, collapsing heavily onto the cushions. Once I'd snagged the game controller on the table, I used it to load up Netflix.

"What do you want to watch?"

Once he'd plopped next to me, Nate twisted away from the TV to face me. "Can we talk first?"

I took in his serious expression and froze. For a moment, I wanted to stop him. I'd had more than enough heavy conversations for one day. I was still trying to get over the one I'd had with Jimmy ten hours ago. But as much as my brain urged me to postpone the conversation, I kept my mouth shut and let him go on.

"Look, I've been thinking recently, and I think you should get back on the ice."

I flinched. Literally flinched. And with his corresponding wince, I knew he'd seen it.

"No." The word was quiet, a little muffled by the sudden thickness in my throat and tightness in my chest.

"Caroline-"

"No, Nate. It's not happening."

I wasn't New Caroline right now. I was another Caroline— right-after-the-accident Caroline. It was my least favorite version of myself, but it didn't matter because right now she was calling the shots.

He groaned and leaned back against the couch. "I don't get it."

"That's fine. You don't have to."

"Are you scared? Is that it?"

I knew exactly what he was doing, but I wasn't about to fall for it. The truth was, I was abso-fucking-lutely scared. No, not scared—terrified. And call me a coward all you want, but I wasn't willing to go back to living with that fear. Not for a second. Learning to walk again had been bad enough. Learning to skate again... I wasn't willing to put myself through it.

Hockey had been my life, once upon a time. Hockey had been how I *defined* myself. The accident took that away. And while I had made my peace with that, I wasn't about to strap myself onto a sled or rig up some sort of prosthetic blade just so I could repeatedly remind myself of everything I had lost.

That was just a little too masochistic, even for me.

"I'm not having this conversation," I finally answered. I wasn't going to lie to him, but I also wasn't going to budge on this. Not ever. "And I'm not sure if I'm up for hanging out. I think I'm just gonna head to bed."

I knew he was annoyed—probably even angry—at my evasion, but thankfully he didn't force the issue. "Yeah, okay." He rose from the couch and headed for the door. I watched him go, but he didn't look back once. Nor did he say another word before the door slammed behind him, and he was gone.

## Chapter Twelve

Jimmy

THE DAYS AFTER LUNCH WITH Caroline sped by. The nights I didn't have practice I spent working, and even though I collapsed into bed exhausted every night, I still made sure that I called Maddie once I was there. Things were... Well, I wouldn't say they were better, but I truly believed we were getting there. At the very least, we were starting to actually talk again—really talk. I'd even gotten her to tell me a little about Italy, which had been surprisingly difficult. As excited as she said she was about the opportunity, every time I brought it up, she tried to change the subject. Still, like Caroline had said, I was stubborn, and I finally got her to tell me at least the barest details.

Besides my work-in-progress relationship, life was good. The team was coming together really well on the ice, which was great because our first game was only two weeks away. Because of that, I'd been putting in extra hours in the weight room in the mornings before classes, which meant I was getting even less sleep, but at this point my motto had become, *Who needs sleep*? I figured I'd catch up at some point.

Like maybe the end of the semester.

My good week didn't last, though. On Saturday Jack was horrible. It happened every once in a while, so I was used to it, in a way. Still, that never made it any easier. When he was having a really bad day, there was nothing I could do to break him out of it. I spent the day just trying to calm the arguments he was determined to have and keep my cool. I'd learned great lessons in patience from Jack over the years, so I was able to at least seem outwardly calm. That said, by the time Mom got home and I could leave, my nerves were shot. I'd been planning on heading out to the bar with a few of the guys from the team, but I bailed in favor of sitting in my living room with three fingers of bourbon in an attempt to unwind.

After the first glass, I was still shaky, so I figured another wouldn't hurt. It didn't, but it didn't help either. I meant to call Maddie after glass number two, but glass number three distracted me. Around glass number four, I remembered that I'd been doing something with the phone in my hand. I didn't know what, though, and that led to glass number five and half an hour of staring at the last messages I'd sent to Caroline before Marco's party.

I wanted to text her. No, I wanted to call her. I wanted to hear her voice for real, not just in my head, like I'd become used to. And I was really used to it. I heard it in the mornings when I showered after my workout. I heard it during class when my thoughts drifted away from me. I especially heard it at night, after every phone call with Maddie.

*Sometimes, when we focus so hard on one thing, we can miss out on something better.*

I was focusing extra hard on blocking out those particular words.

My thumb hovered over the screen, but I couldn't press the button. I wouldn't let myself. It was probably the half bottle of Beam, but the lines were too blurred. Sober, I was able to ignore the thought, but drunk—alone in my silent apartment—I couldn't stop thinking that maybe Caroline was my something better.

There was still a lot that I didn't know about her, but I knew the important things. Caroline was strong. She was kind and smart and funny and so goddamn beautiful that it drove me crazy. When she laughed, every problem in my life seemed to melt away, and I'd never met a better listener. Somehow, she always seemed to know exactly what I needed to hear. And she trusted me, at least enough to share what was on her mind, which seemed to be more than I could say for my own girlfriend these days.

When she'd spoken about Dan and how she didn't know if they were right for each other, it had taken every bit of patience I possessed not to get pissed. She deserved so much better than a relationship of convenience. Sure, I didn't know the guy, and I had no idea what they were like together, but speaking as someone in a long-distance relationship, I wanted better than that for her.

And now I wanted to call her again. I wanted to tell her all the things she deserved to hear. Because she needed to know that she wasn't broken. She was the most whole person I'd ever met. And she needed to hear that I didn't need to see her scars to know that there wasn't an inch of her that was anything less than perfect. Anything less than beautiful.

I poured glass six because I was going to do it. I was going to tell her all the things I needed her to know. Which was an absolutely fucking terrible idea, but six glasses in, I did not give a single fuck.

Really, it couldn't be considered anything less than an act of God that six was the magic number. Before I even knew it was happening, my eyes slid shut, and I passed out.

The first thing I recognized when I woke was the pounding headache. The nausea kicked in shortly after, and I slowly peeled my head off the couch, trying to focus through the spinning of the too-bright room. My neck ached like a motherfucker from sleeping sitting up, and, taking stock, I realized my right hand did too. Probably because I'd somehow managed to sleep all night still clutching the empty glass tumbler. My phone, which I was almost positive had been in my other hand when I'd drifted off, was lying on the floor between my feet.

Giving my stomach a minute to settle, I leaned forward to grab my phone from the floor. I let myself fall backwards once I had it, turning so my head landed on the arm of the couch, and I was finally able to stretch out. The movement set off the spinning again, and my eyes slid shut to block out the motion of the room.

Once it faded, I pried them back open and turned on the screen in the same moment I remembered I'd never called Maddie the night before. I brought up her number and almost pressed send before deciding at the last second that I needed to wait until I was sure I was, one, sober and two, not dying.

Tapping the home button, my gaze passed over the time, and a tired groan escaped my throat. It was already three—I'd lost almost the entire day. Not that I had much of anything to do; Sundays were an easy day, since Dad never put me on the schedule. They were also the one day a week that I didn't practice or work out.

I gave myself another ten minutes on the couch feeling shitty and sorry for myself before I finally forced myself up to shower, stopping along the way to swallow two full glasses of water. I took my time in the steam-filled bathroom, reaming myself over my totally out-of-line thoughts about Caroline the night before. If I was going to make things work with Maddie, I needed to be completely committed. That meant I couldn't afford any more lunches or long walks at night with Caroline. I couldn't afford to spend any more time with her. She'd already started to feel too important. I already cared about her more than I should have.

I was officially going back to avoiding her, or trying to, at least. I knew we'd probably run into each other here and there, and I was okay with that. I could handle that. But I couldn't handle getting to know her any more than I already had—couldn't allow myself to focus on anything besides Maddie and our future together.

That was my last thought as I climbed out from under the water. Once I'd dried off and put clothes on, I was feeling almost 100 percent better. It was probably mostly the water I drank, but it felt good knowing I had a plan, that I was actually doing something. Now, I just needed to keep working. Keep trying. Keep moving forward.

With that thought, I texted Maddie first, just to let her know that I was thinking about her and I loved her. Then I texted Marco to see what he was doing. As soon as he'd told me he was just hanging out at home, I grabbed my keys and was out the door.

I may have always considered Ash my best friend, but, really, Marco Simms wasn't too far behind. In fact, over the last year or so, I'd probably grown even closer to Marco than Ash. Granted, that wasn't really Ash's fault. It's hard to stay close to someone when they're legally not allowed to leave their house. We had talked on the phone a lot while he was on house arrest, and I visited him as much as I could (as much as he would let me). Still, it made sense, in a way, that we'd drifted apart a bit. It made even more sense that Marco and I had grown closer.

That said, I hadn't been lying when I'd told Caroline that she was the only person I talked to anymore. It wasn't that I didn't feel like talking to my friends. I just didn't feel like talking to *anyone*. Anyone except her, at least. But I had decided that needed to change if I was going to cut her out of my life like I had to. And since I still hadn't talked to Ash since the party, which I figured he was probably still a little pissed about, I decided to start with Marco.

By the time I got to his place, it was almost four. I buzzed up at the front door and then made my way up the stairs until I could let myself in the door that he'd already opened for me, shutting it quickly behind me before too much of the smoke wafting through the apartment escaped. I knew, according to Marco at least, that his neighbors were cool, but it still surprised me just how much he wasn't worried about advertising his drug use. Still, I wasn't his dad, and I wasn't going to say a word.

Once the door was shut, I turned to find him on the couch, game controller in hand.

"Hey," he offered as I made my way to the couch and settled in beside him. "How are you?"

I shrugged. "I'm alright. How have you been?"

He smiled a trademark Marco smile, wide and half-vacant. "As good as always."

Moments like this, I missed the old Marco. The Marco who cared about more than getting fucked up all the time. The Marco who talked practically non-stop about computers even though neither Ash nor I ever had any clue what he was saying. The Marco who hadn't had his heart broken.

I was the only one who knew about Emily, or I used to be. I still wasn't sure if he'd ever mentioned her to Ash, but I never had. It wasn't my place. Plus, it was kind of pointless. That girl busted ass out of this town like she was being chased, and once she was gone, she was gone.

It was a shame. Emily was the only girl Marco had ever given a shit about, and her sudden departure destroyed the guy, so much so that he still hadn't fully recovered. Sure, he put on a good front, but I knew what motivated his need to spend night after night wasted and high, filling his apartment with people he didn't know, people who didn't really give a shit about him. I knew what pushed him to sleep with an endless parade of girls, never letting anyone get close. And usually I'd feel bad for the girls because he really did use them, but they used him right back. He handed out party favors like it was his job, and they paid with their bodies.

The whole thing was massively fucked, but I kept my mouth shut and let Ash give him a hard time. That said, with the way he'd been acting lately, I had a feeling I would need to speak up soon.

Marco paused the game and tossed the controller onto the couch next to him. "Wanna smoke a bowl?" I shook my head, and he nodded but packed one anyway. As he brought it to his mouth, my phone vibrated in my pocket, and I pulled it out to find a new text.

Maddie: **Are you at home?**

I quickly typed, **no**, then shoved it back into my pocket. I looked back up just as Marco exhaled a massive cloud of smoke that quickly filled the air between us. Jesus Christ, I might as well be smoking.

"So, have you talked to Ash recently?" I figured I might be able to get a feel for where he was from Marco if they'd hung out at all, but I wasn't really hopeful. Besides Ash's general reluctance to do much of anything since he'd gotten off house arrest, I guessed he was probably spending most of his time with Parker.

"Yeah, why? Have you?"

I shook my head. "Nah. We haven't talked since your party."

"How is that possible? You guys work together," he pointed out as if I didn't know.

"We haven't been scheduled together at all." I shrugged. "I kind of figured he was spending his free time with his girlfriend now."

Marco chuckled and took another hit. His voice was distorted by the exhale as he spoke. "You guys are girls. Just fucking call him and talk to him."

I rolled my eyes. "It's not like that."

"It's exactly like that. He bitched about you too when he was here the other day. Just fucking talk to each other. I don't get why you guys are so weird now."

I had nothing to say to that because he wasn't wrong. Things had gotten kind of weird. And, apparently, I wasn't just fucking up one relationship, but all of them.

Marco must have sensed the turn my thoughts had taken because his voice broke in. "It's not that serious, Jimmy. Just talk to him."

"Yeah, I'll talk to him." And I would. At some point.

He sighed and slid the bowl onto the coffee table. "Whatever. Talk to him. Don't talk to him. I don't give a shit. Wanna play something?"

I didn't. Not at all. But I also didn't have any of the motivation I'd had when I walked in the door, to actually talk to my friend, tell him what was going on in my head, and get some advice. So I went with the next best option.

"Sure." He handed me his controller and got up to grab another from the entertainment system. From there, we didn't say much at all. It wasn't what I went to Marco's looking for, but it helped all the same. Mostly, it helped remind me that I had friends. I had people I could talk to when I was ready to. People to spend time with. I didn't need Caroline.

I didn't need her, and I didn't want her.


I walked back through my front door less than three hours later. Maddie had texted me two more times while I was at Marco's, the first message being, **Please call me when you get home**. That was followed not long after by, **It's important.**

That was when I'd headed out the door.

As soon as I was back on my couch, I called her. It only rang once before she answered. "Hey."

Something in the tone of her voice made the hair rise on the back of my neck.

"Hey," I breathed. "Are you okay?"

There was a brief pause before, "No. I mean, yeah, I'm fine, but I'm not okay."

"What's going on, Maddie?" My words were deathly quiet. I almost expected her not to have heard me, but she must have because after a short pause she answered the question.

"I can't do this anymore."

"What are you talking about?" I wasn't proud of the broken and breathless quality to my voice, but I was past trying to censor myself. "Can't do what?"

There was a long, pregnant pause before she whispered a single word.

"Us."

My heart was pounding, and the only air I was getting was sneaking into my lungs through short, shallow pants, but, strangely, I bit back a laugh when she said the word. Because, *really*? When I spoke, though, there wasn't a trace of humor in my voice. "Are you fucking kidding me?"

"Listen, Jimmy, I've spent a lot of time thinking about this, and-"

I interrupted her because I honestly didn't give a single shit about how much time she'd spent thinking about this. "How the fuck are you breaking up with me right now? Like, right now, on the fucking phone, a week after I told you I was going to fight for you? What, you suddenly decided, fuck it?"

"It's not like that. You know-"

"Apparently, I don't know a goddamn thing. Because I really thought...after everything we've been through and all the time we spent together, I *really* would have thought that I deserved more than this."

I heard a quiet sniffle through the phone, and it took everything I had not to completely lose my mind. As far as I was concerned, she had no fucking right to be upset right now. Not when she'd just ripped my future—my life—away from me.

"I'm sorry, Jimmy. I really am."

"Is that supposed to make me feel better?"

That must have pushed her over the line from upset to pissed because she snapped. "You don't need to be a dick about it!"

That time, I didn't fight the laughter that threatened. I just let it roll. And, sure, I was probably losing my mind because underneath the laughter I still couldn't breathe, and I was pretty sure someone had wrapped a vice around my head and was just slowly, steadily squeezing it tighter and tighter. Still, it felt good to laugh. And since I figured I wouldn't feel good for a while, I seized the moment and made it last.

When I finally calmed myself, I think I surprised us both with the nonchalance in my voice. "You're absolutely right. I don't need to be a dick about it. But I'm sure as fuck going to. Know why? Because fuck you, Maddie. That's why."

It might not have been eloquent, but it was honest. It was real for the first time in a long time.

She started to talk, but I didn't want to listen. Didn't feel like hearing another word of bullshit from someone I was starting to think I had never known at all. Instead, I ended the call and tossed the phone to the table.

I took a long look at the bottle of bourbon that I'd made a massive dent in last night. Then I decided that what I had left wasn't going to be nearly enough. It took fifteen minutes to get from my apartment to the closest liquor store and back home. I spent that fifteen minutes analyzing every conversation I'd had with Maddie over the past week, looking for any clue I could have missed, anything that would have given me a sign that this was coming. I let the anger and the pain mix together into a potent cocktail that filled me up and left me empty at the same time. For fifteen minutes, I thought and raged and broke and thought some more.

Then I was back home. In the silence. With the liquor. After that, I didn't think at all.

## Chapter Thirteen

# Caroline

FOR WHAT WAS POSSIBLY THE first time ever, I was having a phenomenal Monday. For starters, the professor in my first class had emailed everyone Sunday night to let us know he was sick and class was canceled. And there was really nothing I liked more than sleeping in later than I was usually able to. Something about it just made me happy, like little-kid-on-a-snow-day happy.

From there, the day only got better. My second class, Financial Accounting, was the one I struggled with most. Granted, that was mostly because the professor had a habit of mumbling so badly it was impossible to understand a word he said. Still, we'd taken a test last week, and I was super happy to discover that I hadn't bombed like I thought I had. Sure, I scraped by with a C, but that was loads better than I had thought I'd done.

By lunchtime, I'd decided this was probably the best day I'd had since coming to Virginia. And, by default, that made it the best day I'd had since the accident, which in itself was enough to have me smiling as I started the trek to meet Jen. I couldn't help but wonder if Jimmy would be there. It had become something of a Monday tradition for us to run into each other, and I would have been lying if I said I wasn't at least a little bit hopeful that he'd make an appearance.

On that thought, my phone buzzed from my back pocket. I checked the screen and, as if my thoughts had summoned him, found a text message.

Jimmy: **Meet me for lunch**

I narrowed my eyes at the screen and quickly tapped out a message.

Me: **Are you asking me or telling me?**

He responded almost instantly with the words, **Please, Caroline**. Apprehension prickled the back of my neck as I sent a message asking him where he wanted to meet. Once again, I didn't have to wait more than a few seconds before the answer came in.

Jimmy: **My place**

The unease wasn't just tickling my neck now. Goosebumps worked their way down my arms as I pressed the button that would dial his number. He answered after the second ring and didn't waste time with formalities.

"Please come over?"

The words were quiet, but there was something off about the way he spoke and the rhythm of his voice. I just couldn't immediately place it. "What's wrong?"

He chuckled at that. "Why does something have to be wrong? Can't I just invite my friend over to my apartment for lunch?" That time I was able to figure out why his voice sounded so strange, but that just lead to a whole host of other questions.

"Are you drunk right now?"

"It's possible. I've stopped keeping tabs on my sobriety level. Are you coming over?"

"I-"

"*Please* come over, Caro. I really need to talk to you."

*Fuck.* I couldn't say no to him, especially not when he called me Caro and said please. Even worse, part of me didn't *want* to say no. I really did consider Jimmy a friend. Sure, if things were different, he was a friend I would have loved to see naked, but I could keep my attraction separate from my friendship. I had to. Because my friend needed me.

"Okay. I'll come over."

He promised to send me directions, and I told him I'd be there as soon as I could. As I turned to head for the dorms, I called Jen. It took a few minutes to convince her that everything was okay after I canceled our lunch plans and asked to borrow her car. Thankfully, she accepted my promise to explain everything later without much argument. I still had her keys in my bag from using the car the night before, so I made my way straight to where I'd parked it once I had her agreement.

Five minutes later I was navigating away from campus. Jimmy's directions were surprisingly simple. They also surprised me by leading me east to a residential neighborhood that didn't look too different from my town back in Michigan. The houses were all decently big and well kept. Most of the lawns were scattered with at least a few things that would suggest kids lived inside, and I had to wonder if Jimmy still lived at home.

I pulled onto his street a few minutes later and parked in front of the address he'd given me. Next, I turned off the car and dialed his number like I'd been instructed. It rang four times before telling me to leave a message. I considered it for a second before quickly hanging up the call because, really, who leaves messages anymore?

I didn't want to blow up his phone, but I was sitting in the car out front of his house, and that was arguably weirder. I didn't want to be *that* weird, so I tapped the screen to call him again and lifted the phone to my ear. Thankfully, this time he answered.

"Hey, sorry, I was in the other room, and my phone..." He sucked in a breath and then changed topics. "Are you here?"

"Yeah, I'm out front."

"Okay, be right there."

The line went dead, and I climbed from the car with the keys and my phone. I had only taken a few steps toward the house when he appeared from around the side where the driveway was, and I'd be lying if I said the sight of him didn't take my breath away because *oh my God*. He was wearing a pair of loose gray sweatpants that sat low on his hips, low enough that I could see the waistband of the black briefs that hugged his hips. And abs. Abs that I couldn't stop staring at because, for some reason, he wasn't wearing a shirt, and, I repeat: Oh my *God*.

I had to have been struck at least partially brain dead because he was waving and gesturing for me to follow behind him as he headed back around the house, and I still couldn't move, couldn't do anything but run my eyes over smooth skin and muscled...everything. The spell was broken when he vanished from my line of sight, and I stumbled across the grass toward where he had disappeared, scolding my over-eager eyes along the way.

Once I made it around the house, I caught sight of him a few meters ahead, heading for a detached garage at the end of the driveway. Stopping in front of a door to the left of the aluminum garage door, he turned around to wait for me, and I steeled myself against the reappearance of his chest. Forcing my eyes to stay above his neck, I closed the remaining distance between us, and then he was leading us both through the door.

We walked up a short flight of stairs until we were both standing in the center of his apartment. My first thought was that it was much bigger than it looked on the outside. My second thought was that it just felt so Jimmy.

The floor plan was wide open, and windows practically filled the three exterior walls in the main room. Curtains were drawn over them all at the moment, and the only light in the place came from a strip under the cabinets in the kitchen. Still, it was bright enough that I could make out two framed hockey jerseys hanging on the walls. I saw his name stitched across the back of one. The other was a Philadelphia Flyers jersey, which I found interesting, but I stored the information to ask him about it later. Besides the jerseys, the walls were bare, but a few pictures sat on a surprisingly full bookshelf in the far corner of the living room. His TV was exactly as big as I would have expected, and his couch looked unbelievably comfortable. It was part man cave, part bachelor pad and, even as sparsely decorated as it was, it managed to suit him perfectly.

I was pulled away from my slow appraisal of his place when I heard a glass bottle hit wood. I turned away from the living room in time to find him carrying two glasses from the kitchen to join the bottle of what looked like bourbon he'd dropped on the table.

"Want a drink?"

I narrowed my eyes in his direction and slowly appraised the parts of him that I hadn't focused too much on when he'd blindsided me with his shirtlessness. His eyes were red and surrounded by dark circles. There was so much stubble covering his jaw that it probably qualified for beard status, and, don't get me wrong, it looked good, but *he* didn't look good. He looked exhausted.

He must have taken my silence for acquiescence because he held a glass of brown liquid in my direction and used his other hand to pour another for himself.

"Uh, no. Thanks," I managed.

He shrugged and retracted the glass, downing the contents in one gulp before dropping it to the table carelessly. The bang that sounded when the glass hit wood elicited a jump from me, but Jimmy acted as if he either hadn't heard it or didn't care and grabbed the other one before heading away from the table to collapse onto the couch. His movement was so uncontrolled, I waited for the liquid to spill all over the dark green fabric—or his bare chest, which was seriously the last thing I needed. Somehow, though, he managed to keep the liquor contained as he fell to the cushions.

Once he was settled, I lowered myself next to him, leaving as much space as possible between our bodies. It didn't feel like enough with him only half-dressed, and that was before he angled back into the corner of the couch, stretching his body toward me and spreading his legs until his right knee was only inches from my denim-covered prosthesis. For some reason, the proximity had me feeling incredibly self-conscious, and I wiggled myself away a few inches as he opened his mouth.

"Am I an idiot?"

I gave him a pointed look. "I would have said no before today, but you are drunk at 12:30 on a school day. That said, why are you asking?"

His mouth quirked up, but the tiny smile died almost immediately. "Because I'm pretty sure that I'm an idiot." I watched him take a breath that seemed to require a whole lot of effort before he lifted the glass in his hand and took a healthy sip.

"What's going on, Jimmy?" I asked the question gently. Something was obviously wrong, and I had the sinking suspicion it had to do with Maddie. I tried to ignore that thought, though. As much as it felt inspired by common sense and what little information I had, it also felt slightly based on a perverse variety of hope.

Hope that I had absolutely no right to feel.

"Maddie broke up with me yesterday."

My stomach did a weird nosedive as those words landed, and I said the first thing that came to mind. "I'm so sorry." I hadn't even finished the last word before he let out an exasperated groan and snapped his eyes to mine.

"Are you fucking kidding right now?"

I didn't mean to get frustrated, but his words struck a nerve. "What do you want me to say, James? 'That's good, Maddie was a bitch?' Or maybe, 'Don't worry, there are plenty of other fish in the sea?'"

He did the last thing I expected him to. He laughed. It wasn't a roar of hilarity, but it was still certifiable laughter, and at the sound of it, my irritation completely melted away.

"Yes," he finally said as his laughter died. "Either of those would be better than apologizing."

"In that case," I shot him a conciliatory smile, "good for you. Maddie was a bitch, and there are plenty of other fish in the sea."

His smile faded before he sighed and lifted a hand to run it over his face. "Women are bitches."

My head jerked back, and I gave him my most impassive stare. "Wow. Thanks for that."

"Not you, Caro," he said quietly, dropping his eyes to the floor. There was a long pause before he spoke so quietly I almost couldn't make out the words. I had the feeling that was intentional. "I haven't figured out what you are yet."

I was dying to know what that meant, but I wasn't about to question it. Instead, I laced my hands together in my lap and cleared my throat. "So," I finally forced out, "did she at least tell you why?"

"She tried." He shrugged. "I didn't feel like listening."

I didn't try to stop the grin that surfaced at those words. "I'm sure she loved that."

He didn't respond. My smile died, and we were both quiet for a moment. He seemed lost in his own thoughts, eyes once again staring into space, but then he spoke, catching me slightly off guard. "I had decided I was going to ignore you."

"What do you mean?"

"Yesterday, before she dumped me, I had decided that if I was going to make things work with Maddie, I needed to stop spending time with you."

"I..." I trailed off because I really had no idea what to say to that. He continued like I hadn't spoken.

"Now, even though it's the last thing I want to do, I feel like I should stay away from you even more."

"Why?" I shouldn't have asked, but the word burst from my mouth almost on its own.

His eyes finally came back to me, and he slowly ran them from the top of my head, down to my shoes, and back up again. "I don't want to fuck up your relationship, too."

I scoffed. "That's a little presumptuous of you."

"No, it's not."

"Uh, yeah, it is. You being single doesn't change anything between us."

"You're wrong, Caroline. It sure as fuck does. You think I give a shit about your dickhead boyfriend in Michigan? I don't. The only thing that's been keeping me from doing what I've wanted to do since the day we met was Maddie, and now she's gone."

Those words shot through my head with all the force of a shotgun blast, and I forced my face to remain neutral even as they dropped straight through my stomach, leaving an uncomfortable sensation in their wake. Kind of like butterflies, except the butterflies were drunk and pigeon-sized.

"Can I use your bathroom?" I would have been worried about the desperate tone of my voice if I wasn't completely focused on getting off his couch. I needed space. I needed air. And for some reason, there wasn't any in his living room. Or maybe it was just my lungs because he didn't seem to be struggling to pull in each breath like I was. Either way, I needed to escape.

He pointed to a door across the room, and I burst off the couch and beelined for it. Once I was shut inside, I flicked on the light and then collapsed back against the cool wood of the door.

I needed to leave. I just needed to walk back out and tell him that he was right, that we shouldn't be friends. That it was too weird or hard or dangerous. Any of those because they all accurately applied to the situation. Then I needed to head down the stairs and out the door and never come back.

The problem was, all I could hear was Jimmy's quiet voice in front of the sandwich shop telling me that I was the best friend he had. And underneath everything else—the chemistry and the attraction that I now knew we both felt—I didn't want him to be alone. Underneath it all, I'd started to care about the guy on a level that had nothing to do with sexual interest.

I just wanted him to be happy.

Because of that, I quickly washed and dried my hands so it wasn't totally obvious I'd been hiding in the bathroom to pull my shit together. I placed a hand on the doorknob and took one last deep breath before I pulled the door open.

The breath wheezed out of my lungs, and my hand gripped the door tighter at the sight of him standing directly in front of me, one arm extended to rest against the door frame. There was less than a foot of space between us, and even though we'd been this close before, closer even, in the silence of his dark apartment, his proximity affected me to a degree that it never had. Sparks raced along my skin, and heat radiated from between my legs. His eyes locked onto mine, and there was an alertness there that hadn't been present when I'd first walked in the door. When he leaned in even closer, my spine stiffened, and I licked my lips quickly to work some moisture back into my bone-dry mouth.

"Wha- What are you doing?"

"Before you leave, I need you to hear a few things."

"Jimmy-"

"No, Caroline." His voice was low and forceful, and it was blatantly clear, despite how much I didn't want to hear whatever he had to say, I wasn't going to be able to stop him. "I'm going to say what I have to say, and then you can leave, and that will be the end of...whatever this is. But I can't let you leave until you understand something very important."

He needed to shut up because I couldn't breathe again, and it would be really embarrassing if I passed out on his bathroom floor.

"Your scars, they don't mean that you're broken. They mean that you're strong. That you're a fighter. They make you beautiful and unique. And if Dan doesn't see that, if he doesn't appreciate every fucking inch of your body and every piece of your soul, then he doesn't deserve you. You are absolutely perfect, Caroline. Don't settle for anyone who treats you as anything less."

Now I really needed to go. I couldn't handle that. I couldn't handle him. I couldn't handle words that made me feel... I didn't even have a *word* for how I felt, which was okay because I just needed to shut it all down. I couldn't do any of this.

As prepared as I had been to fight him on the we-can't-be-friends thing, the second he'd opened his mouth, there had been no going back.

"I have to go," I whispered. He held my eyes for a long moment, then nodded and dropped his arm from the door, taking a step backwards, so I could fit past him. Once I had enough room, I darted for the stairs, stopping only once I'd reached the top step to turn back in his direction without meeting his eyes.

"Goodbye, James." I directed the words at his feet and didn't wait for a response. As soon as his name passed my lips, I ran down the stairs and out the door. I didn't stop running until I'd gotten into the car, and I didn't start breathing until I'd pulled away from the house and headed for home.

## Chapter Fourteen

Jimmy

SO FAR MY MONDAY HAD been nothing but a series of increasingly bad decisions. Once the biggest one walked out my front door, I decided to make some more. I spent the four hours I had before work drinking. I figured it was worth it, even though I had to leave a solid hour before my shift started since I couldn't drive.

As I headed out the door and started the trip, I had to at least appreciate the weather. The day was fucking beautiful, which was kind of just my luck. Another subtle jab from whatever god I'd pissed off. *Oh, McCarthy's life just went to shit? Well, the rest of the world is awesome, so fuck you very much.*

Walking turned out to be a somewhat shitty decision, and I realized that only two short blocks from home. There was absolutely nothing to do but think. My feet moved over the concrete, and my head played a constant loop of both Maddie and Caroline's voices, and by the time I was closing in on the rink, I was seriously wishing I had just called out. That regret magnified tenfold when I finally walked onto the lot and saw both my dad's SUV and Ash's pick-up truck parked out front.

I made my way inside and headed straight for the back room. Dad was sitting in the office, eyes trained on the computer. He glanced up as I made my way to the time clock to punch in. "Hey, Jim."

I avoided his eyes, muttered a quiet hello, and turned to check the deployment, but he stopped me before I took a step. "Come here, kid. I want to talk for a minute."

Fuck. I sighed and turned around, making my way into the smaller room. I knew the conversation was going to be really bad when he slid the rolling chair toward the door to shut us inside.

"Sit."

"Dad…"

"James, sit."

He was using his don't-fuck-with-me voice.

I sat.

"Look," he started, leaning back and training his eyes on me, "obviously, you look like shit. I also know you didn't leave the apartment today. Normally, I might assume you were sick, but you didn't call out, and you've been to the liquor store twice in the past three days. Wanna tell me what's going on?"

This was a prime example of why it fucking sucked living next to your parents. Not to mention working for them.

"Maddie and I broke up."

I could tell he hadn't been expecting that, which made sense because, hey, I hadn't been expecting it either.

"When?"

"Last night. She called me."

The color rose in his face, and I could tell he was angry on my behalf. I appreciated it, but I really didn't feel like talking about it or listening to him tell me whatever he thought I needed to hear.

"Honestly, I just want to distract myself with work. Can we please talk about this later?"

He hesitated for a moment, and I forced myself to hold in the exasperated sigh that was straining to burst from my mouth. I was physically exhausted, mentally drained, and sobering up. In other words, censoring myself was tough.

I pulled it off, though, and a few seconds later he finally nodded. I escaped the office as fast as humanly possible, scanning the deployment quickly before heading out the door. Dad had me running the floor, which wasn't a surprise, since we were fully staffed for once. More often than not these days, I filled the holes made from call-outs, and I had to admit it was nice not being pinned to one specific place. It meant that I could keep myself busy, keep my mind off everything that wasn't related to this building and its occupants. Minus me, obviously, because avoiding my shit was the entire point.

Unfortunately, half an hour later my shit was staring me in the face. I had avoided visiting the rental booth for as long as I reasonably could, checking in with every other employee at least twice. Finally, I forced myself to walk into the small wooden shack where Ash was seated on a stool behind the counter. I made my way to the back and dropped onto the empty stool next to him.

"Hey," I said, eyes trained on the scratched wooden counter in front of us. "How you been, man?"

"Fine. You?" The words were clipped, the tone curt. I had been right—he was pissed.

I shrugged because the question had obviously been a formality, not actual curiosity. Even if it had been curiosity, I just wasn't going to go there. "How are things with your girl?" I thought the question might break the ice, remind him that I actually did care about his life. It didn't have the intended effect though.

"Why are you even asking? It didn't seem like you gave a shit the other night."

"Sorry, man." I decided to go with a little bit of honesty. "I've just been dealing with some shit, and..."

Yeah, that was all the honesty I could muster up. Even I knew it wasn't enough.

"Honestly, I'm sorry, but I don't really give a fuck."

For the first time since I'd walked in, I trained my narrowed eyes on him. I could get him being annoyed or even a little pissed, but he was completely past that, closing in on livid. And after two days of feeling way too much, but mostly a whole lot of anger, all that emotion was looking for somewhere to go. I knew it wasn't fair, but I also knew that he had just given me a golden opportunity. An outlet, if you will. But first I needed him to come out and admit what he was pissed about. Then we could have the argument we were *clearly* going to have.

"What the hell crawled up your ass?"

"You, motherfucker!" He flew off the stool and spun toward me, face reddening with every word that flew past his lips. "I'm sick of dealing with your bullshit, and I'm pretty over the fact that we only seem to be friends when it's fucking convenient for you!"

Golden. Fucking. Opportunity. Dude might have been my best friend, but every verbal barb he'd just flung my way tipped me over the ledge from regular angry to stupid angry. And I didn't hold back when I was stupid angry. I'd learned that lesson to my dismay quite a few times before.

"My bullshit?" I forced out something that might have been considered a laugh if it hadn't been quite so guttural. "That's really fucking rich, coming from you. Look," I reasoned, "I'm sorry you're having problems with your amazing girlfriend because she doesn't want to tell you how many guys she's fucked, or whatever bullshit you're dealing with, but I actually have a real fucking problem, and where the fuck have you been? Getting your dick wet with your princess?"

Was it uncalled for? Probably. Was it over the line? Yeah. Quite a bit.

I didn't fucking care. It felt great.

It didn't feel great when his fist slammed into my jaw.

I saw it coming but couldn't react fast enough. I took the hit and dropped to center myself. Then I charged off the stool, straight into his stomach. My fist slammed into his ribs once, and as I drew my arm back to hit him again, his knee came up into my solar plexus, completely winding me.

Dad was suddenly there, shouting loud enough to wake the fucking dead. Ash let up, and I slowly stood, trying unsuccessfully to take a full breath. I didn't need to see Dad's face to know that he was beyond livid. I wasn't sure if there was even a word for how angry he had to be.

"Someone needs to fucking explain to me why you two are going at it in the rental booth. Right the fuck *now*!"

I didn't have an answer he would like, or even accept. Apparently, Ash didn't either because we both stayed silent while Dad glared down at us, arms folded across his wide chest.

His eyes came to me, and he nodded slowly. "Right. Jimmy, I get it, you're miserable. That doesn't mean you take that shit out on your best friend. And you, Ash," he slid his gaze from me to the guy standing at my side, "I don't get this, at all, from you. I want you out of here. Don't come back to work until you sort out your shit and pull your head out of your ass."

"Chris," he started, "I'm sorry, but I swear-"

"I don't give a shit. Just fucking sort your shit, yeah?" Ash must have nodded because Dad grunted, "Good. Now get the fuck out of here." He left without a single word or glance in my direction.

As soon as he was gone, Dad turned back to me. "Anything you want to say?"

"It won't happen again."

He shook his head at my lackluster response. "Yeah, I imagine it won't. Still doesn't explain why it happened in the first place." I met his stare head on but kept my mouth shut. After a moment, he realized I wasn't going to talk and sighed, dropping disappointed eyes from mine.

I might have been a twenty-one-year-old college senior, but that still stung.

"Get it together, Jim."

He walked out of the booth I was now stuck manning, and I watched him go, trying desperately to come up with a way to do exactly that.

I failed just as hard as I tried.

Between work and the hour walk home once I'd closed up, I was actually able to lie down and pass out almost the second I got home. I woke Tuesday morning with my alarm, which was earlier than I would have liked, but I still forced myself out of bed and into the shower. I considered shaving but decided against it, hoping the Grizzly Adams beard would help ward off the world because as much as I didn't want to be around people, I knew I couldn't spend another day hiding out.

I dressed in sweatpants and a t-shirt, threw a change of clothes into my backpack, and then I was out the door and driving toward the athletic center. Once I got inside, I made a quick stop in the locker room before heading straight for the weight room. The room was empty but for me, which I appreciated. I needed to work off my almost-twenty-four-hour drinking binge, and I attempted to do that with the most intense workout I'd pushed through in months. Each rep eased away a tiny bit of the anxiety that had settled in once the bulk of my anger faded.

That anxiety was why I'd tried to hold onto the anger as long as I could. Underneath rage was nothing waiting for me but fear. Fear and a heavy doubt that I'd ever be happy living my life in this town.

An hour and a half later, my arms felt ready to fall from my body in defeat. I shuffled back to the locker room and took another quick shower to wash the sweat from my skin. My brain went blissfully blank under the water, and I was able to get dressed and head outside in peace.

That peace lasted, astonishingly enough, through my first two classes. It wasn't until I started thinking about where I was going to grab lunch that thoughts of Caroline assaulted me.

Here's what really got me. I had spent four years with Maddie—four long years. And now that she'd extricated herself from my life, I wasn't missing *her*. I was pissed that she'd decided to throw away our future and I officially had no clue what my future held, now that everything I'd planned for had been tossed away like trash. That said, I didn't want her back. I didn't want the problems and the dishonesty. I didn't want to be with someone who could throw away a four year relationship, completely out of the blue, and over the phone no less. So, besides the moments of panic when I tried to settle on a vision of my future, I didn't think about Maddie at all.

Caroline, on the other hand...

I'd known the girl for less than a month, and yet, at the thought of never talking to her again, never staring into those blue eyes that somehow saw through every layer of bullshit I'd piled around myself, I felt absolutely empty.

I had no idea how it had happened, but Caroline had worked her way into my subconscious with her quiet words and her understanding looks. She had taken up residence in my mind and no matter how hard I tried, no matter how hard I worked to keep her from my mind, she wormed her way through every defense. She was a force of nature, like the raging flow of a flash flood and the dam I'd erected to keep her from washing away the fire in my heart had foundered.

Once I realized that, there was no way to avoid an even scarier epiphany: I was *so* fucked.

Tuesday night was practice night. Thank God, because otherwise I probably would have just spent the night in my apartment getting drunk again and trying to convince myself that I could stay friends with Caroline without putting my hands on her.

I felt better the minute my skates were on my feet. I felt amazing the second I glided onto the ice. The anger, fear, and loss all turned into fuel, something I could actually use. When coach split us up to scrimmage, I was practically fucking *giddy*.

I played better than I ever had before. I was faster, I hit harder, and I scored two goals, one of which came in in the last two minutes of the match-up, pushing my team to a 3-2 win.

As the whistle blew, Brooks skated to a stop at my side and pulled off his mask.

"You okay?"

I pulled off my helmet and jerked my head up once, still riding the high of being on the ice. I wasn't about to let him bring me back down. That would happen all on its own soon enough.

"If you say so. Listen, I'm only saying this because I'm worried you're going to put someone out of commission: Either work it out, or save it for a real game because if you keep this shit up, half our team'll have broken ribs before the opener."

He skated toward where the rest of the team had gathered around Coach, and I followed slowly behind, considering his point. I got a good look at Seth gingerly holding his left side, and I figured it was probably valid. Granted, Seth had had it coming, trying to steal the puck from me the way he had. He would have gotten hit just as hard if this had been a real game, against real opponents, and in my defense, he should have seen how it was going to play out.

Coach gave his typical end-of-practice speech. You played well, but it's still not enough. Push yourselves, both on and off the ice... I tuned out the bulk of it, and then we were dismissed. Before I could follow the team to the locker room, though, his voice rang back out behind me.

"McCarthy."

Fucking A.

The beard was clearly not working.

"Yeah, Coach?" I asked as I backed myself up and turned around to meet his stony expression. It was really the only one he had. Coach Miller was even bigger than my dad, both in terms of height and bulk. I had no doubt he had a soft side that came out when he went home to his wife and kids, but I hadn't seen it.

Frankly, I had no desire to.

"You alright?" His eyes zeroed in on the nasty bruise currently covering the bottom half of my face. I'd known Ash had a nasty right hook but had never experienced it personally. My face regretted my decision to antagonize him.

Ignoring that, I nodded. "Yeah, nothing to worry about."

He watched me for a moment before accepting that and going on. "You looked good tonight."

I stood an inch taller. I had known that already, but it felt good to hear it confirmed.

"Everything okay at home?"

It made sense that he'd think that; Coach and my dad had been friends for years. I knew his kids, and he knew Jack.

"Yes, sir. Everything's fine."

He considered that slowly, then gave me a curt nod. "Good. I'll see you Thursday."

I took longer in the shower than I needed to, refusing to even come out from under the spray until the last voice had faded from the locker room. Once the only sound was the echo of water hitting tile, I climbed out and slowly got dressed. My avoidance tactic worked. By the time I walked out the front doors, everyone else was gone.

The numbness that practice created only lasted through the first two minutes of the drive. So even though I'd decided in the shower that I wasn't going to make yet another stop at the liquor store on the way home, ten minutes later I was pulling into the lot. Once I finally got home, I carried the bottle straight to bed. It only took half an hour before the alcohol—whiskey this time—calmed my nerves enough that I could handle lying in my dark bedroom.

Thank God it only took another ten minutes to pass out because I spent every one of them thinking about Caroline.

Chapter Fifteen

# Caroline

KATY PERRY WOKE ME UP. I mean, not the *actual* Katy Perry. Just her music. I figured out pretty quick that it was coming from a phone, and I impatiently waited for whoever owned the stupid thing to answer it, so I could fall back asleep. It took me another minute and a half to realize that the phone that wouldn't shut the fuck up was mine. I groggily reached a hand out toward the nightstand to find the annoying piece of technology and managed to wrap my fingers around it just as the singing stopped on its own.

*Thank God.*

I cradled the phone to my chest, and my eyes had just slid back shut when the noise started again, jolting me into semi-consciousness. I swiped my thumb across the screen and hoped that by the sudden silence in the room, I had managed to connect the call.

"-lo?" I managed through a dryer-than-dry mouth.

"Morning, Care Bear."

I sat up like I'd just done the ice bucket challenge. And it was *cold*.

"Dan? What's wrong?" Because something had to be. Otherwise, why the fuck would he be calling me at what had to be a pre-6 a.m. hour, his time?

"Nothing, nothing," he assured me quickly. "I just, well... I'm kind of lost."

That made two of us.

"Okaaay," I finally said to fill the silence. "And can I somehow help you?"

"Yeah. You can come find me. I was trying to get to your dorm, but I'm in the complete wrong place."

"Wait, what?" *No fucking way.* "You're here?"

"Surprise."

"Wow," I forced out. "Yeah, it really is."

"I'm going to ignore how completely unexcited you sound right now and assume it's because I just woke you up. So, can you come rescue me?"

I slid to the edge of the bed and reached out to grab my stump sock and liner, holding the phone to my ear with my shoulder. "Yeah, of course. What do you see?"

"Well, I'm standing inside a Panera right now. I didn't get coffee before I left the airport, so I stopped in here to grab one."

"Okay. There's only one nearby, so I know where you are. Just stay put, and give me about fifteen minutes. I'll be there.

"Great," he said brightly. "See you soon, baby."

I hung up and quickly finished putting on my leg before getting dressed. I grabbed a sweatshirt from my closet and headed through my door and across the suite toward Jen's, not bothering to knock before I pushed through it.

"I need you," I moaned, dropping onto her bed where she was lying awake, staring at her ceiling.

"Does this have to do with whoever was just blowing up your phone?"

"That was Dan. He's apparently here."

Her eyes locked onto mine, showing about the same amount of surprise as I felt. "Here as in Virginia, here?"

"Yep. He called me because he couldn't find his way here once his flight landed."

"Hmm," she murmured. "Interesting..."

"Can I please borrow your car to go track him down?"

"Yeah, of course. What are you guys going to do?"

"Fuck if I know. I was just planning to go to the gym and then hang out here. Nate's first game is tonight."

Her eyebrows soared up almost to her hairline. "You're going to that?"

I had told Jen what went down at Jimmy's apartment once I'd gotten home that night, and she knew I was doing my best to avoid going anywhere he could potentially be. That said, I wasn't a total coward, and I definitely wasn't going to miss my best friend's college hockey debut because of some guy.

"Of course I'm going. Are you?"

She shrugged. "Yeah, I'll tag along."

I didn't buy her nonchalance for a second but let it go in favor of getting out the door. The truth was, things had been weird between Nate and Jen for the past week or so. I assumed it had something to do with the pretend "date" they'd gone on, but so far neither one of them had been overly talkative about that particular subject.

I knew this because I'd brought it up repeatedly. No dice.

"Alright," I told her as I slid back to my feet. "Then I'll see you later."

She nodded, and then I headed out the door, keys in hand, to track down my boyfriend.

Dan was easy enough to find. Once I'd parked outside the restaurant, I grabbed the keys and headed toward the storefront. He was sitting at a small table just inside the window, and as if he sensed my approach, he looked up from his coffee and locked his eyes onto me. Through the bright glare on the glass, I still made out his wide smile. It dropped into my stomach like lead.

I made it inside, and as soon as I was standing in front of him, I was hauled against his body. Long arms wrapped around me, and he held me tightly for three of the longest minutes of my life.

While I was trapped in the embrace, I tried to muster up any sort of enthusiasm over the fact that, for the first time in months, the guy I loved was holding me. I just couldn't do it. I couldn't feel anything besides mild irritation at being pulled out of bed for a surprise visit.

It was a sad truth, but the truth nonetheless. In the two weeks since I'd last seen Jimmy, I hadn't been able to get his voice out of my head. I'd questioned my relationship almost nonstop since that day. I was well aware of the irony of the situation, but it didn't change the fact that, despite his good intentions, he'd still managed to fuck things up.

Or maybe I'd done that all on my own—I wasn't sure anymore. Either way, the weekend was guaranteed to be interesting.

Once he'd finally released me, I took a small step back and fully took him in. You wouldn't know from looking at him that he'd spent the morning on an airplane. His sky-blue polo was still wrinkle-free, his khaki pants perfectly pleated down the leg. His pale blond hair was longer at the top than I'd ever seen it and was piled into a messy pompadour that I knew for a fact he labored over each morning. I used to think it was the sexiest thing in the world.

Now? Now I thought he looked kind of ridiculous.

"You look amazing, Care Bear." He beamed down at me throughout the compliment, and I immediately felt completely crappy about my own less-than-complimentary thoughts. "Virginia suits you."

That at least made me smile. "Yeah, I think so too."

The silence that followed felt beyond awkward (at least to me), but Dan just grinned at me like he would have been happy doing nothing but that for hours.

"Well, you want the grand tour?" I finally offered.

"Absolutely. I'm all yours until tomorrow afternoon."

Two days of Dan. I really should have been thrilled. I really *wanted* to be thrilled.

I felt nothing.

Nine hours later, that *nothing* had morphed into full-fledged annoyance.

Here's the thing. I appreciated the fact that Dan had flown out to spend the weekend with me, but I had built a life in Virginia in the two months that I'd been here. I had friends and a social calendar. It was a mostly empty one, but it was a social calendar nonetheless.

I spent all day showing him around. We visited almost every landmark on campus, and, honestly, it wasn't that bad. The weather was fantastic, surprisingly warm for the start of October, and I'd even go so far as to say we had fun when we weren't awkwardly trying to keep a conversation alive for more than two minutes. The problem was that we really didn't know each other anymore. I mean, I knew him, but I didn't know anything about his life. I didn't know what he did or what he liked. In the year we'd been apart, despite the phone calls and perfunctory conversations, it felt like we'd somehow become strangers.

When I'd finally run out of places to show him, I took him home and introduced him to Jen. For half an hour we all just hung at the apartment, and that was nice too.

Then Jen glanced down at her phone before sliding her eyes up to mine. "What time is the game, Caro?"

"Uh, six, I think. Why? What time is it?"

"It's five right now. I'm gonna go get changed. We should probably leave soon."

I nodded, and she disappeared into her room, leaving Dan and I alone on the couch.

"What game is she talking about?" He asked the question quietly, but there was a dissatisfied tone that I had come to know all too well, mostly in the last year or so. It was the same tone he'd used when I told him I was applying to school here. His response was, "Why would you go to school on the East Coast?" So much disappointment. I *hated* that tone.

"Nate's first game," I said with a tiny shrug, a small attempt at placating him. "I promised him I would be there."

He frowned. "I thought we would go get dinner or something. I mean, we only have one night together..."

"I know that, and I'm sorry, but I can't miss it."

The frown turned into an annoyed pout that stayed in place. "Fine. That's fine."

For a second, I considered calling him out on his passive-aggressive attitude. I decided against it because, honestly, I just didn't have the time to start that argument right now. Instead I quietly headed for my room to get ready for the game.

Forty-five minutes later, Jen, Dan, and I were piling out of the car at the arena. Dan's mood had done nothing but deteriorate since we'd left the apartment, but I wasn't willing to let him drag me down. I was beyond excited to see Nate play, and, thankfully, Jen seemed as eager as I was.

The place was fairly packed. Students and alumni crowded around the snack bar and throughout the hall that led to the seating area. There was a familiar charge in the air, an almost breathless anticipation. Granted, that could have just been me. It really wasn't that long ago that feeling this charge in the air meant I was headed onto the ice. I'd always loved that feeling, just like I'd always loved this time right before a game started when there was nothing but possibility in front of me. I could play like shit, or it could be the best game of my life. Either way, I was in complete control—not necessarily of the game, but of my actions, my plays, my movements. I could count on myself to think and react and do. I trusted myself to make the right decisions.

That's why I had loved playing hockey. Life was a game that felt too big, too scary to react to. I didn't always trust my decisions when it came to life. But hockey? I got hockey. I *understood* hockey.

Life was a total fucking mystery.

It took us ten minutes to get around the crowds and into our seats. By the time we'd gotten settled, both teams were already warming up on the ice. I found Nate easily and attempted to keep my eyes focused on him. On more than one occasion, though, they slid to the jersey marked 27, McCarthy displayed brightly across the back in crisp, white lettering. I couldn't help but notice how comfortable he seemed on the ice, how in tune he was with his surroundings. I'd seen hints of his ability before at practices, but it had been nothing compared to this.

When the game started, the air went from charged to absolutely electric. Even so, through the first few minutes, the action was visibly tame. Both teams were clearly trying to get a feel for the matchup, trying to find any weaknesses. I noticed a few between the players of the visiting team, their sloppy passing and an all too frequent habit of going for the easily blocked shots. I couldn't find a single one on our side, though. They played through a few line changes as, slowly but surely, the intensity level rose. Ten minutes into the first period, we scored our first goal, and the crowd went insane, myself included. From there, it was no holds barred. I watched our boys fight hard, fighting to keep control and making their hits count. It was fast, it was rough and, even just watching, it made me feel *alive*.

By the time the first period ended, I was practically beaming. Hockey was my first real love. Even if I couldn't play anymore, even if it hurt sometimes, I would never stop watching. Dan, unfortunately, didn't share my excitement, and as soon as the ice had emptied, he offered to head out to the bar for some food. Jen and I both gave him our orders, and then he was gone, leaving us alone.

"So," she started, as soon as the coast was clear, "he's not exactly having a good time."

I shrugged and avoided her eyes by pretending that the ice cut was the most interesting thing I'd ever seen. "He wanted us to have a date night."

"That's understandable," she ceded.

"That's why surprise trips halfway across the country aren't always a great idea." I felt bad the second the words left my mouth, but it didn't make them any less true.

"You're not wrong. Think you guys will be okay?"

My teeth tugged my bottom lip into my mouth as I considered answering with a deflection. Somehow, though, it felt shitty. After Nate, Jen was the best friend I had. If I had been honest with Jimmy, I could be honest with her.

"I'm not sure, but I know that we're going to spend a lot of time talking before he goes home tomorrow."

"Yeah," she mumbled, "that's probably a good idea."

I nodded and kept my mouth shut for approximately two point five seconds. "So, speaking of conversations that need to be had..."

Her back went straight, and now she was the one concentrating on the ice like she'd never seen any before.

"You *need* to tell me what happened," I pleaded. "Obviously, things are weird between you guys right now. It's been awkward as fuck. We need to talk about it, so we can fix it, so it *stops* being awkward as fuck. I can't handle it, Jen. Please," I begged, lifting my hands and lacing them together in mock prayer, "save me from the awkward."

She didn't react at all to my exuberant plea, and I was a little disappointed.

Okay, more than a little.

"Seriously?" I asked. "You really have nothing to say?"

"I really have nothing to say."

I groaned through my frustration and turned toward her in my seat. "Can you just tell me-"

"There's nothing to tell!" She interrupted with a half-desperate shout. I watched her take a quick breath, and just like that, her face blankly focused on the ice again. "Seriously, Caroline. Nothing happened. Nate's just pissed at me because he can't seal the deal."

My eyes narrowed on her face as I tried to piece together what that could possibly mean. I wasn't sure if she was talking about the girl that the whole sham "date" had been for or herself. Either way, it still didn't make sense. Nate wasn't the type of guy to get pissed because he got turned down. I'd watched him crash and burn enough times to know that for a fact.

Dan was back a few minutes later with cheese fries for everyone, and I tried—unsuccessfully—to get back the high I'd been riding before the intermission, a difficult task since the conversation with Jen and my impending conversation with Dan both weighed heavily on my mind. As the second period started, I munched my fries and stared at the ice, lost in thought.

Despite the guilt I felt over it, it was almost a relief when my gaze drifted to Jimmy. He wasn't hard to find. There was an intensity to the way he played, almost like his life depended on it, that drew my eyes straight to him. He handled his stick like it was an extra appendage and skated like he'd been doing it since before he could walk. Just like I had before the accident.

As physically intense as he was on the ice, there was a mental intensity that I noticed as well. Jimmy played hockey like you would play chess. He wasn't just three steps ahead; he was five. His passes were perfectly timed; his hits were perfectly placed. He was just perfect.

I saw the second goal coming before it happened. With three minutes left in the second period, Jimmy intercepted yet another sloppy pass between the opposing center and right wing. He dumped it back into the offensive zone, and his center, Jake Collins, chased after it, sending the left defenseman into the boards hard in the process. By then, Derek Soto had positioned to receive the pass from Collins. Soto lined up and shot the puck to Jimmy, who sent it careening over the goalie's glove and into the net.

The play was perfectly executed. The crowd went crazy once again, but this time I didn't celebrate with them. I watched Jimmy skate away from the net like nothing had happened, back over to the bench to grab a drink of water. The rest of the team showered him with pats on the back, but, from what I could see, he didn't react at all to their praise. When the lines swapped out and play resumed, he sat alone at the end of the bench, face pointed straight ahead.

The second intermission was decently awkward. Jen spent the entirety of the fifteen-minute break on her phone while Dan and I both stared silently at the ice. I wondered what he was thinking for only a minute before I decided that I'd rather not know. Instead, I did something I hadn't allowed myself to do at length in weeks, something that proved I was, hands-down, the world's worst girlfriend: I thought about Jimmy.

It had been twelve days since I'd visited his apartment. They were not the worst days of my life. I was not dying inside because we weren't friends anymore. That said, saying I hadn't thought about him, that I hadn't missed him at all, would have been a lie. I had liked spending time with Jimmy. He was occasionally funny, and when he actually loosened up and stopped worrying so much, he was nice to have around. Not only that, he was a good guy. A really good guy. The kind of guy who would sacrifice his own happiness to take care of the people he loves. The kind of guy who would punch someone in a bar just because he made a total stranger uncomfortable.

In a lot of ways, he reminded me of Nate. He was someone that I knew I could grow to feel strongly about. But that just brought us to the one major way that he differed from Nate.

Nate had never stolen my breath with a single look or scattered my wits with a smile. In fact, even Dan had never affected me the way Jimmy did. My own boyfriend had never melted my brain the way Jimmy had fried it the first time I'd seen him shirtless. I wasn't sure if that said more about Dan or about me, but, either way, now wasn't the moment to examine it too closely.

Thankfully, the third period flew by. The away team came out fighting and scored one goal around the six-minute mark. Unfortunately for them, our lines changed. Once Jimmy was back on the ice, he stayed there, and they didn't get another opportunity. We scored one last goal with four minutes left and ended the game 3-1.

By the time the final buzzer had blown, I'd gotten back a little of the excitement I'd sported at the start. I was happy for Nate. Jimmy, too. They'd played a good game, and I was glad I'd come.

But I was also tired and really wanted nothing more than to go home and go to bed.

The three of us followed the flow of people out the front doors before I pulled Jen and Dan to the left, finding a quiet place where we could stand to wait. I fired off a quick text to Nate and let him know that we would see him out front, and then the three of us settled into a heavy silence. It didn't take long before players started streaming from the building, all of them clearly riding the high of the win. Nate, following a bunch of guys I didn't know out the door, spotted us instantly, a wide grin stretching across his face.

"Sweet fucking Caroline," he shouted, jogging to me before wrapping his arms around my waist tightly. I let out an alarmed laugh as he picked me up off the ground, spinning us both in a full circle before setting me carefully back on my feet.

"Congratulations, Mr. Baker," I told him with a grin. "You were fantastic."

He snorted a short laugh. "Tomorrow I'm sure you'll have different words for me entirely."

I smiled because he wasn't totally wrong, but I didn't get a chance to respond before his eyes were scanning the space over my shoulder. I couldn't tell if it was the sight of Dan or Jen that shut his face down as he took a quick step away.

"Wow. Hey, man. Long time no see." Dan and Nate exchanged an all-guy hand-slapping thing, but my eyes were on Jen, who was staring at Nate like she wasn't sure if she wanted to kiss him or kill him.

*Nothing happened, my ass.* I made a silent vow that even if it took every trick in my arsenal, I was going to find out what went down from one of them.

"You guys have to come!" Nate's exuberant shout brought me back to the conversation, but it was Dan's excited, "I'm in" that really got my attention.

"Wait, what? Come where?"

"Team party," Nate answered in a tone that implied an unspoken, *Duh.* I ignored that and turned to Dan.

"You seriously want to go? 'Cause I kind of just want to go home."

Dan gave me a look I couldn't interpret. "We've already wasted the night. Might as well do something fun. Besides, we haven't been to a party together since..."

Mentally, I was daring him to finish that sentence. The last party I'd attended with Dan had ended with me in the hospital, minus an appendage.

Thankfully, Jen piped up before I had time to vocalize my challenge. "I'm with Caro. I want to go home."

Nate turned his eyes on her for the first time since we'd all started talking and gave her an almost clinical once-over. His eyes were hard as he slowly ran them across her body. "Come on, Jen," he goaded. "Don't be such a coward."

My mouth dropped open while her face turned bright red. Things might have been weird, but he hadn't resorted to straight up provocation. At least, not until now. I waited for her to say something to him, to come back with something snarky like she always did. Instead, her lips snapped shut, and she looked to me pleadingly.

I resisted my strong urge to give her an I-told-you-that-we-should-have-talked-about-this face and picked up the gauntlet. "I really don't think it's a good idea, Nate..."

His attention shifted back to me, but before either one of us could say another word, Dan sighed. "Whatever. You guys talk. I need to take a leak." With that, he turned around and headed back for the arena.

"Please, Caro," Nate pleaded as soon as he was gone. "Just come."

I glanced around to make sure Dan was out of earshot before I spoke quietly to him. "Besides the fact that I'm tired and I really just want to go home, can we keep in mind that we all," I gestured to Nate, Jen, and myself, "agreed that I should attempt to stay away from Jimmy? I came to the game. I don't think going to the party is a smart idea."

"He won't be there."

"You can't promise that."

"Yes, I can. I already asked him. He told me himself he wasn't going."

An odd sensation passed through me. It was part relief and part disappointment, and I forced it away before it had time to settle. "Jen doesn't want to go either," I pointed out. I felt especially bad for drawing her back into the argument when her eyes widened with panic and she shook her head quickly at me. Nate didn't notice. He responded without glancing in her direction.

"Yeah, well, Jen has a habit of not knowing what's good for her."

Ouch.

Her eyes slid to the ground while I tried to come up with another argument. Before I could find anything to say, any possible way to get out of going to this party, Dan appeared back at my side and looked to me. "We going?"

Nate answered for me. "Yeah, we're all going. And I need a ride, so shotgun."

If looks could kill, the glare Jen shot my way would have sliced a hole through my insides. I didn't have to withstand it too long, though, because almost immediately she transferred her laser eyes to Nate, and they somehow turned even more murderous.

Yeah, I definitely needed to find out what was going on there. It was going to have to wait though because apparently we were going to the party. The four of us headed to the car, and I reasoned that it couldn't possibly be that bad. We'd show up, celebrate with the team for a little bit, and then head home. There was no way the night could turn into a total disaster.

It was actually frightening just how wrong I was.

## Chapter Sixteen

*Jimmy*

THE GAME PASSED BY IN a blur. Don't get me wrong, I was completely focused. I was so focused that I just saw and processed, no thinking involved. No feeling either. I played using pure instinct, and somehow it worked. I knew I was playing better than ever before, but I'd never managed to shut myself off to the world so effectively before. So, that was a first.

Coach's post-game talk was relatively short because, honestly, there wasn't a whole lot to say. It had been an easy game, and we dominated it. We would all show up to practice ready to push ourselves harder to get ready for the next game, one that might not be so simple.

For tonight, we were winners.

The rest of the team was riding the high of the victory, but I couldn't get myself to a place where I felt good enough to celebrate with them. I was already sinking back into my leave-me-alone-and-don't-talk-to-me head space. It wasn't a place I wanted to be. It wasn't even a place I liked. It just felt like the only thing holding me together.

I took my time in the locker room, as was becoming standard for me. As much as I wanted to, I couldn't wait for everyone to leave. I knew that Mom,

Dad, and Jack were outside waiting for me, and I didn't want to keep them there too long. Still, most of the guys had disappeared by the time I finished getting dressed, all eagerly flying out the door to get to the hockey house for what was guaranteed to be a shit-show. It was one I had no plans on attending.

Over the past two weeks, most of my teammates had realized that it was a good idea to give me space, and now that the game was over, that unspoken rule was followed by almost everyone. I say "almost" because there were three motherfuckers on this team who didn't give a shit that I wanted nothing to do with people in general, and two of them felt the need to stop by my locker on the way out. Nate was first.

"Good game, man."

I gave him a nod, hoping he would take it and move on. He didn't.

"You going to the party tonight?"

That didn't even deserve a verbal response. I stared at him blankly until he dropped his eyes uncomfortably to the floor.

"Right, you hate people now. Listen, I know this is probably a long shot, but I wanted to ask... It's just, Caro mentioned that your dad owns a rink, and I thought..." He lifted his eyes to glance quickly at mine, which had narrowed at the mention of Caroline's name, and shook his head, quickly regretting whatever he had been about to say. "Never mind, it's fucking stupid." He gave me one more quick look before shaking his head again and turning away. "Have a good night, man."

I considered calling him back because watching him walk away made me feel every bit of the dick I knew I was being. Maybe it was how little actual speaking I'd done recently, but I couldn't force his name past my throat. It sat there, heavy and constricting, until he'd reached the far end of the room and disappeared out the door.

Once he was gone, I attempted to forget about it. I grabbed the last of my things from the locker and swung the door shut, turning around to find Brooks standing two feet away. Sighing heavily, I crossed my arms across my chest and settled my shoulder against the wall of lockers, ready to hear whatever he had to say.

I'd known Eric Brooks for going on four years now. He was our captain, a fellow senior, and a really good guy. Tough, quiet, and always in control. I envied him a little for that. I knew that he was the one the guys went to when they had problems, and for the past couple weeks, he'd been almost relentlessly trying to get me to open up about mine.

I had yet to take him up on that offer.

"I take it you haven't sorted out your shit yet."

I shrugged. "At this point, I think it'd only hurt the team if I did."

He ran a hand across the dark layer of stubble on his jaw and smiled slowly. "Solid point."

I started to move past him, but he stepped in my way to block me before I could escape. "You should come out tonight."

"No."

"It'll be good for the team."

I smirked at that. "Really? Since when is getting drunk and finding a groupie to fuck a team-building activity?"

"That just goes to show how much you need to get out," he argued. "There's more to do at a party than get wasted and laid. Besides, we'll be celebrating. And it'll be good for the guys to see you being a real person again. They might be a little less scared of you."

I pretended to think it over for a moment and only felt a little bad about the hope that lit behind his eyes. "If they're not scared of me, they'll talk to me. That doesn't work for me. So, no. Sorry, but I'm gonna pass."

I pushed straight past him and headed for the door, ready to be out of this locker room, this entire arena. The emotional blankness I'd managed to secure around myself during the game had disappeared completely, leaving me tense and jittery, almost as if all the adrenaline I'd built up during the game had settled in my stomach and was now eating its way through my body like cancer. I felt it invading every inch of my skin, and all I wanted to do was get home. Get a little drunk. Think about Caroline a little. Maybe Maddie too, if I was feeling especially shitty. Finally fall asleep.

That was what my nights had, for the most part, become. I didn't drink every night, but I wasn't opposed to it when my thoughts got darker than I could handle, when I started thinking about all the things I wished I could be, the things I wished I could do.

The things I wished I could change.

It was all pointless, so those were the nights I drank. Tonight was definitely going to be one of those nights. I could tell.

The last stragglers were still making their way out of the arena by the time I made it outside. I scanned the area for Mom and Dad and finally spotted them to my left, standing well away from where the last crowds of people were roving toward their cars. I headed in their direction, and Jack spotted me first, interrupting what looked like a conversation between him and Mom as he turned my way.

For just a moment, I got the best gift Jack ever gave: eye contact. It was fleeting, but for one single second his excited eyes met mine, and, bright smile on his face, he shouted, "Jim!"

That fast, he'd closed the remaining distance between us and wrapped thin arms around me. All the panic and anxiety that had crept in since I'd gotten off the ice felt miles away while I accepted the tight hug, another rare occurrence. It was always like this when Jack came to games. No matter how I played, no matter if we won or lost, Jack always looked at me afterwards like I was his hero.

I lived for those moments.

The hug ended abruptly, and he stepped back as Mom and Dad finally reached us, both wearing smiles as well. Mom's radiated pure happiness. She didn't care what I did or how well I did it; she just wanted me to be happy, and why wouldn't I be right now? I tugged my lips up a bit further, not sure if it was for her benefit or my own, but wanting to make the effort regardless. My gaze slid to Dad, whose smile wasn't as bright, but filled with every bit of the pride I'd been so desperate for when I was younger.

Taking it in, I realized that it didn't really do it for me like it had in the past. Sure, if felt good. Sure, I liked knowing that he was proud of the way I played. That said, I didn't find even close to the amount of satisfaction in it that I had when I was younger. I didn't feel fulfilled the way I had in high school.

Dad might have been proud of me because of hockey, but I couldn't appreciate that anymore. I wasn't proud of me. What's worse, I knew it wouldn't be as simple as improving my game play to feel like I was the person I needed to be. The person I *wanted* to be.

Because, the person that I had become? I wasn't really a fan of him.

"Good game, Jim," Dad murmured gruffly, and I nodded.

"Thanks."

"You were awesome," Jack interjected, eyes focused somewhere around my hairline. The hero-worship window was closing quickly, and I found myself especially sad to see it go.

"Thanks, dude," I told him, ignoring the way my voice hitched on the words. Mom leaned in to give me a quick hug and kiss before we all said our goodbyes and they turned toward the parking lot. Dad hadn't taken a step before he twisted back, eyes trained heavily on me.

"You should do something tonight. Something fun," he clarified, like I hadn't understood the implication. "You keep spending every night at home, and you'll end up old faster than you can blink."

I chuckled at that and shrugged. "You know me, Dad, always been an old soul anyway. I'm just embracing it."

He shook his head disapprovingly but smiled through it. "Embrace life instead, Jim. You only get one."

Twenty minutes later I was pulling out of the liquor store, headed for home. My phone had already gone off twice during the drive from the arena, but I was resolutely ignoring the thing. I had no doubt it was the only other person who hadn't attempted to get me to come out tonight, and I figured I could wait until I'd gotten home to deal with him.

As I pulled up to the house, though, the phone went off three more times in quick succession, the vibration causing it to rattle angrily in the plastic-lined cup holder where I'd stashed it. I slid the car into park but grabbed the phone before turning off the engine, quickly pulling up the messages that were indeed from Soto, fellow senior and, along with Nate and Brooks, my only other teammate who apparently hadn't given up all hope for me.

Derek: **where the fuck r u?**
Derek: **get ur ass here now, mccarthy!!!!!!!!!**
Derek: **didnt want to have to mention this, but ur girl is here...**

Derek: **...the one from the bar**
Derek: **she brought a date**

By the time I'd finished reading the texts my shoulders had risen to my ears and my fingers were clenched around the phone so tightly, I half expected the screen to shatter. There was no way. Caroline couldn't have brought a date to the hockey party. Not with Dickhead Dan in Michigan.

*Unless he's out of the picture...* The thought drifted through my mind like the smell of rain before a thunderstorm—barely there at first, but growing stronger as the clouds approached. When that storm hit, it hit hard.

Thoughts of her with some other guy—some new guy—had my heart racing and my hands shaking. There was no fucking way. Even if she'd ditched the dick, why wouldn't she...?

I forced myself to abandon that thought before I'd even completed it. She didn't owe me anything. What had I ever been to her? A bullshit excuse for a "friend," and even that only lasted a few weeks before I fucked it up. Because the reality of the situation was, I'd never wanted to be her friend in the first place. I wanted to be so much more than that.

I wanted to be her beginning and her end. I wanted to be her everything.

Suddenly, even though I knew it wasn't fair, I was pissed. I'd all but defined the fact that I had feelings for her. She had to know that. There was no way that I could feel this lost, this hopelessly consumed by a girl, without her knowing it. *Right*?

I decided it didn't matter. It didn't matter if she didn't know that she wouldn't leave my mind, that I couldn't make it through a single day without thinking about her countless times. Innocent things—curiosities—like what she was doing or what she'd had for lunch. There were quite a few not-so-innocent curiosities as well, like what she sounded like when she came and what it would feel like to finally press my lips against hers like I was dying to do. What she would taste like.

I adjusted myself in the sweatpants I was wearing before turning the key and sliding it from the ignition. I climbed from the car and made my way inside, only staying long enough to change my clothes. Once I had on jeans and an old Flogging Molly t-shirt, I headed straight back out the front door.

I was just going to stop at the party, get a look at the guy she was with, then leave, I reasoned as I started the car and pulled away from the curb. I wasn't even going to talk to her. I just needed to see her.

The list of things I wanted was a lot fucking longer, but I didn't let myself go there.

I just needed to see her.

It took about fifteen minutes to get to the hockey house. It was called the hockey house—uncreatively—because five of the guys on the team currently lived inside it. Soto was one of them, along with Dan Fisher, Eddie Garcia, Ryan Turner, and Oliver Cole.

Even under normal circumstances, I did my best to avoid the house. That wasn't because of its inhabitants, although Turner *was* a grade-A douchebag. The problem was five college-aged guys—hockey players no less—living together. The place was almost always disgusting. That said, I was sure Nate and the other freshmen had been cleaning for at least a day. Probably longer.

Hopefully longer.

I parked a few houses down and slipped my phone and keys into my pockets before making my way quickly toward the front door. I heard music pulsing from the tall Victorian monstrosity before I'd even started up the walkway, and I sent up a silent prayer to anybody who felt like listening that the night ended without any arrests or injuries.

Dodging some groupies on my way up the front stairs, I let myself in, into fucking mayhem. Bodies filled the wide front hall, and I had to work to avoid all the moving limbs and gyrating figures as I headed further inside. The hall led past a dark living room filled with more people and the heavy odor of lots of pot. I scanned the room as well as I could, not really thinking I'd find her there but wanting to be sure before I moved on.

I was doing one sweep of the house. If I found her, I'd check out the guy, feel out the situation, and then I'd leave. If I didn't find her, I'd leave right away and go home to agonize over every aspect of the shitty situation I had gotten myself into.

Once I determined she wasn't in the living room, I headed further down the hall, scanning heads while continuing to navigate the churning sea of students. For as early as it was, there were quite a few people who looked to be nearing the end of their nights. I didn't even want to imagine what the guys were going to wake up to tomorrow. Besides how wrecked this place was guaranteed to be, I was positive there'd be at least a handful of passed out strangers littered across the property. There was always at least one in the yard.

Or so I'd heard.

At the end of the hall, I headed left toward the kitchen instead of the dining room to the right, where I could just make out a game of beer pong being played through the heaving bodies. I didn't find Caroline in the kitchen, but I did find Soto seated on the counter that ran the length of the far wall. Once I was sure she was nowhere nearby, I made my way across the room.

"Holy shit," he laughed when he finally caught sight of me. "You fucking asshole..."

I faked affronted innocence. "What did I do?"

"You don't show up for your team, but you'll show up for fucking pussy."

That word used to describe Caroline had my fist tightening at my side but I forced the anger away. It was just Soto. If I cursed like a sailor, he cursed like the fucking captain. I wasn't going to take it personally.

"I'm not here for her. I figured I could at least make an appearance. You know, show up for my team." I felt a small twinge of guilt as I threw the words back at him because they were a total fucking lie. I was 100 percent here for Caroline. He just didn't need to know that.

"Sure you did," he said. "Whatever it took, man, I'm fucking glad you're here. You need to get over that cunt. Plenty of bitches here, dude... Use Oliver's bed. Fuck knows it could use some action 'cause he sure doesn't see any."

I smiled as Oliver, our goalie, shouted a colorful, "Fuck you" from just a few feet away. "I'll get right on that. I'm gonna go," I pressed my lips into a line and gestured with one hand in the air, "socialize."

Derek laughed and nodded. "You do that. And have some fun while you're at it!" The shout followed me across the kitchen as I headed for the hall.

I'd just turned toward the dining room to give it a quick pass when I looked up and immediately locked eyes with person number two on my Make-Sure-to-Avoid List: Nate Baker.

"Shit," he muttered, glancing over his shoulder toward the basement door. I immediately followed his gaze, expecting Caroline to materialize any second. When she didn't appear, I breathed a sigh of relief and looked back at him.

"Uh, hey man..." He reached up to push the hair back off his forehead. His nervous fidgeting made me feel even worse about how I'd brushed him off at the arena. "What are you doing here? I thought..." He trailed off, and I jumped in quickly.

"Yeah, I figured I'd give the party a shot. No time like the present to stop being an antisocial dick, right?" My smile might have been self-deprecating, but it was still an improvement over blank stares and aggressive glares. I think I had even grunted at someone.

*Jesus Christ, I'm turning into a fucking caveman...*

Thankfully, he laughed, and I relaxed the tiniest bit. "Yeah...no time like the present."

We were both quiet for a moment, and I used it to consider my options. I could finish my sweep of the house and call it a night, head home to work on the unopened bottle of Johnnie Walker in my backseat. Or I could man the fuck up, find Caroline, and just talk to her. Say hi. See how she'd been.

*Find out who she's here with...*

I weighed both scenarios and suddenly found the first much more unappealing than I had when I'd walked in the door.

"So, is Caroline here?" *Subtlety never was my strong suit.*

This time his eyes darted toward the dining room, and again I followed his lead, searching the space I could make out from where we stood.

"Uh, yeah," he finally admitted nervously, drawing my eyes away from the crowded room. "She's downstairs with Jen."

I nodded and smiled tightly. "Thanks, man. I'll probably see you later."

I heard him call my name as I turned toward the open door at the top of the basement stairs, but I ignored it, taking the steps two at a time. The lights in the basement had all been turned off, and a heavy bass thumped through the walls louder down here than anywhere else. The only illumination came from strips of black lights that lined the ceiling, plus the walls that had been painted a few years ago with stuff that glowed underneath them. As cheesy as it was, I had to admit, it looked kind of cool.

The walls weren't the only things glowing, I noticed on closer inspection. A gaggle of groupies stood crowded around a table on the far side of the basement. I watched them decorate their skin with lines of bright, fluorescent paint. My gaze shifted to the makeshift dance floor between the groupies and myself, and I noticed more paint-covered bodies, colors shifting hypnotically with the movement of the crowd.

It was while I stared at the dancers that I spotted her, standing in the far corner of the room with Jen. Her back was toward me, but even if I hadn't seen her roommate, I would have known it was her. There was something about the way she stood—the way she held herself—that always caught my attention.

She'd been capturing my attention since the first second I'd laid eyes on her.

I started around the throng of dancers toward the two girls, neither of whom noticed me. Jen was staring intently at Caro, holding a small brush up to her cheeks carefully. I noticed Jen already had swirls of paint up and down her arms, and I wondered if Caroline had painted them.

By the time I'd made it to them, Jen was dropping the brush and turning away to place it with the paint sitting on the small table beside them. As she looked back up, her eyes slid right past Caroline's and crashed into mine, growing wide before they darted back to the girl in front of me.

*Less than two feet away. For the first time in weeks.*

I let out a shaky breath as she slowly turned around. Or maybe it was only happening in slow motion in my head, but every millisecond of time between when she started to turn and when her eyes locked with mine felt branded into my consciousness.

She didn't show Jen's surprise or Nate's nerves. Instead, as I took in the small lines that Jen had painted across her cheekbones, I got the wide flash of a smile before it quickly faded, almost as if she had forgotten where we left off in my apartment that day.

Her eyes glanced over my shoulder nervously and then flitted back to mine, as if she was afraid to be seen with me. Even though I tried to tell myself that it didn't bother me, that was a lie too big to swallow.

"Hey." The word came out too rough, like I hadn't used my voice in years. And it felt like I hadn't. Every word I'd ever spoken that wasn't directed at the girl standing in front of me felt pointless, inconsequential. Like they had all never even happened.

She licked her lips quickly, and I tried not to get lost in the sight, but, fuck, I wanted to know what that felt like. I wanted to know what it would be like to run my tongue across her lips, to coax my way into her mouth.

I wanted to earn my place there. And once I'd earned it, I never wanted to leave.

I watched her mouth move through a near silent, "Hey" before I was able to lift my eyes back to hers.

"Congrats on the win." Her quiet compliment meant more to me than all the others I'd received tonight, and the tiny smile she served it with slammed straight into my chest with all the shocking power of a defibrillator.

"Thanks," I mumbled around a tongue that suddenly seemed too thick. I didn't know if it was because I hadn't seen her in a while or because, for the first time in the month that I'd known the girl, I was finally allowing myself to entertain visions of her and I together, but either way I'd officially become the guy that didn't know how to keep his cool around beautiful girls.

In my defense, it was really only this beautiful girl. And beautiful almost didn't cover it.

She glanced over my shoulder again, and I barely resisted turning around to see who she was looking for.

"How have you been?" I forced out quickly, bringing her attention back to me. Kind of. Her eyes fluttered to mine for a second before landing on my ear, Jack style.

"Uh, I've been good." She slid her gaze to Jen, who was staring at her phone like we didn't exist. I had to admit, I kind of liked that girl. Caroline sent her a glare she didn't notice before meeting my eyes and, thank fuck, keeping them there. "How about you?"

I shrugged because I wasn't about to lie to her. "I've been better." Her face fell a little at that, and I hurried on quickly. "I'm okay, though."

She nodded and dropped her eyes. "I should probably go..." She grabbed Jen and angled around me quickly, turning back as I spun to face her. "It was good seeing you."

They started to move away, and at the thought of watching her leave again, at the thought of letting her walk away from me for what I knew would be the last time, I panicked. I took a quick step in her direction and wrapped my fingers gently enough around her wrist as to not hurt her, but firmly enough that I had her attention.

"Wait," I forced out, and I gratefully noticed Jen take a few more steps to give us at least the semblance of privacy in the crowded room. "I miss you." She tried to tug her arm from my hand, but I refused to let go, taking a step closer instead. "I know this is weird and complicated but-"

"Jimmy, I can't-"

"No, just listen-"

We both stopped speaking at the sound of a male shout echoing down the basement stairs loudly enough to be heard over the music. "Care Bear, you down there?"

Her eyes darted to the steps, and she pulled her arm away from my hand again. This time, I let her go, and she took a quick step back before I could react. I was too busy trying to stay calm, trying to keep breathing normally.

"I really have to go."

"Who is that, Caroline?"

"Jimmy, I-"

"Who is that?"

"That's Dan. He flew in this morning, and I really need to go find him. I'll see you later, or whatever, okay?"

She didn't give me a chance to respond before she was darting around the edge of the room, grabbing Jen by the arm on the way to the stairs. I watched her go and tried to process the information she'd just dropped on me.

It wasn't a new guy. It was Dickhead Dan. Which meant they were still together, and I'd essentially freaked the fuck out for no reason.

A new opportunity presented itself once she'd disappeared out of the basement. This time I convinced myself I wasn't going to talk to her. This time I just wanted to watch them together a bit. Just wanted to see how he was with her.

I wanted to prove, even if only to myself, that she deserved better than him.

I slowly headed for the stairs and up into the kitchen where Soto was still sitting on the counter, groupie standing between his spread legs. He laughed when I grabbed a cup and filled it from the keg on the floor by his foot before taking a slow sip, beer falling quickly into my empty stomach.

The night had suddenly become much more interesting than I'd initially thought it would be. It seemed I was sticking around after all.

## Chapter Seventeen

# Caroline

I GOT OUT OF THAT basement like someone had shouted, "Fire!" dragging Jen roughly behind me. My stomach twisted itself into aggravated knots as we made our way toward the dining room where we'd left Dan at the pong table. A new team stood where he and his partner had been, so I quickly turned toward the living room, eyes scanning the crowd along the way.

I didn't find Dan, but I did spot Nate just as he turned off the stairs that led to the upper floors. His gaze moved over me quickly and locked onto Jen before he started toward us with a determined gait, practically shoving people out of his way to get to her.

Her arm was yanked from my hand as he took her hand in his and pulled her toward the back of the house. "I need to borrow Jen, Caroline. She'll find you in a little bit."

I watched him steer her away and gave a small shrug at the desperate glance she sent my way. The glance quickly became a glare that lasted until they had disappeared into the crowd.

My mood had been generally crappy since we'd arrived, but it was suddenly declining at a serious rate. I finally made it to the living room, and through the darkness and heavy clouds of smoke in the air, I scanned the space for a shock of blond hair, coming up empty. I turned around to make for the stairs and jumped when I felt an arm wrap around my shoulders, locking me in place.

Glancing over my shoulder, I took in dark hair and eyes that looked vaguely familiar. I knew he was one of the guys on the team, but I had no fucking clue what his name was. He was decently attractive, but there was a darkness in his eyes that didn't sit right with me, and as I tried to get some space, his hand locked onto my shoulder, keeping our sides pressed together tightly.

"You look lost," he commented, and I made no attempt to stop the eye roll his words provoked.

"I'm fine," I responded. "You can let go now."

He didn't.

"Who you looking for, gorgeous?"

"My boyfriend. So, I'll just be going..."

Even that didn't deter him. His arm curled to swing me around until we were facing each other, and he leaned in even closer. *Way* too close. "If he wandered away from you, he's an idiot. Hang with me instead."

I lifted my hands to push off Mr. Handsy, but before they could make contact, his fingers were pulled from my shoulder, and he went flying across the floor, crashing into innocent bystanders before he was able to regain his balance.

"Back the fuck off, Turner."

At the sound of Jimmy's baritone, I wanted to scream. Once again, he was coming to my rescue when I didn't need it. Once again, he was doing something nice. *Once again*, I appreciated it, but I wanted him to stop being nice. I wanted him to stop being a good guy, so I could forget about him. And I really wanted him to let me handle my own fucking problems.

*Is that really so much to ask?*

I turned to face him quickly and used my still-raised hands to push angrily against his chest. He didn't move an inch, and, irrationally, that only made me angrier.

"I don't need your help."

A muscle twitched in his jaw as he stared down at me, but that was the only movement he made. "Turner is a douchebag. I was doing you a favor."

"Well, stop doing me favors!" I was shouting now. As the people closest to us turned toward us, I forced my voice to drop. "Just stop."

I spun away from him and finally spotted Dan descending the stairs. His eyes found me in the same second. As I darted through the people to get to him, he shouted, "Babe!"

The second I reached his side at the bottom of the stairs, his arms reached out to grab me, and he slammed our bodies together. My teeth clattered with the impact, but besides swaying drunkenly against me, he didn't react to the bone-jarring collision. Instead, his mouth came to the spot below my ear, and he laid a sloppy kiss against my skin.

"I was looking for you." I think the words were meant to be a whisper, but they came out too loud. I jerked my head back to spare my eardrum while he continued to shout into it. "Where'd you go, baby?" he leaned back without releasing my waist and ran bright eyes over my face, narrowing them slowly, "And what the fuck is all over you?"

I blinked and brought a hand to my face distractedly before remembering. "Paint," I answered. "There was some downstairs. Jen did it..." I shrugged and stepped back out of his hold. He swayed a little before he was supporting his own weight again, and I let out a silent sigh at the visible proof of his drunkenness.

I hated drunk Dan. He wasn't too bad for the first few hours. That was Happy Drunk Dan. But he didn't know how to stop drinking, and Happy Drunk Dan almost always turned into Mean Drunk Dan before the end of the night.

"You look ridiculous," he muttered before taking a step toward me and grabbing my hand. "Come on. I need another beer."

"Seriously?" I asked as he led us both toward the kitchen. "Because I'm ready to leave whenever you are."

"Fuck that!" he shouted back at me as we entered the brightly lit kitchen. I looked around for any sight of Nate and Jen, but I guessed they had headed through the door that led to the backyard because I didn't see either one of them. I *did* see Jimmy, though. He was hard to miss, standing a few feet from the keg that had been placed against the far counter, surrounded by an assortment of players, all almost as big as him. I recognized the guys who'd gone to the bar with us, and I noticed and ignored the curious glances a few of them sent my way as I followed Dan to the keg no less than three feet from the crowd.

He filled his cup before leaning back against the counter. After taking a long sip, he lowered his drink and used his other hand to grab mine, giving me a sharp tug that had me stumbling into his chest. By the time I'd gotten my balance back, he'd wrapped his arm around my waist, locking our hips together.

Seriously, though, I was sick and fucking tired of being manhandled.

"So," he smiled down at me, "you haven't told me yet how glad you are that I flew to see you."

My mouth felt coated in ice when I tried to force a smile. "I'm glad you came."

He frowned. "You can do better than that, Caroline."

I opened my lips to respond to that, but before a single word could escape, his mouth landed on mine, and his tongue darted out eagerly. My gut reaction was to pull away, but I forced myself to return the kiss. His lips worked against mine, and I tried to get into it, but it was just...awkward. I didn't feel swept away. I was all too aware of exactly where I was and who was around me. I was also very aware of the burn of a heavy stare boring into the back of my head, and I didn't need a full three guesses to figure out who it was coming from.

For all those reasons, I let the kiss last only a few more seconds before pulling away. Dan followed me, though, pulling his arm even tighter around my waist and pressing wet lips against my neck. I chuckled uncomfortably and lightly pushed at his chest, but he just leaned in closer.

"Dan..."

"Fuck, Care Bear," he murmured into my ear, "I've missed you."

When I felt his hips rub against mine once lightly, then again a bit harder, I straightened my back, planted my hands on his chest, and shoved. He hadn't been ready for it, and he flew backwards half a step, his lower back hitting the counter violently as his full cup of beer flew into the air before raining back down, missing him entirely but covering my leg just enough to send me from irritated to full on pissed.

"What the fuck, Caroline?!"

"Can you please just *shut up*?" I forced out through gritted teeth. I was trying really hard not to slap him, but the urge was growing stronger. Too strong for me to hold back much longer.

"What's your fucking problem?!"

I had just opened my mouth to tell him exactly what my problem was when heat hit my back, and I heard a quiet voice in my ear.

"You okay, Caro?"

It was too much. It was just way too much. Sandwiched between Dan and Jimmy, my head felt ready to explode, and my heart felt ready to burst, and I needed to get out of the fucking kitchen.

I bolted.

It was far from my finest moment, but in that second I couldn't have cared less. I dodged around bodies until I'd reached the staircase and made my way quickly upstairs. Once I hit the second floor landing, I turned to the right and headed for the bathroom to find a closed door. I pounded against the wood for a solid ten seconds before pressing my forehead against the grain. My heart was racing, my head was spinning, and I needed to lock myself inside a room by myself until I could pull it together.

"I'm gonna need another-" The weak voice on the other side of the door was suddenly replaced by the sound of vomiting, and I pushed unsteadily off the door to lean against the wall, cursing under my breath.

At the sound of a nearly identical curse coming from the stairs behind me, I spun around as quickly as I could manage. I breathed a sigh of relief at the sight of Derek moving across the landing toward me. "Are you okay?"

I nodded but must not have convinced him. "You sure? Because you look like you're gonna throw up."

"I'm fine. I just need quiet. Please tell me this place has another bathroom I can hide in for a few minutes."

He gave me an appraising look before sighing. "Come on. You can use mine." He led me past the bathroom to a second staircase and up to the third floor, where a short hall led to three doors. He stopped us both outside the middle door and pulled a small key from his pocket, sliding it into the knob and twisting it open to reveal an almost pristine bathroom.

"If you throw up, please do it in the toilet. I don't wanna clean that shit up. That's why I lock the door."

"No worries. I won't throw up."

His look implied he didn't believe me, but I didn't really care. I slid past him as he said, "Lock up on your way out," agreeing and flicking the light on before I slammed the door shut.

Once I'd sealed myself inside, I turned on the faucet and splashed my cheeks with icy water. My skin felt too hot, and a quick glance in the mirror confirmed that not only was my face bright red, the paint that had outlined my eyes was dripping down my cheeks in sad streaks.

I used the running water to quickly wash the last of the paint from my face, then turned off the sink. There was no towel, so I grabbed a few tissues from the box sitting on the back of the toilet. Resolutely blocking all thoughts of what the box was probably kept there for, I used them to dry my face and hands before tossing them into the trash.

With another long look in the mirror, I took a few slow breaths that did little to ease the apprehension I felt at the prospect of heading back downstairs. I couldn't hide up here forever, as much as I wanted to. I needed to go back downstairs even if it was just to get the hell out of this house and away from this fucking party. Away from this entire night.

With one last deep breath, I grabbed the doorknob and pulled it open. The sight of a determined-looking Jimmy spanning the door frame had me stopping short. Before I had a chance to react, he was pressing a gentle hand into my stomach, forcing me backwards until he could step inside the bathroom and shut the door behind him. I wasn't ready to look at him, hadn't been prepared to experience the intense sensations that his presence brought forth in me. Because of that, when his eyes latched onto mine, I snapped out a preemptive strike. "What is it with you and trapping me in bathrooms?"

"We need to talk."

"I thought you already said what you had to say," I responded cattily, crossing my arms across my chest and sticking out a hip to lean it against the sink.

"Yeah, that was before I saw you with Dickhead Dan."

"Don't call him that," I argued weakly. He ignored my quiet words and took a slow step toward me.

"What was that down there, Caroline?"

I shook my head gently. "It was nothing, Jimmy."

"Bullshit. Is he always like that with you?"

"No," I said quickly, "of course not. He's drunk," I explained with a small shrug.

"That's not a fucking excuse."

I nodded because he was not wrong.

We both fell quiet for a moment, communicating through the eye contact we both refused to break. His eyes were saying, *You can do so much better than that guy, Caroline.*

Mine responded, *Trust me, I know.*

His said, *I'm so much better than that guy, Caroline.*

Mine replied, *Trust me, I know that too.*

"I don't want you to leave with him," he suddenly said, his voice coming out rough, like his throat had been lined with sandpaper.

"That's not your call to make."

"You think I don't fucking know that?" he asked quickly, eyes narrowing on my face as he took another step in my direction. It was too close—he was too close—and I spun around him and backed quickly toward the door.

Horrible, terrible idea. He stalked toward me, following until I was pressed to the wood with no more room for retreat. Once he had me trapped, he leaned one hand against the wood over my shoulder, his chest less than an inch from mine. If I had been able to pull in air, a full lungful would have pushed my breasts against the tight t-shirt that covered a chest I remembered more than a little too well. Even without the actual contact, his proximity sent heat rushing to my belly, and my heart pounded so hard I felt the pulse across every nerve ending in my body. I froze when his eyes dropped to my mouth for a long moment before lifting slowly back up.

"I know it's not my call. Doesn't mean I don't wish like hell it was. Doesn't mean I don't know that he will never, *never* in a million years deserve you. You're going to do what you want to do..." He stopped and shook his head gently, "What you need to do. I know that. But that doesn't mean it doesn't hurt me to see you with him. It might not be fair, and it might not make sense, but that doesn't make it a lie."

I officially needed an escape from my escape.

"I have to go."

"Caro, please-"

"What do you want me to say?" The words came out fast and angry, but I was past the point of trying to hold it together. "Please fucking tell me what I'm supposed to do right now because I'm just trying to figure my life out, day by day and second by second. But since you apparently have all the answers, tell me, James. Tell me what I'm supposed to say."

"That you're going to ditch that guy. He's not right for you. And if you can't do that, at the very least tell me that I'm not fucking crazy. Tell me that you feel this between us, and I didn't completely imagine every second we've ever spent together."

His eyes held mine, the light in them dimming as the seconds passed with no response from me. I wanted so badly to tell him what he wanted to hear. It almost physically hurt me to see him bracing nervously, as if my answer had the power to knock him off his foundation. I just wasn't able give him what he wanted. What we both wanted.

I couldn't give him the truth.

"I can't," I whispered, my voice a broken exhale that still somehow managed to echo through the silent room. I watched him shut down, watched the shutters fall over his eyes as he pushed off the door and took a few steps backwards. "Jimmy-"

"Just go, Caro." He was the one leaning against the sink now, eyes trained lifelessly on the tiled floor. I watched his chest rise with a deep inhale, and I took a longer look than I should have. The way he held his shoulders, the slight slump of his spine; he looked strong but somehow weak as well. They weren't easy to spot, but I knew his tells; I knew him. I saw the way his hands trembled as he slipped them quickly into his pockets and the tight jaw that revealed his frustration.

Frustration I understood all too well.

I placed a hand on the knob and turned it quickly. The door swung open behind me, and I whispered one last apology. Before he had a chance to respond, I escaped from the room.

After almost killing myself during my mad dash down the stairs, I emerged back into the party alone and ready to fucking leave.

*Stat.*

I pulled my phone from my pocket and dialed Jen, shoving roughly past partygoers on my way to the kitchen. By the time I'd reached the back door, the phone had connected with her voicemail, and I cursed under my breath as I stumbled down another three steps into the backyard.

"Jen!"

I didn't give a fuck what time it was or who could hear me shouting like an absolute crazy person. I just needed to get home. That was my only concern as I headed toward the side of the house. I could hear muffled voices and what sounded like... *Fuck.* Definite sex sounds. On one hand, I really didn't want to interrupt Nate and Jen (if that really *was* Nate and Jen) if they were in the process of, ahem, working out their shit. On the other hand, I needed to leave, and I couldn't do that until I found my friends.

Bracing myself for the possibility of seeing something that could not be unseen, I took a deep breath and rounded the corner, stopping short at the sight of a pasty white ass, thrusting furiously in the moonlight. I had just started to turn back because, sadly enough, I had seen Nate's ass before and that wasn't it. For some unknown reason—call it a woman's intuition—I turned back, took another look, and froze at the sight of the stupidest tattoo I had ever seen, stamped across his glowing left cheek. A tattoo I had hated since the first time I'd laid eyes on it.

That had been last Christmas.

"Are you fucking shitting me right now?"

My stomach rolled, and I was glad I wasn't in Soto's bathroom because now I really was about to throw up. I thought the situation couldn't have possibly been more nauseating, but that was before Dan quickly pulled out of the shadowed figure he was sticking it in and spun around, wilting hard-on flapping in the cool night air.

*Fuck, I'm really going to be sick.*

"Shit," he slurred, tucking himself away quickly and zipping up his pants as he took one step toward me. "Care Bear."

I was already gone.

Spinning around, I darted back around the house and practically fell up the stairs. Once, I'd pushed through the door, I slammed it shut behind me and stormed through the kitchen. I heard his voice call my name as I forced my way through the hall. I gave up on finding Jen and Nate, taking off for the front door instead.

I blew through the door, careening into a small group of girls standing on the small front porch. Apologizing quickly, I squeezed through them and started down the sidewalk. Once the music had faded behind me, I finally pulled my phone from my pocket. Somehow, since the time I'd called Jen at the house, I had acquired four new texts and three missed calls. Two of the calls and three of the texts were from Dan, and I didn't even bother reading them before I hit delete. The last message was from Jen; I ignored it to pull up her number.

Before the call could connect, my phone was ringing in my hand. Dan's smiling face popped up on the screen, and it took everything I had not to throw the phone to the ground. I wanted to smash that face into a thousand pieces.

I ignored the call and again attempted to dial Jen. And, *again*, the fucker called me before I could place the call.

This time, I answered.

"Allow me to make this perfectly clear, Daniel, because after I say what I have to say, we will not be speaking again. You are not to call me. Don't text me.

Don't talk to me online. I want absolutely nothing to do with you."

"Care Bear-"

"No, Dan. *Fuck* no. I just saw you..." I stopped as the nausea rose again, and I forced the image from my mind. "Just no. Seriously, I don't want to fight, and I don't want to talk about it. I'll put your shit outside the apartment door, and then we're done. Just leave me the fuck alone."

I didn't wait for confirmation from him before disconnecting the call and dialing Jen.

"Hey," she answered breathlessly after the second ring, music pumping loudly in the background. "I've been looking everywhere for you. Where did you go?"

"I left. Can you please come pick me up?"

"Wait, what? What do you mean you left? I just saw Dan, like, a second ago."

I knew I had to tell her what had happened. I needed to tell her what I'd seen, and I would. I was just pretty sure I'd lose the tenuous hold I was keeping over my gag reflex if I had to recount that particular story at this particular second.

"Please just come get me. I'm not far, just right down the street. I can't go back there."

"Okay, yeah," she agreed quickly. "Of course. I'll be right there. Just, real quick, should I bring him or...?"

"No. I don't give a shit what he does. It's not my problem."

"Right. I'm on my way."

Once I'd hung up and slipped the phone into my pocket, I shuffled across the pavement and sank gracelessly to the curb. I was still a little in shock, and I was more than a little pissed. That said, I wasn't sad. I wasn't heartbroken. If anything, I was actually kind of relieved. Don't get me wrong, it really sucked watching your boyfriend fuck some bitch at a party. It more than sucked. It straight up swallowed.

Nonetheless, it felt like a weight had been lifted from my shoulders. Even if I'd been refusing to admit it, I'd known for a while that our relationship was coming to an end. Granted, I totally hadn't seen it playing out like this. Still, it had ended, and I refused to feel bad over the fact that I was totally okay with that.

Headlights flashed down the street, and I got to my feet as Jen pulled to a stop at the curb. I quickly climbed into the car and buckled my seatbelt, grateful for her silence as she headed toward home. A quick glance into the empty backseat had me wondering where Nate was, so I asked. She kept her eyes trained on the road and pulled her lip into her mouth, chewing on it lightly for a minute before answering.

"He found another ride home. He wanted to stay."

The words slipped out quietly, and I considered questioning it further but decided against it. The second I started prying into her love life, she would return the favor, and I still wasn't ready for that. Instead, I leaned forward and switched on the radio, scanning the stations until an old Maroon 5 song filled the space around us. Between the music and the thoughts that I knew were filling both of our minds, there was no room for the words that neither of us wanted to say.

We were both silent for the remainder of the drive. Once we'd gotten into the apartment, I headed for the kitchen while Jen slumped straight to her bedroom, slamming the door shut behind her. I wasn't sure how to feel about that, so I decided to feel nothing at all, focusing instead on quickly grabbing a bottle of water before I made my way into my own bedroom.

I pulled my phone from my pocket to plug it into the charger and noticed two new texts. Both from Dickhead Dan.

*I need to thank Jimmy for that nickname. It's quite appropriate.*

I deleted the messages without reading them and dropped the phone onto my desk a little more forcefully than necessary. It clattered across the wood before falling off and sliding into the space between the back of the desk and the wall. I groaned softly and left it there to grab his overnight bag from where it sat on the floor. One handle slipped from my hand and my smoldering anger burst back to life as a strip of condoms fell from the bag to the floor. Cursing under my breath, I kicked them across the floor and searched his bag. Two more strips (*the optimistic bastard*) were inside and I took those, too before I zipped it closed. I carried the bag out of the apartment and into the hallway, dropping it by the door before I shut myself back in and locked up for the night.

Shuffling to the bathroom, I quickly washed my face and teeth. I still felt the party clinging to my skin like the smell of smoke after a campfire. I wanted to wash it away, but I also knew that once I got under the water, I'd want to sit there for an hour, and then I'd probably fall asleep. With the way my luck was going, I didn't want to risk falling from the chair, a move that would probably end with me dead on the floor of the shower.

I wasn't afraid to die. I'd come to terms with my mortality since the accident, and I had no problems with it. That said, I *really* didn't want to die naked.

Deciding the shower needed to wait until morning, I padded back to my room. Once I'd shut myself inside, I turned off the overhead light and carefully navigated by what little moonlight there was to the lamp next to my bed. Once it was on, I quickly changed into shorts and a t-shirt before dropping onto the bed to remove my leg. The skin at the bottom of my thigh was red and irritated, and I took a few minutes to wipe it down with the baby wipes I kept on hand for this exact reason before rubbing a salve onto the irritated skin. Putting on the prosthesis was going to suck in the morning.

I smiled slowly as I realized, with Dan gone, I suddenly had nothing to do for the rest of the weekend. A day of doing nothing but lying on the couch eating junk food sounded like the greatest thing in the world.

Because, hey, everything else might have sucked, but I could still take pleasure in the little things.

I had just finished sliding under the covers when a soft knock came at the door before it opened slowly. Jen closed it behind her, then shuffled across the floor toward my bed. I pulled back the covers and slid toward the wall as she climbed in and situated herself onto her side, curling her body to mirror mine. Her knees brushed mine in the tiny bed, and, force of habit, I tensed for a moment before compelling myself to relax. Her eyes still hadn't met mine, but I let her get comfortable without pushing.

Just like I knew she would, she spoke after a few quiet minutes. "Nate and I fought tonight." She swallowed slowly before looking at me. "He's kind of a dick when he's pissed."

I let out a short breath and nodded against the pillow we shared. "Yeah, it's one of his less charming traits."

She was quiet for another moment before, "So...what happened with Dan?"

Turning onto my back, I let out a heavy sigh and trained my eyes on the ceiling. "I found him fucking someone in the backyard."

Her body jerked up, rising onto one elbow to more effectively stare down at me in shock. "Are you fucking kidding me right now?"

I wanted to laugh because it sounded like a joke. A joke at my expense, but a good one nonetheless.

I couldn't laugh because this was actually my life.

"I really wish I was. I was looking for you and found him going to town between someone's legs against the house."

And that memory still didn't fail to make me sick. I really hoped that changed with time.

"What a prick," she muttered. After a moment, she huffed angrily. "Really though, who *does* that?"

I sighed. "Dickhead Dan, apparently."

She settled her head against the pillow and let out a soft chuckle. "Dickhead Dan. I like that."

"Thank Jimmy," I muttered. "He coined the phrase."

I could see her out of the corner of my eye, so I saw the way her lips twisted into a smile before they opened. "You know, I wasn't even going to bring your latest admirer up, but what are you going to do about him?"

I turned my head and gave her a blank look. "Can I remind you that I just broke up with my boyfriend like, an hour ago? Regardless of the fact that it happened because I caught him buried dick-deep in some chick, I still think it might be a little classless of me to go running straight to some other guy."

"Okay, no," she stated, propping her elbow against the pillow again, this time to support her head with her hand. "First off, he cheated. That means you automatically get out of the customary waiting period. Besides," she grinned, "you know what they say…"

I rolled my eyes but asked anyway. "No, Jen. What do they say?"

"The best way to get over someone is to get under someone else. And don't even pretend that you don't want to get under him. He is the *definition* of sex on a stick."

I chuckled and felt warmth hit my cheeks as I considered her words. "I'm not going to pretend I'm not...interested," I said slowly. "But after tonight I don't really think he's my biggest fan."

Her stare turned incredulous. "What the fuck are you even talking about? I was in that basement. I saw the way he looked at you. That boy is *seriously* into you, Caro."

"Yeah, well... We may have had another conversation that you weren't present for."

"Where?"

"The bathroom."

"When?"

"Shortly after the fight Dan and I got into in the kitchen. Which Jimmy saw."

Her mouth fell open slightly, and her eyes widened. "How did I miss all this?"

"You were... How'd you put it? *Arguing*? ...with Nate."

Her cheeks flushed slightly, and she shifted onto her back so our shoulders just brushed. One arm reached out to turn off the light, and as we settled into the darkness, we both let out identical sighs at the exact same time. The moment had my lips lifting into the smallest of smiles.

"Tonight sucked," I said quietly. "But I'm glad you're here."

I heard a small sniffle before, "Yeah, me too." Then, even quieter, "Thanks, Caroline."

"For what?" I asked. I wasn't fishing; I honestly didn't know what I had done for her. In fact, her problems began and ended with my boneheaded best friend, so, really, I should have been apologizing.

I had to wait for an answer. A few minutes later, it came as a whisper. "For just...being you."

She was asleep before I could question her further. Before I could ask the question that had already been plaguing my mind for weeks.

*"But who exactly is that?"*

## Chapter Eighteen

*Jimmy*

SUNDAY MORNING CAME TOO EARLY. I hadn't even stayed out late the night before. In fact, I'd bolted from that house immediately after my conversation with Caroline upstairs, getting home just before eleven. I'd headed straight to bed, sans liquor, and I'd only spent about an hour tearing myself apart for being stupid enough to put myself out there before I had managed to fall asleep.

It had been a dumb and risky move, but at the time it had seemed like my only option. And that guy was just *such* a tool. It had taken every ounce of self-control I possessed to keep from ripping the motherfucker apart when he went at her in the kitchen. I mean, on one hand, I understood his pain. If Caroline was mine, I'd have a hard time keeping my hands off her too.

On the other hand, no fucking meant *no*. Everyone in that kitchen had known that she wasn't into it. I'd seen her try to push him away. I don't give a shit how drunk you are; if a girl pushes you away, you back the fuck off.

Apparently, being a handsy asshole wasn't enough to convince her though.

*I can't...*

Those two words had ripped me apart. It had been a struggle to stay calm when all I wanted to do was fall to my knees and beg her. *Please, please pick me. I promise, I'll treat you so much fucking better than him.* I wasn't going to beg Caroline for anything because I had just enough self-respect not to, but I had *wanted* to.

*I can't...*

It made no fucking sense. I literally couldn't wrap my head around why it hurt so much to hear her say those words. Maddie breaking up with me had hurt less. Scratch that. Maddie breaking up with me hadn't even hurt. Not in comparison to this.

This was agony.

This was *torture.*

It made no fucking sense, but those two words had demolished me, so much so, I was still recovering Sunday morning.

I shuffled out of bed and absently rubbed a hand across my chest as if that could cure the ache that wouldn't let up. As if it could dull the pain of rejection and the sting of embarrassment. Because there was definitely a good amount of embarrassment mixed up in the shitty emotional blender that had somehow managed to plant itself in the space normally reserved for my heart.

The morning passed quickly enough. I took a shower to wash the night away before throwing on sweatpants and a t-shirt. Despite the general exhaustion that had become an ever-present part of my life, I was filled with nervous energy. That, combined with my racing thoughts, propelled me out the door and down the street, feet pounding the ground as I jogged.

I used to run outside every day. I still ran; I just did nearly all of it on a treadmill. There was something gratifying about running outside, though. There was actual progress. I could map how far I'd gone just by glancing around, and the changing scenery was enough to keep me mostly distracted from my jumbled thoughts.

The day was overcast and chilly, but the streets were still busy enough. I passed plenty of people leaving their homes dressed for church, families smiling happily at each other as they headed off in their mini-vans.

I'd always known I wanted kids. The honest truth was, relationships were great while they lasted. I truly believed that we, as intelligent, self-aware humans, had the potential to make relationships last as long as we wanted to. It just took compromise, hard work, and occasionally depriving yourself of what you wanted to do in order to do what you needed to do.

I was capable of all that.

That said, I couldn't control everything, and I knew that. That's what kids were for.

Kids were love. Kids were people to take care of you when you got old. Kids were security—a guarantee that as long as you didn't fuck up too massively while raising them, you would always have someone to love you. And I wanted that security.

I also wanted stability; someone to come home to, a family that I looked forward to seeing at the end of the day.

That's what I had wanted from Maddie. Maddie was safety and security. Maddie was knowing that I could do whatever it took to make it work; whatever it took, so long as it wasn't the one thing I'd always told her I couldn't do.

I couldn't leave.

Maddie had been all those things until she suddenly wasn't anymore.

Then there was Caroline.

Caroline was the opposite of safety. Caroline was heading into the offensive zone a man down and taking on two defenders who each outweighed you by 100 pounds. Caroline was hanging over a cliff, dangling over hundreds of feet of open air, just praying that someone was there to catch you when you inevitably fell.

I had fallen. And she hadn't bothered to catch me.

I was starting to think I didn't know what love was. Because after loving Maddie for four years, her defection had been an inconvenience, an interruption along the course of my life, one that changed the details of the trip but didn't cancel it entirely.

Caroline's most recent departure from my life, on the other hand, felt like a cracked radiator and a flat tire with no spare. That car was stuck, and it wasn't fucking moving on its own anytime soon.

Maybe what I felt for Maddie hadn't been love, but, pounding a heavy rhythm against the sidewalk, I decided I didn't care one way or another. I'd still take the safety of that relationship over the feeling of being eviscerated. I'd still take something stable, something secure, something that I could work at and improve, just like any other skill, over the unrestrained, unbridled, absolute recklessness that was how I felt about Caroline.

If that was how it really felt to fall in love, I wanted nothing to fucking do with it.

Since the day in the sandwich shop, I had spent a lot of time considering the words that Caroline had said to me, about things happening for a reason. In all honesty, I probably *wanted* to believe them more than I actually *did*. Nevertheless, I had committed myself to trying to see the bigger picture in life. With that in mind, the knock that came at my front door an hour after my second shower of the day was proof that someone, somewhere, was fucking with me.

Jogging down the steps, I used my hand to push aside the thin curtain that covered the window and sucked in a surprised breath. I considered turning around, walking back upstairs, and ignoring any further knocks, but before I had the chance, brown eyes locked onto mine, and I was trapped. I dropped the curtain and wiped my suddenly moist hands against my cotton-covered thighs before grasping the door to pull it open.

Maddie stared up at me for a moment before shaking her head as if to clear it. "Hey."

I raised one eyebrow and waited.

"I was hoping we could talk."

*Fuck.* My head was way too fucked at the moment to have whatever conversation she wanted to have, so I took a deep breath and prepared to send her on her way. She must have seen it coming because she took a quick step forward and placed her hand on my arm.

"Please, Jimmy. I know I don't deserve it, but please."

Before I could process the decision, I stretched out my arm, opening the door enough for her to slide past me and up the stairs. I followed behind slowly, tracing her steps as she led a path to the couch and lowered herself onto it.

I didn't want to be a total dick, but I also didn't want to sit down next to her in the last place we'd had sex. I settled for climbing onto the arm, pulling my bare feet up onto the seat as I angled myself toward her. Then, I waited.

Two minutes later, it was still silent in the apartment, and I'd had about enough. "Look, Maddie..."

"I fucked up." Her voice sounded utterly broken, the words sharp shards that stung to hear. I couldn't imagine how they felt to say. "I fucked up so bad."

I suspected I knew where this was going, but I kept quiet in case she felt like surprising me.

"I thought I knew what I was doing. I thought it was the best decision." Her eyes finally lifted from the floor and locked onto mine. They were bright, and I saw the tears collecting on her bottom lids, but they hadn't started to fall. Yet. "I threw away the best thing that ever happened to me."

I ran a hand across my face while sliding down onto the cushions. There was still a good foot of space between us, but it felt closer than we'd been in ages. She was finally being honest.

At least, I *hoped* she was finally being honest.

"Maddie, I don't think-"

"Wait. Please, don't say it. Not yet. I miss you. I miss us." She took a breath and said the only words that would have made me consider going back to her. "I miss feeling safe."

Just another coincidence that couldn't have been anything less than a higher plan.

An hour later, I'd agreed to give us another shot. This agreement had been tentative on my part, but after quite a few tears and even more promises (all from Maddie,) I'd finally caved. Really, what reason did I have not to?

Maddie had said she was sorry. Caroline had told me to fuck off. And I just wanted to get my life back under control. Maddie and I together seemed like the first logical step toward carrying that plan out. It might not have been the best way to go about things, but it was the only real option I could see.

We spent the afternoon on the couch, watching a movie. When it was over, we migrated to the kitchen, and I grabbed stuff from the fridge to make us each a sandwich. I also grabbed two cans of Coke from the bottom shelf before shutting the door. As I turned around, arms wrapped around my waist, knocking one of the cans to the floor. The force of the impact cracked the top of the can, and suddenly brown, syrupy liquid was shooting into the air and raining down on both of us.

I couldn't help but laugh as Maddie shrieked and tried to duck under my arm. I wrapped my arm around her waist, not to shield her from the fountain of soda still somehow shooting from the floor but to push her into it. She shouted again, slapping me lightly on the arm, but her smile was wide, and she was chuckling softly next to me.

Once the soda had stopped raining down, I sent Maddie into the bathroom with a t-shirt and a pair of sweatpants to take a shower while I cleaned up the kitchen. Half an hour later she reemerged, wearing the shirt but no pants.

"Yeah," she said as my eyes skated quickly over her bare legs, "those things weren't staying up without the help of some permanent alterations." I nodded and looked away quickly, weirdly uncomfortable with her walking around my place half-naked.

It was a fucking annoying sensation.

I left Maddie on the couch while I took shower number three of the day. I wasn't under the water for more than five minutes, just long enough to wash the sticky residue from my skin. I dried off quickly and wrapped a towel around my waist before heading out of the bathroom toward my bedroom to get dressed. I emerged a minute later and scanned the relatively small space for Maddie, coming up empty.

Then I heard quiet voices and Maddie calling, "Okay, bye," before the door shut at the bottom of the stairs.

"Who was that?" I asked, moving toward the stairs as she walked back up.

Her brow wrinkled, probably at the annoyed tone of my voice, but that was beyond my control at the moment. I wasn't really a fan of Maddie answering my front door at all. I was decidedly less a fan of her answering my door in nothing but a t-shirt.

"Someone from one of your classes?" I gave her a look that accurately portrayed just how poor that description was, and she continued. "I don't know. I asked her name, but she didn't tell me. Just said she needed something for a class but she could get it later."

My heart actually stopped. Just stopped beating altogether. Because there was only one girl in the entire student populace who knew where I lived.

"Oh," I said quickly, moving down the stairs. "Right. I'll be right back. I need to tell her something before class tomorrow."

The lie settled heavily into my chest as I headed out the door, pulling it shut behind me. I took off at a sprint down the driveway, spotting her as soon as my bare feet hit the front yard. She was still parked at the curb, directly in front of Maddie's bright pink beetle, engine off. As I walked closer, I noticed her lips moving quickly, and I wasn't sure if she was talking on the phone or to herself, but either way, I interrupted the conversation by knocking lightly on the driver's side window.

Startled eyes flew to mine, and her hands shot into action. Suddenly, the engine roared to life. I moved fast, grabbing onto the handle of the door that was thankfully unlocked before tugging it open. I took a quick step backwards, just in case she still decided to drive off, sparing my feet from potentially being crushed by a tire.

I stared into the car as she reached out a hand to grab the door, attempting to tug it closed. Somehow, in this beyond fucked situation, I found myself smiling as she pulled on the door that I held open with a strong hand on the frame. Really, though, it was kind of adorable that she thought she was going to get it shut.

Once she realized her attempt was an exercise in futility, she groaned loudly and glared at me. "Has anyone ever told you that you're incredibly annoying?"

"Once or twice," I answered as the smile faded. "What are you doing here?"

"I..." She trailed off and stared at me for a second, the anger gone. In its place was something else entirely, something I didn't recognize but that had my heart clenching tightly in my chest nonetheless. "It doesn't matter," she finally finished. "I need to go."

"Caroline, why did you come here?"

She just looked at me for a long moment before shaking her head. Her eyes slid toward the windshield, staring through it blankly before speaking again. "Go back inside to your girlfriend, James."

When she pulled on the door that time, I let the metal slip from my hand. Before I could take an unsteady step onto the sidewalk, she pulled away and disappeared down the street. I watched until she was out of sight.

Later that night, hours after she was gone, I still couldn't ignore the feeling that penetrated in her absence.

Watching her leave felt like the biggest mistake of my life.

In an annoyingly convenient way, life went on like the last two weeks hadn't even happened. I did finally shave. I know, I know, big deal, right? Except I'd kind of gotten attached to the beard. Sure, at first it had been purely a defense mechanism, but over time it had grown on me (No pun intended.), and I'd gotten used to it.

Still, when Maddie told me in no uncertain terms before she left my place Sunday night that it needed to go, I didn't argue. I just got rid of it.

That was what I'd signed up to do, after all. Work. Compromise. The things that needed to be done. That was what I was willing to do for normalcy. And normalcy was what I got.

Sure, there wasn't any happiness. True happiness. I didn't even really feel fake happiness, the kind that coats the surface in just enough sweet to cover a bitter aftertaste. But I also didn't have any of that bitter aftertaste. I just felt...okay. My life was okay. My job was okay. School was okay. Hockey was...

Hockey was shit. Tuesday's practice had gone about as bad as a practice could go. Thursday had gone even worse. I just couldn't clear my head the way I'd done less than a week ago. Couldn't tune out the okay long enough to sink into the moment, to really feel the ice.

I could tell Coach was disappointed. It was written clear across his face as he dismissed the team Thursday night, once again holding me back as the guys cleared out. When he'd asked if everything was okay at home for a second time, I'd wanted to laugh. Since I'd just suffered through the worst practice of my life, it was easy to refrain.

There was just something funny about the fact that three weeks ago, he'd asked that question because I was playing better than ever. And three weeks ago my life had been falling apart around me.

Now my life was back on track. It was *okay*. And apparently I didn't know how to fucking skate anymore.

Once I'd assured him that everything was alright for a second time, I followed the guys back to the locker room and prepared to head home. Even worse than Coach's disappointment were the frustrated faces of my teammates as we all got ready to leave. I avoided the eyes that snuck looks surreptitiously in my direction, not needing to see their glares to know they weren't happy. We had two games this weekend that were both guaranteed to be harder than the opener. In other words, it was a really bad time for my game play to fall offline.

For the first time in a long time, I didn't drag my feet after practice. I was in and out of the shower, getting dressed in about three minutes. I didn't want to be there, listening to the muted voices and curious whispers. Feeling the burn of their stares.

I was wound so tightly, I actually jumped when Nate appeared at my side the second after I'd grabbed the last of my things from the locker and slammed it shut.

"If your plan is to play like shit so I see some ice time, it's appreciated, but really not necessary."

I appreciated his attempt to play off my shitty night (*week*), but I wasn't distanced enough from the situation yet to find it humorous. Still, I nodded and played along. "Gotcha. I'll take back over then."

He let out an awkward chuckle and wrapped a hand around the back of his neck. "Look, I wanted to know... Have you talked to Caroline recently? She's been blowing me off since the party, and I didn't know..."

I spoke quickly to shut him up. "No, I haven't talked to her all week. Sorry, man." I stepped around him to head toward the door, cursing him internally for bringing her up.

Since Sunday, I'd forced myself to forget about the girl entirely. It was worse than when we'd first met. Anytime a thought of her drifted through my brain, I wiped it clear by focusing on the worst things I could think about. Auschwitz, the Rwandan genocide, smallpox blankets.

It was my own form of aversion therapy.

The problem with my fucked method of clearing Caroline from my thoughts was that it meant, on top of thinking about her in the first place, my head was also almost constantly filled with images I could really do without.

And every night I still felt guilty for the thoughts I hadn't been able to purge.

Once home, I collapsed into my bed with my phone to call Maddie. She answered after the second ring, laughter echoing across the line before, "Hi."

"Hey," I responded. "What are you up to?"

"Susi, Trish, and I are watching How I Met Your Mother."

"Ah," I replied with as much enthusiasm as I could muster. "Indulging your NPH obsession?"

"Hey, Neil is not only a comedic genius, he's a social icon."

I smiled despite my heavy mood. "You just think he's sexy."

"That too."

I heard her roommates laughing in the background, and I sighed quietly. "I'll let you go then. Get back to your show."

"Okay," she said slowly. "You okay?"

Yes. That's the problem.

"Rough night at practice. I'm beat."

"Oh, alright. Well, go get some sleep."

"I will. Have fun with the girls."

"Okay. I'll talk to you tomorrow. And Jimmy?"

"Yeah?"

"Love you."

"Love you too, Mads."

Despite my almost overwhelming exhaustion, I spent another hour lying in bed trying to figure out what the fuck was wrong with me. I'd gotten my shit together. My life was moving forward like it was supposed to. I should have been happy.

*Why can't I be happy?*

For all Caroline talked about being broken, I was starting to suspect that I was the damaged one. Something was wrong; something had broken loose inside me, and until I knew what it was—until I knew exactly what was missing from my life—I couldn't do a goddamn thing to fix it.

Chapter Nineteen

# Caroline

ONE WEEK AFTER WHAT I'D started calling "the weekend from hell," I was sick of myself.

A small part of me felt totally at ease with hiding out in my apartment, avoiding the world whenever I wasn't in class. That part of me reasoned that after what had possibly been the most humiliating series of events I'd ever personally experienced, it was totally natural to want to spend all my free time by myself. The worst part was, it wasn't even really the break-up that had me feeling two inches tall. I mean, sure, watching Dan cheat on me was definitely one of the lowest moments of my relatively short life. That said, the intensity of the emotions provoked by that event paled in comparison to the way I'd felt when I'd been forced to come face to face with the person I just *knew* was Jimmy's ex-girlfriend. Or his not-ex-girlfriend because that was the only logical conclusion I could draw when she answered his door wearing only his t-shirt.

I felt my face burn just thinking about it. Me, stupidly thinking I should go over to tell him the truth, to tell him all the things I'd wanted to say in the bathroom at the party. I'd convinced myself that he and I could finally work out the tempest of emotions that seemed to hit whenever we were in a room together.

Then that perfectly adorable girl had answered the door in a faded UVA hockey t-shirt that hugged her body loosely in places, but still tight enough that I could see exactly how gorgeous she was. Like a fucking pin-up girl — tiny waist, generous assets, legs that somehow went on forever even though she was a good three inches shorter than I was. What really drew my eye, though, was the smooth, unblemished skin that flowed out from under the hem of the oversized t-shirt. Two knees, two slender ankles. A perfectly painted manicure on all ten toes.

It was stupid and emotional and *so* insecure, but I hated her a little bit for those ten toes.

When she'd smiled at me brightly before asking if she could help me, it had taken me a few seconds to find my voice, to stammer out something about classes and homework. She offered to give Jimmy a message for me and asked for my name, but I'd muttered the least sincere, "Thanks, no thanks" in human history before bolting for the car.

Still, I would have suffered through that conversation a thousand times over if it meant I would have avoided the one that came after it when Jimmy followed me out to the street.

I found it best to not think about that little chat.

Like I said, part of me felt totally natural avoiding the world for a week, although I fucking missed my best friend.

I felt absolutely horrible dodging Nate's calls and texts. I knew it wasn't a permanent solution, but I didn't really know what else to do. Jen had made it clear that she didn't want to be around him. She asked for a heads-up before he came over, but it was her apartment, too, and I didn't want to run her out of her home. Since I was avoiding the outside world like I was in quarantine, it meant I'd been blowing off my best friend in the entire world for a full seven days. And I absolutely hated it.

It was almost a relief when he decided to force the issue of our not speaking on Sunday afternoon. Jen and I were sprawled across the couch watching TV, which was really all we did anymore, when urgent knocking echoed across the apartment loudly enough to make us both jump. Matching surprised expressions turned toward the door in time to hear his shout.

"Caroline Delia Olsen, I'm not fucking leaving until you talk to me!" Nate's voice boomed from the other side of the door before the pounding resumed, and I sank back onto the couch with an aggravated groan.

Jen sighed loudly before turning to me. "You should probably answer that."

"He can't stay out there forever. Besides, I'm sure someone will call security soon." The tail end of my response was drowned out by even louder knocking, some of the hits coming so hard I thought the door would fly from the hinges. She rolled her eyes and climbed to her feet.

"I have to go to the library anyway. Let him in, and talk to him. Stop ignoring him because you're afraid of how I'll feel. He's your friend, Caro."

And I officially felt like shit. I tried to come up with an argument against that, but she was right, and I was a jerk. She grabbed her backpack from her room before heading toward the noise, and I watched her shoulders rise and fall with a quick breath before she grasped the handle and pulled it open quickly.

Nate froze at the sight of her, fist stuck next to his face, but she didn't give him a chance to react before she was pushing past him, out into the hall without a word.

Once she was gone, he shook the startled expression from his face before closing the door behind him. He still looked slightly dazed as he crossed the floor between us, but by the time he dropped onto the seat Jen had vacated, his expression cleared, and his eyes were pissed. He took a moment to pause the show playing in the background, but once the room was silent, he turned to face me.

"Look, I get that me being here makes shit weird with Jen. Just do me a fucking favor and answer my goddamn phone calls. You might not give a shit, but I worry about you."

*Nope.* Now *I officially feel like shit.*

"I'm so sorry, Nate."

"I don't want you to apologize," he argued. "Just tell me that you won't do it again."

I nodded quickly. "I won't do it again."

He nodded slowly and dropped his eyes from mine before leaning back against the couch. "Okay. Thank you."

"I really am sorry," I repeated. "I've had a really shitty week, so it wasn't just the stuff with Jen. I've kind of been hiding out."

His gaze came back to mine, and even though I'd been a total dick to him, his expression showed nothing but pure concern. "Why? What happened?"

I didn't want to talk about Jimmy. Couldn't talk about Jimmy. So I gave my next best excuse. "Well, Dan and I broke up."

"The fuck? When?"

"At the hockey party. After I found him having sex in the backyard." His eyes narrowed, and I clarified, "With someone who was not me."

"You're shitting me, right?"

"I really wish I was."

"I'm gonna fucking kill him."

I rolled my eyes. "He's hardly worth a life sentence."

"You think I care?" he retorted. "What a dickhead. Really, who the fuck does that?"

I smiled at the words that matched Jen's, almost to a T. "Apparently him."

He was silent for a moment, glaring at the table in front of him, before he shook his head angrily. "Tell me you at least kicked him in the balls."

"Uh, no. I was trying to avoid throwing up pure stomach acid at the sight of him flapping in the breeze." Nate snickered beside me, and I wanted to laugh too, but this was the first time I'd talked about that night without feeling sick. With that annoying sensation gone, I was just plain angry. "Seriously, he just turned around mid-thrust and called me fucking *Care Bear*. God, now I wish I *had* kicked him in the balls. How big of a dick do you have to be to have sex at a party with someone who isn't your girlfriend? While you're on a trip to visit said girlfriend for the first time in *months*? GAH!"

Nate was quietly laughing beside me by the end of my rant. Once I'd taken a breath, I turned toward him with a scowl. "I'm so glad you find this funny."

"He's just such a fucking tool. I'm sorry," he forced out around the last of his laughter, "really. So, what did you do?"

"I left him there. Jen and I went home."

At her name, his entire frame stilled for a moment. He played it off quickly, reaching up to run a hand through his hair, but I saw it for the sign it was. He was just as uncomfortable as she was.

"What did you do, Baker?"

He rolled his eyes and leaned back against the couch, arms crossed against his chest defensively. "I didn't do anything, Caroline. Nothing happened."

"Yeah," I sighed, annoyance dripping from my every word. "I stopped buying the 'nothing happened' lie a week ago. Look, I'm not in the mood to fight with you, so I'm just going to say this. If you can't figure your shit out and at least find a way to co-exist with my roommate peacefully, then we need to find a new place to hang out. And I don't want to find a new place to hang out. So please just fix it."

"I tried to fix it at the party." His voice fell, and his eyes stared blankly across the room. When he spoke again, the words were almost a whisper. "I don't know how to make it better."

Shit. I chewed my lip and scanned his slumped shoulders and defeated expression. Then I turned my butt in the seat to pull my legs onto the couch, propping them up before wrapping my arms around them. Once I'd repositioned myself, I asked gently, "You really like her, don't you?"

He was quiet for a moment, and still. So still I thought he must not have heard me. I had just opened my mouth to ask again when he suddenly leaned forward and braced his elbows against his knees. With a loud groan, he wiped both palms along his face before dropping them between his legs. "It doesn't matter."

"Nate, just talk to her. I'm sure-"

"I have talked to her," he interrupted. "Trust me, Jen knows how I feel. It still doesn't matter."

I didn't like it, but I couldn't exactly tell him he was wrong. The truth was, sometimes the way we felt meant absolutely nothing. Sometimes emotions just weren't enough to overcome obligations. Sometimes things just never worked out, and we were left to work through those feelings alone.

That was just life.

"Well, I'm sorry for that," I said quietly. "And I promise I'll let it go."

"Thanks," he said with a small smile. "Can we please talk about something else?"

Finally, I laughed. "Yes, we can. How'd you guys do this weekend?"

His smile evaporated. "I'd rather talk about Jen."

"That bad?" I asked with a wince.

"Yesterday we managed to get an early lead that we held onto, but it was an ugly game. I'm still fucking sore."

"And today?"

His face turned positively thunderous. "Today was bullshit."

"Yikes."

"We got annihilated. Everyone was still trying to recover from yesterday, which didn't help, and Sean was straight up out of commission. He took a nasty headfirst hit into the boards, so Coach didn't want to play him. Jimmy just fucking..." At the sound of his name, I sucked in a breath that Nate thankfully didn't notice. "I have no fucking clue what's up with him, but it essentially left me playing left wing by myself and getting fucking demolished for my efforts. Remember the championship game we played against that team from Illinois? They had that guy..."

"Oh, God," I groaned. "Of course I remember that game. That motherfucker broke my collarbone."

"Yup. And our entire team almost got kicked out of the tournament for the brawl that ensued."

I grinned. "Instead, I went to the hospital while you guys won me a trophy."

"Yeah, well, today's game was like that, minus the win."

I dropped a shoulder sympathetically. "It's alright. It's early in the season. You guys can get it back."

He nodded, but it wasn't enthusiastic. "We'll see. You should come to practice one night this week. I'm going to need all the help I can get if McCarthy doesn't figure his shit out soon."

I nodded noncommittally but chose to keep my mouth shut. There wasn't a chance in hell I was going to sit in on one of their practices. I was fine with going to a game and blending into a crowd where I'd remain mostly hidden. Practice in a nearly empty arena where it would be almost impossible to avoid running into Jimmy?

Yeah, that was another story entirely.

Nate and I spent another two hours on the couch talking before Jen blew back through the front door. Her face was carefully blank as she scanned the two of us before heading straight to her room without a word. Before she could escape through the door, I managed a quick look at Nate to find him watching her like a man possessed. For a moment, I regretted agreeing to butt out of their issues.

Once she'd disappeared, his eyes dimmed, and he glanced down at the floor. "I should probably go." I started to argue, but he shook his head. "No, really. It's fine. And I'm exhausted anyway. I'm just going to go crash. Talk to you tomorrow, though?"

"Yeah," I assured him with a quick nod, "Tomorrow."

When Nate was gone, I headed to Jen's door and knocked lightly. "He's gone. You can stop hiding."

She didn't respond, not that I'd really expected her to. Without another word, I left her to sulk and headed for bed. If I was going to stop hiding, I decided, I was going to do it well-rested.

The week that followed was better, at least marginally. The weather turned cold, and the skies stayed dark and dreary, threatening a storm without delivery. It had me on edge, waiting for something to strike, but I stayed busy to block out the sensation. I hung out with Nate. I attended a few study groups. When I was at home, I focused on school work. When there wasn't any school work to focus on, I played and beat the newest Grand Theft Auto game in its entirety. Life was good.

I did skip both of Nate's practices, despite his near-endless pleading. I still wasn't ready to tell him about everything that had gone down with Jimmy, so he didn't really understand my reticence. Regardless, I held out both nights, promising to come to the game on Friday instead.

It was a move I hadn't planned out well. Once I realized I'd be attending by myself, I was reluctant to go. I wouldn't normally have a problem sitting at a game by myself, but I didn't want to sit and stare at Jimmy for hours with nothing and no one to distract me. I knew Jen was going to say no before I even asked her to go. I still asked because I was praying for a miracle, but she actually laughed at me like it was the most ridiculous thing she'd ever heard.

It actually might have been.

Since I didn't have any other friends, Friday night I walked into the arena alone, a tight ten minutes before the game started. I shuffled through a crowd that was only slightly less populated than the last game I'd attended, and by the time I found a seat, the ice had already been refinished, and the game was about to start.

Five minutes in, I felt bad for Nate. I felt arguably worse for Jimmy. I hadn't realized just how bad it was when Nate and I'd talked, but Jimmy's playing was almost unrecognizable from the last time I'd seen him. All that natural ability had disappeared, and during the short periods of time he spent on the ice, it was almost hard to watch him play. He flubbed passes left and right, and I stopped counting after his fourth forced conversion. It was ugly.

Oliver Cole saved the game, literally. The goalie stood on his head, pulling off save after magnificent save, not that he had any other choice. Our defense wasn't doing a single thing to keep the visiting forwards out of the offensive zone. Brooks got lucky ten minutes through the third period and scored the single goal of the game. Cole stepped up again to survive a brutal attack to close out the clock, and the boys managed to win a game that they *really* shouldn't have won.

Once the final buzzer had blown, I gave the crowds a few minutes to die down before heading outside. I'd worn a light jacket, but the wind had picked up during the game, and it blew straight through the thin layers I was wearing. By the time players started streaming through the doors, I was shivering.

Nate only took another five minutes to get outside. I started to head his way but stopped when I noticed the man beside him. I figured he was talking to the coach about the game and wanted to give him his space. A second later, though, his eyes looked up and met mine. He smiled. Pointed at me. Then they were both moving in my direction. I watched them close the distance between us and tried to figure why Nate could possibly be leading his hockey coach in my direction.

None of my ideas were good.

I seriously considered running, and that was even before my eyes drifted over Nate's shoulder and locked with Jimmy's. Before I could take off down the street, my gaze flicked back to Nate and the coach who was standing two feet in front of me, a large, tanned hand held out in my direction.

"Ms. Olsen? I'm Rick Miller."

The rumbling tone of his voice had me jolting into action, quickly pushing out my hand to return the proffered handshake.

"It's nice to meet you, sir."

"I've heard quite a bit about you, and not just from Baker. I'm honestly surprised Wade let you leave the state. I figured he'd have you on staff as soon as it was legal."

At the mention of my coach from Michigan, the coach who'd helped me win all three of my national championships, my eyes widened. "You know Coach Russell?"

He nodded. "We played together in college. We've stayed in touch over the years, so I got all my Mighty Mite news firsthand."

I'm not sure, but I think I blanched at the nickname. If there was one thing I hated more than being called Care Bear, it was hearing the words Mighty Mite.

Thankfully, he didn't wait for me to speak. I really wasn't sure I was capable. "Look, I know you're not playing anymore, but I'll be honest, we could use you on staff. What's your major?"

"I'm double majoring in business and art."

The look he gave me was pure bewilderment. "Can I ask why?"

*No.*

"Sir, I appreciate what you're trying to do, but I'm done with hockey. I left it behind, and I really have no desire to come back now."

His lips tilted down into a disapproving frown, and it was like quitting the team all over again. Even more so when he threw the exact same words Coach Russell had used at me.

"I have to say, I think that's a mistake." With a quiet sigh, he shrugged. "Look, you're still young. You don't know me, so I don't expect you to listen to what I have to say. Still, you got a God-given talent, one it'd be foolish not to use."

I couldn't help it; I got pissed. I fought the urge to glare at Nate, who I could see from the corner of my eye, staring at the ground like he knew exactly what was coming for him once we were alone. Instead, I focused all my attention on the man in front of me and forced out my next words through gritted teeth. "With all due respect, *sir*, you don't know me, either. Whether or not I'm being foolish, what I do with my life is really none of your concern."

Miller was unfazed by the acid in my tone. He stared down at me for a long moment with what I assumed was his most intimidating *I'm the boss* face and then shook his head gently. "Fair enough. I apologize. However, at the risk of getting my head bitten off, I'm going to ask you to think about what I said. I can always find a place for you here. I also have a friend who works with outreach groups for different kids, both physically and mentally handicapped. He runs hockey camps and leagues and what not. Might be a good fit for you. I'm not saying you need to play, but from what I've always heard, you loved hockey and hockey loved you back. Just think about it."

I opened my mouth to give him a resolute "No thanks," but he was already gone, leaving me with Nate.

"Caro?" The deep voice resonated from three feet to my left, and I revised my head count.

He'd left me with Nate and Jimmy.

*Fuck.*

Chapter Twenty

*Jimmy*

WHEN CAROLINE SPUN TO FACE me, I thought I was about to get hit. She looked *that* angry. Thankfully, she only glanced in my direction for a short second before she shook her head roughly and turned back to Baker.

"I can't fucking *believe* you."

His expression was bland, almost dismissive. "I'm not sure why. I think I've proven that I don't really give a shit about pissing you off when it's your future that's at stake."

"I told you to let it go, Nate. I told you no. And you went to your *coach*?!"

I knew I should walk away. I mean, I'd already eavesdropped through her entire conversation with Coach, but it felt like things were about to get really personal. And really ugly. Even knowing that, I couldn't force myself to move.

"Guess what, asshole? He came to me after the season opener. He saw you after the game and recognized you. So, yes, you told me to let it go, but when he asked me to introduce him, I figured what the hell? I thought maybe someone could pull your head out of your ass long enough to make you realize that you're being stupid. A fucking *art gallery*, Caro?

You don't want to open an art gallery! It makes no fucking sense. You have loved exactly one thing your entire life, and it's not fucking art!"

Nate took a jerky step backwards, breathing heavily, eyes locked on Caro's. Caroline, on the other hand, stood frozen on the pavement, one hand pressing against her sternum like she couldn't catch her breath. My posture mirrored hers, stuck solid. I was still trying to process all the information that had just been thrown at me.

Caroline was the fucking *Mighty Mite*. Of course I knew who she was. I'd known who she was for years. Even halfway across the country, it had been almost impossible not to hear about the tragic accident that had ended the career of one of the best youth hockey players in history. Hell, she *was* considered the best youth hockey player in the entire state of Michigan's history.

ESPN had reported on the accident; she was *that* revered. For weeks after the crash that had taken her leg, I'd seen pictures and footage of her playing, and somehow I hadn't fucking known.

Caroline's broken voice pulled me back to the present. "I can't do this. I'll talk to you later."

"Caro..." Nate argued weakly, but she was already heading down the sidewalk, away from us both without another look back.

I glanced at Nate and waited for him to move, to follow her. When he didn't, I couldn't stop the word that rolled past my lips. "Really?"

He shot surprised eyes my way before accurately reading my expression. "Trust me, man. I cannot fix this right now. I know Caro, and she won't want to look at me for at least a day."

I didn't hesitate for another second. Leaving Baker behind, I quickly jogged behind her, closing the distance between us before falling into step beside her silently.

It was another minute before she acknowledged my presence. "I can get home just fine by myself, Jimmy."

"I know." My words came out just as quietly as hers had. I saw the exaggerated eye roll without turning her way, heard her heavy sigh, but didn't respond. We walked in silence for a moment before I tentatively spoke. "Do you wanna talk about it?"

"No."

"Come on," I softly pleaded. "You've listened to me unload tons of times. Let me return the favor." I could sense her hesitance, so I gently nudged her shoulder with my own before adding, "I'm a good listener, I promise. Maybe not as good as you, but still."

That earned me a tiny smile, and even when it disappeared almost immediately, I had to restrain myself against the urge to pump my fist in the air.

I want to make you smile every day, Caroline.

"He doesn't get it." I sent her a confused glance, and she clarified. "Nate. He just keeps pushing. I've told him over and over that I don't want anything to do with hockey anymore, but he doesn't get it."

I licked my lips slowly, considering the safest way to phrase my question. "Can I ask why?"

"Why what? Why doesn't he get it? I don't know; he's Nate."

"No," I quickly corrected. "Why don't you want anything to do with hockey?"

I watched her nostrils flare on a long inhale before the air slowly leaked back out her mouth. She looked like she was weighing her options, trying to decide what exactly to say.

"It doesn't matter."

"It does to me."

I watched from the corner of my eye as she bit her lip, worrying it between her teeth for a long moment. When she finally spoke again, it was a whisper. "It shouldn't."

My eyes darted to her, narrowed with sudden irritation. "Why *wouldn't* it matter to me, Caroline?"

"Really?" She stopped walking and glared up at me as I stumbled to a halt in front of her. "You're really going to ask me that?"

"Yeah, I really am," I tossed back, crossing my arms over my chest. It probably wasn't fair, but it pissed me off to hear her tell me that I shouldn't give a shit, especially since we both knew that my biggest problem, when it came to Caroline, was caring *way* too much.

"I'm sorry, did I just imagine meeting your half-naked girlfriend at your apartment last weekend?"

*No, but that reminds me...*

"Why did you come to my place?"

Her eyes flitted from mine, and she turned quickly, resuming her furious pace over the sidewalk.

Once I'd caught up, I asked again. "I'm not going to let it go this time, Caro. Why did you come over?"

"You want to know why I came to your place? First tell me why you and Maddie are back together."

"Seriously? We're going to play this game?"

"You answer my question, I'll answer yours," she goaded.

I sighed and rubbed a hand across my jaw uncomfortably. I didn't want to think about Maddie right now. I didn't want to think about Dan. I wanted this moment—this night with Caroline—without any of the other bullshit. It might have been wrong, but it was how I felt.

"Honestly?" I shrugged. "She asked, and I couldn't find a single reason to say no."

"You're joking, right?" When I shook my head, she scoffed loudly. "That is *such* bullshit." Stopping again, she swung toward me with more ease this time. "You want to know what I think? I think you're so fucking scared of being alone that you'd rather settle for some girl who doesn't give a shit about you than risk taking a chance on something better. You say you love her, but if you really loved her the way you should, nothing would stop you from being with her; not an ocean, not your brother, *nothing*. And if she really loved you, she wouldn't have thought twice about moving to Italy. I think you made some bullshit plan up in your head when you were eighteen out of fear, and now you're going to throw away your entire life over a girl who doesn't deserve it."

Feet planted on the sidewalk, I took her in and tried to temper my reaction to her words. I tried and tried, and I still failed just a little bit. "This coming from the girl who's committed to a long-distance relationship with the douchebag of the fucking century. Forgive me if I don't feel the need to take relationship advice from someone who clearly sucks at them as much as I apparently do." I took a quick breath and ignored the way her cheeks flushed and her eyes fell. "You might not like the answer, but I gave you one. It's my turn. Why did you come to my place?"

"It doesn't matter, Jimmy."

"Why did you come to my place?"

"If you're with Maddie, it doesn't matter."

"Why did you come to my place, Caroline?!"

Breathing heavily, her fingers curled into tiny fists, and she exploded. "Because I was more upset about lying to you in that bathroom than I was about finding my boyfriend fucking someone else in the backyard! Because I wanted to tell you that you were right! That there is something between us. Or was. But it doesn't fucking matter anymore!"

She tried to take a step around me to continue her path down the sidewalk, but my hand wrapped around her arm to keep her in place. I stared down into eyes that cautiously held mine, like she was bracing for whatever was going to come next.

That sight had me lowering my voice, speaking softly even though I was completely losing my shit on the inside. "You found Dan in the backyard with someone else?"

She nodded without breaking eye contact, and I had to take a deep breath to ward off the cloud of rage that descended with the simple movement. I wanted to find him. I wanted to hurt him. I wanted to...

*Fuck. Calm down, McCarthy.*

I focused on the rest of what she'd said to force away the supremely satisfying images blasting across my mind. Images of me breaking every bone in that dickhead's body.

"You lied to me?"

She nodded again.

"About what, specifically?"

Her tongue ran over her lips slowly, pulling my gaze to her mouth, where it stayed. "You're not crazy." The words were spoken quietly and with reluctance, almost like she wished they weren't true. Which I understood completely. Part of me wished they weren't true too.

"Caroline, if I-"

"Don't," she interrupted quickly. "Whatever you're about to say, just don't. It doesn't change anything." She gently pulled her arm from my grip and took a small step back. "Look, I was wrong earlier. If Maddie makes you happy, then you should be with her."

*She doesn't. You make me happy.*

"Caro-" I started, but she stopped me again.

"Please, don't. I just... I need to go. Please, James. *Please* let me go."

With a quick step around me, she propelled herself down the sidewalk, away from where I was stuck to the cement. I watched her until she'd disappeared from view around a corner. Even then I stayed frozen in place, wondering why it always hurt to watch her leave. Wondering if I'd ever be able to do what she asked.

The problem was, I didn't know how to let her go. I wasn't even sure I wanted to. That didn't change the fact that I knew she was right.

For both our sakes, I needed to let her go.

Chapter Twenty One

# Caroline

UP UNTIL I TURNED SIX, if you had asked me what my favorite holiday was, I'd have told you it was a tie between Christmas and Halloween. I imagine it's the same answer many young American children give because, really, presents and chocolate are basically God to a five-year-old.

Then my mom married Steve. My dad had been dead for four years by that point, so it had really always only been the two of us. Suddenly, I had a dad and a sister. The house was full. After that, my answer changed, and Thanksgiving ruled.

Thanksgiving was still my favorite holiday thirteen years later. But getting dressed to go to a hockey game with Nate, I couldn't help but think that this day was going to be drastically different from every other Thanksgiving I'd ever had.

Once I finished getting ready, I headed out to the living room to wait for Nate. Jen emerged from her room a few minutes later, still dressed in her pajamas, and flopped herself down onto the couch next to me. "When are you guys going to be back?"

"Maybe three hours?" I guessed. "I'm not totally sure, but I'll text and keep you updated."

She nodded and stretched out along the couch, groaning through the motion. It gave me a moment to once again consider her relationship (or non-relationship) with my best friend. For the past five weeks, I think I'd spent half my time trying to figure out what was going on between the two most important people in my life. And I was still almost completely clueless.

The good news was they were getting along again. At least, I was pretty sure they were getting along. Either they didn't talk much, or they just weren't talking when I was in the room because I'd caught them whispering heatedly a few times when they didn't know I was watching. Besides that, the few words they'd exchanged in my presence weren't exactly substantial.

Still, something had changed, and although I didn't know what that something was, I appreciated it, especially since it meant we'd been able to plan a Friendsgiving in the apartment. Initially, it was supposed to be just the three of us. Somehow, though, Nate had ended up inviting one of the guys from the team who also had nowhere to go. Then Jen decided to invite one of our neighbors from down the hall. So now we (and by we I meant Jen and I because I knew firsthand that Nate could not be trusted in a kitchen) were cooking dinner for five.

We'd planned all this before Nate had asked me to come to a Thanksgiving Day game with him first thing in the morning. I'd been reluctant to say yes, but he'd also asked Jen, so I agreed in the hope that she would as well. She hadn't, and Nate had refused to let me back out after the fact.

He was annoying like that.

The annoying man himself showed up two minutes later. I let him in and then watched in rapt fascination as he walked past me without a word, straight to the living room to stop a foot behind the couch, eyes locked on Jen. "Hey," he said quietly. "You okay?"

I couldn't see her from where I stood by the door, and I didn't hear her either, but she must have responded because he nodded slowly. "You sure you don't want to come?"

Again, I missed her response to the question. I did hear a quietly murmured, "Keys are on the counter," though, so I guessed it was a no.

I was still staring at the spot where he'd been standing long after he moved away to grab the keys and make for me. When he grabbed my arm gently, I shook off the daze and looked up.

"You ready?"

Putting the odd conversation to the back of my head for later, I nodded and followed him out the door.

Ten minutes later, once I'd realized we weren't headed toward the school arena, I turned to Nate, eyebrows narrowed curiously. "Where are we going?"

"I told you: a game."

At his short response, I grew suspicious. "Not what I asked, Nathaniel. Where are we going?"

He didn't speak, didn't even glance in my direction.

"Nate Baker, if you don't tell me where we're going..." I left the threat unfinished, hoping he wouldn't force me to make it. Instead of caving, he laughed.

"Yeah? What exactly are you going to do?"

I chewed on the corner of my lip for a moment, considering my options. Once I'd decided, my mouth curved into a truly depraved smile. "Do I need to remind you of our trip to Nevada? I have pictures, Nate. Pictures I could very easily distribute to the world."

He glared at me through the red light we were stopped at. "That's fucked up, Caro. You told me you got rid of those."

"Who gets rid of pictures? I sure as hell don't. I figured I'd save 'em until you got engaged. Make sure the person who snags you knows what they're signing up for."

He turned through the intersection, chuckling softly before muttering an insincere, "Bitch."

For a few minutes we drove in silence. I broke it by laughing quietly. "Nicely played, Nate; you almost got me. Now answer the question. Where are we going?"

"Just chill. We're almost there anyway."

I sighed and attempted to shed the apprehension that had settled around my spine, leaning back into the seat to stare blankly out the window. The day was cold—bitter cold—and a thin but persistent layer of clouds blocked out most of the sunlight. Every few minutes, though, the clouds cleared in just the right spot, and the sun burst through.

I couldn't help but feel like my time at this school was just like this sky. My days all felt dark—not necessarily bad, but gray. Cold. Lifeless. Then, for brief, bright moments, my world exploded into glorious Technicolor. Everything became amplified, heightened to a level I hadn't even known existed.

I wasn't ignorant enough to pretend I didn't know that Jimmy was the cause of that color, that sunlight. There was just nothing to do about it. I hadn't seen him once since I'd asked him to let me go, besides the little bit of staring I'd done at the few games I actually attended. Other than that, I hadn't seen him at all. And I was totally fine with that. Really. I was enjoying being single, since I'd never really done it before, and I was enjoying my life, or trying to. At the very least, it was nice not to have to answer to anyone besides my mom. And Nate, of course.

When I was alone, though, usually while I was lying in bed at night, I still missed him. And I wasn't sure how that was possible, since I had never really *had* him in the first place, but I also didn't let myself spend too much time contemplating it.

When we turned off the road and into a parking lot, I forced my eyes to take in our surroundings. My stomach dropped into my ovaries as I read the sign announcing our location. More specifically, the *name* on that sign.

"You're shitting me, right? Are we actually here right now?"

Here was Jimmy's rink. Or his dad's rink. I didn't really know or care about the particulars. They didn't matter because I wasn't going in either way.

"Okay, listen," he started once he'd pulled the car into an empty parking space, a commodity in the packed lot. "I know it may have been a dick move to not tell you where we were going, but in my defense, I never would have gotten you in the car if you had known. Also, before you tell me that you're not going in, I'm just going to tell you that I brought you here for a good cause. I really want you to do this with me." He must have seen the reluctance on my face because he quickly added, "Please, Caroline."

With a groan that could not be misinterpreted, I grudgingly climbed from the car, and we headed inside. Once we got through the door, Nate led me across the lobby and into the main room, where small groups of people milled about the wide perimeter surrounding the ice. My eyes focused on the wide white banners that hung from the walls, bright red letters proudly announcing that we were attending the 9th Annual Jack Attack Thanksgiving Classic.

My attention was pulled from the wall when sharp chills broke out along my skin. A second later I heard a familiar voice rumble out a greeting behind me, and I turned in time to watch Nate and Jimmy shake/slap hands. I sucked in a shaky breath when his eyes dropped to mine. Holding his gaze, I allowed the force of it to roll through me. My hands felt clammy, and I seriously thought my heart might burst from my chest, but, God, he looked better than ever. He must have gotten a haircut recently because it was shorter than I'd ever seen it, and while he'd been clean shaven the last time I'd seen him, he was currently sporting a seriously sexy amount of stubble. It worked for me.

Big time.

I tried to force my tongue into motion—tried to do something other than gawk—but it was like my entire body had completely shut down. We were still locked in our silent staring match when, suddenly, a high-pitched voice echoed over the sound of my pulse crashing through my ears.

"Hey, babe? Your dad is looking for you. I told him that- Oh! I remember you!"

My eyes shifted over Jimmy's shoulder, and I got my first real (fully clothed) look at the glory that was Maddie. Dressed in perfectly ironed, bright white linen pants and a black silk shirt, hair perfectly curled into dark spirals, she looked gorgeous. Meanwhile, I was rocking jeans, three-year-old Uggs, and a long-sleeved Red Wings t-shirt under my seriously attractive puffy coat, hair messily pulled into a crooked ponytail. I looked like I couldn't have cared less what I'd worn because, really, I hadn't.

But I cared now. And that sucked.

I forced away the suck and pulled my lips into what I'm sure was a completely lifeless smile. "Yeah, hey."

I caught Nate's quick glance in my direction, but I was focused on the next words coming out of her mouth. "Jimmy, you going to introduce me?"

*Shitfuckshit.* I had *so* not signed up for this.

"Uh, yeah, sorry," he quickly muttered, appearing almost as uncomfortable as I felt. "Guys, this is Maddie. Mads, this is Nate. He's on the team at school, and-"

"This is Caroline," Nate said quickly, grabbing my hand. I turned to face him and caught his wide smile before he pulled me into his side. "My girlfriend."

My head jerked back. Jimmy's did as well, but Maddie just smiled as Nate planted a swift kiss on my cheek. "Aw, that's adorable. Well, it's great to meet you guys!" She gave us one last smile and turned back to Jimmy, whose eyes were still anchored to all the places my body pressed against Nate's.

"Babe? You coming?" She took a step away from Nate and me, grabbing onto Jimmy's hand before giving him a light tug. It was enough to get his attention, and he jerked away without a word to follow her across the room.

The second they were out of earshot, I turned toward Nate angrily, pinning his eyes with mine. "What the fuck was that?!" I whisper-shouted, doing my best to avoid causing a scene, even though part of me *really* wanted to.

"That was me saving you from looking like a total idiot back there." He paused and looked at me thoughtfully for a long second. "It also had the added benefit of throwing him off, although it looks like I succeeded in that regard a little too well." He glanced over my shoulder and quickly back at me. "Motherfucker is still looking at us. What a dick..."

I tried to pull away, and he let me have space but didn't drop my hand. "Nate..."

"No," he said quickly, smiling in a way that I'm sure made it look like we were just a young couple having a private conversation. "You know, I kept my mouth shut when you told me about everything he put you through, but if you want the truth, I'm pissed the fuck off. He doesn't know what he wants, and that's fine. What's not fine is that he messed with you while he tried to figure it out." His smile turned positively wicked, and he took a step closer. "Just smile and pretend to be as happily in love with me as everyone already assumes you are."

Against my will, the corner of my mouth lifted the tiniest bit. "This is a horrible, terrible thing you're doing, Nate. In fact, after this entire morning, you might not make it onto my list of things I'm thankful for at dinner tonight."

He rolled his eyes. "You know full well you don't know what you'd do without me. Now go find somewhere to sit while I get ready."

"Good luck, Mr. Baker."

"Thanks, Ms. Olsen." He leaned in and gave my cheek another quick kiss before he headed off, laughing softly to himself.

I shook my head and turned around to head for the small set of bleachers that extended from the longer wall. There were already quite a few people settled into seats, and almost the entire front row was blocked by an assortment of wheelchairs, both manual and electric. I gave the sight a curious glance before ignoring it to climb to the top of the seating area, dropping onto the small wooden bench heavily.

A few minutes had passed with me staring blankly across the room when I felt someone settle onto the bench next to me. My eyes dropped to see slender knees covered in white, and I suppressed the groan that threatened to crawl from my throat.

"I'm so glad you're here," Maddie whispered conspiratorially. I turned slightly and caught her small smile, which made me feel about a thousand times worse than I already did. "I always have to sit by myself at these things. Jimmy doesn't usually invite any of the guys on the team, and, between us, not a whole lot of them are boyfriend material." She laughed softly, and the sound grated my eardrums. Even her laugh was perfect—like bells or windchimes. "Nate must really have it bad for you."

I tripped over an uncomfortable laugh and dropped a shoulder pathetically. "I don't know. The whole thing is still pretty new."

She scoffed. "Maybe, but I saw the way he looked at you. Trust me, I'm good at reading people."

I had no response for that, so I was relieved when bodies slowly started filling the ice. It didn't take long for me to realize that this wasn't a normal game. I mean, the banners had hinted at that already, but there was something else odd about it as well. I saw Nate, and Jimmy too, but neither of them were actually playing—more like reffing while providing a good amount of hands-on assistance to players who, for the most part, were all much shorter than them. And generally much less coordinated. For a moment,

I considered the possibility that it was just a regular youth game, but it wasn't even really a game — more like a lighthearted scrimmage, since the players seemed more interested in helping each other than actually playing.

I don't know what it was that pulled my gaze from the ice, but my eyes skimmed over the stands to my left, falling on a woman who I knew in an instant was Jimmy's mom. They didn't even look that similar, but there was something about the curve of her lips as I stared at her profile, something about the way she held her shoulders, that told me in my gut I was right. My eyes trailed to the person sitting by her side, and the air in my lungs wheezed out at the sight of a boy who I guessed was around twelve or thirteen, though I couldn't be sure. That wasn't what had stolen my breath though. Besides the hair two shades darker than Jimmy's already dark blonde, they could have been twins, albeit twins separated by eight or so years.

It was almost eerie. Jack's nose was straighter, without the slight bump of Jimmy's, but  I imagined that if I ever got my hands on pictures of Jimmy as a kid, he would have looked exactly like the boy sitting to my left.

I forced my eyes away from Jimmy's brother and back onto the ice, forcing my mind blank beyond anything not related to applauding when it seemed appropriate. I wasn't fully sure why Nate had dragged me here, unless it really was just to make me uncomfortable, but I couldn't help thinking he had a bigger plan than that.

By the time the final whistle blew, my butt hurt from sitting on the hard bench, and my head hurt from having to nod and smile every time Maddie chose to make an observation. I quickly excused myself before carefully navigating my way down the steps to the edge of the ice.

Nate skated to a stop in front of me opposite the waist-high barrier, and, before I could react, leaned in to plant a swift, closed-mouth kiss against my lips. He pulled away as fast as he'd approached, and as I opened my mouth to complain, my eyes drifted to Jimmy standing behind him on the ice, staring in our direction. The tightness of his jaw and the way his eyes sparkled with irritation had me holding in the words I'd been ready to say.

"He's staring, isn't he?"

Nate's words brought my eyes back to him, and I nodded slowly.

"Dick." He shook his head softly and gave me a short smile. "I'm going to get changed. I need to talk to someone before we go, but then we'll be on our way, okay?" I nodded again, and then he was gone, leaving me alone.

Not for long though.

I saw the shadow first—a slight blur of darkness that caught my attention and had me turning to the side. I was completely unprepared to find Jimmy's mini-me standing a foot away, staring somewhere in the vicinity of my chin.

"Know you," he mumbled, the tips of his ears turning pink. I took a small step forward to hear him better, but he tensed, and I froze.

"Hey there. You're Jack right?" He reacted to that, pulling his shoulders an inch further up his neck, and I continued quickly, "I'm a friend of your brother's."

That was clearly the right thing to say because the tension evaporated, and his smile was wide. "You know Jimmy?"

I couldn't help it; his grin was infectious. It wasn't just that, though; the way he said his brother's name, so full of love and almost...reverence. I smiled back at him and nodded as his eyes trailed over my mouth to my cheekbone.

"Jimmy's the best."

"Can you keep a secret?" I asked quietly, leaning in an inch. This time, instead of backing up, he leaned in as well, clearly excited to be told something that no one else knew. "I kind of think he's the best too."

His smile drooped a bit, and his eyes fell back to my chin. "You should tell him." My lungs dragged in a painful breath at the quiet, almost somber words. "Think he's sad a lot. Try to make him happy, but it's hard."

Shit. Tears stung the corners of my eyes, and I took a slow, deep breath to will them away. "Do you want to know what he told me, Jack?"

He considered it for a moment, staring at my ear now, before nodding slowly. "He told me the thing that makes him happiest in the world is spending time with his brother. And that he loves you more than anything."

I could tell he was really thinking about the words. He must have deemed them acceptable because a moment later he nodded. Then shrugged. "Should still tell him. The Mighty Mite said he was the best. Think it'd make him happy."

I smiled because that was definitely one of the nicer things anyone had ever said to me.

"I got another secret, Jack. Do you wanna hear it?" He nodded, and we both leaned in again. "The way you look after your brother, the way you love him? I think that's the best, too."

The grin he shot me then was absolutely blinding, so much so that I almost didn't notice that his eyes had landed on mine. They stayed there for a few seconds, warmly and confidently holding my gaze before dropping back to my cheekbone. The smile lingered, though, all through his next statement. "You didn't skate today."

Apparently it wasn't just Jimmy, but all the McCarthy boys who had the power to send me careening from the highest of highs to the absolute lowest of lows. My heart lodged itself somewhere just south of my windpipe, and it took me a moment to find something to say. "I don't skate anymore."

"Are you like...?" He gestured to himself, and I gazed at him curiously for a second before allowing my lips to tip up.

"You mean, am I painfully handsome?"

He shook his head quickly and laughed, but before he was able to clarify, I noticed movement over his shoulder and looked up, straight into Jimmy's eyes. He was radiating tension, and there was a slight hint of concern on his face as he closed the distance between us. I hadn't noticed while talking to Jack, but the rink was largely empty, a few small groups of people still scattered around the space. I noticed Maddie standing with the woman I'd identified as Jimmy's mom, but she didn't seem to be paying too much attention to whatever the other woman was saying because her eyes were trained on Jimmy's back. When they slid to me, I quickly looked away in time to see Jimmy come to a halt beside his brother.

"You bugging Caroline, bud?" He gave his brother a small smile, but I noticed the way it didn't reach his eyes.

Jack's ears turned red again, and I jumped in quickly. "Not at all." The smile I snuck him was small but reassuring. "Jack and I were just getting to know one another."

Jimmy nodded slowly in my direction before turning back toward his brother. "Mom wants you. Can you go find her for me?"

Jack sighed heavily but nodded before giving my chin one last glance.

"It was nice to meet you, Jack," I said quietly. He gave me a shy smile and nodded again, more quickly this time, before turning toward the stands and walking away. I expected Jimmy to follow behind, but he just turned back to me, a completely unreadable expression on his face.

"Everything okay?" I asked cautiously. I mean, all the evidence suggested that the answer was a big, fat no, but, hey, pointless questions were kind of my thing.

"You guys aren't really together, right?"

I cocked one eyebrow, unamused. "Really?"

"I just want to know whether you lied to me months ago or he lied to me hours ago."

"You're absolutely ridiculous." I took a step closer and lowered my voice. "You're really going to stand here and give me shit about this when you're still hiding under your safety blanket? I gotta say, James, the hypocrisy is *really* getting old."

His eyes flared with anger, and his lips parted, probably to argue a point that, in my opinion, he had no right arguing. Before that could happen though, a wide hand came down hard on his shoulder.

I stepped back quickly before looking up into eyes almost identical to the ones I'd just been staring into. Identical, but a good deal less angry.

Jimmy's dad stared down at me, Nate at his side, and I felt the flush come to my cheeks. I couldn't get a good enough read on either of their expressions to figure out whether they'd heard me or not. I figured, either way, it didn't really matter now, and I fought to bring the most sincere smile I could manage to my face.

"I take it you're Caroline?" The older McCarthy's voice was warm and laced with humor I didn't fully understand, but I nodded nonetheless.

"I take it you're Mr. McCarthy?"

"Yes, but no. Call me Chris." He extended his hand, and I shook it tentatively, feeling an odd sense of déjà vu. "I gotta say, I'm kind of thrilled to be meeting you."

I smiled and shrugged because what was I supposed to say to that? He just laughed off my discomfort.

"Yeah, I heard you're not too crazy about reliving the glory days. Look, I'll keep this short and sweet. I know you have no interest in playing again. That's your choice, and I'm not stupid enough to tell you what I think about it. That said, when Nate said he'd brought you with him, I wanted to introduce myself at least. And tell you that if you ever decide you miss it, I'd love to bring you on board here. I run a couple of programs, and there's a few I think you'd be great for. Like I said, though, it's your call. I just ask that you think about it."

"Can I ask you a question?" He seemed a bit surprised that I wasn't flat out denying him like I had Coach Miller, who I could only assume he had spoken to. Once he nodded, I continued. "Why would you do this for me? I have literally zero experience coaching. I'm not qualified at all. I don't get it."

He stared at me for a long moment before smirking. "Can I ask *you* a question?" I hesitated, then nodded slowly. "When you were eleven, did you really score on an NHL goalie?"

"He was a rookie," I argued. "And they traded him a year later for a reason."

He simply laughed. "Just think about it, Caroline. You know where to find me." Turning to his son, he gave his shoulder a tight squeeze before pulling him away, and then it was just Nate and I.

"Are you mad?"

I faced him slowly, letting my mind fully process this entire mindfuck of a morning. Surprisingly, I wasn't angry. I had liked meeting Jack. Chris, too. If things had been different, I probably wouldn't have hesitated before agreeing to his offer.

But the ugly truth was, if things were different, I wouldn't be in Virginia. If things were different, I'd be in Michigan. If things were different, I'd still be with Dan, playing and training and living the life I'd always imagined.

So it didn't matter. None of it mattered because things *weren't* different.

"No," I assured him, "I'm not mad. I *am* ready to leave though."

"Gotcha. Well, let's get out of here and go cook us a turkey."

We headed out to the car, and I reflected for a moment on just how right I'd been. The day wasn't even half over, and I could already confidently say that this was the weirdest Thanksgiving ever.

## Chapter Twenty Two

*Jimmy*

HALFWAY TO MADDIE'S PARENTS HOUSE, I was still pissed. I was only getting away with it because Maddie had decided, since she was spending the night there, that we needed to take separate cars to dinner. I hadn't argued the point because, truth be told, I knew I needed to get myself together. The twenty-minute car ride that I would be spending alone seemed like the perfect opportunity to do that.

Caroline had been 100 percent correct, as usual. I had no right whatsoever to be upset about her and Nate, if there even was a her and Nate. I didn't believe it was true, but I had no idea why he would lie. I had even less of a clue as to why she would go along with it.

None of that mattered though. At least not right now. Right now I needed to focus on getting through dinner. Normally, I wouldn't be worried about my ability to make it through a meal with Maddie's family. But things hadn't exactly been normal for a while.

It had been five weeks—five fucking long weeks—since I'd last seen Caroline, and, more than anything, I missed her. That was the worst part of it. When she had walked into the rink with Nate earlier,

I had trailed off mid-fucking-sentence talking to my mom and Jack. Mouth wide open, I'd just fucking stared at her. Captivated.

By the girl I was supposed to be forgetting about.

She was impossible to forget, though. Even more so, her words were impossible to forget. At least once a day I thought about the things she'd said to me the last night we'd talked. About me being afraid. About me not loving Maddie the way I should.

I knew she was right. I'd decided she was right weeks ago. I just hadn't found the right time to do anything about it.

As I liked to do, I had made a plan. The day after Thanksgiving. That was the day I was going to end it with Maddie. I reasoned that only assholes broke up with someone right before a holiday. On the actual holiday was probably even worse. I didn't want to be that guy, so I decided to give us both the day before I closed the book on an exceptionally long chapter of my life.

The decision had nothing to do with Caroline, beyond the fact that she'd opened my eyes to how I really felt about Maddie. Did I love my girlfriend? Yes, I did. But I wasn't *in* love with her. I wasn't crazy about her. Maybe I had been once, but that had died a long time ago. Maddie deserved more than what I had left to give her. So did I.

So, it needed to end.

By the time I'd parked in front of the Campbells' home, I'd managed to relax just enough that I wasn't risking a cracked tooth with the force of my clenched jaw. I slid my phone into my pocket and took two last deep breaths before climbing from the car to meet Maddie on the sidewalk. We didn't speak, didn't touch. She just headed straight for the door, and I followed.

The house was quiet when we entered, and seemingly empty. There was no one in the small living room, so we kept moving toward the dining room, which was also empty, and into the kitchen. There we finally found Maddie's mom at the counter, smashing a bowl of potatoes. Maddie gave her a quick kiss, and I smiled and waved.

"I don't think so," she said playfully. "Get over here and hug me, kid."

I chuckled but did as she demanded, giving her a short but genuine hug. Mrs. Campbell had always liked me, from the first time Maddie had brought me home. Her dad was a somewhat different story, but he didn't outright hate me.

At least not anymore.

"So, how have you been, James? We haven't seen you in a while."

"I've been alright. Keeping busy with work and school."

"I'm sure. Senior year." She smiled brightly, and I returned it with as much enthusiasm as I had. For all my high hopes at the start of the year, at this point I was just trying to survive. Classes weren't going terribly, which was the one bright spot, I guess. I'd also managed to find a solid middle ground between royally sucking and being the best guy on the team, and I was okay with that. It was just everything else that had my year turning out nothing like I'd expected.

*Everything happens for a reason, right?*

I was still undecided, but I couldn't say I wasn't hopeful.

Despite my concerns, dinner passed fairly uneventfully for me. This was mostly because Maddie's sister Noelle had unexpectedly flown in for the holiday since she'd just broken up with her fiancée. It was probably a little fucked on my part, but I appreciated the distraction her appearance provided for me. As soon as she'd walked her tear-stained self in the door, she and Maddie had disappeared upstairs, leaving me alone with Mr. Campbell. We spent the time until dinner watching a football game in silence. It worked for me.

The actual meal was mostly quiet, Noelle's bad mood coating the conversation like a layer of ash. It seemed to be affecting Maddie particularly hard; she spent the bulk of our time at the table distractedly scraping her fork against her plate, leaving me to make stilted conversation with Mrs. Campbell. Dessert passed much in the same fashion, and before long, I was standing from the table and offering to help clear it.

Once I'd been waved off, I turned to head for the living room to wait for Mads, but then she was at my side, grabbing my hand gently. "Can we talk?"

I took in her downcast eyes and slight frown before nodding slowly. She pulled me through the living room and straight out the front door, onto the porch.

Before she even sat down on the wicker bench, I knew what was coming.

"Look, Jimmy, I think-"

"It's okay. I get it."

Her eyes flashed up to mine, clouded with confusion. "You get what?"

"It's over, right?" The guilty look that crossed her face confirmed what she hadn't yet said. "It's okay, Mads, really. I understand."

Her gaze searched mine and grew contemplative. "You have a thing for her, don't you?" I must have made a face because she continued. "Caroline. I saw the way you looked at her earlier. And I'm sorry if this comes out wrong, but you seem really okay with this being over. More than I expected."

I thought about lying but realized there was really no reason to anymore. "I do, but she doesn't have anything to do with us. I've realized that I don't really care about you the way you deserve. It's just... We're not the same people we were in high school. And that's okay. That's normal. But this," I gestured between us, "it just doesn't work anymore."

She nodded and shot me a small, quick smile that faded almost instantly. "We tried, though, didn't we?"

"Yeah," I said with a nod of my own. "We tried."

She leaned in to give me one last hug, and I returned it tightly. I cared about this girl, and I wanted her to be happy. I just couldn't be the one to make her happy. And she couldn't do it for me either.

As we pulled away, she found my eyes and held them for a moment. "I hope you're happy, James. Whatever you decide to do, wherever your life ends up, I really hope you're happy."

"Me too, Mads. I hope you're happy, too."

With a final goodbye, I turned around, stepped off the porch, and walked away from all my best-laid plans.

It took about twenty minutes to drive myself home. I managed to keep my mind off Caroline and Nate until I walked in the door. After that, my determination completely withered away. For almost an hour, I sat on my couch and thought of nothing but the girl who'd asked me to let her go.

I had no clue why I wasn't able to do that.

I pulled my phone out of my pocket and let my thumb hover over the screen for a full five minutes before shoving the thing back in my pocket, trading it for my keys and then heading straight out the door.

Half an hour later, I'd pulled into a spot in front of her building. I sat in my car for a few more minutes, trying to talk myself out of walking inside. I knew there was a good possibility that my showing up was about to make everything even worse between us. I also knew that if she really was with Nate, I didn't stand a chance. Not when he'd already had at least fifteen years' worth of earning a place in her heart. You don't start dating your best friend unless you know it's going to last.

I finally shoved myself out the door, reasoning that I just needed to know, one way or another, if they were together or not. I pushed my way into the building and practically jogged down the hall.

Quickly wiping my palms against my jeans, I knocked on the door a bit harder than I intended to. The sound echoed through the empty hall, and the quiet voices I'd heard on the other side of the wall stopped immediately. Less than six seconds later, it swung open, revealing a happily smiling Nate.

The smile disappeared almost instantly, and his eyes narrowed. "What are you doing here?"

I swallowed, feeling like a total asshole. I had come all the way here, though; I wasn't about to back down now. "I'm sorry, man, I just... I need to talk to Caro. Can I come in?"

He stared at me without saying a word, but I heard her voice from inside the apartment. "Knock it off, and let him in, Nathaniel."

Grudgingly, he stepped back and let me walk through the door. I glanced around the room and found Caroline almost instantly. She was seated at a small card table they'd set up in the living room, loaded with half-empty bowls and plates. I forced my eyes off of her to scan the rest of the room, noticing Jen and another girl I didn't recognize before spotting someone familiar.

"Sean?"

The forward looked surprised to see me, which I could understand. Frankly, I was surprised to see him too.

"Hey, man. You okay?"

I nodded quickly and looked back to Caroline. She was watching me curiously, and I blocked out the rest of the room to ask quietly, "Can I talk to you?" She glanced around quickly, and I added, "Privately, I mean."

The small frown on her face deepened, and she nodded slowly. Rising carefully from the folding chair she'd been seated on, she scooted around the table and headed toward her bedroom, calling out behind her as she went, "Jen and I cooked. The rest of you are in charge of clean-up." I followed her through the door, and she closed it behind us, blocking out the sound of the guys grumbling and the clanging of plates being cleared.

"Are you sure you're okay?" she asked, once we were safely inside. She leaned against the desk and faced me, eyes sweeping over my face slowly. "You look...stressed."

"I'm okay. Really. I just..." I took a step toward her and held her eyes. "I need to know, Caroline."

I watched her drag in a breath and blow it out softly, eyes narrowing slightly. "Why?"

"Because Baker is a good guy. And if you honestly tell me that you and him are together, at least I can walk away knowing that someone is going to take care of you."

"I don't need anyone to take care of me," she fired back angrily.

"I know that," I ground out. "I just..." Shaking my head gently, I took another step closer. "Just tell me, Caro. Please just tell me the truth."

Her eyes held mine, deep blue pools of uncertainty. For a long minute, she just stared up at me, lower lip tucked safely between her teeth. When she finally released it, my gaze dropped to her mouth, and I forced it back up before I did something really reckless.

"No." I had to strain to hear the whispered word, even in the silent room.

"No what?"

"No, Nate and I are not together."

I processed that slowly, holding her gaze the entire time. Slowly, the nervous tension I'd been holding onto since this morning dissipated, leaving an even more nervous energy in its wake. My skin felt tight, my heart pounded like it was attempting to break free, and I had to wipe my palms against my jeans to clear the moisture that had gathered there.

"I need to ask you something else." Taking another slow step forward, I brought us close enough that I had to spread my feet to fit her bent knees between my legs. Close enough that I could feel her breath ghosting across my skin as she practically panted.

"What?"

My eyes dropped to her mouth with purpose. I watched as she darted her tongue out to moisten her lips, and I had to suppress a groan. I managed that but had no control over the tightening of my groin.

But fuck it. I was single. So was she. There was nothing wrong about this situation.

In fact, I would have bet that standing inches from Caroline was the most *right* place I'd ever been.

"I need to kiss you. *Please* let me kiss you, Caroline."

## Chapter Twenty Three

# Caroline

I WAS IN FULL PANIC MODE.

Buzzers, alarms, sirens. They were all blaring through my head, warning me to back up, get away, slow this *the fuck* down. At least long enough to get a few answers.

Jimmy's eyes hadn't left my mouth, and the hot, heavy feel of his determined stare was almost paralyzing. Worse, he was getting closer, moving toward me with a singular purpose that was written plain across his face.

I just barely managed to pull a hand up in time to place it flat against his chest. And, God, was it a chest. Sure, I'd seen it. From a relatively close distance, too. But it felt like my hand was pressed against warm, cotton-covered steel. I felt the contours of his muscles through the thin t-shirt he was wearing, and for a second, I considered saying, "The hell with it" and pulling him in for what we both had been dying to do for weeks, if not months.

"Wait," I finally choked out. "Maddie?"

He shook his head without moving his eyes. "We broke up."

I scanned his face carefully, trying to find any emotion in the words, but I came up empty.

"So..." I took a breath. "You're single."

He nodded, still fully focused on the lower half of my face. "And you're single."

"Yep." The word was more wheeze than anything. He must have noticed because his eyes slowly came back up to mine. They were warm, comforting, but still somehow terrifying. The pure hunger on his face... I'd never seen anything like it. No one had ever looked at me like that, even before the accident. But Jimmy... He stared at me like he'd die if he didn't get to taste me. Like I was integral to his very survival.

"Let me kiss you, Caroline," he said softly, placing his hands on either side of the desk I was leaning against. It brought him even closer, close enough that he was easily able to bring his mouth to the skin at my jaw. He pressed a soft kiss there before whispering against my skin, "I need to kiss you, Caroline."

Trailing a path with his lips, the gentle kisses he laid along my jaw had heat flooding my body. My skin felt tight, my breasts felt heavy, and the juncture of my thighs was radiating so much warmth that if he got any closer, he was going to feel it through both our pants.

He hadn't even kissed me properly yet, and I was already more turned on than I'd ever been in my life. I tried to find my voice, but it was lost, carried away on the sea of sensations he provoked in me. I didn't know what it was about him, but no one else had ever made me feel the way he always made me feel.

Jimmy made things bigger. He made them more. The highs with him were higher, the lows were lower, but it was all just so intense. I still hadn't decided whether that was actually a good thing or a bad thing, but right then the word "bad" wasn't even in my vocabulary. Shit, I didn't even have a vocabulary. That had taken a hike with my brain.

No thinking. Just feeling.

Feeling his lips place soft kisses against my jaw, my neck. Feeling them work up to the spot behind my ear before tugging the lobe between his teeth gently. That maneuver pulled a shaky groan from between my lips, and I felt him smile against my skin.

"Can I kiss you yet?" He didn't bother removing his mouth from my skin to ask the question, and the vibration that traveled over my nerve endings sent chills shooting down my spine. I brought my other hand up to his chest to join the first and pulled his body toward mine gently. When he started to pull his mouth from my neck, I gripped his shirt in my hands and held him immobile, softly shaking my head.

His low chuckle rumbled over my skin, the air lightly tickling my neck as it passed. Then his mouth was pressed against me once again. I dropped the cotton from my hands to let them roam. One trailed around to his back while the other slowly descended along his stomach, gently feeling the grooves and ridges that composed the landscape of his body. A body I wanted to discover. Explore. Map. I wanted to learn every contour, every freckle, every scar. I wanted to memorize it all.

One of his hands slid from the desk onto my hip, moving gently up my side until he was able to weave his fingers into my ponytail. With a light tug, he pulled my head backwards until my neck was bared to him. Then his mouth was moving again, tracing the curve of my throat. His head dipped, and I felt his tongue slip into the hollow between my collarbones.

At my shudder, he withdrew enough to bring his eyes to me. The normally light brown was dark and shining with need, capturing mine from less than two inches away. "Can I-"

I plastered my mouth to his, swallowing the rest of the words. With his mouth open to speak, I was able to slide my tongue against his tentatively, once. That was all it took before he commandeered the kiss, retuning it almost frantically. I was just as frantic. His lips worked against mine forcefully, letting me know just how much he'd been dying to do exactly this. And, *God*, I'd been dying for it too.

When his teeth snagged my bottom lip gently, giving it a quick nip before soothing it with his tongue, I practically melted against the desk. He swallowed my moan and dropped his hands to my hips. Grabbing me tightly, he lifted me just enough to slide me back onto the desk before his hands moved to my knees. I couldn't even process what was happening quickly enough to get self-conscious when he encountered the metal of my prosthesis.

In less than a second, he had pulled my thighs far enough apart that he could fit his hips between them, and he did that all without pulling his lips from mine.

When I felt him press against the spot between my legs, I trembled. He must have felt it because his arms wrapped around my waist, and he pulled his mouth from mine to rest our foreheads together.

"Sorry." The word was guttural, filled with lust and barely there restraint.

I shook my head gently against his, trying to catch my breath as well and failing pretty spectacularly. But seriously? I didn't even know it was possible to kiss someone the way he'd just kissed me.

A sudden knock at the door had us both jumping before Jimmy dropped his arms and took a quick step backwards. I felt the loss of him like a cold draft through a poorly fitted window.

Sliding shakily off the desk, I took two steps to face the door. Once there, I ignored the second, more insistent knock to take a deep breath before grasping the handle and cracking it enough to pop out my head.

Unsurprisingly, it was Nate.

"You okay?"

"Yeah, I'm fine. Are you going home?"

His eyes narrowed before he nodded slowly. "Do I need to take anyone with me?"

Shaking my head, I gave him a small, only slightly annoyed smile. "'Night, Nate. I'll talk to you tomorrow."

By the time I'd closed the door and turned around, Jimmy had kicked off his shoes and settled onto my bed.

"Little presumptuous of you, don't you think?"

He grinned. "I'm not exactly stripping off my clothes and asking you to get on your knees, am I? I didn't come here to get laid."

I cocked an eyebrow and glanced over my shoulder to the desk before making my way across the room toward him. "So why did you come?"

I was only a foot and a half away from him, but he must have thought it was too far because one hand darted out to grab mine, and then he was lightly pulling me closer and closer still, until I had to either straddle him or drop to the mattress beside him. I chose the latter after a few frantic seconds of deliberation.

Once I was sitting, his fingers laced through mine, and he rested his hand against my right thigh. "I missed you. I went home after everything went down with her, and I just...couldn't stop thinking about you." His thumb traced a path over my palm, and his eyes glanced up at mine briefly. "I think about you more than I probably should."

*Well, at least I'm not alone there...*

"I missed you, too," I told him honestly. "I didn't want to, but I did."

His eyes lifted to mine, and I could tell he was happy, maybe even a little relieved, to hear that. "Can I ask you a question?"

I gave him a look that he must have read because he asked, "Two questions?"

"I mean, technically that *was* two, but..."

He laughed softly, and that low rumble slid over my skin like velvet, warm and soft and utterly decadent. "Why did Nate introduce you as his girlfriend?"

I gave him an apologetic smile. "Mostly to piss you off. I mean, it wasn't completely motivated by that, but..." I shrugged. "It's a weird thing about Nate: He seems to think that inventing fake relationships solves all manner of problems."

"And I was a problem?"

Angling my lower half toward him, my face scrunched up as I considered how bad that had probably sounded. "Not quite. He just knew that I had feelings for you, and he was trying to protect me."

"And piss me off. Don't leave that part out. It's my favorite." The words sounded grumpy, but the smile he delivered them through told me he was mostly joking.

"Mine, too."

We were both grinning, just watching each other the way we always seemed to end up doing. This time, though, he ended the staring match by leaning in slowly to press a soft kiss against my lips.

His mouth slowly worked against mine, at least at first. When his tongue swiped across the seam

of my lips, I gasped, and then he was in, tasting—
no—*devouring* me. His exploration was thorough, and
his commitment to it absolutely intoxicating. Best of
all, it just went on and on, like he wanted nothing
more than to spend the rest of his life inside my
mouth.

It was the best kiss in the history of my life.

Hell, it might have been the best kiss in the
history of the universe. Fueled by two months of
longing and angst, it burned and raged, and before I
knew it, we had moved across the bed, ending up
with me on my back, Jimmy suspended above me,
hips notched between my thighs. He held himself up
with one arm while the other softly trailed from my
hip up to my breast, swiping gently along the swell
there, and my back arched off the bed desperately. I
felt his smile against my lips, and then he was doing
it again, lightly tracing a path that came closer to my
pebbled nipple than the last had.

I didn't even know nipples could get that
hard.

*First time for everything, I guess.*

When his thumb finally trailed exactly where I
wanted it, I sucked in a breath as heat flooded the
lower half of my body. My hips jerked up again,
pressing into his, and the groan he let out was so
incredibly sexy that I couldn't stop myself from doing
it again. His thumb continued to rub over my breast,
and his hips dropped just enough to lightly press
against mine, rocking slowly but steadily.

Another potential first?

It was very possible that I was about to have my first fully clothed orgasm. He wasn't even actually touching my skin, and I still felt ready to combust, ready to explode from the almost overwhelming number of sensations that feeling his body pressed to mine created.

When his fingers slid to the skin next to the waistband of my jeans, I shivered, and he broke the never-ending kiss to meet my gaze.

"This okay?" The words came out gruffly, and I nodded quickly, almost desperately. I was too far gone to stop this now. Too far gone to tell him no. In that moment, there was nothing in the world I wanted more than Jimmy's hands on me—in me.

His mouth dropped back to mine, his fingers deftly popping the button and undoing the zipper before I felt his hand slide under the fabric that covered me. When he finally reached his destination, fingers eagerly filling me in a way that had me gasping for breath, I was completely lost.

I couldn't focus on anything, couldn't control anything. Time didn't exist. In fact, I wasn't sure that the world existed. It was just Jimmy and me, in this moment, separate from the universe and every single other thing in it.

It wasn't long before my body tightened. My mouth fell open, and my head fell onto the pillow as I exploded. The release was pure, unadulterated, unchecked pleasure, and it turned me into nothing more than a quivering pile of mush on the mattress.

It took me a few minutes to pry my eyes open once the sensations had passed. I hadn't even noticed him pulling his hand away or shifting to my side, but there he was, lying quietly next to me, smug smile across his face. I returned it with a lazy grin of my own, and the smugness disappeared. His eyes warmed, and the air grew heavy.

That look... It wasn't lust. It wasn't sexual at all. It was something else entirely, something I was completely unprepared to face.

I snuck a glance down to see him straining against the zipper of his pants, and I shifted up to sitting. He must have realized my intention when I slid myself further down the bed because he sat up quickly.

"Caroline, you don't-"

"I know," I interrupted quietly. "You think I do anything I don't want to?"

"Good point." He smiled tightly and leaned back. "In that case, carry on."

I smiled and reached out a hand to flick open the button of his jeans and pull down the zipper.

"Don't mind if I do."

It was after I'd taken him between my lips and against my tongue. After I'd gotten myself worked up all over again just from watching him lose control. After I'd pushed him over the edge, relentlessly working him until he was coming with a breathless groan and my name on his lips.

It was also after I'd decided that blowjobs were my new favorite thing ever.

Once he had tucked himself back away, he leaned across the space between us and gave me a swift kiss before climbing over me and off the bed.

"Yeah, so I'm gonna head home..."

My mouth dropped open just as his face split into a giant grin. I transitioned from a look of shock to a playful glare, and he leaned down and planted another feather-light kiss on my lips, pulling away just enough to stare into my eyes.

"Just kidding. I'm going to the bathroom, and then, so long as you don't kick me out, I was hoping I could crawl into bed with you. Is it okay if I stay?"

My heart did a strange, stuttering pirouette, and I smiled slowly before nodding. "Yeah, that's okay."

His response was a warm look that heated my insides before he headed through the door, closing it softly behind him.

The second I was alone, I launched myself off the bed and raced for the dresser. Based on what I knew about guys in the bathroom, I figured I had less than a minute to get ready for bed, a process that usually took closer to ten. I grabbed shorts before vaulting back onto the bed with a loud thump. Shimmying out of my jeans was made even harder than usual by my frantic pace, and I let a rapid-fire stream of obscenities flow from my lips as the denim snagged repeatedly over the metal and plastic of the prosthesis.

Thankfully, I managed to get them all the way off, quickly popping the seal before tossing the leg as carefully as possible out of the way. I was able to pull on the knee-length shorts, wriggling across the mattress to pull them hastily to my waist, before the door opened and shut with Jimmy back inside. He glanced at the jeans dropped carelessly on the floor next to the bed and the shorts I'd changed into before dragging his eyes back up to mine with a knowing look and a slight frown.

"Question time. Is this a We're-still-getting-to-know-each-other-so-I'm-still-keeping-some-secrets thing, or is it an I'm-super-self-conscious-of-my-scars-so-I'm-going-to-try-to-hide-them thing? Because if it's the former, I'll turn back around and give you a couple more minutes, but if it's the latter..." He trailed off, and I dropped my eyes to attempt to hide the unfortunate truth.

I guessed he saw through the maneuver because the door didn't open and close. Instead, the mattress dipped slightly, and I glanced back up to find him sitting beside me.

"I don't want you to hide from me." The words were soft but so strong; I didn't doubt that he meant them for a second. Eyes boring into mine, his hand came to my thigh—my left thigh—and I tensed but didn't drop my gaze. "Please believe me when I tell you that nothing about you, not a single fucking thing, is a turn-off to me." His fingers gripped the mesh of my shorts and slowly started dragging it up.

I clenched my fists tight enough that I could feel the sharp bite of my nails as they threatened to cut through my palms, but I didn't stop him. I didn't say a word. Just held his eyes as he pulled the hem of the shorts above the bottom of my leg, baring the skin enough to reveal the gnarled flesh and misshapen thigh above where the liner ended. His fingers moved to lightly grip the liner wrapped around my stump and his eyes lifted to mine questioningly. Only once I had nodded did he begin to slowly peel the fabric back, baring the carnage of my accident in all its glory. Dropping the liner to the floor next to us, his hand softly came to rest on my skin, right over one of the largest scars on my body, and it took everything I had—every single ounce of restraint—not to flinch.

Besides my doctors and myself, no one, not even Dan, had ever touched the patchwork skin of what remained of my left leg.

Only him.

"This," he said, flexing his fingers lightly, "makes you even more beautiful. Because you survived. Not even that, you're *thriving*. You didn't let losing a leg stop you from living your life. You didn't let it turn you bitter and cynical. You still look for the good in life. I'm in awe of you, Caroline."

I couldn't breathe. Couldn't speak. So I kissed him instead. It wasn't like the kisses earlier, stoked by lust and need. It was calm and slow, but it said everything that I couldn't. Things like, *"Thank you,"* and, *"I could fall in love with you."*

In fact, I was probably already halfway there.

After a minute he pulled away and stood to strip off his jeans and t-shirt. I let my eyes trail over every inch of skin that wasn't covered by his black boxer briefs, soaking in the smooth flesh stretched over corded muscles. Until he laughed, I didn't even notice that he'd stopped moving to stand, nearly naked, three feet from the bed. My eyes lifted to find him watching me.

"You done staring, or should I stand here some more?"

I grinned despite the burn spreading across my cheeks. "Just give me a slow turn, and I'll be all set."

He laughed but did as I'd asked, spinning in a patient circle for my perusal, and my grin stretched even wider. Once he'd turned back to face me (taking away the glorious view of his fantastic ass covered by only a thin layer of black cotton), his crinkled eyes came back to mine.

"Good?"

I nodded, and then he was dropping to the mattress next to me. I scooted over to press myself against the wall, and together we pulled the covers down far enough to slide underneath them. Once they were settled on top of us, his arms reached out to wrap around me, and then I was being pulled into his side. I hid my smile in his neck as he settled me against the warmth of his body, and I let one of my hands trail softly up to rest on his rippled stomach.

The overhead light was off, and the room was bathed in a soft glow that illuminated the three small freckles that dotted his chest. My finger traced a path between the marks and then traveled to the ridges that punctuated his abdomen. He let me explore the lines for a few moments before his stomach tightened, and his hand lightly grabbed mine.

"Ticklish?"

"Horribly ticklish," he answered. "I get violent."

I smiled against the plane of his chest. "Nate is too. I used to torture him when we were younger."

I heard a quiet hum before, "How'd you guys meet?"

"My home town was really small, so when I decided I wanted to play hockey, there wasn't anywhere nearby for me to go. None of the youth leagues had a team for girls that was closer than 100 miles from my house.

"My mom refused to accept that. She's all about equal opportunities for women and all that jazz, so she petitioned our local league to start a team for girls. When they told her there wasn't enough interest, she threatened a lawsuit until they agreed to let me play with the boys.

"I still remember my first practice. I showed up—this tiny little girl with all these bigger boys who thought I was just a joke. They didn't know I'd been skating for three years by then. They didn't know that I watched hockey games like other kids watched Barney.

"This one kid, he was a good foot taller than me and probably outweighed me by about fifteen pounds. He looked at me before we got on the ice and said, 'Girls can't play hockey with boys. They're not tough enough.'

"So, to prove him wrong, I tackled him. Got in a couple good hits too. The coach had to separate us, and we both had to sit out of practice as punishment.

Somehow, by the end of the night, he'd become my best friend."

"Wow," he said softly, and I could hear the smile in his voice. "So you've been putting Nate in his place for years?"

"I like to think I'm helping to make him a better person. But, yes, I'm not afraid to call him out when he's being an asshole."

"That's nice to hear. I'm glad it's not just me."

Pushing up onto one elbow, I levered my head off his chest and turned to find his eyes. The content smile on his relaxed face settled into my gut like a shot of morphine, warm and slow and soothing.

"I have to admit, I'm glad too," I told him honestly. "I can't regret anything that got us to where we are right now."

When his eyes darkened, I knew he understood the full implication of my admission. One hand lifted to curve around my jaw, and his thumb reached out to stroke my cheekbone. "Everything happens for a reason, right?"

I nodded slowly. Then, just because I finally, *finally* could, I dropped my lips to his and kissed him again.

## Chapter Twenty Four

*Jimmy*

WAKING UP PRESSED TO CAROLINE for the first time was an experience I would never forget. The room was dark when I opened my eyes, surprising me a little. After our talk about Nate the night before, we'd spent another couple of glorious hours doing a lot less talking and a lot more touching. And kissing. And tasting. By the time we'd both passed out, it had been well after midnight, and I'd expected to sleep late into the morning.

That seemed not to be the case as I glanced around the darkened room and took in my surroundings. And by surroundings, I mean the girl fastened to my side like she was worried I would disappear. Her head rested on my shoulder, tucked into the curve of my neck, and her weight was piled more on me than on the mattress. One arm was securely draped over my abdomen, and her good leg wrapped around both of mine like ivy.

She wasn't the only one holding on tightly. My arm snaked around her waist, and my fingers gripped her hip like she was a lifeline.

Something about the simple act of watching her sleep put me at ease, and I didn't dare risk moving a single muscle; I didn't want to disturb her at all.

I have no idea how long I laid in bed, just watching her take slow, steady breaths, but the sun was scattering its first rays across the floor by the time she stirred and slowly lifted sleepy eyes to me. The smile that broke across her face the second her gaze found mine shot straight into my chest like a bolt of lightning.

"Hey." Her throaty whisper was sleep-filled and sexy as all fuck. I resisted the urge to press my mouth against hers.

"Morning."

"Did you sleep okay?" she asked quietly, and I nodded.

"Did you?"

Her lip tucked between her teeth as she nodded. "I slept great, actually."

"Good," I grinned and tried to drop my head for a kiss, but she pulled away and slapped her palm to her mouth.

"No! I have morning breath!"

I rolled my eyes and moved quickly, swinging my weight up onto my forearms, which pressed into the bed on either side of her head. Her upper body stilled, frozen in place even as her thighs parted to welcome my hips between them. But she didn't move her hands from her mouth.

"Kiss me, Caroline," I demanded quietly, allowing no more than a two millimeter tilt to my lips. She shook her head quickly, pressing her fingers even more firmly against her mouth, but I could see the smile in her eyes as they sparkled up at me. She mumbled something softly, her eyes dropping quickly to my mouth before sliding back up just as fast. Arching one eyebrow, I watched her eyes crinkle with more humor, but I ignored it and pushed up to my hands and knees before dropping back onto my heels.

"Fine, then I'll just have to kiss you."

Holding her gaze the entire time, which had turned slightly cautious, I slowly brought my hands to the waistband of the shorts she was wearing. I watched her chest start to heave as I gently tugged the fabric down. It slid easily along the bedding despite her weight on top of it, but I didn't drop my eyes to what I was revealing. My eyes stayed focused on hers, noting her reaction through the periphery — the flush of her cheeks where they peeked out from behind her fingertips; the way her chest moved with quick, frantic breaths. She hadn't stopped me yet, and that was enough to fuel my hands through the final few inches.

Once I had carefully pulled the shorts off and tossed them to the ground, I finally dropped my eyes from hers. Resting back on my heels, I trailed my gaze over the smooth, unblemished skin of her right leg, the rippled skin of her left, and the black underwear that sat above them both. From there, my eyes kept moving to the scars that ran along her left side. When my gaze collided with the hem of the t-shirt she was wearing, I gripped it between my fingers and tugged it up until she was forced to lean forward and lift her arms. The motion had the added bonus of finally removing her hands from her mouth. Once the shirt was off, I dropped it to join the discarded shorts on the ground.

She settled back against the mattress, hair spread across the pillow and legs widened just enough to accommodate my body between them, in nothing but simple black underwear, and I couldn't breathe. The sight of her body, stretched out in front of me, was the most incredible thing I'd ever seen.

"You are impossibly beautiful." I didn't even realize I had spoken the words aloud until she shifted slightly. I sensed her discomfort, but I wasn't about to drop the subject. "You might not think so, but you are."

She sighed and brought her eyes to mine, but the brightness from just a few minutes ago was gone. "Trust me, I was better before."

"I don't believe that," I replied quickly, stretching out so my arms were above her shoulders again. "You can't improve perfection."

"Oh, God," she groaned, but I saw the hint of a smile touch her lips. "This is never going to work if you think I'm perfect."

I grinned and shook my head. "Don't worry about that. Personality wise, you've got your fair share of flaws. I'm just talking physical perfection."

Her look of affronted shock was only slightly ruined by the smirk that curved her lips. "Aren't you supposed to argue with me? Even if it's a lie?"

"That's not our thing," I disagreed. "If anything, we've always been too honest with one another. And, in the spirit of that tradition, I'll just tell you now that you're stubborn, you're occasionally rude, and you're almost obnoxiously oblivious to how absolutely fucking gorgeous you are."

"Well, you're stubborn, too," she parried. "And you like to avoid problems, and you can occasionally be a hypocritical asshole."

Her cheeks were flushed, and her chest was heaving again, but this time it was with anger. I couldn't help it; I shoved my face into her neck and burst out laughing. She stiffened and held herself as tightly removed as she could while lying under my shaking body.

Once I'd calmed myself, I lifted back up and found her unamused eyes. "This is good. We already know each other's issues. And unless you kick me out of bed right this second, I'm going to assume that all involved parties are acknowledging the aforementioned flaws and choosing to move ahead regardless. Any objections?"

A reluctant smile tugged at her lips, and she shook her head gently. Once I had her agreement, I smiled and shifted back onto my heels. "Good. Then, if you don't mind, I believe I was in the middle of something before you rudely distracted me."

She rolled her eyes, but the earlier tension was gone. I let my hands trail to her thighs before leaning down to press a kiss to her left hipbone, directly over the largest scar on her waist. It branched out from under the black waistband, and I let my lips trail the raised line up to where it ended before reversing my trajectory. I followed the path of the line over the black fabric, picking the trail back up on the other side where it ran down the length of what remained of her thigh. I moved to her other leg and trailed my lips along the inside of her calf, pressing wet kisses into her skin softly as I traveled back up her body, past her knee and up to her good thigh. She shifted restlessly on the bed, and I smiled against her skin before pulling my mouth away.

A quick glance up revealed that her head had fallen back onto the pillow and her eyes had drifted shut, but at the loss of the sensation, her head jerked up, just in time to watch me wrap my mouth around one budded nipple. I sucked it into my mouth, and the keening moan that rattled from her throat caused my dick to harden even further, almost painfully. I wrapped my hand around her other breast while my mouth worked against her skin, and a low, steady flow of words tumbled past her lips too quickly and quietly for me to hear.

Asking her to clarify would have required pulling my mouth off of her, and that was something I just wasn't willing to do.

Instead, I slid my tongue along the swell of her breast and down to her sternum before tracing my way back up the other side. I repeated the process from before, and within minutes her hips were rising off the bed, seeking contact. I took that as my cue and slid my mouth down, over her ribs, to the soft skin of her stomach. I circled my tongue around her belly button and heard her quiet giggle but didn't stop my journey. Once my tongue had reached the skin just above the waistband of her underwear, I grabbed the fabric and tugged it free, finally baring her to me.

Fucking glorious.

The vision of her spread before me frayed what little control I had left, and I dropped my mouth to her eagerly, consuming her like she was a cool drink of water and I'd been stranded in the desert for years. I was absolutely voracious.

I'm not going to pretend that going down on a girl was my favorite activity. At least, it never had been before. But there was something about being between Caroline's legs that affected me like nothing else ever had. Every noise she made, every restless movement... It was like the ultimate aphrodisiac. I was painfully hard by the time I added two fingers to what my mouth was doing. Then she was shaking and crying out and coming on my face and I never wanted it to end.

I pulled away slowly, wiping an arm across my mouth before crawling back up over her body. I dropped what was meant to be a quick kiss against her lips, but, in the aftermath of her orgasm, her supposed morning breath was completely forgotten. Her tongue darted out to find mine, and her hands wrapped securely around my neck, anchoring my mouth to hers in a wet exploration, a slow but heated perusal of my mouth.

I couldn't stop the groan that rumbled from my throat when she hooked her calf around my thigh, tugging my hips into hers. *Fuck*.

"Caro," I groaned against her mouth, trying to keep this from going too far. I wasn't going to push her for anything more until she was ready.

"Please tell me you have condoms," she breathed, and I quickly pulled my mouth from hers to scan her face. Besides a small pout that appeared when I dodged her attempts to reattach her mouth to mine, she seemed completely serious, and I was suddenly really fucking upset that I wasn't a normal, twenty-one-year-old guy who always carried a condom, just in case. I had never needed that insurance, and now I was really regretting it.

I shook my head slowly, but before I could say a word, her eyes flew open, and she grinned. "Oh my God. I totally have condoms."

I eyed her curiously, tilting my head. "From the look on your face, I'm not sure I want to know why."

Her body shook with silent laughter as she slid across the bed, pushing my arm out of the way to reach into the top drawer of her nightstand. She haphazardly shuffled through the contents before pulling out a foil square and returning to me. "Dickhead Dan had them in his bag, and I kind of stole them before I put his shit out in the hallway."

"Seems fair," I acknowledged with a shrug.

"No," she argued, pushing the condom into my hand. Her hands dropped to the band of my boxer briefs, and she eagerly pulled them down. "Fair will be having sex with you using condoms that he generously donated."

I started to respond, but her hand wrapped around me tightly before sliding up and back down slowly. The sensation tore the words from my throat, and I dropped my forehead against hers carefully.

"I want you," she whispered softly. "Please."
The gentle request staggered me. I wasn't about to
admit it, but she could have asked for the world in
that quiet, imploring tone, and I would have broken
my back to give it to her.

It took a few short seconds to get my briefs the
rest of the way off and the condom open and on. Her
hands grabbed at my hips and pulled along my back,
tugging me down to her, and then, with one quick
thrust, I sank fully inside.

The motion elicited near matching groans
from both of us, and I froze, memorizing every single
nuance of this moment—her face, mouth dropped
open and cheeks flushed; her hands, gripping my
back tightly as if she never wanted to let go. Most
spectacularly, the feel of her, wet and warm, wrapped
around me.

I never wanted to be anywhere else.

Finally, when I couldn't take it anymore, I
moved, and our actions became completely
instinctual. It was like she had been created solely for
me; when I moved, she matched it. When I needed
something, she somehow just knew to give it to me. I
had no idea how, but we connected like we had done
it a thousand times, like we knew each other inside
and out.

Never before had sex been *this* good.

For as long as it had been since I'd been with
anyone, I managed to hold off my own orgasm
astonishingly well. That said, as soon as I felt her start
to tighten around me, felt her body shaking and
heard the sounds I was beginning to recognize (and

crave), my final shred of control snapped, and I pounded into her—fast, hard, and deep. I followed her quickly over the edge in the most intense orgasm of my life and collapsed, shaking against her body.

I would have been embarrassed by my reaction if I hadn't felt her legs trembling just as badly against my hips, if I couldn't hear the frantic pounding of her heart telling me it had been just as monumental for her as it had been for me. I gave myself a long minute to catch my breath before pushing up onto my arms, pulling out and away to dispose of the condom. Before I could get far, though, she latched onto my torso, pulling my weight back down onto her.

"I'm gonna crush you," I mumbled into her collarbone, a lazy smile stretching across my lips. I felt her shake her head, but she didn't reply except to wrap her arms tighter around me. Something about the gesture had my heart beating a little bit harder, even as something in me settled. I brought one hand to the base of her neck and wrapped my fingers around it carefully, rubbing my thumb against her skin gently. For a few quiet minutes, neither of us spoke, but that didn't mean we weren't communicating.

In fact, I heard every single word she didn't say.

Chapter Twenty Five

# Caroline

WITH THE EXCEPTION OF TWO trips to the kitchen and a few short bathroom breaks, Jimmy and I didn't leave my bed at all on Friday. Also, that day was officially the best I'd ever had.

There was lots of sex. Incredible sex. Amazing sex. Superlative sex.

I cannot stress enough how fucking good the sex was.

It was a relief in more ways than one.

We did more than just have great sex, though. We also talked—a lot. I told Jimmy about Mom and Steve, about my younger half-brother and my older step-sister. When he asked me what home had been like, I told him about my two drastically different experiences, both pre- and post-accident. He seemed to understand why I had been so keen to get away from Michigan and all the people I'd grown up around.

I'd asked about his family, and he told me all about his parents and Jack. He said Jack had been diagnosed at age four, and Jimmy, only twelve at the time, had struggled to understand what it meant. He also told me how much Jack had improved, how much he'd grown, and how much brighter his future looked when compared to what the doctors had initially told their family to expect. But he also told me, in an absolutely heartbreaking voice, how much he worried about the future Jack had to look forward to, how scared he was that Jack wouldn't be able to live the life he deserved, or even wanted.

I worried that Jimmy placed a little too much pressure on himself when it came to his brother's happiness, but, at the same time, I didn't know how it felt to worry about a siblings' future, about their limitations, and about the way the world would treat them. Regardless, I didn't want Jimmy to bear that responsibility alone, but I wasn't sure there was a whole lot I could do about it.

I half expected him to stay another night, which I would have welcomed enthusiastically, but by the time the sunlight streaming through my window had faded, he climbed from the bed and started throwing his rumpled clothes back on. I thought about putting on my leg but decided against it. Days that I could go completely legless were rare but treasured commodities, and I figured since I'd made it this far, I was going to enjoy the break. At my request, Jimmy helpfully tossed me a pair of shorts and a fresh shirt from my dresser, and I pulled them on hastily before grabbing my crutches from the wall.

I didn't question the smile that curved his lips as we headed out into the living room, mostly because I was too caught off guard by the sight of both Nate and Jen seated on the couch playing a video game that was quickly paused at our entrance.

"Well, what do you know?" Nate commented, turning his gaze to Jen instead of us. "They're alive."

Jen chuckled and nodded in greeting at Jimmy and I, but I ignored it to glare at the back of Nate's head. "Why are you even here?"

He chuckled and un-paused the game, leaving Jen to claw for the controller she'd dropped in her lap while she cursed my annoying friend. "I just came for the PlayStation."

I rolled my eyes and crutched to the front door, leaving Jimmy to follow behind. I heard him direct a goodbye toward the couch before he traced my steps, only coming to a halt when his chest brushed mine. I felt his hands land on my hips, and his eyes locked with mine as a small smile grew on his lips.

"Thank you." My brow crinkled, and he clarified, "For today." Before I could brush off the sentiment, his mouth descended, and my breath was stolen by his lips against mine. The kiss he gave me was devastating, setting fire to my insides and burning through every thought in my mind. When he finally pulled away, I swayed in his direction dazedly, and his fingers tightened just enough to keep me standing. "I'll call, okay?"

I nodded distractedly as his head dropped once again, this time to press a firm kiss against my forehead. Then he pulled away, opened the door, and disappeared behind it.

Eyes vacantly staring at the closed door, I stood balanced between the crutches for a full minute after he'd left. It didn't make sense, and it scared me a little, but I already missed him. I was already anticipating the next time I could see him and that was just... crazy.

I was in the process of willing the sensation away when Nate's voice echoed through the apartment, "You alright over there, Care Bear?"

With one last shake of my head, I turned and headed back into the room. Once I was able to place my hands against the back of the couch, I carelessly dropped the crutches from under my arms and pitched myself over into the space between Nate's back and the couch. From there, I used my weight to shove him forcefully onto the floor before stretching out across the seat he'd been in. Jen laughed from her spot near my foot as he turned to glare at both of us, game controller dropped and forgotten on the floor by his knee.

"I told you not to call me that," I said in response to the look on his face. I took his silence as acknowledgment of my point and let my lips tip up as he pushed himself up off the floor. With one hand he lifted my calf and then flopped to the cushions beneath it, throwing his empty arm around Jen's shoulders comfortably as he settled in with my foot in his lap. I raised one eyebrow curiously, but he steadfastly ignored me by training his eyes on the game that Jen was now playing alone.

"So?" His question came after a minute and a half of relative silence, ruined only by the sound effects that quietly surged from the TV as Jen continued to ignore us both by focusing on the NPCs she was mass-murdering.

"So what?"

He sighed and turned to face me. "Don't play stupid, Caroline."

"Then don't ask stupid questions that don't actually mean anything. If you want to know something, ask."

"Okay. Are you two together now?"

*Good question.* I chewed my lip and considered it carefully. Despite all the talking we'd done, Jimmy and I hadn't actually discussed what was happening between us, which, in retrospect, might have been an unfortunate oversight. I mean, it's generally considered wise to discuss the parameters of your relationship (or non-relationship, as it may be) before you engage in eighteen hours' worth of frisky business.

My internal monologue stuttered over that phrase, and I giggled, completely losing my train of thought.

"Do you think someone has already re-made Risky Business into a porno? Cause, I mean, come on," I said, turning toward Nate, who was staring at me like I'd completely lost my mind. "You don't even need to change the plot. Fill a house with people, tape them all getting it on, and call it Frisky Business. Simple, but absolutely genius."

Jen paused her game to collapse into Nate's chest, holding her side as the bellows of laughter burst from her mouth.

Nate wasn't nearly as amused. "Did an entire day of sex kill your ability to think about anything else?"

I smirked because, if that was even possible, I figured Jimmy would be the one to pull it off. "Ha ha, Nathaniel."

"Seriously, Caroline." He was undeterred. "What's going on with you two? And, more importantly, what's up with his girlfriend?"

I sobered and met his eyes as Jen finally collected herself. Instead of starting the game, she turned further into Nate's side, and then they were both staring at me contemplatively, waiting for my answer.

"They broke up, and, honestly, I'm not sure."

"How are you not sure?" Nate asked skeptically.

"I mean, yeah, we had sex, but we didn't talk about what it meant."

Jen pulled her lip into her mouth and dropped her eyes, which I didn't read as a good sign. I also wasn't crazy about the sigh Nate blew out, so I attempted to appease them both. "Look, I appreciate your guys' concern, but it's really not necessary. This isn't that serious."

"I don't know, Caro," Nate said carefully. "I mean, the guy did end a four-year relationship for you."

"No, he didn't." I shook my head because this was something we had talked about. "I asked what happened. He said they both just agreed that it wasn't really working anymore. It wasn't about me."

Nate looked unconvinced, and Jen still steadfastly avoided my eyes. "If you say so." I sighed, but he continued quickly. "Look, all I'm saying is that you should probably make sure you guys are on the same page, whatever that page is." He paused and considered me thoughtfully. "Do you even want a relationship right now?"

I frowned and shook my head gently. "It's not a relationship."

"Says you," he parried.

I groaned and dropped my head back to the couch. "Point taken, Nate. I'll talk to him. Not that I wasn't already going to."

"Hey," he said quietly, squeezing my ankle gently. I lifted up to find him staring at me, a gentle expression on his face. "I'm not trying to be a jerk. I'm your best friend, and I'm allowed to worry. I just want to make sure you're okay."

"I know," I nodded and mustered up a small smile. "But I am, really."

"Then okay." He turned toward the image frozen on the TV and sighed. "I'm bored. We should do something."

I looked to Jen and was surprised to see her nodding against him. Then again, at this point, I was learning to expect the unexpected when it came to my friend and my roommate. Since I hadn't done anything all day and figured it really wouldn't hurt to get out of the apartment, I gave up my hope for a legless day and agreed as well. After fumbling for my crutches over the back of the couch, I headed toward my room to get dressed.

After a quick stop through a nearby drive-through for a giant box of chicken nuggets and a healthy (or unhealthy, depending on the way you viewed it) number of French fries, Jen used her long list of cell phone contacts to find out what was happening across campus while Nate drove and I munched quietly in the backseat. The radio stuttered faintly in the background, but I wasn't focused enough to know what song was playing. My mind was going over everything that had happened over the past twenty-four hours, up to and including my conversation with Nate.

He hadn't been wrong. I really didn't want a relationship, at least not right now. More specifically, I didn't want a relationship with Jimmy right now. That's not to say I didn't love being around him and everything that had happened between us, because I absolutely did.

The problem was that I didn't know what he wanted. Worse than that, I still worried that he didn't know what he wanted. He might have realized that his relationship with Maddie existed for all the wrong reasons, but that didn't mean he'd learned what the right reasons actually were. And I wasn't about to become another Maddie—another stop-gap solution to the greater problem of his life.

So, I was just going to talk to him and explain that I liked where we were headed—wherever that was. But where it was not headed was a relationship. Or at least not a relationship anytime soon. I was fine with what we'd done and what we'd shared. Fine wasn't even the word; I'd loved every second we had spent together, and I wanted more of that. But for both our sakes, that was all I was willing to give. That was all I was willing to *take*.

Since my thoughts were heavy, not to mention somewhat irrelevant until I did what I needed to do (namely, talk to him), I pushed them away as Jen started spouting off directions to a party at a house off campus. I focused on my food and the car, as well as its occupants, and forced each of my concerns about my non-relationship with Jimmy to the back of my mind. Tonight was about being out with my friends, my normal, benefits-not-included friends, and I wasn't going to let anything—or anyone—ruin that, even, or maybe especially, Jimmy.

As it turned out, Jimmy wasn't the one I needed to worry about.

The rest of the ride had been good. The walk to the house had been good. Our first hour at the house was also good. Jen had agreed to drive home, so Nate and I were both partaking of the keg, and we may have been doing so slowly, but we were both doing it steadily. This meant that I was definitely buzzed—probably closer to drunk—by the time Nate dropped his empty cup on a table and started attempting to pull Jen toward the dance floor. Admittedly, this dance floor was more of an empty space in the middle of the living room, currently packed with swaying and writhing forms moving in the stuttering strobe light. The song was fast but overtly sexual, and from what I saw at the edges of the crowd, the dancing bodies were really getting into the music.

Jen must have seen it too because she laughed and wormed her hand out of Nate's grip. He gave it two more tries, but since Nate was probably drunk too, she dodged him easily, tempering the rejection with a wide smile. I didn't have time to process this because before I could grin at him along with her, his arm was around my waist, my cup was gone from my hand, and we were moving across the floor.

My surprised shriek turned into laughter as he pulled us through the crowd, but it died quickly for me to murmur his name in a low tone, one that he recognized.

"Shut up, Caro," he replied, pulling me around and into his arms, "and dance with me."

I was drunk. I was with my friends. I was having a good time, and that good time had not yet been tainted by a drunk, cheating boyfriend or an emotionally intense non-boyfriend or any of the other kinds of drama that somehow always followed me to parties.

Fuck it.

I was going to dance with my best friend.

So I did exactly that.

And she didn't know it, but Jen was really missing out.

Nate was a fantastic dancer. This was not news to me, as Nate and I had danced together quite a lot over the years. He had such an intense control over his body and the way it moved, which not only made him an excellent dance partner, it was also one of the things that made him as good as he was on the ice. But, like his natural hockey ability, his ability to dance had been honed, not by a coach but by a mother who'd been a dancer her entire life. She was a woman who spent her nights after dinner listening to music and grabbing anyone in reach to dance with. Throughout our childhood, this had included, on occasion, me. This had also included, with much more frequency, Nate.

It didn't take long for me to fall into the moment, to sink into the music and the pulsing light that turned my surroundings into a stop-motion film. My mind went blank as he moved against and with me, pushing me away and pulling me back in the little space we had. I didn't think about the people I brushed elbows with. I didn't think about my life or my problems or anything that existed outside of this small circle of carefree happiness.

I wasn't a terrible dancer. Well, I hadn't been. I, like Nate, knew how to move and control my body, and I knew how to settle into the tempo. I knew how to lose myself in the rhythm, to really feel the emotion in the music and move my body to match it. And sure, I hadn't danced since the accident, and some of my steps were awkward and a little unbalanced, but I barely even noticed. I moved with Nate like I had always moved with Nate: freely, without thought or concern for how I looked or what I did, without thinking about anything more than an instinctual knowledge of what came next, and next, and next.

For what couldn't have been more than two minutes, but what felt like an hour, I got back the feeling I'd been desperately missing for the last two years. The feeling that had only ever come when I stepped onto the ice, skating away from the real world and into a world where I was in control.

By the time the song had ended, my face was stretched into a wide grin, and I was soaring. I was practically giddy. So much so, that when the next song started, a slow song that had the dance floor thinning considerably around us, I didn't object when Nate pulled me back into his arms, resting his forehead lightly against mine before he started swaying gently. I went willingly, folding into an embrace that had been there for so long, an embrace that had been nothing but steady and safe for almost my entire life. An embrace that felt like home. My smile dimmed a little but had by no means faded when I felt his head lift, and I pulled back to meet his eyes.

"Are you happy here?" His question was softly spoken, and I read the words from his lips more than I heard them over the pumping of the bass, the droning beat covering the sound of our conversation. I scanned his face and noticed a heaviness there that didn't look like Nate's normal drunken sappiness, something which, although it didn't come out that frequently, wouldn't have been unprecedented. It looked like something else entirely, and while I wasn't sure what it actually was, I nodded quickly to reassure him all the same.

"Yeah," I choked out around a voice that had grown thick. "I'm happy."

His eyes scanned my face for a moment, almost distrustfully, and I opened my mouth to question it. Before I could get the words out, though, his gaze traveled over his shoulder, and his jaw grew hard. Then, as proof that I couldn't get through a single night out without something going wrong, I turned out of his tight arms and spotted the reason for his sudden irritation.

Sammi Preston was standing two feet away and staring at us with a strange mixture of malice and glee. The first, I thought, was extreme. The second I didn't understand at all.

"That didn't take long, did it?"

I was trying to decipher the meaning behind that when Nate spoke from behind me, his voice low and angry. "You need to get lost, now."

Sammi laughed and ignored him. "You two are just sad. No wonder Dan was tired of you."

"Seriously, Sammi," Nate urged, again before I could respond. "I did you a fucking favor. A mistake I won't make again. You do this shit, I won't hold her back."

I was silently trying to figure out what he was talking about, what she was talking about, what the *fuck* was going on around me, and I had no clue. Thankfully, she just kept on going.

"I'm not afraid of Caroline, Nate, and I'm even less afraid of you. You've followed this girl around like a lost puppy your entire life, and the way I see it, you should be thanking me. Because of me, you got her," she jerked a thumb toward me without sparing a glance in my direction, "on the rebound, which, let's be honest, was the only way you two were ever going to happen." She smiled, but it was cold and empty.

"It's either really funny or really sad, all things considered."

Nate's hand grabbed onto my arm, trying to pull me away, but I wrested out of his grip and stared at her. My lungs turned to granite in my chest over the four seconds it took me to piece together what she'd said. Well, most of what she'd said. At the very least, I had grasped the basics, and slowly, like the tumblers in a lock turning with a key, I started to understand.

"It was you," I said quietly as Nate once again gently grabbed my arm to pull me away. Once again, I shook his hand loose without taking my eyes off Sammi. Her smug grin had grown, her malicious eyes were dancing, and, God, I wanted to hit her just for being a bitch, but the truth was, she wasn't wrong.

I mean, *yes*, she was wrong, but at the same time, she wasn't.

I smiled. It wasn't wide, it wasn't full of joy, but it was a real smile, and her face fell, just a bit.

"The only person you did a favor was me, so thanks for that. Honestly, Sammi, I wish you and Dan all the best. You two deserve each other."

That brought her smile back in full force, and she looked over my shoulder in Nate's direction for a long moment before chuckling. "As do you two. Really, Nate. I know you've wanted this for a while, so congrats."

With that, and without another glance in my direction, she turned and walked away. I was still staring, still trying to figure out what that last statement meant—and not just that one; there had been quite a few sentences uttered over the course of the two-minute conversation that made zero sense to me. As I started to fit together the other half of the puzzle, I slowly turned toward Nate to catch sight of him shoving his way through the crowd in the opposite direction, moving fast. I took off after him and saw him head straight out of the room before turning into the hall that led to the front door.

It took way longer than it should have to push my way through the bodies, and by the time I had burst through the door and out into the front yard, I had no idea where he was. Thankfully, a quick search along the front of the house revealed him, leaning heavily against the siding, nearly hidden in the shadows.

It might have been anger, it might have been frustration, it might have been fear, but some emotion—something strong and gripping and toxic—fueled the eight fierce steps I took in his direction. Once I was close enough to see his face in the darkness, I crossed my arms over my chest, stuck out a hip, and stared at him for a long, silent moment before opening my mouth. "You knew, didn't you?"

He didn't move, didn't speak—I don't even think he was breathing. Both his fists were clenched tightly, knuckles pressed to the wall at his back, and his head was pointed straight at the ground, eyes open and unblinking.

"Nate-" I started roughly.

His head shot up, and his eyes met mine. The look in them made my mouth snap shut. "Yeah, I knew."

"How?"

He sighed. "Caro-"

"How, Nate? How did you find out?"

"I knew that night. You and Jen had left. I was at the house and..." He trailed off and dropped his eyes back toward the ground, which only sent blood racing through my veins even faster.

"And?" The word snapped out like the lash of a whip, and his eyes jerked back to mine.

"And I saw them walk in the kitchen together, looking like they'd obviously done what they had just done. I flipped. Dan was freaking the fuck out. He took off, and Sammi and I had a conversation. That's how I knew."

I took a deep breath. Then I took another. Neither one helped to ease the fury flooding my system. They also didn't soothe the sting of betrayal I felt. When I thought I could speak without my voice further giving away the emotion I was sure was plastered across my face, I asked my next question.

"So why didn't you tell me?" I shook my head quickly and swallowed. "Actually, no. Why did you lie to me?"

"Caroline-"

"Why did you lie to me, Nate?"

His lips pressed into an unhappy line, and he held my gaze, strongly, apologetically, but silently. I snapped. I took two quick steps in his direction and shoved my hands into his shoulders, slamming him back into the wall with all the force I had. I saw the breath wheeze out of his lungs, but I didn't hear the accompanying sound because I was too busy shouting.

"Tell me why you lied, Nate!"

"Because she threatened me, okay?!" He took a step in my direction, forcing me back, and continued, voice raised almost as loudly as mine had been. "She has shit... She knows...things about me that I didn't want out there. She told me you had seen them together, but you hadn't seen her. I stupidly agreed to keep quiet, not realizing that she just wanted to deliver that news in person because she's a bitch." He broke off, breathing heavily, eyes scanning my face, and, I could only guess, not liking what he saw.

Not that that was a surprise.

"Caroline-" he started, but I interrupted him once again.

"What does she have?"

"Caroline, listen-" he tried again, ignoring my question entirely, which did nothing but piss me off even more.

"No, Nate, you listen to me. I know…God do I know that I am not a perfect friend. I fuck up—a lot. I can be a bitch—a lot. But I have never, never, stared into your eyes and purposefully misled you. I would never do that to you. No. Matter. What. So right the fuck now, you need to tell me what she has that was so fucking dangerous—so fucking important—that you were willing to risk ruining a lifetime of friendship by lying to my face."

Neither one of us moved. Neither one of us drew in a single breath. I could see him working through his answer in his mind, and I silently begged him to say something, anything, that would make this go away. Anything that would fix this.

I didn't want to be mad at Nate. I downright *hated* being mad at Nate. But I couldn't not be mad about this, so he needed to fix it.

"Please, Nate," I whispered, utterly detesting how broken my voice sounded around those words. "Just tell me."

Another thirty seconds of silence passed, and I was done. I spun for the front of the house and marched quickly away. He didn't say a word, nor did he stop me.

He just let me go.

## Chapter Twenty Six

*Jimmy*

SAYING THAT IT HAD BEEN hard to pull myself out of Caroline's bed to head home would have been an epic understatement. I'd struggled with that decision so much, I had seriously considered spending another night. Once I'd finally convinced myself that it probably wasn't a smart move, I dragged myself out the door. We had a game scheduled for Saturday afternoon, and if I had let myself stay, I wouldn't have gotten nearly enough sleep.

I climbed into my car just after six. The sun had already set, and the sky was clear as stars started to shine against the black. I planned on heading straight home to eat a quick dinner before falling into bed. It was early, but I hadn't gotten more than four hours of sleep the night before, and with all the physical...activities, I figured it would be pretty easy to pass out.

My plan was quickly altered by a lucky run-in with my dad in the driveway. I'd just parked my car when he shared that my mom had made meatloaf. That was all it took to get me in the door.

I ended up spending longer at their house than I meant to, but Jack asked me to stay to play a board game after dinner. One game turned into two, but Mom rescued me from game number three by initiating the battle that would end with Jack heading upstairs to shower and get ready for bed.

I finally got into the apartment a little after eight. After a quick shower of my own, I threw on a pair of shorts and fell into bed.

An hour and a half later, I was still lying wide awake in the dark room, staring unseeing at the ceiling. I'd already picked up and put down my phone at least ten times. As much as I wanted to call Caro, for some reason I wouldn't let myself push the buttons. As much as I wanted to know what she was doing, what she was thinking about, I was also terrified of actually getting those answers. Since I'd left her apartment, she hadn't left my mind, and I was afraid of discovering that I was the only one who couldn't stop wondering what the past twenty-four hours or so had meant for us.

I finally switched on the light and grabbed a textbook from the small desk in my room, attempting to bore myself into unconsciousness with some reading for my macro policies class.

I was rereading the first paragraph for the fifth time when I heard the first tentative knock at my door. I froze, listening hard. It was possible that the quiet thump had been Dad slamming the back door of the house shut, and I was ready to play it off as exactly that when a second knock, decidedly stronger than the first, echoed up the stairs.

Tossing the book onto the nightstand, I climbed from my spot in bed and headed for the door. At ten-thirty at night, I had no idea who would be here. Even though it was stupid, not to mention more than a little reckless, I couldn't beat back the thought—the tiny glimmer of hope—that whispered, "*Maybe it's her.*"

I descended the steps slowly, taking a breath to diffuse the tension thrumming through my shoulders before I put a hand to the lock, flipped it open, and yanked on the door. The air I'd been holding in my lungs punched out in a second when I got a good look at the exact person I'd been hoping to see, looking both incredibly fucking sexy and incredibly fucking pissed.

"Hi," she almost growled. "Can I come in?"

I took a quick step back, pulling the door wide as she stalked through it without another glance in my direction. By the time I'd gotten the door shut and locked and followed her upstairs, she had tossed her coat onto the dining room table and was heading straight for the dark kitchen. Without flipping on the light, she started looking through the cabinets, angrily slamming each one after no more than a two-second glance.

As soon as I stepped into the space, I flicked the switch and saw her jump as light flooded the room. She was staring into another cabinet, and her hand had started to push it closed when I wrapped my fingers around her wrist. I pressed my front along her back, pushing us both forward until her hips were against the counter. Dropping her wrist, I gently grabbed both her hands in mine and spread them flat against the counter. Once I had her still, albeit tense, I pressed my nose into her hair and inhaled deeply, breathing in the subtle smell of summer.

*Fuck.* This was not the time to be fighting against getting hard, with her obviously upset about something. Granted, around Caroline, the space between my head and my dick was practically a war zone. Every single thing she did turned me on, and I lost that fight far more often than I won it.

Forcing my mind back to the situation at hand, I took a breath and pulled my head out of her neck. "I'm not sure my cabinets can handle that kind of abuse. Wanna tell me what you're looking for?"

"I need liquor," was her immediate reply.

I took a deep breath before stepping back. She turned to face me immediately, her arm brushing along the front of my body and, yep, there went another battle.

"What's wrong?" I asked quietly, crossing my arms over my chest in hopes that the movement would distract her from the lower half of my body. These shorts weren't gonna hide shit if I couldn't get it under control. My maneuver only half worked because while it definitely distracted her from anything else, the way she stared at my bare chest wasn't fucking helping at all. I gave her a few seconds to answer, but when she made no move to do anything other than stare, I finally muttered a low, "Caro..."

Her eyes snapped up to mine, and the anger from just a minute ago was gone, replaced by a look that had my mouth going dry. When I licked my lips and her eyes dropped to watch, I had to lock my knees to keep from reclaiming the space between us to pull her into my arms. Thankfully, before my self-control completely snapped, she looked away, to the wall over my shoulder, and the heat in her eyes faded.

I expected the anger to make another appearance, but it never did. Instead, I saw devastation. There were no tears, and she wasn't falling over under the weight of her grief, but the grief was there all the same. I saw it when her eyes slowly came back to mine, open and shining and hurt—so filled with hurt that I started to panic, thinking that someone had to have died.

Again, I said her name. It was almost a whisper, but it echoed like a gunshot across the silent apartment, and she jumped. Dropping her face to the floor, I saw her eyes drift shut and when she finally looked back up, the emotion had faded. It was still there, but she'd hidden some of it, sliced it up and stored the bulk of it to deal with in small doses.

"I decided to go to a party tonight," she finally said, voice coming out more forcefully than I think either one of us had expected. She softened it a bit before continuing, "Why, I have no idea, but trust me, I've officially learned my lesson."

"Who'd you go with?" I asked quietly, praying for the answer to be either Baker or her roommate.

"Nate and Jen."

I took a relieved breath. "So, what happened?"

"Sammi Preston happened." She chewed on her lip for a moment, and I could tell she was preparing to go on, so I stayed quiet. "No, you know what? That's not even fair because, yeah, that bitch is a bitch, but I can't even blame her for this. At the very least, *she* was honest."

I was trying to follow along, but I had no clue who Sammi Preston was, and, more than that, she wasn't making a whole lot of sense.

"Caro, baby, I don't know what you're talking about," I finally told her when she'd fallen silently back into her own thoughts.

"Nate and I got into a fight. It was ugly. I found out he lied to me, and we had words, and..." She shrugged. "They weren't nice ones."

"That sucks."

She made a noise that I thought was supposed to be a laugh, but it fell flat. "Yeah, it does."

I turned toward the fridge and pulled open the cabinet hanging over the top before returning to her with the half-full bottle of whiskey.

"Will this work?"

She gave me a grateful smile and nodded, reaching out a hand to grab the bottle once I had set it on the counter. By the time I had two tumblers out of the cabinet, she had the cap off and was pressing the bottle to her lips, hair falling behind her as her head tipped back.

Shit.

It was bad enough that I was completely obsessed with her neck—watching it stretch and move as she chugged from the bottle affected me the same way I'd been affected by her hands wrapping around my dick not seven hours earlier. To make matters worse, there was something about this girl—

dressed casually in dark blue jeans that hugged her ass like they'd been made for her and a lowcut green shirt that was simple and still the sexiest fucking thing I had ever seen—drinking Jack like it was apple juice.

I was not only in awe, I was more turned on than I had ever been in my life.

Turning to press my hips flat against the counter, I adjusted myself as subtly as possible before she finally dropped the bottle and passed it to me. I grabbed it and focused on pouring a glass and then on throwing it back. Once I'd downed the entire thing, I poured another and filled the other glass before leaving the bottle on the counter. I pressed hers into her hand and grabbed my own before wrapping her fingers in mine and leading her toward the couch. Halfway there, I froze mid-step and decided the couch was too dangerous. Instead, I turned us both toward the dining room table, pulled a chair out for her, and then took the seat caddy-corner from hers.

Once I'd gotten settled and taken a long sip from my glass, I looked up to find her staring at me curiously. "Why are we at the table?"

"Because I want to talk, and I don't think we'll do that if we're on the couch."

"We could try talking in your bed."

At her grin, I smiled but shook my head. "If we get in that bed, I can promise I'll have other things on my mind."

She lifted the glass to her lips and drank half the contents around her smile. Dropping it back to the table, she leaned forward and licked her lips slowly as her arms settled against the table.

"Trust me, James, I'd much rather be thinking about other things right now. And, for the record, I don't want to talk."

I took a quick pull from the glass and then dropped it to lock eyes with her. "Are you okay?"

She stared at me for a long moment, chewing on her lip lightly before releasing it and running her tongue over it once. "No, but I will be."

In two quick swallows, I finished the last of my whiskey and stood, taking a quick step toward her before placing one hand on the back of her neck and the other on her glass. Her head tipped back to follow me, and I slid the glass into her hand gently while giving her neck a soft squeeze. "Talk's over. Drink up."

Her eyes stayed on mine as she lifted the glass to her lips and drained it. I took it from her hand, dropped it to the table, and used my hand on her neck to guide her out of the chair and toward the bedroom. As we made it inside, I felt her shoulders rise under my hand, and I released her to shut the door. By the time I had it closed and had turned back around, she was standing next to the bed, back toward me, face pointed down at the mattress.

I watched her hands move to her shirt, which she lifted slowly, revealing inch after inch of pale skin. I noticed a few scars on the left side of her lower back, but they were small compared to the marks she carried in the front. I barely had time to take in the black lace bra that I really wanted to get a look at before my eyes moved up and caught on something that had my feet moving fast across the room toward her.

She'd just dropped the shirt to the floor when I reached her and pulled her long hair over her shoulder. "Holy fuck, Caro. How did I not see this earlier?"

My hands had landed on the skin at her hips, just above her jeans, but I wasn't even processing how good it felt. All I could focus on was the black ink that stretched across her back, just above her shoulder blades, from the top of one arm to the other. The line jerked up and down to form the steady path of a strong heartbeat as it would appear on a hospital monitor. In between the peaks and valleys, spaced so that one fell over one shoulder blade, one over the other, and one directly over her spine, were the words *I am*, repeated three times.

I knew her head was turned to look at me over her shoulder, but I couldn't drag my eyes away from the black ink, stark against her skin, to meet her eyes. I also couldn't stop myself from lifting a hand to trace one finger over the design. She shivered, but I trailed the entire length before looking to her.

"'*I took a deep breath and listened to the old brag of my heart: I am, I am, I am.*'" She shrugged gently, and one side of her mouth tipped up. "It's from The Bell Jar. It seemed appropriate after the accident, and I've loved Plath since high school."

I knew who Sylvia Plath was, and I even remembered some of her poetry from classes, but I'd never read the book. Ash had read it when we were younger, though, and I'd gotten the CliffsNotes version from him.

"Isn't it about her almost constant and eventually successful attempts to kill herself?"

"No, Esther didn't kill herself. The author did."

I gave her a skeptical look, and she sighed but continued. "Yes, it's about her struggle with mental illness, but, really, it's a story about suffering so deeply that you lose yourself in the process, and then coming out on the other side of that. It's about life and death and rebirth. It's about knowing that bad things happen, but we can still find a way to move on and keep living."

She was breathing hard by the time she'd finished speaking, and I gave her a few moments to settle before I pressed my lips to her shoulder.

"Then it's perfect for you." I dropped a kiss to her neck and heard the soft sigh that fell past her lips as my hands slid to the button of her jeans.

Her hands landed on mine, which had already undone the button and zipper and were now just holding onto the denim loosely. With a slight squeeze, she pulled them away and then spun in my arms before laying her hands against my chest. Standing in front of me, with her hands on my skin, barely half dressed, I couldn't stop myself from bending down to press my mouth against hers. The second my lips hit hers, she latched on and returned the kiss fiercely. My mind went blank for a second, and one hand wrapped around her back, pulling her tightly against me.

Rationally, I knew I should probably back off. I also knew that I really should have done a better job at having that talk earlier. We already had a load of shit that needed to be said, and we were adding more by the minute. Not to mention, I was more than a little afraid she was using sex to block out the bad from her night, and, while I could understand that, it still unnerved me a bit, mostly because, since I had the unfortunate problem of not being able to control myself around her, I didn't know where I stood with her.

That's the part that really killed me.

Still, since I couldn't control myself, when her fingers wrapped around the elastic waistband of my shorts—not even to pull them down, just to steady herself, or maybe to drive me crazy—I couldn't think about anything but getting inside her.

I let my palms skate to her thighs and wrapped my hands around them before urging, "Hold on" against her mouth. She looked at me dazedly, so I moved her hands for her, placing them around my neck before grabbing her thighs again to lift her against me. She giggled as my hands pulled her legs up around my waist, but she listened, tightening her arms and wrapping her good leg securely around my waist. I slid one hand to her ass before crawling into the bed with the other. Her arms held onto my neck, and her head dropped back, hair flowing over the sheets as I carried her up to the pillows.

Once I'd laid her down, my hands dropped to her jeans, and I gently started to work them down her thighs. I got as far as halfway to her knee before her hands brushed mine away and pulled them another three inches to reveal the top of her prosthesis. I watched as she pressed a quarter-sized silver button with her thumb, and then, with a quiet rush of air, she pulled the prosthesis, still in the denim, away from her thigh.

From there, it only took a second to get her other leg out of the pants, which she dropped in a bundle to the floor before lifting her hands to my sides to pull me down. I wasn't about to argue. I dropped until my bare chest hit hers, covered in nothing but a tiny scrap of black lace. My forehead fell to rest against hers, and her eyes stared into mine as I slid a hand into her hair loosely.

"I'm sorry you had a bad night," I muttered quietly, needing to get it out. "But I'm really glad you're here right now."

For a moment, she didn't react. Then, slowly, her lips curved, and one eyebrow crept up. "I thought our talk was over."

I dropped my mouth back to hers and didn't say another word.

Chapter Twenty Seven

# CaroLine

SATURDAY MORNING CAME MUCH TOO early for my liking. I woke up with Jimmy's alarm at 7:30, and once I'd taken two minutes to realize that this was real, not a dream, and he really had set an alarm for 7:30 a.m. on a Saturday, I groaned and shoved my face back into his neck, where it had been when I'd opened my eyes.

"Are you serious right now?"

He laughed at my disgruntled muttering, and his arm around my shoulder gave me a tight squeeze. "I'm sorry. I should have warned you last night."

"Why do you even need to be up this early?"

I felt his lips press against my forehead softly, and I pulled my cheek from his skin to look up at him. His eyes were incredible in the morning—warm, soft, and bright. I'd noticed it yesterday morning too. It was like the moments after waking were his favorite of the entire day. I had yet to see that *exact* look any other time.

"I have a game this afternoon, the last before the break, and I usually go to the athletic center before report time when I can. I was planning on heading over around nine."

I frowned, and his smile somehow grew. "Damn. Is it weird to say that I wanted to spend today the same way we spent yesterday?"

"Trust me," he murmured, rolling suddenly so he was leaning over me with one arm still wrapped around my neck and his knees on either side of my hips, "there's nothing I'd rather do."

His mouth dropped to mine, and I didn't even think about dodging him. The kiss was wet, long, and by the time he had pulled away, my entire body felt like it had been electrified. Heat had pooled low in my belly, and I snuck a quick glance at the clock before looking back up at him.

"How long will it take you to get ready?"

His eyes traced my face in a way that I was starting to recognize. He had done the same thing more than a few times the day before, and, while I didn't know what it meant, I was coming to love it.

The soft look faded, and when his eyes came back to mine, they were smiling. "We have time."

That was the last intelligent thought either one of us expressed for at least an hour. And we made full use of every second of that time.

Jimmy didn't make it to the arena by nine because he didn't drop me off at home until a half hour after that. It wasn't until we had gotten in the car to head toward my apartment that he asked if I would come to the game. I thought about it, and, while part of me wanted to avoid Nate for the foreseeable future, I knew that we needed to talk. I couldn't just leave the status of our friendship in limbo, so I agreed and promised to see him there.

After a kiss that felt much too short, I finally climbed from the car and headed inside, waving from the door to where Jimmy still idled in the lot. He grinned and shook his head before driving away, and I headed down the hall to the apartment.

Jen was on the phone—I guessed in the living room—arguing with someone loudly enough that I could hear her voice as I turned the key in the door. As soon as it had swung open, her eyes shot toward mine from her spot behind the couch, and her voice dropped as she lifted a hand to wave.

"Look, I told you, it's not my job. I have to go. I'll talk to you later." She tapped the screen aggressively and dropped the phone to the couch before looking at me with a sympathetic—emphasis on pathetic—look on her face.

"Hey." I walked straight past her to head into my room, dodging her attempts to make eye contact. I had been hoping that she would take the hint and leave me alone, but I looked up once I'd stopped in front of my dresser to see her watching me from the door.

"You okay?"

I held in the sigh that almost broke loose and nodded. "Yep."

"Look, Caro, I talked to Nate, and he's really upset. I think you should talk to him-"

"I'm going to," I interrupted her as I grabbed clean clothes from the drawers before slamming them shut a little harder than necessary. "I'm going to the game, and I planned to talk to him afterwards."

She looked a little surprised, but she covered it quickly, sliding the sympathy back in place and nodding slowly.

"I'm going to take a shower and get ready," I told her, heading across the floor to stand in front of the door she was still blocking. "Do you want to go?"

"To the game?"

I nodded, and she jerked her head up once before stepping back to let me pass. "Uh, sure. What time is it at?"

"One. We can leave at twelve-thirty."

I barely saw her nod before I escaped into the bathroom and closed the door behind me.

Thankfully, by the time we were walking into the arena, Jen had wiped the sad eyes away, for which I was incredibly grateful. I hadn't been at a game in a few weeks because most of them had been away, and, despite the circumstances, I was excited to be back in the building.

Not to mention, this was the first time I would actually feel like I was allowed to watch Jimmy on the ice, and I was thrilled to get to experience one of his games without the guilt that had until now invariably accompanied it.

Still, as the clock started ticking, my eyes kept flitting to Nate, and the scene from the night before continually crawled into my head. As the first period wound down, the butterflies in my stomach became termites, chewing through the muscle and sinew.

I had racked my brain the entire way to Jimmy's after my conversation with Nate, and I couldn't figure out what Sammi could possibly know, what she could be holding over him. I also couldn't believe there was something he wasn't willing to tell me, something he was so afraid of saying that he'd risk demolishing the very foundation of not just our friendship but my entire life.

I barely remembered my life before Nate became a part of it. For years, he'd been my world. Then I'd started dating Dan, and things changed a bit, but Nate was still the one person I'd always known I couldn't live without. I had always known, no matter where we went or what our lives became, that he would be a constant. He would always be my best friend.

If this managed to turn into the end of Nate and me, I honestly didn't know what I was going to do without him. And while there were a lot of things that I could forgive, lying really wasn't on that list. I needed him to explain it to me; I needed him to tell me what he seemingly wasn't willing to tell me before I could consider moving past this.

The tension of the game didn't help the tension in my mind. The guys played great; that wasn't the problem. Even Jimmy looked better than I'd seen him since the season opener, and I tried not to take a totally unjustified amount of satisfaction from that.

The problem was that the team they played against put up a seriously tough fight. The game was rough, fast, and a pretty even match-up, which led to frustration from players on both sides. As the scoreless game continued into the second period, I found myself wincing more than once as guys got slammed increasingly harder into the boards. Jimmy took one particularly nasty hit a few minutes before the end of the second period, and even though I knew really fucking well how brutal this game could be, I sucked in a breath of both fear and surprise as I watched him skate away from the hit and out of the crease, chasing after the puck.

Just like we had during the first, neither Jen nor I said a word through the second intermission. The energy ramped up when the guys finally streamed back onto the ice. I knew that every single player on both teams was giving it everything they had.

About five minutes in, I watched Nate take a hard hit behind the net, and I saw his elbow shoot backwards into the defender. The puck was gone, sliding into the corner, where Eric Brooks got a hold of it, pulling it back into scoring position. Still, I wasn't watching him line up to shoot for the net because my eyes were locked on Nate and the guy who'd hit him, still standing in the corner of ice, in a quickly deteriorating standoff. Just as the buzzer went off with the score, I watched Nate's fist slam into the defender, and I flew to my feet.

The refs rushed toward them and pulled them apart, but Nate just wouldn't back down, and finally Brooks grabbed his back and hauled him away, throwing him across the ice so hard that Nate lost his balance and went down onto his knees. Quickly and angrily, he picked himself up and headed straight for the edge of the rink, throwing himself onto the bench once he'd gotten around the wall. I watched as he yanked the helmet from his head and threw it at the ground before grabbing a water bottle and lifting it to his mouth, totally ignoring the seriously pissed looks his teammates were sending his way.

An admirable accomplishment, I thought, since even I found it hard to ignore the ire shooting from their eyes, and I was across the room.

They had every right to be pissed, though. On top of the five-minute, one-man advantage he'd just given the opposing team, I also knew he'd be suspended, not just from the rest of this game, but for the next one as well.

Despite the disadvantage, the guys held up well. Jimmy managed to somehow exist in two places at once while the team was a man down, and Oliver Cole deserved a fucking award for some of the saves he pulled off. Still, five minutes was a long time, and with thirty seconds left before getting back to full strength, the opposing mountain of a right wing faked both Collins and Cole to sneak a shot into the net, tying the game up at one to one with about five minutes of regulation time left.

As a player who'd always hated going into overtime, my heart pounded as the clock wound closer and closer to zero. I didn't know what the guys' OT record was like, but, for my own sake, I wanted the game to end as soon as possible. I didn't think my nerves could stand up under the pressure for that much longer.

Unlike the only other goal I'd ever seen him score, I didn't see this one coming. I watched Jimmy break away from his defender clear enough, then I watched the puck sweep across the ice to Soto. Derek spun to get around his match, and I watched the puck shoot back to Jimmy, who was charging toward the net. Before I could blink, the buzzer had sounded, and he was flying away from the zone to celebrate with Soto. A quick glance toward the clock confirmed what I already knew. With barely thirty seconds left, the game was all but wrapped up. Still, the celebration didn't last long. Quickly, the guys lined up, and I watched as they gained control of the puck and held it until the final buzzer sounded.

I was grinning when Jimmy pulled his helmet off and somehow knowing where I was, looked directly at me. His smile was wide, and it eased the nerves in my stomach enough that as the teams headed off the ice, I was able to take one deep, confident breath before he disappeared from sight, taking the comfort with him as the termites burrowed right back in.

The excited, if not exhausted, shouts from the guys as they started to file out of the arena brought another smile to my face ten minutes after Jen and I had gotten outside. She'd finally broken the game-long silence between us to ask, again, if I was okay. I had told her the truth: No, I wasn't. And neither one of us had said another word since.

Jimmy was out the door at the tail end of the first surge of players. I saw him scan the space before his eyes fell on us, and then he bee-lined straight for me. As soon as he was close enough, his hands wrapped around my jaw, and his mouth landed on mine, hard. I melted into the kiss instantly, and by the time he pulled away, my lips felt bruised. Despite the tenderness, they stretched into a wide smile.

"I gotta say," I told him quietly as his forehead came to rest against mine, "you played a fantastic game, McCarthy."

"Damn," he whispered heavily, as a small smile played on his lips. "A compliment from the Mighty Mite. That feels really fucking good."

I started to pull away, not nearly as annoyed with his use of that name as I pretended to be, but before I could gain any distance, his hands were in my hair and his lips were back on mine. This kiss wasn't nearly as hard—didn't contain the quiet desperation that the first had. It was slow and wet and long, and by the time I heard a throat clearing from two feet away, my arms were wrapped around his back, under his open jacket, and I couldn't remember where we were.

A quick glance to the left revealed Nate staring blankly at both of us, and I remembered all too quickly. Jimmy's hands dropped from my neck to give me space, but his fingers wound between mine, keeping me close as I turned to face Nate. I took a breath and felt Jimmy squeeze my hand lightly once, a message that I received loud and clear. He wanted me to know that he was there, that he had my back. As much as I appreciated it, this was something I needed to handle on my own.

"Hey," Nate said before I could find my voice. "Can we talk?"

I nodded and gave Jimmy's hand a quick squeeze back before dropping it to take a step toward Nate. "Yeah, I hoped we would. Do you want to take a walk?"

He nodded and then stepped away from the group as I turned back to face our two-person audience. I addressed Jen first and promised her I'd be home soon, then I stepped back toward Jimmy and lifted up onto my toes, hands gripping his waist for balance, in order to press a quick kiss against his lips. Once I'd dropped back to my feet, I met his eyes and promised to call him later before I turned and walked away to follow Nate.

Despite the fact that he'd asked me to talk, Nate didn't say a word as we headed toward campus. I didn't say a word either, mostly because I had no idea how to start this conversation or, more accurately, how to start it in a way that could possibly lead to a happy ending.

This meant that fifteen minutes passed with us walking but not actually talking, and by the time we'd cleared Greek Row, I was more than a little annoyed. "So, did you actually want to talk, or...?"

His head snapped around to face me, and his eyes narrowed. Instantly, I realized I should have stayed silent. Thankfully, he didn't express the irritation that flooded his face. Instead, his voice was low and rough when he turned away and muttered, "Just hold on. We're almost there."

I had no idea where there was, but I shut my mouth and followed along for another block. We passed a grassy lawn that led to a small park, spotted with bright flowers and a few benches surrounding a tall playground, complete with at least six slides and tons of places to crawl and climb.

Nate led me straight to the playground, and I silently thanked the powers that be that there were no small kids running over the contraption that was definitely not designed for almost-adults our age. I followed him up the most straightforward path to the top of the plastic mountain, and when he dropped his ass onto the highest platform, I slid my back along the plastic wall to sit beside him.

"Do you remember," he said suddenly, not wasting any more time now that we'd apparently arrived at our destination, "the summer before senior year? My senior year," he clarified unnecessarily because as he went on, I knew exactly what he was talking about. "You went to that camp—the hockey camp—and I was so pissed because I wanted to go so badly, and, worse than that, you were going to be gone for three weeks, and I didn't know what to do with myself."

I smiled despite myself because he had pouted for the entire week before I left. Finally, the night before my flight to California, he'd shown up at my window, using the tree that we'd both been using for a decade to sneak in and out of my bedroom to climb inside at one in the morning to apologize for being a jerk. We'd spent at least an hour talking before we both fell asleep in my bed.

It wasn't the first time we had spent a night together, but it was the first and only time he'd ever wrapped me up in his arms and slept with his body pressed to mine.

The memory was a good one, and my smile grew until the words he said next shattered everything I thought I'd ever known.

"That night before you left was the first time I realized how easy it is to hate someone that you love. It was the first time I realized that, as much as I loved you, a part of me hated you, too."

I turned to face him, but his eyes were focused up at the clouds, almost as if he'd forgotten I was there entirely.

"That was the night I realized, no matter how much I loved you, no matter what I did, you would never see me as anything other than your friend. I took that night, and I moved on. I told myself that I'd given up hope, and I decided to just focus on being the best friend I could be. I decided that that needed to be enough."

I'd officially been stunned into silence, not that I needed to say anything. Nate clearly had a lot he had to get off his chest.

"Fast-forward nine months. There was this...bonfire. It was right after graduation, and I... I was a mess, Caro. You were out of the hospital by then, in the chair, and things looked so bad." He took a deep, shaky breath that rattled on its way into his chest. "You were so miserable, so depressed, and it killed me to see you like that, to hear you tell me that you wished you hadn't survived the accident. You have no idea..." His voice broke off, and he took another unsteady breath.

"So, I decided to go to this bonfire, and I got... I was trashed. More drunk than I've ever been. I don't really remember most of the night, but at some point Sammi found me by the water.

"To this day, I have no idea what I told her, but I know that we slept together. And I know that when I woke up on the fucking shore the next morning, two things were missing from my wallet. Two things that I told myself had just fallen out, even though I knew... Somehow I knew she had them."

He fell back into silence, and my mind spun, trying to find any possible response to everything he'd just unloaded onto me. Looking at it as a whole felt too overwhelming—too oppressively massive—to deal with at once, so instead, I decided to start at the end and work backwards. That decision led me to the most logical question. "What did she take?"

He sighed heavily and rubbed his hands across his face before, for the first time since we'd gotten here, his eyes finally met mine. "Two letters. The first I wrote right after we started high school, when I decided that I wanted you to know how I felt. I carried it around for weeks, trying to work up the courage to give it to you. Then you and Dan got together, and I stuck it in my wallet to save because— trust me, Caro—I never in a thousand years thought you guys would last as long as you did. So, I kept it for four fucking years."

I had to swallow, to clear my throat, before I could ask, "And the second?"

"The second..." I heard his heavy exhale, and he dropped his gaze before continuing. "I wrote that one the day I graduated, the day I decided I needed to leave. I couldn't handle..." He shook his head quickly, almost as if to clear it. "I just couldn't handle it. Couldn't handle you. I was going to take off, spend the summer before school in my car trying to... I don't even know what."

Through everything he'd said so far, I'd been almost numb, as if shocked into total apathy. That last piece of information, though, filled my empty spaces with anger that bristled under my skin. "If you were planning on leaving, why did you stay?" I tried to hold back the aggression in my voice, but the thinnest layer of it threaded through the words, underlining the question. I didn't want the anger. I didn't want the aggression. I didn't want this at all.

Right now he wasn't making anything better, and I didn't know how much more I could take.

"I put in my two weeks at work the day after graduation. A week later was the bonfire, and, trust me, after that I was more than ready to go. I worked out my last day and went straight to your house to say goodbye and..."

He took another steadying breath, and I matched it. As hard as I knew this was for him to say, it was just as hard for me to hear. I remembered what I was like when he and Dan had graduated, despite how much I tried not to.

And I tried really fucking hard. That version of myself was—hands down—the absolute worst.

"Dan was there. He was losing his mind. You hadn't been eating, and your mom didn't know what to do; no one knew what to do. He begged me to do something. He told me I was the only one you would listen to, that if I couldn't get through to you, no one could." He shrugged like it was the hardest thing he'd ever done, like his shoulders had become too heavy to lift. "And I knew he was right. I knew that if I walked away, you would keep falling apart until you maybe one day pulled your head out of your ass. So, I stayed."

I knew it wasn't fair to be angry. Nate had given up more than I had even known to help get me back to myself after the accident, and I'd always be grateful for that. Grateful for him. But I felt vulnerable in a way that I never had before, and anger was the easiest thing to cling to when everything else seemed to be falling away.

"Okay. Well, I appreciate that. But if you hated me that much, why did you put off school to stay home with me? Why did you tell me to apply here? I could have stayed in Michigan, and you could have gotten all the distance you needed."

"Things changed again," he said, so quietly I had to strain to hear him. "You started getting better, started getting back to yourself. I watched it happen, and I knew I had been the one to get you there. I realized that it didn't matter how you felt about me; all that mattered was that you needed me. And, in a lot of ways, I needed you, too. You've always been the one I've relied on to make me feel...important. You make me feel like someone would miss me if I wasn't around, and I was able to get over everything else because that was enough."

I chewed on my lip and searched for something to say, but my thoughts swirled into and out of my consciousness so fast—too fast for me to grab onto any single one of them. The only thing I fully knew was that I knew absolutely nothing.

"Nate-" I started slowly, but he cut me off quickly.

"The thing you need to understand is that I never thought... I told myself I was over it. Over you. And for the most part, I am. I know what we are, and I know that's all we'll ever be. I know you don't look at me the way you look at Jimmy, like I'm the air you need to breathe. You don't even look at me the way you used to look at Dan, and I get it. Maybe I should have told you sooner. Maybe I should have told you in fucking high school, but I can't say I wish I had. I'm glad I got to spend the past two years—fuck, the past sixteen years—with you, even if I had to lie or keep things from you to do it.

"Still, I'm sorry I hurt you because that was never my intention. I'm sorry for keeping things from you, things that I should have been the one to tell you. You need to know that, no matter what, I love you. You are and always have been my best friend, even when it was hard.

"And I'm sure you're probably mad beyond all reason, so this is probably going to sound crazy, but I need time, Caro. Time away from you."

"Nate-"

"And I'm sure you need time too," he continued, pushing up to his feet quickly. "I just think we both need to get some space. I'm just... I'm not in a good place right now, and I need to sort out my head while I figure shit out."

He started to shuffle toward the stairs, and I climbed to my feet as fast as possible. As I straightened, he paused and turned back toward me. "I promise I'll figure it out as fast as I can."

Taking the wide stairs at close to a run, he made it to the grass and then headed toward the sidewalk, walking away from me without even a second glance.

## Chapter Twenty Eight

*Jimmy*

THE LAST MONTH HAD BEEN, in a word, strange.

Strange in the sense that, while nothing was technically wrong, I was constantly waiting for the other shoe to drop. I felt something coming, something big and ugly, but I had no clue what it was. And since I didn't know what it was, I had no way to prepare for it.

Caroline had been Caroline but *less*, somehow, since her fight with Nate. We had talked about it at length in the days following their...breakup, for lack of a better word, and she had sworn, repeatedly, that she was fine, but I knew their conversation—and his confessions—had rocked her. The constant energy— the pure liveliness that she radiated all the time—had dimmed, and I didn't know how to coax it back to full strength. That didn't mean I wasn't trying. It was just that nothing I'd tried so far had worked.

Besides that, though, things were good between us. We spent as much time as we could together, which admittedly wasn't as much as I would have liked. Still, between hockey, work, Jack, school, and finding time for Caroline, I was running on empty.

I had been looking forward to the holiday break for a few reasons, the least of which had to do with getting away from classes until the new year. I was also looking forward to a break from hockey because our last game—the one we'd barely managed to win two days after Thanksgiving—had turned me into a walking, talking bruise for a week.

More than any of that, though, I was looking forward to spending seven uninterrupted days with Caroline between Christmas and New Year's. Since I was a kid, Dad had shut down the rink for the entire holiday week, and I planned on spending every second of my time of zero responsibilities with the girl who continued to work her way deeper and deeper under my skin every single time I saw her.

I was so excited, in fact, that when Caroline told me she had decided to head home for a week to spend the holidays with her family, it hit me like a physical blow. As disappointed as I was, I managed to keep my reaction to myself, and the two days before her flight had been as close to heaven on earth as I imagined you could get while still living.

Then I'd driven her to the airport, given her a kiss, and told her to have a good flight before waving goodbye.

That had been two days ago, and the comparison of those two days to the two before them was so stark, it was almost funny. It felt like Caroline had taken the sun with her across the country. The days felt unendingly long, and the nights were almost oppressively empty. As much as I didn't want to admit it out loud, I just wanted her back.

Here's the thing. We'd been having sex for a month now. She'd spent countless nights in my bed, and I'd spent more than a few in hers. We'd even gone to dinner a few times. Small, relationship-type milestones were passed without attention or remark, and, somehow, in all that time, we still hadn't taken a single minute to actually define what was happening between us.

Part of me rationalized that we didn't need to define our relationship. We didn't need to apply labels to whatever we were. We didn't need to box and package our feelings to make them easily understood.

The other part of me was just begging to understand.

I'd tried more than once to bring the subject up. Each time, Caroline brushed me off with a generic statement about living in the now, and then we'd ended up in bed. Or on the couch. Or the floor.

*There was that one time on the stairs too...*

Yeah, we definitely didn't have a problem with the physical part of our...whatever it was. And it wasn't like we didn't talk about anything and everything else. Caroline had no problem telling me about school, home, or her childhood. Every night we spent in bed together, once we had finished losing ourselves in each other, I asked her questions, mostly just to hear her voice. She would talk and talk, and then we'd eventually start round two or both drop off into sleep. I already knew more about Caroline's life than I had ever known about Maddie's, and I still soaked up every new piece of information she chose to share with me. So far, no question had gone unanswered.

Unless it was a question about us.

I'd been really good at distracting myself from how much the whole situation bothered me, at least while I had her in front of me to make up for my lack of certainty. Then she'd gotten on a plane, and all I had left was doubt.

Mom sensed my bad mood at dinner. It was Christmas Eve, and my mom had always loved the night before Christmas more than the actual holiday itself. This was a preference she had passed on to me. There was something about the anticipation that thrilled and excited me more than actually experiencing the day that all the fuss led up to. There was also something about the stillness of Christmas Eve. It was like the world took a collective pause and just let out a breath.

I loved that breath.

It wasn't hard to see that I wasn't myself at dinner. I tried to shake the feeling—tried to pull myself out of the doubtful fog I'd fallen into since Caroline had left the state—but it stabbed at my sanity through dinner and into dessert. It wasn't until Jack started telling me about the caroling he had done the day before with a few school friends that I was able to fully focus on spending time with my family and being thankful for what I actually did have instead of fixating on what I didn't.

From there, the night improved, but Mom continued to glance my way with furrowed eyebrows, searching my face as if what was bothering me would appear, suddenly written across my forehead. I ignored her worried looks as much as possible and focused on Jack, who was more animated than I'd seen him in weeks.

By the time we'd finished dessert and rounded out the night in the living room watching A Muppet Christmas Carol, I felt good—better than I had in days (two to be exact). I headed home, committed to hanging onto that positivity.

Ten minutes later I was struggling. I knew I needed to do something or the fog would roll back in, and the doubt would take back over. My first thought was to call Ash, but I decided against that pretty quickly.

Things were better between him and I. We had finally talked the Monday after Thanksgiving and a few times since then. I had told him about Maddie. I hadn't told him about Caroline. It was partly because I had no idea how to talk about Caroline—no idea how to put the way she made me feel into words. Besides, he'd broken up with his girlfriend and was pretty much constantly miserable, so it had never seemed like a good time to bring up something so...big.

While I wouldn't have minded talking to Ash, I needed to avoid being miserable, and, around him I knew that was an impossibility.

I dialed Marco instead; it rang twice before he answered. "Yo."

"You doing anything?"

"Nah."

"Do you want to do something?"

"Yeah. Come pick me up. I need to get the fuck out of this apartment."

I told him I'd be by in ten before I hung up and headed out the door.

He was waiting by the street when I pulled up to his place nine minutes later, covered in a fine dusting of the light snow that had started falling a few hours earlier. I dropped the phone I'd been reaching for and pulled to the curb, watching as he climbed into the car. He looked rough, like he hadn't slept in days, and the clothes under his open, tattered, black-leather jacket looked like they'd been hanging off his body for at least forty-eight hours. I decided to address that once we had a destination and pulled back out onto the empty street.

"Where to?" I asked, as I made it out of his neighborhood. He directed me toward the highway, and in minutes we were headed east on I-64.

I waited until we had merged onto the empty freeway to speak again. "You know you look like shit, right?"

He chuckled quietly and turned to stare out the window before answering. "Yeah. I didn't get a lot of sleep last night."

"Just last night?"

He didn't respond to my prompt, and we were both quiet for so long that I finally leaned forward and turned on the radio. We had traveled another twenty miles when I looked in his direction again. "Where are we actually going?"

"Just drive."

So much for hoping that Marco would help beat back the doubt. In the near silence of the car, there was nothing to keep it out, and every mile I drove, I felt just a little bit worse.

We'd been driving for half an hour before he finally directed me off the highway and onto a dark road surrounded by nothing but forest. Another five minutes, and he told me to turn onto a tiny road that I wouldn't have even seen if he didn't point it out. A mile later, the road ended abruptly with a cleared space just large enough to turn a car around in before the trees took back over.

I hesitated, hand frozen on the shifter, and turned toward the passenger seat. "Are you sure-"

"Just park the car," he interrupted swiftly, before climbing out into the darkness. I parked, shut off the engine, and then followed him outside. As the headlights faded, I took a minute to allow my eyes to adjust to the dark before zipping my jacket higher against the cold and shuffling toward the noise Marco made as he forged a path into the trees.

I had no fucking clue how he knew where we were going, but I didn't say a word, just kept the dark shadow of his back in my line of sight as we moved through the woods. Five minutes later, I almost killed us both when I walked directly into Marco's back. Unbeknownst to me, he had stopped moving because the ground just ended. Trees, too. They were both there, and then they weren't. Once I made sure neither of us were going to fall to our deaths, I stepped around him and took in the view.

Away from the shadow of the evergreens, the weak light of the moon lit up the valley enough for me to see a gaping hole in the forest below us. Filling that hole was a wide, gleaming, black lake. I barely made out a few cabins and what looked to be a dock at the far side shore, but it was both too dark and too far away for me to see clearly. My eyes fell back to the lake, and I stared at the stars reflected on the calm, clear surface.

When Marco dropped to sit at the edge of the rock, feet hanging over the edge, I carefully lowered myself to the sheet of stone under my feet and sat beside him. The ground was freezing, but the snow had stopped, and none had actually settled on the ground.

We'd both been staring at the landscape below for at least ten minutes when he finally broke a silence so penetrating it would have been eerie any other night of the year.

"This is where we used to hang out." At my sideways glance, he clarified. "Emily and I. She showed it to me, and I loved it."

He took a deep breath and looked down at his lap. "I still come here at least once a week, usually more. It's fucking stupid, but sometimes when I'm here..." His voice trailed off, and he shook his head roughly. "Fuck, I'm sorry."

"No," I said, surprised that he'd mentioned her. "If you need to talk, or get it out, or whatever..."

He smiled appreciatively, but it was sad. "There's nothing left to get out. Trust me. And anyway, you called me, on your favorite day of the year, no less. What's up with you? I don't even know the last time you and I talked."

"Yeah, I, uh... It's been a crazy month and a half."

Who was I kidding? It had been a crazy year.

"How so?"

I let out a low laugh and looked toward him. "How long do you have?"

The sad smile reappeared, and he met my eyes for just a moment before turning back to the view. "I have absolutely nowhere to be and nothing to do until school starts, so I think I have time."

The words came out without a single trace of bitterness, but I knew thoughts of Emily weren't the only thing weighing heavily on his mind tonight. "You and your dad aren't doing anything tomorrow?"

It was his turn to laugh. "Yeah, right. He worked today, and he's spending tomorrow with his girlfriend and her kids. I was specifically told I wasn't invited."

*Fuck.*

"Shit, man. I'm sorry."

"Not your fault he's a dick. And I want to talk about that prick less than I want to talk about Em. Tell me what's going on with you."

I took a breath and leaned back, pressing my palms to the rock where it bled through the forest floor. Once I had tipped my head back to focus on the real stars instead of the reproductions, I felt calm enough to open my mouth.

"Well, for starters, Maddie and I broke up." I felt more than saw him turn toward me, and I hurried on so he couldn't get a word in. "I'm fine, and...it's fine. Honestly, it was seriously fucking overdue. I just didn't realize...a lot of things."

In truth, I had been clueless. I had been so willingly blind, and it had taken meeting Caroline—getting to know her and her worldview—to open my eyes to what I really wanted out of life. And while I was still trying to figure out exactly where I wanted to be in ten years, I knew I didn't want to be just okay. I didn't want to spend my life going through the motions, planning every day, month, and year. I didn't want to follow a course that had been prepared for me.

I wanted to set my own.

"Well," Marco finally said, drawing me out of my head, "then I'm happy for you. We should go out and celebrate your singledom."

I didn't say a word, but my face must have betrayed something because he chuckled. "Wow. Seriously?" He laughed a bit harder before going on without giving me a chance to respond. "I gotta say, man, your serial monogamy is really something else."

"I'm not," I started, shaking my head. "It's not like that. We're not..."

"What?" He pressed when I failed to continue. "Dating? In a relationship?"

I sighed and finally dropped my face to look at him. "Honestly, I have no fucking clue. It feels like a relationship. We do all the things people in relationships do. We're just refusing to actually call it that, I guess."

"Both of you?"

I shrugged. "Mostly her."

It was quiet for a moment as Marco's eyes slid to the view at our feet. Then he huffed out the least amused breath of laughter in history. "Man, if I understood women... Jesus, *fuck*. My life would be unrecognizable from this joke of an existence I'm living right now."

"That's bullshit, dude."

His gaze snapped to me, and before he even opened his mouth, I knew he was pissed.

"You don't have a goddamn clue. Fuck, Jimmy, you have no idea what my life has turned into."

"Then tell me," I returned. "If I'm so clueless, tell me what the fuck is going on with you. You can fucking talk to me."

He stared at me, eyes blazing in the moonlight, tension pouring off his shoulders before, with one deep breath, it all just melted away. I watched it happen, watched the anger slide away, and when his eyes came back to mine, it was like it had never been there at all.

"Just forget I said anything." He pushed himself up off the ledge and turned for the trees. "Come on. We've got a long drive, and I want to get back."

By the time I made it to my feet, he was plunging back into the darkness of the forest. Ignoring the desperate feeling in my gut, the tiny voice that urged me to press him, to figure out what was going on with my friend, I let the conversation die in favor of following his quickly retreating form back to the car.

The only other word Marco spoke for the rest of the night was a quiet, "Later" when I had finally pulled the car to the curb at his place. Without even giving me a chance to respond, he was slamming the car door before jogging into the building.

My drive home was spent trying to come up with a way to help him realize he had so much more going for him than he thought he did. Marco was fucking brilliant, smarter even than Ash, and more than once I had wondered why they had both chosen to go to UVA when their SAT scores alone would have given them their pick of Ivys.

On top of that, though, Marco was a genuinely good guy. He might have made a few bad choices here and there, but he'd dealt with more than his fair share of shit over the years, and he needed to realize that he couldn't treat that as a reflection of himself.

It wasn't until I walked in my front door that I realized how well his issues had worked as a distraction from my own problems. And, of course, as soon as that thought surfaced, I was assaulted by all things Caroline.

After a quick shower, I slid into bed and considered my phone for five minutes before dialing her number. We had exchanged a handful of texts since she'd landed in Michigan, but I hadn't heard her voice in two days and I missed it more than I was willing to admit.

I heard the smile in her, "Hey" when she finally answered after the third ring.

After a quick glance at the clock, confirming what I already knew, I murmured, "Merry Christmas."

She laughed quietly, and the sound shot straight to my dick. "Merry Christmas, James."

Her low voice saying my name, especially when it followed her quiet laughter, was all it took to get me hard. This girl turned me into a sixteen-year-old boy, made me completely unable to control my own body.

I heard movement on the other end of the line, the sound of sheets rustling, and instantly my mind pictured her lying in bed, an image I was intimately acquainted with. In other words, I didn't have to work hard to summon up the visual.

"What are you doing?" Her quiet voice came through the line as I was fighting off the urge to wrap my hand around my dick, and every word was a well-placed shot to my defenses.

"Lying in bed, thinking about you," I answered honestly. "What are you doing?"

I heard a quiet hum before, "Lying in bed, thinking about you." I heard the smile in her tone, and it lingered through, "How was your day?"

"It was okay."

"Just okay?"

I smiled. "It's getting better by the second."

She seemed satisfied with that, so I turned the question around.

"My day was okay," she answered. "Mom and I spent most of it in the kitchen, getting stuff ready for the church thing tomorrow."

She had already told me about the community dinner their church hosted for people who had nowhere to go for the holiday. She'd also told me about how her mom had not only agreed to lend a hand but had guilted Caroline into helping out as well. Caro had grumbled to me about it when she'd found out a few days before leaving, but I also detected a note of appreciation in her voice as she told me how their church community had banded together during the months Caroline spent in the hospital. I knew she was thankful for what they'd done for her mother, who, from what I gathered, had barely managed to hold it together after the accident.

"You say that like it annoys you, but I know how much you like cooking with her."

She sighed softly. "Yeah, you're right. I just... I don't know. I've been kind of...disconnected."

"How come?"

She was quiet for a moment, and I could picture her perfectly; I'd gotten so used to our quiet conversation during the nights we spent together. I knew her pause meant she was considering her words—searching for the truth—and I knew if I could see her face, her eyebrows would be slightly furrowed, her lip sandwiched between her teeth.

"I think," she finally said slowly, "it's just being back here. It feels...unreal. Or maybe I'm the one who's not real." She exhaled a frustrated breath. "Everything is so different from when I left not even six months ago. I'm a completely different person, or at least I feel like one. I just don't really know how the new Caroline fits in Michigan."

My first thought was that she didn't fit in Michigan, not anymore. She didn't belong there. She belonged here, in Virginia and in my arms.

My second thought was that while her circumstances may have changed, she hadn't. Not at all. She was still beautiful. Bold. Occasionally brash. Brilliant. She was vital and fresh and unique. She was fierce—a born fighter—but she still possessed a vulnerability that made me want to protect her, keep her safe and happy and smiling for the rest of my life.

My third thought was, *Holy fuck. I'm in love with her*.

The second I admitted it, even just to myself, my body flooded with the knowledge that this girl was it for me. No matter where she went, I would follow. No matter how she felt, it wouldn't change the fact that I cared about her, loved her, needed her like I had never needed anyone in my life.

Knowing what it felt like to truly believe and accept that I'd met the person I was supposed to spend my life with—I barely suppressed my overbearing urge to laugh. I had never, not once, felt this way about Maddie, the girl I'd been so convinced was my future. Definitely not at the end, but not even at the beginning, when things were good and we were happy.

When I had pictured my life with Maddie, she was filling a role I needed filled. She was playing a part in a scene that I'd constructed, but she didn't define the scene. She wasn't even the focus or the point of my desperate planning. The focus was survival; she was just a tool to achieve that.

Caroline, on the other hand... She was the scene. She was the entire show. She would be the focus of every plan I would make for the rest of my life.

*As long as she lets me...*

"Jimmy?"

Shit. I cleared my throat quickly and tried to clear my mouth of the words that almost desperately wanted to make themselves heard. Entire sentences and questions that started with words like *Are we*, and *Can we*, and *You should know...* There were thousands of reasons why telling her how I felt was a terrible fucking idea, but the only one I really needed was the simple thought of her rejection, the image in my mind of her searching for words to end this thing between us, whatever it was. Because there was a huge difference between living in the present and telling someone you loved them. The very act alone implied a permanence, a future that, while remaining flexible, led to a predetermined destination.

"I think you could fit in anywhere you truly wanted to. That said, I'm happy to hear you didn't decide to move home in the two days since you've been back."

She laughed quietly at that. "Yeah, you don't have to worry about that at all. This place doesn't even feel like home anymore. I'm more than ready to get out of here."

"Well, I'm more than ready to have you back. My bed feels unusually empty without you here hogging the mattress."

"Excuse me?" The affront in her tone brought a grin to my lips. "Half the time I sleep in your bed, you don't even let me feel the mattress. I wake up completely on top of you. And, not that you're not aware, I'm not the one mounting you in my sleep."

I chuckled because she wasn't lying. "I can't help it. I like you there, straddling me and wrapped up in my arms. And don't think for a second I'll believe you if you try to tell me you don't like it just as much as I do."

Based on the way she attacked me every time we woke up like that (which was more than you might expect—unconscious me liked Caroline *close*), I knew for a fact she appreciated the opportunities those mornings presented.

"I'm not going to tell you I don't like it." Her voice had lost the hint of humor from just a minute before, and I braced as she took a breath to continue, so quietly I barely heard the words. "There's not a whole lot about you that I don't like, if I'm honest."

I internally celebrated that revelation like it was a billion-dollar lottery payoff. Since we'd started having sex, I told her how incredible I thought she was. Maybe not all the time, but I did it.

Caroline didn't. In fact, the last thing she'd said to me that even indirectly hinted at the feelings (I hoped) she had for me was when she had told me she had no regrets, and that had been Thanksgiving night.

As my celebration wound down, I took a breath and stuck myself over the ledge I'd been clinging to for weeks.

"I like honest Caroline. And I like that you like me."

I heard her breath hitch and a low hum before, "You want to know what I really like about you?"

I hesitated before answering the question. The tone of her voice—the low, seductive glide of her words—told me that the answer I was going to get wasn't the one I really wanted.

Despite that, I still said yes.

"I really like that thing you do with your fingers when your mouth is between my legs."

*What was I saying about not really wanting this?*

"Oh yeah?" Those two words were gruff, choked, and scratchy, as what felt like not just all the blood but all the liquid in my body headed straight for my dick. I licked my lips and pushed my sweatpants down over my hips just enough to free myself from the cotton. It had been barely two days since I'd been inside her, but it felt like a decade.

Part of me acknowledged what she was doing. A very small, incredibly vulnerable, and impossibly quiet part of me. That part told me to stop letting her use sex to avoid talking about the things she either wasn't willing or wasn't comfortable talking about. It told me I needed to man up and force the issue, pull her out of her head and away from whatever was causing her to keep me at a distance.

The rest of me was too on board with the idea of phone sex to care that this was a piss poor attempt at emotional deflection.

I did what I had gotten so good at doing—not just with Caroline but with all the problems in my life.

It was stupid. It was shortsighted. It was the very epitome of my biggest problem, my largest hurdle on the path toward making myself the better person I desperately wanted to be.

It was all of those things and so many more, but I did it nonetheless.

I decided to worry about it later.

Chapter Twenty Nine

# CaroLine

I HAD KNOWN, EVEN BEFORE leaving Virginia that spending a week at home was going to be tough. That said, if I'd known exactly how hard it would be, I would never have gotten on that plane.

It was a combination of a few factors, really. For starters, in the first two days I spent at home, I had no less than five conversations with Mom about Dan. I had shied away from telling her exactly why we had broken up, and she took each opportunity she could find to pry and prod into the situation. In her mind, after what Dan had done for me post-accident, there was nothing that couldn't be overlooked. She had no idea why I'd chosen to end the "perfect relationship" (her words, not mine), and I just couldn't bring myself to put it all into perspective for her. Instead, I suffered through her endless emotional instigation and assured her that I knew what I was doing.

Which was true, at least as far as Dan was concerned.

When Mom wasn't pressuring me about my ex, she hovered. It was worse than it had been when I'd first been released from the hospital. At least back then, I'd been in such a deep depression, locked so tightly inside my own mind, I had barely noticed her overbearing concern. Now, it wasn't so easy to escape.

In an attempt to set her at ease, I had tried to tell her about my life at school. I tried to explain to her how happy I was, how good I felt (uncertain relationship status and fight with my best friend notwithstanding), and how much I had changed since leaving home.

That plan had failed spectacularly. Instead of relaxing, Mom walked away from the conversation with tears in her eyes, and I had felt even worse than before.

New Caroline didn't belong in Michigan. She had no place here, and every day I spent inside my childhood home, I felt her slipping further and further back inside, like a turtle retreating into its shell. I fought it, tried to hold onto her as tightly as I could, but it was about as effective as trying to grab smoke with my fingers.

It didn't help that I was bored. Even more than bored, I was lonely. I hadn't really stayed friends with any of the people I had grown up with, the people I should have graduated with. I also hadn't been looking to make friends during my second stab at senior year. There was no one for me to call up, no excuse to get out of the house, even if just for an hour. And I really needed to get out of the house.

I knew that the root of most of my anxiety was Nate. I had neither seen nor heard from my best friend since the day at the playground. An entire month with zero contact, whatsoever. While that might not seem so bad to the average person, I hadn't gone an entire month without seeing Nate since I had met him. I barely ever went a day without calling or texting him. He was woven into the very fabric of my life, but now those stitches were crooked, like someone had found a loose string and tugged on it, forcing all the rest out of order.

I had no idea how to fix it.

Hell, I could barely even manage to *think* about fixing it without falling into a self-deprecating circle of depressing thoughts. Tons and tons of what-ifs that meant absolutely nothing because the only reality that mattered was the one I was currently living.

Which was a pretty surreal reality at that. Never once would I have guessed that Nate had anything more than platonic feelings for me. Never once would I have thought that he'd been, at some point, holding out hope that the two of us would end up together. It seemed so strange to me, and I found myself spending hours in my room looking for clues among the many memories. Coming up with question after question, none of which I knew I would ever allow myself to ask.

But despite all that, despite the curiosity and the confusion, more than anything else, I just missed him. I understood where he was coming from, and I respected his need for space. Still, that didn't mean it was easy. Forcing myself to maintain radio silence got harder by the day.

Nate wasn't the only person I was missing, though. I missed Jimmy. I mean, I *really* missed Jimmy. It had only been eight days since I'd last seen him, but those eight days had been much harder than I expected. For the first few days, I'd attempted to blame my out-of-control libido. I'd convinced myself that my sex drive was at fault for the way I couldn't seem to get comfortable. For the past month, Jimmy and I had been having sex nearly non-stop. I kept expecting it to wane, the almost desperate need I felt for him, for the way his body could make me feel. It was a need I struggled with almost constantly. It was also a need I had been indulging in quite regularly. And it was something that I seriously worried I was becoming addicted to. That said, the high was just too intoxicating for me to quit.

Day three was when I realized it wasn't just his body I missed. It was after the phone call. After the orgasm that was almost (but not quite) as good as the ones he gave me in person. After he'd convinced me to stay on the phone until we both fell asleep because, as he'd said, "I don't sleep as well when I can't hear you breathing next to me. If I can't hold you, just let me hear you."

I hadn't even been able to breathe, so there was no way for me to tell him no.

I wasn't able to find my voice after that. Instead, I listened to him speak quietly in my ear, telling me a story about his first out-of-state tournament in high school. I was barely listening to the words he said, too wrapped up in the way his voice rolled over the consonants and vowels. The low rumble of his laugh elicited goosebumps over my skin, and as much as I reveled in the reaction that his voice provoked in me, I was also completely terrified by it.

When his voice petered out mid-story, turning quickly into soft, steady breathing, a rhythm I knew as well as my own heartbeat, I still clung to the phone. I oscillated between panic and denial, and the only moments of relative peace came when I quieted the voices raging in my head to focus on the sound of his even breath. The gentle ebb and flow of air flooding his lungs.

It was in those moments—and only those moments—that I found a tentative calm, one that kept me from breaking apart completely under the weight of my fear. And it was in one of those moments, almost three hours after his voice had drifted away, that I finally slipped into a dark and restless sleep.

Christmas Day passed in a blur that bled into the next forty-eight hours. I wasn't engaged; I wasn't present. I went through the motions and faked a smile and felt so much like Old Caroline that I started seriously considering leaving early, just to get myself out of the rut I'd fallen into. I fought against the urge because I knew once I headed back to Virginia, barring an unforeseen emergency, I wasn't coming back to Michigan for a long time. With that decision made, I decided to give Mom as much time as possible before I got the fuck out of dodge. But despite my determination to hold out for my original departure date, ultimately it was Mom who made the decision that pushed me over the edge and sent me home early.

Jordy and I had stayed up late watching movies the night before, and because of that, I woke up later than usual on New Year's Eve. After a quick trip to the bathroom down the hall, I headed for the stairs and descended to the sound of muted voices coming from the back of the house. Halfway through the hall that led to the kitchen, I froze as recognition filtered through the sleepy haze I'd still been in the process of abandoning.

I stood motionless for another two minutes, listening to the quiet, lighthearted conversation that was punctuated occasionally by Mom's soft laughter, and for the first time in three days, I felt something other than detachment.

The problem was, that *something* was blind rage.

I didn't want to go nuclear in the presence of my mother, despite the fact that she probably deserved a little bit of the fallout herself. I'd save that conversation for later, once I dealt with the problem that required my immediate attention.

Taking a deep breath for fortitude and self-control, I counted backwards from ten and exhaled slowly. Once I felt like I wasn't going to explode all over Mom's shiny kitchen counters, I finished my trip down the hall and walked into the kitchen.

The bastard was sitting at the counter, back to the hall, telling Mom a story about Christmas dinner as I propped myself against the door frame silently. I saw Mom's eyes come to me and widen. Then, he was up and off his stool, turning quickly to face me.

"Care Bear..."

Before I could say a word, Mom was rushing around the counter toward me. "Isn't this so nice, Caroline?" she asked with a tight smile as her hand looped itself around my arm. "Dan stopped by to see you. I was going to wake you, but he told me to let you sleep, so we've just been doing a little catching up."

With a firm but gentle pull, Mom tugged me across the floor toward my fuckhead ex with a strength that surprised me. The closest the woman ever got to actual physical exercise was lugging crockpots around to her book clubs and church groups. Mom was tiny in every sense of the word— three inches shorter than me and probably a good twenty pounds lighter—and I didn't put up a fight. As much as I didn't want to stand any closer to Dan, it wasn't worth hurting her to keep my distance.

Once she'd decided I was close enough, her arm released mine, and she took a small step backwards. "Well, I've got some laundry that's not going to do itself, so you kids just settle in and have yourselves a nice chat."

Dan and I both watched her go. The second she turned out of view in the hall, I felt his fingers graze my elbow. I flinched away from the touch, crossing my arms over my chest as I took two steps away from him.

"Caroline, I-"

"Why are you here?"

His eyes searched mine for a long minute, and I held his gaze boldly, refusing to shy away. "I was just hoping we could talk."

"You really want to talk?" A choked laugh burst from my lips, and he winced at the sound. "What could you possibly have to say to me? And, better yet, what in the fuck makes you think I'd want to hear a single word of it?"

"Care Bear, I-"

"I swear to God, Dan, I'll slap you if I ever hear you call me that again."

He looked affronted, and I waited for him to call me on it, but he shifted focus and his expression turned back to pleading. "Caroline, please, just give me five minutes. I just... I'm so sorry. I never thought..." He trailed off and shook his head gently as his gaze left mine. My blood pressure rose even higher.

"No, really, finish that sentence. You never thought what? That you'd get caught? That I'd find you? Because, in case you don't remember, you weren't exactly hiding what you were doing. You had your dick in someone else in the fucking backyard, of all places. Right there for the world to see."

"That's not what I was going to say Care-" He caught himself, or he noticed the threatening rise of my eyebrows. Either way, his mouth slammed shut, and he swallowed thickly. "I just... I hate myself for doing this to us. I hate myself for doing this to you."

"Don't. Honestly, Dan, I'm over it. I'm over you. That night sucked, and, yeah, you're a dick for cheating on me. You're even more of a dick for doing it with Sammi Preston, of all people."

His face paled at her name, but I ignored it to continue, "But really, I don't hate you. I'm completely ambivalent toward you, actually. At least, as long as you're not sitting in my kitchen when I wake up, talking to my mom."

I watched him process my words, watched him realize that I wholeheartedly meant each and every one. His face transformed slowly, taking on the look someone gets when you tell them someone has died, somebody young and vibrant, somebody taken much too soon. It's a sort of stunned disbelief—a moment of blissful confusion that preempts the grief—and even before he opened his mouth, I knew he was in shock.

"You're really over me? Over us?" The way he asked, the very tone of his voice told me he was very much *not* over us. A tiny part of me felt bad, but I wasn't about to lie to him just to make him happy. Nodding slowly, I saw the way he deflated, his confused eyes slowly filling with a resigned sadness. Finally, his lips mashed together into a tight line, and he nodded.

He shuffled toward the hall but stopped in the door and turned back to face where I was still standing, staring in his direction. "I'm not going to apologize again because I know it doesn't mean anything after what I did. But I just... I never wanted to hurt you. Not ever. I hope you know that. And, more than anything else, I hope you have an amazing life, Caroline."

Without another word, he left. I couldn't contain my relieved sigh when I heard the front door click quietly closed behind him. The second he was gone, I headed out of the kitchen and straight upstairs to my room. Sitting down at the desk, I opened my laptop, and in less than five minutes I had switched my return flight to one leaving in four hours. It gave me about an hour to get packed and on the road, so I didn't waste a second.

I changed quickly out of my pajamas and considered my clothes carefully, trying to decide on an outfit to wear. I wanted to be comfortable, since I would be flying, but I also wanted to look good enough that when I got off the plane, I could head straight to Jimmy's without having to swing by my place to get changed.

I'd finally decided on a pair of jeans and a cute v-neck t-shirt that managed to look good without looking like I was actually trying to look good when I heard the quiet knock on my bedroom door. I called for just a minute and got dressed as quickly as I could manage.

Once I was decent, I yanked open the door and found Mom standing in the hall, worrying her hands together nervously. I backed away from the door and left it open for her to follow, which she did, eyeing the suitcase on my bed and the clothes scattered in and around it. "Cary..."

"I changed my flight. I need to leave in," I twisted to check the clock, "about forty-five minutes. If you can drive me to the airport, I'd appreciate it; otherwise, I'll take a cab."

"Caroline, I'm sorry if I upset you, but you don't need to leave. Please, let's just talk about this."

I dropped the armful of clothes I'd pulled from the dresser into the case before turning to face her. "Fine. Let's talk. I told you repeatedly that Dan and I were over. You obviously don't respect me as an adult, nor do you trust me to make the right decisions for myself. I have a problem with that, so, yes, I'm sorry, Mom, but I do need to leave."

"That's not fair, Cary. You know I trust and respect you. I let you go to Virginia for school, didn't I?"

"You *let* me? Because I'm pretty sure I'm an adult, and, as such, it's not up to you to *let* me do anything. You might have a leg to stand on if you were actually paying for my education, but since you're not, that decision was entirely mine to make."

"This is all beside the point, Caroline," she said dismissively, and I had to take a deep breath to rid my voice of the irritation swamping my body.

"It's really not. I'm nineteen years old. I'll be the first to admit I still have some growing up to do. I make mistakes, and I'm far from perfect, but I can't deal with you treating me like I'm still twelve. Forcing me to talk to my ex-boyfriend even though I told you over and over that we were done just proves that you don't respect my decisions. I don't want to be around that. I *can't* be around that."

"Don't leave just because you're mad at me. I'm sorry, Cary, and I promise I'll do better, but Steve and Jordy... We were all looking forward to spending this time with you."

"I know, Mom, but I need to go home. I'm not happy here. Don't get me wrong, I love being with you guys, but I just... I need to go home."

She sniffled but didn't cry, which I appreciated. "I'll wait for you downstairs to finish packing."

Without waiting for my nod, she turned and headed back out the door, closing it quietly behind her.

Once I was alone, I couldn't help but feel guilty. I knew she loved me and just wanted the best for me. She just didn't understand that right now what I really needed was her unconditional support.

Lately, I'd had a lot of reasons to doubt myself and my decisions. Between whatever was going on with Jimmy and I and the murky situation with Nate, I was starting to lose faith in myself. I just wanted my mom to tell me that everything would be okay, no matter what I did. I wanted her to tell me that she was proud of me and how I was living my life. More than anything, I wanted her to tell me that even when I screwed up, she trusted me to fix it. I wanted her to believe in me.

I wanted her to help me believe in myself.

That said, I was starting to think that the only one who could help me believe in myself was me.

The flight flew by, no pun intended. I listened to music the entire time but barely heard a note. All I could think about was Jimmy. I had considered calling him from the airport to let him know I was headed back early, but I decided to surprise him and called Jen instead. She had gone home for Christmas but had been back in Charlottesville for two days and happily agreed to pick me up when I landed.

As soon as I got off the plane, I quickly stepped into a bathroom to freshen up. I pulled my hair out of the ponytail I'd rocked through the flight and examined myself in the mirror. A little wrinkled, a little pale, but my eyes were bright. I looked excited. I *felt* excited. And despite the rocky start to the day, I smiled.

In no time at all, I had my bags and found Jen idling at the curb of the pickup area outside the arrivals gate. She spotted me quickly and climbed out to help me throw my bags in the trunk after giving me a huge hug. From the force of it, you would have thought I'd been gone for a year, not a week.

Traffic was light, and we made good time on the drive back to Charlottesville. I listened to Jen talk about going home to see her Mom and sister and answered her questions about my own trip. When she asked why I had come home early, I didn't tell her about Dan or the fight with Mom. Instead, I told her I'd just needed to get out of Michigan, and she accepted that answer readily.

After the first half hour, conversation petered off, and we both listened to music quietly while she drove. I must have zoned out because next thing I knew, Jen was gently shaking my arm. My eyes focused out the window, and I realized  the car was stopped in front of the McCarthy's house. I shook off the lingering fog and thanked her for the ride. She just smiled and told me she'd stick my bags in my room, leaving me free to climb from the car with just my phone. Once I'd waved, she pulled away, and I watched her go, taking the moment to calm the sudden nerves parading through my belly.

When my hands felt slightly steadier, I turned toward the house and made my way down the driveway. Sometime during the trip from the airport, the sun had set fully and the night was dark. Thankfully, the light outside the back door of the main house was lit, brightly illuminating the small garage that my feet carried me toward. I knew he was there. Even if I hadn't seen his car sitting out front, he'd already told me he planned on spending the night at home.

I saw light shining through the curtained window on the door as I brought my fist up and knocked quickly. I waited for noise or footsteps on the stairs, but after two minutes of total silence, I lifted my hand and knocked again, a bit louder. Again, nothing. My left hand traveled to my pocket, fingering the cool plastic of my cell phone, and I pulled it out but hesitated with my thumb over the screen. I didn't want to call him. I'd been so looking forward to knocking on his door and seeing his face, anything else felt like an epic disappointment.

I was still trying to get over my totally ridiculous hang-up when a noise behind me startled the silence of the night. I spun quickly, losing my balance for a second, but I was able to correct it before falling on my ass. My cheeks felt extra hot in the cool air, and that heat only grew when I finally caught sight of Mr. McCarthy standing in the open back door, one hand on the handle, the other holding a trash bag. His eyes were confused, but before I could say a word, the puzzled expression faded, and he gave me a small but genuine smile before stepping the rest of the way out of the house and pulling the door shut behind him.

"Can't say I expected to see you, but I also can't say I'm surprised," he said as he moved down the small set of stairs, toward the side of the house where two trashcans stood at attention. He opened one and tossed in the bag before turning back toward me. "I'm guessin' you're looking for Jim?"

I nodded, for some reason unable to form words. His smile just widened, and then he was headed back up the stairs and into the house. I took the open door as invitation to follow and quickly shuffled after him, not wanting to let too much heat escape.

As I closed the door from inside the warmth of the kitchen, his voice rang out behind me. "Jim! I found something of yours. It's in the kitchen."

As awkward as that was, I grinned, and that grin widened as I turned around to find the kitchen empty, Jimmy's dad already gone. Two seconds later, it practically split my face in half when Jimmy walked through the wide doorway, eyes instantly landing on mine.

I caught the flash of his own smile, and then he was across the room, my face pressed against his chest as his arms wrapped around my waist and held on tightly. I laughed and grabbed onto his shoulders when he lifted me from the floor and raised me so he could bury his face in my neck. He was warm and hard and safe, and I relaxed instantly into his embrace. I thought I'd known how much I missed him in Michigan, but now that I was actually here, standing next to him, it scared me to realize just how much I had needed this. Just how much I needed him.

He pressed a soft kiss just below my jaw before gently setting me back on the ground and loosening his arms enough to lean back and meet my gaze. "What are you doing here? Is everything okay?"

I nodded, fingers playing with the collar of his t-shirt absentmindedly. "Everything's fine. I just... I needed to come home." He still looked worried, so I slid my hands to his neck and squeezed gently. "I promise to tell you all about it later. But I'm here, and I'm happy, and I really want to spend New Year's Eve with you, if that's okay..."

"Are you kidding?" He laughed. "*Fuck*, Caro, I'm so happy you're here." His arms tightened again, and he pulled me into another hug, this one not quite as tight as the first but somehow more tender. I felt his breath across my neck and then his lips moving against my skin as he whispered, "I missed you. So fucking much."

It took me a minute to find my voice, and when I did, it came out thick, full of everything I wouldn't let myself say. "I missed you too."

It was the most, and the least, I could give him.

## Chapter Thirty

Jimmy

MAYBE I SHOULDN'T HAVE BEEN, but I was both amazingly satisfied and seriously fucking thrilled to hear her say she had missed me too. God, it was almost sad how completely gone I was for this girl. When I'd walked into the kitchen to see her standing there, smiling at me, my heart had just stopped. Seeing her for the first time since I'd realized I loved her... It had felt like a rough jab to the stomach. Strangely enough, as much as it hurt, it was a pain that I craved.

Having her body pressed against mine after eleven long days was incredible. That said, having it happen in my parents' kitchen was a unique form of torture. Half of me wanted to pull her out the door, across the driveway, and straight into my bed. I wanted to ring in the new year inside her, wanted to spend every day until the new semester started in my apartment, sans clothes. I wanted to reacquaint myself with her body over and over again.

Unfortunately, I'd promised to watch the ball drop with Jack. That simple fact made the hard-on I was sporting really fucking inconvenient.

I grudgingly let Caroline go and took a quick step back. She smirked when I adjusted myself in my jeans, and I shook my head. "You have no idea how much I want to take you home right now." Her eyes lit up and she licked her lips, obviously on board with that. I couldn't help but laugh. "I want to, but I promised I'd stay 'til midnight. You mind hanging here with me?"

The excitement faded from her eyes, and she looked a little nervous, but she shook her head all the same. "Not at all."

"You sure?"

"Yeah, of course," she urged with a smile. I studied her for a moment before I grabbed her hand, giving her a gentle tug to get her moving. I led her through the dining room and then into the living room, where Mom, Dad, and Jack were all sitting, Jack on the floor, Mom and Dad on the couch. The Times Square broadcast was playing softly in the background, but no one was paying much attention to it. Jack was in the middle of saying something to Mom and Dad, but his voice cut out when I cleared my throat from the doorway.

All three of them turned to face us, and I opened my mouth to speak, but Jack beat me to the punch. "Holy *shit*!"

Dad's jaw dropped. Mine slammed shut, my lips fighting to hold in the laughter that was dying to come out. I really shouldn't have been laughing, since Mom was *absolutely* going to blame me for this, but I just couldn't help it. The way Jack stared at Caroline, you'd think Wayne Gretzky had just walked into our living room.

"Jack Andrew!" Mom finally managed to snap after a long moment of shocked silence. "Watch your mouth! And James, you better wipe that smirk off your face this second. I know he didn't hear that from your father or I."

She was maybe half right. Jack definitely wouldn't have heard it from Mom; Dad was another story entirely. But, yes, I was definitely the most likely culprit.

"Hey, Jack," Caroline said, forging bravely into the conversation. I say *"bravely"* because Mom was still glaring daggers at both Jack and me.

"And you must be Mrs. McCarthy." Mom's angry face fled, and she focused on Caroline, a small, embarrassed smile stretching across her face.

"Hello there..." Mom trailed off and glanced at me uncomfortably.

It took me a second, but I figured it out. "Sorry, Ma, this is Caroline."

"Well," Mom said, "it's a pleasure to meet you, Caroline. And, please, call me Pat."

Caro smiled and nodded at her as Jack finally recovered from his star-struck moment to ask, "Why're you here?"

Her eyes darted to mine, and I smirked as I led her to the loveseat. We both sat, Caroline leaving a few inches between us that I quickly closed. She'd been too far away for far too long, and I wanted her as close as I could have her, present company considered. It still didn't feel close enough, but I figured I could make do until I could get her alone. "She's here to hang out."

"Your girlfriend?" I felt Caro tense at Jack's question, and I forced myself to keep breathing naturally. Surely that reaction was a bad sign, but this wasn't the time or place to talk to her about it.

"She's a girl, and she's my friend," I told him, hoping that just once he'd accept the answer and realize that this was something I didn't want to talk about. Unfortunately, that wasn't Jack's style.

"A girl who's a friend is a girlfriend."

My focus pleadingly shot to Dad, begging him to do anything to get us off this subject, but he looked way too amused by Jack's line of questioning (and my reaction to it) to say a word. Mom just looked confused, like she wanted the answer almost as badly as Jack did.

With no help at all from my parents, I raced to find an appropriate response because the silence was quickly becoming awkward. The problem was, I had no idea what the right answer was. Part of me wanted to say yes, because that's what it felt like and because that's what I wanted the answer to be. The rest of me was terrified that the g-word would freak Caroline out and send her running.

Before I could come up with a way to skirt the landmine Jack had tossed at my feet, Caroline cleared her throat. "I'm pretty sure Jimmy just hangs out with me because he's hoping I'll help him out on the ice. He's jealous of my mad skills."

I watched Jack consider that carefully, the breath holding in my lungs while he came to his decision. Finally, he smiled and nodded. "Makes sense. You're better at hockey than he is."

Caro and Dad both laughed, but I couldn't even respond to the shade he'd just thrown my way. I was too thrown off by the way he looked at her, not to mention the way she looked at him. I'd seen them together once before, but I hadn't really gotten a chance to watch it, and doing so now... The easy way she interacted with him would have been enough to make an impact, but it was the way he spoke to her that really stunned me. He was completely calm, seemed totally comfortable around her in a way that I'd never seen in the presence of anyone but our immediate family.

"You play hockey, Caroline?" That was from Mom, and the reactions it garnered were both varied and priceless. Dad burst out laughing again while Jack looked at Mom like she was out of her mind. I followed closer to Dad's route, chucking softly until I turned and saw the way Caro's smile had dimmed, becoming decidedly more forced.

"I used to," she said quietly, just as Jack shouted, "She's the Mighty Mite, Mom!" His tone implied that not knowing exactly who Caroline was (or, if you were asking her, who she *used* to be) was a crime of the greatest offense. Like he was personally offended that Mom hadn't recognized her on sight.

That said, Mom lived with us. The second Jack used Caroline's nickname, her face was pure recognition. "I thought you looked familiar! You were at the benefit, weren't you? On Thanksgiving?"

Caroline relaxed a little, but her smile was still less than genuine. "Yeah, I was there."

"Caroline's best friend is on the team at school, Ma," I added, feeling the need to get involved in the conversation. It wasn't until after I had spoken, when Caroline shifted next to me and I glanced up to catch her biting her bottom lip, that I realized my mistake in bringing up Nate.

Thankfully, Mom didn't notice the damage my comment had done. Or maybe she did. Either way, she naturally shifted the conversation toward school and how Caro was liking Virginia. I felt Caroline slowly relax next to me, and, as she did, her confidence grew. Mom got along with just about everyone, so I wasn't surprised by how quickly she took to Caro. Dad was usually harder to crack, but then again, whether she liked to admit it or not, Caroline *was* the Mighty Mite. I'm pretty sure Dad had seriously considered moving us to Michigan at one point, just to get the chance to work with her, so it really wasn't a surprise how quickly they bonded.

Jack was the one who surprised me, though. Or maybe it was Caro who surprised me by being as good as she was with him. I was transfixed by the way they interacted. As simple as it was, and as stupid as it might have been, I fell a little bit further in love with her just for the way she treated my brother. She didn't talk down to him, and she didn't single him out or act uncomfortable, even when he asked an uncomfortable question—unless, of course, that question was related to relationship statuses. She was just Caro, and she just let him be Jack, and it was beautiful.

After about an hour of easy conversation, Jack started begging to play Guess Who. I reluctantly agreed and grabbed the box from the game cabinet, but before I could set it up, he pulled it from my grip and turned to Caro. They played five rounds before we talked Jack into playing something that everyone could play. Once he'd finally accepted that, we spent the next three hours playing almost every single board and card game we owned, some more than once. It was comfortable, it was easy, and it was fun.

And I wanted it for the rest of my life.

Because, really, it was all Caro. She was comfortable. She was easy. She was fun. No matter where we were or what she was doing, she made my life better. She made the world around her better. And I wanted that—wanted her—for as long as she would let me have her.

At around eleven, Jack started dragging. We put away the games and settled in to watch the ball drop, quiet conversation flaring to life during the commercial breaks. I had to smother an inappropriately exultant cheer when Caroline curled up against my side on the loveseat, allowing my arm to drop around her shoulders possessively.

By eleven-thirty, Jack had passed out, and Mom didn't look to be too far behind. Dad gave me a look I couldn't interpret before he climbed off the couch, pulling Mom up with him.

I stood with them, tugging Caro to standing at my side. Mom gave us both a drowsy goodbye, told

Caroline how nice it had been to meet her and how much she hoped to see her again, and then headed toward the stairs behind Dad, who was already carrying a dead-to-the-world Jack up to bed.

Without waiting to say goodbye to Dad, I led us both through the back door, locking it before shutting it behind us. We quickly made our way to the garage door, and I used my key to let us both inside. She let go of my hand, so I could shut and lock that door as well, and then I turned to follow her up the stairs.

She was waiting for me at the top, but I stopped her when she turned to head straight for my bedroom. We still had twenty-five minutes till midnight, and while I now wholeheartedly planned to start the new year inside Caroline, I wanted to make sure she was okay—we were okay—before I let us get into bed.

I used my hold on her hand to lead her to the kitchen counter and then dropped her hand to grab her hips. A second later, she was seated on the counter's surface, laughing softly.

"Have I told you how much I hate being manhandled?"

I grinned and slid my hands to her knees, widening them just enough to fit my hips between them. My arms wrapped around her back. I slid her forward until we were pressed tightly together and then ran my nose along hers.

"Yes, you have. But we both know you love the way I do it."

She smiled and leaned forward, eyes closed and lips searching, and I forced myself to dodge the kiss. Turning my head so she landed on my cheek, I pressed my mouth against her neck twice before sliding up her earlobe. The desperate groan that rumbled from her mouth when I sucked the skin gently into my mouth had me straining against the zipper of my jeans, and I forced myself to take a breath.

"I have something for you."

Her hands, which had been resting on my waist, tensed, and I leaned back to gauge her expression. We hadn't discussed gift-giving at all, and I had no clue how she was going to react. Thankfully, she was smiling excitedly by the time I met her gaze.

"A present?" Her hands came up, and she rubbed them together like she needed to warm them up for whatever I was about to place between them. I couldn't have held in my laughter if I'd tried.

"I take it you like presents?"

She rolled her eyes impatiently. "Everyone likes presents. Anyone who says they don't is lying."

I shook my head and backed away from the counter to head toward the cabinet I had stashed her gift in. "Well, don't get too excited. Trust me, it's not much." Which wasn't entirely true. The twenty-one-year-old scotch had put a nice dent in my savings account, but it was nothing compared to her other gift.

And on that note, I decided to wait to give her the other gift. Not that I thought she would freak out or anything, but...just in case. Because there was definitely a chance that she would, in fact, freak out.

Retrieving the bottle carefully, I turned to hand it to her, watching her face closely to see her reaction. It was almost exactly what I expected.

"No way, Jimmy. This is *way* too much."

"It's really not."

"It really is," she argued. "How did you even...?"

I gave her a small smile and shrugged. "You mentioned it one night."

She had told me about the party they'd gone to after winning finals their junior year and about the bottle Nate had snatched from the unattended hotel bar on their way up to bed. At the time, they'd had no idea how much it was worth, and they'd gotten drunk in her hotel room after curfew. She'd also told me it was *that* scotch in particular that had kicked off her love affair with single-malts.

"Look," I said, "it's barely even a gift. In fact, if it makes you feel better, you can keep it here. I bought it with the intention of drinking it with you, so..."

Her lips tipped up, and she glanced up at me and then back down to the bottle in my hand. Her hand shot out and wrapped around the neck, carefully pulling it from my grip. She examined the bottle carefully while I set about grabbing glasses, and by the time I returned, she had it open and waiting. She poured the liquor and then replaced the cap before taking her glass from my waiting hand.

"We should toast to something." She was staring into the amber liquid, sloshing it carefully around the bottom of the tumbler.

"Like what?"

Her bottom lip disappeared between her teeth, and her eyes flashed up to mine. "The new year?"

"That's too easy. We need something better."

"What's better than the new year? It's three hundred and sixty-five new chances. Three hundred, sixty-five new opportunities to get it right."

Her quiet words resonated somewhere deep inside of me. Some dark, secret place that dreamed of a different life, a different dream, a different future. As much as I loved my family—as much as I loved my brother—the life I was living felt...wrong.

And more than anything, I wanted to get it right.

I wanted to get my life right. I wanted to get my future right. I wanted to get *myself* right.

I hadn't made a New Year's resolution since grade school, but standing in front of Caroline, I permitted myself to make a vow. I was going to allow myself to want the life I deserved. I was going to give myself a true chance at happiness, and not just for myself. I was going to do it for the girl in my arms because she deserved it just as much as I did.

We *both* deserved a true chance at happiness.

Lifting my glass in her direction, I met her eyes with a renewed sense of determination.

"To the new year...and getting it right."

## Chapter Thirty One

# Caroline

I HAD BEEN HAVING AN absolutely incredible dream. It began with fingers lightly dancing over my skin, teasing and touching just enough to get the blood stirring in my veins. Soft lips pressed even softer kisses against my neck, my shoulder, my collarbone. The mouth dropped lower, brushing a kiss here, a taste there. Then warmth covered one nipple, sucking hard, forcing my back to arch straight off the bed.

I realized the dream wasn't a dream pretty quickly after that, but kept my eyes closed, trying to hold onto the moment—the mindlessness of sleep and the haze of lust I'd awoken to. Jimmy's mouth lifted from my skin, and then his breath was brushing past my ear. "I know you're awake."

He dropped a light kiss against my lips but disappeared before I could return it. Then his mouth was skating back over my skin, dropping a flurry of kisses over every inch of my conveniently naked body. It wasn't my usual style, but I'd passed out almost immediately after round three the night before.

Yep. That's right. Round three.

Jimmy had missed me *bad*.

Apparently, he wasn't done showing me just how much because before I could even fully adjust to being awake, he had settled onto his knees, palms pressed to my thighs, holding them open while his mouth devastated me. He did it slowly, purposefully, alternating long drags of his tongue with slow circles around my clit. It didn't take long until my hips were pushing urgently against his mouth and the hands that held me down.

I needed more. I needed his fingers or his cock or *something* because all he was doing was driving me absolutely crazy. And, worst of all, the bastard knew it. He'd have to be deaf not to, what with the way I was moaning and begging and practically crying his name.

His mouth picked up speed, pushing me closer to the edge, and thank God for that because I needed to come more than I needed my next breath. Just as my legs began to tense and my back began to arch, Jimmy lifted his head, and I nearly screamed in frustration. My eyes were squeezed shut. My fingers gripped the sheet at my side tightly. And I'm pretty sure I was just mindlessly begging, but I was too far gone to be sure.

Before I could process what was happening, I felt his lips brush across my jaw just as his weight settled between my thighs. His body came to rest on top of mine for only a second before he rolled us, quickly and effortlessly positioning me on top. I wobbled unsteadily with only one leg to keep my balance, and his hands gripped my hips, holding me in place. I felt him between my legs, hard and ready, and as much as I wanted to shift back and let him slide inside, I froze, stuck somewhere between panicked and full-out terrified.

Either he read my expression or the tension holding me rigid gave me away, but either way, one hand left my hip to brush against my cheek before his fingers were sliding into my hair. When his hand started gently guiding my face down toward his, I used my hands on his chest to control the fall, and I let him bring our mouths together. The kiss was gentle, reassuring, and tender, so tender that my heart clenched painfully in my chest at the reverent way he explored my lips.

With Jimmy, every kiss felt like the first kiss, full of passion and want and need. But somehow, at the same time, every kiss also felt like the thousandth kiss, the millionth. Comfortable, familiar, safe. His kisses felt like home.

By the time he used his grip in my hair to lift my face from him, I'd forgotten where we were completely, my entire focus pinpointed on the perfection of his mouth. But then his hand still at my hip gave a gentle squeeze, and my shoulders rose completely on instinct.

"Tell me," he murmured.

"I, uh... I just haven't..." I glanced down at where I sat on his hips, hoping he'd let me off the hook. He didn't.

"Haven't what?"

I fought against rolling my eyes because I knew he knew exactly what I was talking about. "I haven't...been on top." Licking my lips, I quickly added, "Since the accident, I mean."

"Okay..." he said slowly, as if he wasn't entirely sure what that had to do with anything.

"I just, I'm not sure..."

His hand in my hair fell away, moving back down to my hips before both palms moved back to grab my ass. Slowly, as if to prove a point, he used his hands to lift me an inch into the air before pushing me back down against his length. His hands pulled me back and forth easily, coating him in the overwhelming wetness between my thighs and driving us both absolutely wild. My hands trailed restlessly across his chest, down to his abs, reaching between my legs to feel him pressed against me.

When my fingers brushed the head of his cock just as he slid himself against my clit, we both groaned, and his grip on me tightened to the point of pain for just a second before relaxing. That slight bite of his fingers on my skin was all I needed to wipe away the last of my inhibitions, leaving them all behind in the wake of the vicious force of the need that barreled through my body.

I used the hand already in place to grab him, meeting Jimmy's eyes in a silent plea. He read it and complied, lifting my hips securely as I guided him into place. Then, slowly, he lowered me around him, inch by mind-blowing inch, until my ass rested against his thighs, and he was further inside of me than he'd ever been before.

For a few quiet moments, we both adjusted to the sensation. Not only was it my first time on top, but we were both still getting used to having sex without a condom. I had put my time at home to good use, not just securing birth control but also managing to get my period while I'd been in Michigan. It meant I'd been able to start the pills, so we were good to go. I'd surprised him with that little fact the night before, and he'd quite graciously expressed his gratitude.

Now, though, I was the one feeling grateful. There was something about feeling him—just him— with no barriers. Nothing between us at all. It felt...intimate. And incredible. And so amazingly perfect, I knew, down to my soul, I'd never manage to find anything better than this. I knew it like I knew my own name. Every single time he slid inside me, James McCarthy ruined me just a little bit more. Every time his hands or his mouth or his cock drove me over the edge, he worked at destroying any chance that I'd ever manage to feel satisfied with anyone else.

When I felt him jerk inside me, I adjusted my hips, tipping them forward and he managed to slide in deeper, pressing at a spot that sent shockwaves ricocheting along my spine. His fingers were gripping my skin, holding me tightly, but I used my good leg and my hands at his chest to push myself up, reveling in the desperate groan that rumbled in his throat and the way he uttered my name like it was a prayer.

Like I was his deliverance.

My downward slide was much faster than the upward one, and he cursed tightly under his breath as I slid him home hard, forcing a ragged groan out of me as well. It felt so fucking good, I couldn't stop myself from doing it again. And again. And then again.

It didn't take long for my rhythm to begin to stutter. My muscles were tightening, my breathing had grown shallow, and my fingers clutched at him like I wanted to claim him, my nails leaving faint scratch marks along the smooth skin covering his sculpted pecs. As my motions turned jerky, his hands took over, lifting and dropping my weight with ease while also tipping me forward another inch. The new angle rubbed my clit against the skin below his stomach, and that last bit of sensation was all I needed.

I came with a mangled shout, words tumbling past my lips in a fervent litany of pleasure. As I tightened around him, Jimmy's hands gripped my ass and secured my position, and then he was powering his hips off the bed, driving up into me in a frantic cadence that prolonged the pristine agony of my orgasm. It was powerful, it was intense, and it went on and on until, with one final, thought-obliterating thrust, he pulled my body down, wrapping me tightly in his arms as he came with a grated groan that was punctuated by ragged exaltation and my name on his lips.

I'm not sure how long we lay there, my thighs straddling his hips, with him gradually softening inside me. My cheek was pressed to his chest, and as I slowly came back to Earth, I noticed his fingers running carefully through my hair. The soothing motion wasn't helping me regain use of my body, but I didn't care enough to fight the drugging effect of his tender movements.

After what could have been an hour, his lips dropped a gentle kiss to the crown of my head before he shifted us both onto our sides. I frowned when he slipped from inside me, and through heavily lidded eyes, I watched a satisfied smirk curl his lips before he was sliding across the mattress and out of bed. I still hadn't fully re-entered my body, so I didn't even bother moving to watch him go.

The quiet rushing of the sink barely penetrated my mind, and then he was back, gently wrapping a hand around my scarred thigh and lifting it carefully. A warm washcloth passed between my legs and my eyes drifted closed, overwhelmed by the tender look on his face and the earnestly affectionate way he took care of me.

The washcloth disappeared, and then he was back, crawling into bed beside me and pulling me once again into his arms. He shifted me up against his chest until my head was beside his on the pillow and then tangled my leg between his comfortably as one hand skated down my hip and slid to rest on my ass. I winced slightly, the skin surprisingly tender from his rough fingers, and he frowned.

"I didn't mean to hurt you."

He looked genuinely upset, and I shook my head quickly. "Trust me, you didn't. Every second of that was absolutely incredible." His brows stayed furrowed, his lip kept its adorable pout, and I couldn't resist shifting forward to lightly kiss the pink skin.

By the time I pulled away, his expression had relaxed, and I curved my mouth into a small smile. "Good morning, by the way."

He grinned and pressed a soft kiss to my nose. "It was a good morning, wasn't it? Best I've had in a while."

"Last night was kind of phenomenal too, you know."

"Oh, I know. It's all phenomenal with you."

That statement settled onto my chest with the heat and weight of an African elephant. I was pretty sure one had sat its massive rear-end onto my ribcage because my lungs were screaming for air, but I just couldn't manage to drag any in. Thankfully, he either didn't notice or chose to ignore the way my hands trembled against his waist.

"I've never really been a fan of New Year's, but I have to admit, it's kind of growing on me," he said suddenly, and I ran with his change of subject gratefully.

"I love New Year's."

"Is it your favorite?" He must have read my confusion because he clarified. "Favorite holiday, I mean."

"Oh. No, Thanksgiving is my favorite. New Year's is probably my runner-up. How about you?"

"I love Christmas Eve." I must have made a face because he laughed. "I know, it's a little weird. It's just, all the pre-holiday craziness is over, and there's just one night of peace and serenity before all the gift-giving and family gatherings. Just one more night of anticipation for the kids who are dying to wake up to presents from Santa. And it's just... It's like the world takes a breath. For just one night, everything is calm and happy and...right."

I thought about that, about what that said about him, and I barely noticed the way his eyes softened as my lips curved into an affectionate smile. Something about him loving the peace of Christmas Eve was so beautiful to me, and I considered telling him, but I wasn't sure how he'd take it.

Before I had the chance to say anything, though, he changed the subject again. "So, I need to ask you a question."

I searched his face for any emotion, but it was carefully blank. "Okay..."

"How do you feel about road trips?"

I felt myself relax at the innocuous question and answered honestly. "I used to love them. In high school, riding the bus to games and just traveling in general, I liked the trip as much as I usually enjoyed the actual destination. But I haven't actually done any long-distance driving since the accident."

He frowned at that, tongue peeking out to wet his lips, and it took a serious effort to keep from leaning in to kiss the pout away again.

"Is that... Are you uncomfortable in cars?"

"Yeah. It's gotten a lot better, trust me. I used to panic anytime I had to get in one, and I flat out refused to drive myself at all. I was in therapy for a while after the accident, though, and that was one of the things we worked on."

"Can you…" he started but then trailed off, his eyes shifting across my face nervously. "I'd like to hear about it. The accident, I mean, and what came after. You don't have to talk about it if you don't want to, but I'd just like to know."

His nervous rambling was adorable, and it gave me the strength I needed to actually tell this story. We'd skated around the topic a few times before, but he'd never directly asked me about it, and I hadn't volunteered. I wasn't sure what had changed—why he wanted to know now—but I didn't care. Drugged on him and sex and a lazy morning in bed, I couldn't deny him anything.

"I don't mind, really. It's just…" I took a deep breath and closed my eyes for a second before opening them to meet his steady gaze. "I'm not proud of that night, or a lot of what came after it."

"That's okay. You've seen me do a lot of shit I'm not proud of, and nothing you tell me could change the way I see you now."

I *really* hoped that was true.

"So," I began, pointing my eyes away from his. I might have been able to talk about this with him, but I definitely couldn't look at him while I did it. "During my first senior year, Dan and I went to a Halloween party. I hadn't wanted to go; the party was way out in the middle of nowhere, and I had to be up early the next morning for practice. Plus, the forecasters were calling for a really bad snowstorm, and I was worried we would end up getting stuck out at this dude's house if it got as bad as they said it was going to.

"He just wouldn't let up, though, and I finally agreed to tag along if he promised we wouldn't stay long.

"So, we got to this house, and even though he promised to limit himself to three beers, an hour later he was trashed. We fought about it a little, and he told me he was going to start sobering up so he could drive us home because he knew I hated driving his car. It was a stick, which I can handle if I need to, but the clutch used to stick, and...

"Anyway, he disappeared for a while, and when I finally went to find him—to see if he was ready to leave—he couldn't even stand up straight. We got into the world's most pointless argument because I could barely understand a single word he shouted at me, and I just stormed off. I found his coat and stole his keys and left him there.

"By the time I got outside, it was already snowing pretty badly, but I figured I could get home. I was so angry, I barely even remember the drive. Just the snow; big, fat snowflakes, the kind I had always loved as a kid. Every mile they came down faster and faster until I could barely see the road in front of me. But I was still angry, and I was driving fast—way too fast for the weather and the road I was on.

"I remember coming around a curve and then headlights. There was nothing but white and a bright, blinding light. I remember the sound of metal on metal, the way that Dan's car practically disintegrated, and I remember..."

My throat was closing, the words sticking in my chest like molasses. Jimmy's hand came to my face, and he wiped away a single tear, one I hadn't even realized had fallen. I swallowed the emotion back down and sucked in a deep breath before lifting my eyes up to him. I needed to see him, I suddenly realized. I needed the quiet comfort that his eyes provided.

"I remember the way the car wrapped around my leg. I felt the metal cut into my skin, and I felt every bone in my leg being crushed. And then the car was in the air, and I... Well, I hadn't remembered to put my seatbelt on, and I got thrown around pretty hard.

"Thankfully, I guess, the metal didn't completely cut through my leg, and it kept me pinned enough that I didn't sustain any fatal head injuries. But I blacked out, and the rest I only know because the doctors told me.

"The way the metal had wrapped around my leg, it acted as a sort of tourniquet, keeping me alive until the ambulance could reach us. Thankfully, the guy in the other car was fine, and he was able to call 911. He apparently freaked, thought I was dead at the scene, and, from what I understand, it's kind of a miracle that I wasn't.

"The EMTs had to remove my leg to even get me out of the car. I was airlifted to the hospital, and once they stabilized my leg, they induced a coma to try and reduce the swelling in my brain. But they told my parents not to get their hopes up, and my mom..."

*Nope. Can't go there.*

"They kept me sedated for a month, and then it took another month before I woke up."

His thumb rubbed soothing circles over the skin at my waist, and his eyes burned into mine, telling me something I refused to hear.

"And then?"

*And then comes the part I'm not proud of...*

"I spent another month in the hospital. I had some memory loss—little stuff, really, but it messed with me. I was frustrated with that and with myself. I hated being in a wheelchair, and I was told that I'd probably never walk again, which just... It wasn't pretty.

"I alternated between rage and pretty severe depression, to the point that they worried about sending me home. The hospital was its own sort of suicide watch, and my mom was against them releasing me when they did.

"They did, though, and I was even more miserable at home. Mom set me up for PT and tons of therapy, and I just slowly came back to myself, I guess. There wasn't really any other option."

He nodded slowly and then leaned forward to give me an incredibly long, incredibly sweet kiss. It cleared the last of the memories from my mind, for which I was entirely grateful.

"Thank you for telling me," he whispered against my lips, once he'd finally ended the kiss, and my lips tipped up against his.

"Thanks for listening."

I settled back against the pillow and remembered how we had gotten to that conversation, curiosity taking over everything else in the air. "Why did you ask about road trips?"

"Ah," he hedged, nerves suffusing his face in a way that only had me wanting to know more. "Well, I kind of got something else for you, to go with the liquor, but it requires some travel.

"Speaking of which, how do you feel about planes? I originally thought we could just drive—it's only about six hours—but I don't want you in the car for that long if you can't handle it. You didn't seem worried when I dropped you at the airport last week, so if you're okay with that, I'll just get tickets, and we can fly up-"

"Wait," I interrupted quickly. "What are you talking about? What requires travel?"

"First, let me tell you that this barely counts as a gift either. It's something that I want to do, and I want you with me, so you can't get mad."

"Jimmy..."

"Promise you won't get mad, Caro."

"You know, when people say that, it's because they know whatever they're about to say is worth getting angry over."

"I know, but I just don't want you to-"

"Just tell me."

He let out a defeated sigh, and, by his expression, I could only assume that he was bracing. "The Red Wings are playing the Flyers in a month, and I might have gotten us tickets to go see them."

"See them where? In Philly?"

He nodded carefully, and the smile that ripped across my face was so wide it almost hurt. I pushed up out of his arms, one hand on the mattress, so I could look down at him. "Are you serious right now?"

His eyebrows furrowed like he was attempting to work out an extremely challenging puzzle, and then he nodded. "Yeah."

"Oh my God! Why the hell would I be mad about that?!"

He must have realized that I wasn't screwing with him because his face relaxed, and he smiled happily. "Honestly, I have no fucking clue. But you tried to tell me the liquor was too much, so..."

"Well, yeah," I told him frankly, "but that's only because that was a disgustingly expensive bottle of alcohol. Spending that much on a bottle of liquor is just stupid."

He narrowed his eyes, and I smiled apologetically. "It was sweet, but it was still stupid."

"I don't know," he said thoughtfully. "That shit was the best scotch I've ever had."

"I know, right?" I laughed quietly before getting back on topic. "Anyway, this is all beside the point. We're talking about a Wings game. And I kind of have a rule against turning down tickets to NHL games, no matter who's playing."

He chuckled and lifted a hand to shove my loose hair behind one ear tenderly. "That sounds like a good rule."

"It's an exceptionally good rule," I agreed, sliding back down into the circle of his arms. I pressed my lips to his and attempted to show him just how thankful I was—and not just for the tickets. I was thankful for *him*.

It didn't take long for the kiss to smolder, and then it went rogue. It was mouths and skin and tasting and feeling, and there was so much emotion, barely contained but still carefully concealed, as if we were both choosing to ignore our feelings, so we could just *feel* them.

I didn't think about the future. I didn't even think about the present. I didn't second-guess a minute of our time together. I trusted myself, and I trusted him, and I just let myself live in the bubble we'd built around ourselves, the bubble that kept things easy and simple because there was no one to ask questions or pass judgment. There was no need to evaluate and process what was happening. We were free to just let it happen.

Somewhere, deep in the back of my mind, I knew I couldn't avoid facing reality forever. But I was living inside the bubble, and I planned on staying there until the very second it popped.

I convinced Jimmy to take me home after dinner. He had actually cooked, something I knew he didn't do, and it made his effort that much more adorable. And, honestly, his spaghetti wasn't half bad.

We had sat together at his dining table—just the two of us in his quiet apartment—and it all felt so perfectly domestic that it stole my breath. After we had eaten, I insisted on doing the dishes, but he puttered around the kitchen with me, drying and putting things away while we continued to tell stories about our time apart. I'd told him about Dan's visit to the house and my fight with my mom, and he told me about hanging out with his friend Marco on Christmas Eve.

He'd told me quite a bit about his best friends over the course of our time together. Enough that I was curious why I hadn't met them yet. Not that I thought he needed to introduce me to his friends, but as close as he made them all sound, I just wondered why he didn't seem to spend much time with them. I also wondered if he wasn't spending time with them because of me, and then I decided that, either way, I didn't want to know.

Once the kitchen was clean, he tried to pull me back into his bedroom, but I told him that I really needed to go home, which wasn't a lie. I'd been gone for over a week, and I'd come straight to Jimmy's when my plane landed. I wanted to check in with Jen and check on the apartment, and I desperately needed to shower and do laundry since I hadn't had time to do it before leaving, like I'd intended. I knew he wasn't happy about it, but he finally grabbed his keys and led me out to his car.

The ride home was quiet, but not uncomfortably so. When we finally pulled into the complex, I heard his quiet sigh, and I couldn't help but smile. "Stop pouting. We have almost two weeks until classes start. You're going to be sick of me by the time we go back to school."

I'd hoped to get a smile out of him, but he seemed upset—maybe even a little angry—though I wasn't sure. His gaze stayed focused out the windshield, and his fists tightened on the wheel for just a second before relaxing.

"Trust me, Caro," he finally said. "I won't ever get tired of having you around."

I wasn't entirely sure how to respond to that, so I kept my mouth shut until we had pulled up in front of my building. Before I could say a word, his body was stretching across the center console toward me. His hands secured my face, and his mouth landed hard on mine. This kiss was slightly different from every one that had come before. It was more possessive. It was a claiming kiss, and I allowed it. More than that, I completely *reveled* in it. For the first time in my relatively short life, I wanted to be claimed. I *wanted* him to make me his own.

That thought was followed by a quick slice of unease. Tendrils of doubt invaded my consciousness as he finally pulled away, leaving us both breathless in the quiet car.

"Go, before I turn the car around and take you back home. I'll text you when I get home." Finally, he gave me a smile, but it was small and sad.

I couldn't resist pressing one last, closed-mouth kiss against his lips before I threw open the door and climbed from the car. Turning back at the door, I waved toward where he continued to idle, and then I slid inside, the hard thud of the door behind me sounding strangely final.

I arrived home to an empty apartment. My suitcase was sitting directly in front of my bedroom door, and I took it to my room and sorted through the jumbled mass of clothing quickly. Once I'd gathered up my dirty laundry, I grabbed the basket and hiked it down the hall to the laundry room. I loaded and started the washer and left the basket in the small room to head back.

Next, I grabbed a pair of sweats and a t-shirt from my dresser before shuffling into the bathroom. I took the world's longest shower, washing away the flight and almost twenty-four hours of near non-stop sex. Even after I'd turned the water off, I could still feel the echo of his fingers against my skin. I could still feel his heat and weight pressing me into the softness of a mattress. I could still feel the ghost of his breath skating over my skin, leaving goosebumps in its wake.

I got dressed and headed back to my room, and I'd just laid down across my bed, phone in hand to text Jimmy, when I heard the door open. A minute later, Jen's face popped into my open doorway, and her wide smile greeted me happily. "Hey! I wasn't sure when you were going to be back. I texted you..."

*Shit.*

Sex made me really stupid. I had already started to understand this, but she managed to hit it home with three well-placed words.

"Sorry, my phone died last night, and I didn't think to charge it there."

This was only partly true. I honestly hadn't bothered charging it there because I didn't think I needed to worry about talking to anyone else. And *that*... Something about that really bothered me.

"No worries. I was just worried about you getting home, but I'm assuming he dropped you off?"

I nodded, but I did it distractedly. Her question had stuck my mind back in the car with Jimmy and his strange despondency. I had no clue what had happened to bum him out, but I planned on finding out.

"You alright?"

I refocused and found Jen standing a few feet inside the door. She was watching me cautiously, and I considered nodding, just to deflect the question.

Instead, I pulled my lip into my mouth and searched for an honest answer. I finally settled for the closest thing to truth I could find. "I'm not sure. I think so?"

"Are you asking me?" Her smile was small and fleeting, and then she was crossing the floor to flop onto the bed at my side. "What's up?"

"I don't really know. Jimmy was just kind of weird earlier, but I'm sure it was nothing."

"How was he weird?"

"He just seemed...sad."

She frowned and glanced at me quickly. "Did anything seem off before that?"

"No, not at all. Last night was great. We hung out at his parents' house and then went back to his place a little before midnight. And today was..."

I must have made a face because she laughed and nudged her shoulder into mine. "You can spare me the details. I get it."

I grinned and turned onto my side to face her. "Well, yeah, there was a lot of that. But it was just a good day. And then I told him I needed to come home, and he just kind of...deflated."

She was still and silent for a minute before her shoulders shrugged against the mattress. "I'm sure it was nothing. He was probably just bummed that you wanted to leave."

I nodded, not entirely convinced but placated for the moment.

Another thought crossed my mind, and a quick smile flooded my face. "Dude, guess where I'm going in a month?"

She looked toward me, and I continued once I had her attention. "The fucking City of Brotherly Love!"

Her head swished against the pillow as she turned to look at me more closely. "You're going to Philly?"

When I nodded, she asked, "Why?"

"Jimmy got us tickets to a Flyers-Red Wings game. He wanted to drive up, but then he said something about flying because I'm not a huge fan of cars, but I should probably talk to him about that. He already paid for the tickets, and he argued with me when I said I'd pay for the room, but..."

My excited rambling trailed off when I focused on her face and noticed the goofy grin she was flashing in my direction. There was something in her eyes, something so sickeningly sweet that I couldn't help but ask, "What?"

"What what?" she replied, smile not fading in the least.

"Why are you looking at me like that?"

"I just think it's cute. You guys are all settled and in love. It's nice seeing you happy."

I *was* happy. But I couldn't focus on that because I was so jarred by the rest of what she'd said.

"We're not settled *or* in love. We're not even together."

She looked at me like I was absolutely insane and then rolled her eyes. "Please, Caroline. You flew home from Michigan early, and despite your whole, 'I just needed to come home' line, obviously a big part of that had to do with him, considering you didn't even come home first. You went straight to him. Not to mention, you spent New Year's Eve with his family, meaning you *met* his family, which literally only means one thing.

"Oh! And let's not forget that he's taking you to Pennsylvania as a Christmas gift, which, sure, seems weird to me, but the point is that *you* like it, and he knew you would.

"Seriously, you're obviously into him, and that boy couldn't be more glaringly in love with you unless he hired a freaking sky-writer to spell it out word-for-word."

I was trying to process that, coming up with argument after argument, but before I could speak a single one, she went on.

"No offense, Caro, but you're not exactly the most observant person in the world. You see things, but you're really good at blinding yourself when you want to. But listen, none of this is bad. I'll admit, I was worried at first. I didn't want you to get hurt because he wanted a rebound or because he wanted the thing that he hadn't been able to have, you know? But I think he's been good for you. I mean, I haven't seen you two together a whole lot, but from what I *have* seen, you guys have a good thing going."

We *did* have a good thing going. I knew that, and I loved it, and I wasn't ready to give it up. But Jen had just slammed a pickaxe into the bubble, and that bitch was demolished.

"Caro, you don't look very good. What are you thinking right now?"

I shook my head and shut my eyes tightly, desperately searching for another solution. Anything else that would get us both where we needed to be, but I knew I didn't have another option.

"Caro," Jen repeated, "please tell me what's wrong. What did I say?"

"You didn't-" I had to stop, swallow, and suck in a shallow breath. Peeling my eyes open, I forced myself to meet her eyes. "It wasn't anything you said really. But you're right. I never meant to let this get so...big. And Jimmy..."

She waited for a minute and then urged me on impatiently. "Jimmy what? You're making absolutely zero sense right now."

"Jimmy was with Maddie for over four years. That relationship finally ended because he realized he didn't know what he wants. Then, less than twelve hours later, he's in my bed. And the sex... God, the sex is so incredible. Of course neither one of us wanted to stop, but I should have realized... Fuck! Sex makes me stupid!"

"What the hell are you talking about, Caroline?"

"I'm talking about the fact that he still doesn't know what he wants! And he's not going to figure that out if he thinks he's in love with me!"

Her head jerked back, pushing deeper into the pillow, and she stared at me like I'd spontaneously grown a second head. Granted, I was shouting at her, so it might have been warranted. "What does that even mean, if he *thinks* he's in love with you?" The words were quiet but completely bewildered, like the thought was so absurd, she couldn't put even an ounce of force behind it.

"I just mean...I didn't mean to let things get so serious. I thought if we didn't define it... And I told him… I told him we were going to take it one day at a time. He can't love me. He can't even think he loves me, or he'll never figure out what he actually wants. And I don't want him to settle for me the way he was going to settle for Maddie."

That last thought was the one that bothered me most. Jimmy had never experienced college as a single, unattached, carefree guy. Granted, his life wasn't entirely carefree even without annoying things like girlfriends—or even theoretical girlfriends—fucking with it. But I was convinced he needed that; he needed to experience what life had to offer, and he wouldn't do that if I was in the picture. Which meant I needed to remove myself from the picture.

Jen was still staring at me, but she no longer looked like she thought I was crazy. She just looked impossibly sad. "I can't believe you think that anyone would ever be settling with you. And, I have to say, I think you're wrong. I also think you should talk to him before *you* start making decisions about what *he* needs and wants."

"But that's my point. He doesn't *know* what he wants."

"How could you *possibly* know that? You didn't even know he was in love with you until I pointed it out!"

"Look, I don't expect you to understand. It's not like you have a great track record with relationships-"

"Wait a second," she said shortly, cutting me off mid-sentence and shooting up to a sitting position beside me. "*I* don't have a great track record with relationships? Can we talk about Nate for a second? How you managed to blind yourself for over a decade to the fact that your best friend was in love with you, just so you could keep him in the neat little box you'd placed him in?"

Tears burned behind my eyes at the harsh tone of the even harsher words she'd flung at me, but I blinked them away and wore my anger like armor.

"I'm not really sure what that has to do with anything," I responded coldly as she pushed off the bed before turning to face me.

"It has *everything* to do with this, Caroline! You're just *once again* refusing to see it! You made decisions about how Nate felt about you; you convinced yourself that he didn't care about you as anything more than a friend, and you fucked up that relationship entirely on your own. You didn't pay attention, and you didn't talk to him. You let your assumptions ruin what you and Nate had, and you're about to do the exact same thing with Jimmy."

"Nate never said a word to me-"

"He didn't have to! *I* fucking told you, Caroline. I told you a week after meeting you that I thought he had feelings for you. You refused to listen. You're *still* refusing to listen. And if you don't learn to do it pretty fucking quick, this won't be the last relationship you destroy."

With that, she spun on her heel and marched from the room. Angry footsteps pounded across the living room, and the last sound I heard before a deafening silence filled the apartment was the biting crack of her bedroom door slamming shut.

## Chapter Thirty Two

$\mathcal{J}inny$

I HAD DEFINITELY FUCKED UP during the drive to her house. I knew this, and I had agonized over it for the entire trip back home. The problem was that I already fucking missed her. Hell, I'd started missing her the second she had said she needed to go. And, if I was really honest, I think a part of me missed her even when we were together.

*Problem number one right there, folks.*

There was just still so much distance between us. Don't get me wrong, the day had been incredible. No surprise there, since everything was incredible with Caroline. But I felt like I constantly needed to hold myself back. In truth, I don't know how Nate managed to keep his feelings for her a secret for as long as he did. I'd only been fully aware of mine for a handful of days, and I was close to bursting with the secret.

Which was exactly why I'd fucked up. I'd been so bummed about her going home that I spent our time in the car anxiously trying to come up with a plan. I had meant every word of my spur-of-the-moment New Year's resolution. I was going to get my life straight—I was going to start living right—and the first place I needed to start was with the girl at my side. I needed to clear the air between us, needed to close the distance and tell her exactly where I stood.

Unfortunately, despite all my determination, I was still scared shitless at the prospect. She could totally shoot me down. In fact, a large part of me fully *expected* her to. I'd even formulated a contingency plan in the event that she did, in fact, laugh in the face of my feelings. I was desperately hoping it wouldn't come to that, but I wanted to be prepared for anything and everything.

As soon as I'd gotten home, I sent her a text. I only stared at my phone waiting for a response for two minutes, which was good because that response never came. I tried to ignore the ominously silent device and the way it churned my stomach, cursing myself all over again for acting like the world's saddest sack in the car. I had never been like this with Maddie. I had never felt like every second spent away from someone was an exercise in agony. When it came to Caro, though... I felt utterly lost without her.

I thought about showering but decided against it. I could still smell her on my skin, and I wasn't ready to wash her away. Instead, I collapsed on the couch, phone in hand, and watched SportsCenter until I finally passed out. Thankfully, that happened before I was able to send a second text, one that would have been decidedly more pathetic than the first. Although, let's face it, I would totally get pathetic if I had to. If that's what it took, I'd make myself as pathetic as she wanted me to be.

And that was definitely problem number two.

The next morning, I awoke to the same churning in my stomach and still no messages from Caro. It was already almost noon. I figured there was no way she was still sleeping, so I sent another text, this one asking if she wanted to meet for lunch. I waited a full five minutes this time before heaving myself off the couch to toss the silent phone on the dining table.

I didn't look at it again until after I'd showered, shaved, and dressed, but she hadn't answered that message either. My insides twisted harder, but I ignored the sensation and pocketed the phone before grabbing my keys and heading out the door.

I spent two hours driving around aimlessly. Then I stopped for gas and did it for another four. I didn't stop driving until I had worked out every angle of what I wanted to say to Caroline. I considered every possible outcome, from her declaring her undying love for me to her telling me she never wanted to see me again, and I formulated a response to each possible scenario. The one common denominator, though, was my determination.

I wasn't giving up on her. Hell, I *couldn't* give up on her. I hadn't been able to do it months ago, and there was no way I could do it now, not now that I knew how absolutely incredible we were together. I would do whatever I had to do to convince her to give us a real shot.

At six-thirty I was parked in front of her building. I didn't go up, though. Instead, I pulled her number up and hit the screen to dial it. It rang four times before going to voicemail, and the second I heard her voice instructing me to leave a message, I ended the call and dropped the phone in the center console. I zipped my jacket and turned off the car before climbing out and up to the outer door. Once I'd let myself in, I shuffled down the hall and knocked on her front door quietly.

It was Jen who answered, locking eyes with me a second before a small, sympathetic smile stretched her face. On one hand, I realized that was a bad sign, but I took the sympathy to mean that maybe, just maybe, she was on my side. That suspicion grew when she waved me in without announcing my presence, shutting the door quietly before turning back toward me. She silently gestured me toward Caroline's room, and I gave her a grateful smile before heading toward the open door.

Caroline was lying in bed on her stomach, attention completely focused on the paperback in her hands. My attention, however, was completely focused on what she was wearing. The tank top was small. The shorts were short. More specifically, they were the shortest shorts I'd ever seen her in. Usually she wore long basketball shorts—I'd always assumed to hide her scars—but the pale blue cotton ended less than an inch below her ass and showed off so much skin that for a minute I was pissed about our fight, if that's what it even was. There was no way I could stare at her dressed like that and not touch her. It was going to drive me fucking crazy.

She still hadn't noticed me leaning against the door frame, so I took a moment to get myself under control. I also took the opportunity to wipe my hands on my jeans. They shook against the denim, and I crossed my arms over my chest to give them somewhere to hide. Once I'd managed that, I swallowed and opened my mouth. "I called you."

She jumped against the mattress, and the book slipped from her grip to land on the bedspread as she turned to face me. Her cheeks reddened, and I wasn't quite sure whether she was embarrassed or just plain angry that I had shown up at her place when she was obviously trying to blow me off.

"I know," was her short, certain reply, and I had to admit, knowing she had the balls to own up to it had me both proud and weirdly turned on.

"So, were you planning on calling me back? Or maybe answering one of the texts I sent you?"

"Yes."

I waited for her to go on, and when she didn't, I couldn't help but smile. "And when were you planning to do that, sweetheart?"

"It's not like you gave me much of a chance," she snapped, pushing up from the mattress to angle herself toward me. "What did you do, call me from the parking lot?"

"Yep." I watched her react to that as I crossed the floor to sit beside her on the mattress. I barely had a chance to settle onto my ass before she was sliding frantically toward the foot of the bed. She wasn't wearing her prosthesis, and with her crutches leaning against the wall behind me, she was stuck. Still, she put as much space between us as possible and I resisted the urge to close the distance, not wanting her to feel any more trapped than she probably already did.

"We need to talk."

"We do," I agreed.

"I can't do this anymore."

"I can't either."

Her head jerked back, and her eyes narrowed in my direction. She watched me carefully for a moment before nodding slowly, and when she spoke, the words came out hesitantly. "Okay. Good."

"Good," I echoed with a resolute nod. Then, because I couldn't help myself, I smiled in her direction. "So, what time can I pick you up tomorrow for dinner?"

"What?" The word was an alarmed wheeze, and it took everything I had not to laugh.

Instead, I schooled my expression into a mask of innocence. "What what?"

"Why would we go to dinner? We just broke up."

"No, we didn't."

"Yes, James, we did."

"We didn't, Caro. Because you can't break up if you're not actually together. Unless..." I paused hopefully. "Are you saying we're together?"

"No, but-" Her mouth snapped shut angrily, and the look she gave me was filled with so much angry heat, it could have boiled water.

Through gritted teeth, she spoke quietly. "What are you doing right now?"

I thought about answering the question directly but decided to take another, more subtle route. So far, I'd only pissed her off further, and that was definitely counter-productive to my efforts. Not to mention every aspect of the plan had flown out of my head the second I'd seen those shorts—six hours coming up with strategies lost to a tiny piece of blue cotton. I was left with no other option than to wing it. "I have a proposition."

She eyed me warily, and I figured it was probably in my best interest to continue before she started pushing me straight out the door. "The past month has been incredible. Really incredible. I don't want it to stop. Fuck, Caro..." I laughed softly, unable to stop myself from saying the words, "I don't *ever* want it to stop."

"Jimmy-"

"No, just listen, please. I like spending time with you. I like being around you. I think you're amazing in just about every way that it's possible for a person to be amazing. From the first second I saw you, you made me feel...invincible. Like I can do anything in the world, which, trust me, is a totally new thing for me. Before you, I didn't dream about wanting a better life. I didn't dream about *anything*."

"Dreams aren't always a good thing to have, James. And it hurts like a bitch when they fall apart."

My eyebrows slammed down, and I eyed her critically. That negativity... That wasn't Caro. "What happened?"

She stared at me blankly, so I elaborated impatiently, "Between yesterday and today, what happened to change your mind?"

"Nothing happened."

"Bullshit. What happened? What scared you?"

That brought the fire back to her eyes. "I'm not scared."

"Then why are you running?"

Her mouth dropped open and I waited for her to explode. Before the angry words could escape she froze, took one deep breath, and then closed her mouth. Her eyes dropped to the mattress and I watched the anger fade.

Once she'd reclaimed her composure, she finally met my eyes again. "Look, I just didn't mean to let this turn into such a..." She frowned while searching for a word, and it was so fucking adorable that I would have smiled if I hadn't been so anxious to hear what she was about to say. "A *thing*. It's not that I don't like you, because I do. It's not that I don't enjoy spending time with you, because I like that too. But I didn't break up with Dan all that long ago, and you and Maddie..."

I'd been irritated when she brought up the Dickhead, but the second Maddie's name entered the conversation, I shot straight through irritation to anger. "Me and Maddie what?"

She glanced at me carefully, having accurately read my tone to mean *tread carefully*. "You and Maddie were together for a long time. You don't know what it's like to really be single, and if you just settle for the first thing that comes along, you'll never get a chance to figure out what you actually want."

And with that, I was pissed. Pissed that she didn't believe I actually wanted her. Pissed that she was once again acting like I hadn't been single for over a month already. But mostly, I was pissed that she thought being with her could ever be considered settling.

Slowly, I lifted myself off the mattress. I needed to stand to relieve some of the anxious tension thrumming through my veins. Getting angry was not going to help anything, but I was having a hard time breathing away the useless emotion.

My fingers curled into painfully clenched fists, and I could feel my pulse thumping at my temple as I turned to face her. She slid back and settled against the wall as I took a deep breath, and although my jaw was still clenched when I finally managed to speak, I was at least able to relax my fists and keep from shouting. "Didn't we just establish that we are not together?" She nodded quickly, and I continued. "So I have been single, for over a month now. Which brings me to my next point: Don't you find it at least a little telling that, in the month that I've been single, I've spent almost all my free time with you? Because I happen to think that's a pretty good indicator of just how much I want you."

"But-"

I raised one finger in her direction, and her voice cut out instantly. "What really bothers me, though, is the fact that you somehow believe being with you would be anything less than a dream come true. I'm not settling. I'm doing the opposite. I'm claiming you."

I watched the indecision play out on her face, like she couldn't decide if she wanted to argue that or not. I sighed when she decided on the former. "You can't claim me. Like it or not, I do have some say in who I date."

"I know. But I also know I can make it clear as fuck that I'm in love with you, so anyone who thinks about making a play will know to back off."

Her jaw dropped then, and I knew mine had too. I hadn't meant for the words to come out like that. I definitely hadn't planned on telling her for the first time while we were fighting.

"Fuck," I muttered. "Can we pretend I didn't just say that?"

Again, she looked like she was considering whether or not she wanted to argue. Thankfully, this time she decided against it. "Yes, we can." I nodded and watched as she nervously weaved her fingers together before continuing. "Because, honestly, none of it matters. I'm telling you now that whatever we had is over."

"Good, because I don't want what we had. I want more. And I'm not going to give up until I get it."

She snorted and crossed her arms across her chest. It pushed her breasts further up and out of the tank top, and I had to wonder if she was doing it on purpose to distract me.

If so, it was definitely working.

"Well, don't hold your breath. I don't have any more to give, so you'll be waiting forever."

"Not forever. Just until you're ready to admit what I already know."

"And what's that?"

"That you're mine and I'm yours."

She shook her head and laughed softly. "Like I said, don't hold your breath."

That time, it was my turn to laugh. "Caro, I give it two weeks. A month tops, and you'll be at my front door."

"Wow. I'm actually amazed your ego is fitting in this room right now."

I managed to hold onto my laughter because she truly had no idea that my confidence was mostly bravado. Caroline was stubborn, almost as stubborn as me. But the keyword there for me was *"almost."*

I was positive I could outlast her.

"It's not ego; it's confidence. You don't know the details of my plan to win you over."

One brow rose, and the corner of her mouth lifted. "You have a plan?"

"Of course I have a plan. I make plans for everything important."

She shook her head like she was annoyed, but I recognized the resignation in her eyes and in her voice when she finally muttered, "Whatever. Does this plan involve anything else tonight, or can I get back to what I was doing before you showed up unannounced and uninvited?"

"As long as we're clear..."

"Crystal. Now please go."

I figured I had pressed my luck enough for one night, so I went.

## Chapter Thirty Three

# Caroline

JIMMY HADN'T BEEN LYING ABOUT having a plan. And it wasn't just any plan. It was the mother of all plans. At least, all the plans that had ever been created to facilitate winning someone's affections.

He didn't realize he'd already won mine. I just wasn't going to give in and let him know that.

Truthfully, I hadn't known what to expect when he left my place that day. I figured he'd text, probably call a few times, and maybe try to invite me on a few more dates before he finally realized I wasn't going to back down.

That's not what happened at all.

It started with a letter, written on a piece of spiral-bound notebook paper carefully torn from its bindings. The letter had been folded into fours and shoved under the door of the apartment after our non-break-up. I had no clue what time it had been dropped off, but I'd noticed it on my way out the door in the morning.

From its spot on the floor, I could make out my name across the paper in Jimmy's slanted scrawl, and I hesitated before leaning down to pick it up.

With shaky fingers, I stood frozen in my spot by the door and unfolded the paper.

> *Caroline,*
>
> *I know we agreed to forget I said the words, but they're already out there. You already know, and I'm tired of hiding how I feel about you. So, I'm telling you again now. I LOVE YOU! So much and for so many different reasons that it'll take me a lifetime to list them all. A lifetime I'm excited to give.*
>
> *To start the task of making you understand just how incredible you are—how perfect you are for me—I began that list last night. So far, it has 138 items. That's barely the tip of the iceberg. I just fell asleep before I could get any further.*
>
> *I dreamt about you, by the way. I dream about you every single night.*
>
> *I don't want to overwhelm you (any more than I already have), so I'm going to give you one reason at a time until you realize that I'm not going anywhere. Until you realize that what we have is bigger than anything else I've ever known. It's unlike anything else I've ever felt, and it's something I want for the rest of my life.*
>
> *I'll be here whenever you realize that you want it, too.*
>
> *Jimmy*
>
> *P.S. Reason #1: I love the way you see the best in people—the way you've always seen the best in me. I know I didn't really give you a lot of reasons to at first, but you've always seen something better in me. You've always tempered who I am with who I could be, and you've never*

*been judgmental, even as you helped push me to become a better man. I love you for the person you've helped me become.*

*P.P.S That might seem like more than one reason, but most of my reasons are really compound reasons, so it's only one. Don't freak out (any more than you already did).*

I honestly didn't know whether I wanted to laugh or cry or punch something. It was easily the most romantic gesture I'd ever been on the receiving end of, and I had to admire him for it. He was clearly giving this all he had. But what he didn't account for was the way the letter solidified every notion I had about what was best for both of us.

He clearly needed space and time to realize that, whatever we had, it wasn't permanent. It wouldn't last—it wouldn't be able to last—because one day he would realize he wanted more. He would realize he had been blinding himself to the world because he'd been too focused on trying to love me.

The letter, though... I stared at the words on the creased paper, re-read them over and over. So many times that I could have replicated it word-for-word from memory if it was ever lost or destroyed.

I neither heard nor noticed Jen until she was standing a foot away, staring at me and calling my name impatiently. When her voice finally broke the spell I'd been under, I flinched and folded the paper quickly, shoving it carefully into my pocket before meeting her gaze.

"Jesus, I've only been..." She let out a frustrated breath and shook her head. "Are you alright? I thought you left, like, half an hour ago?" Her eyes were narrowed suspiciously on me, and she was obviously still pissed about our fight the night before. While she had every right to be angry, I wasn't in the headspace to even remotely have the conversation the two of us needed to have. Jimmy's letter had temporarily broken me.

"Yeah," I finally managed, "I'm going now, I just...got distracted." And then I still didn't move. In fact, I didn't move for so long that she eventually arched a brow in my direction and shook her head like I was quite possibly the most ridiculous person on the planet.

"Sorry, yeah," I muttered, spinning toward the door and waving a hand back in her direction limply. "I'll see you later."

The only response was the sound of the door closing behind me.

I spent the bulk of the day out of the apartment. It had started as a legitimate need to run a few errands, but my reluctance to go home came after I'd spent another half an hour sitting on a bench in the middle of campus, reading and obsessing over the letter.

I'd clearly underestimated him. I wasn't worried about him breaking through my resolve. I was worried about getting my heart mangled while he figured out that whatever he thought was love would fade. I had real, genuine feelings for the guy, and I knew it wasn't going to feel great forcing myself to cut him off. But it needed to happen, quickly and cleanly, if it was ever going to heal right. It was like a gangrenous limb; you just have to get ahead of it— chop that shit off before it can do any permanent damage.

Death, for instance. Death was pretty permanent.

So that's what I was doing. I was cutting us apart, quickly and cleanly, before I became the death of him. The death of those dreams he'd started having. The death of his chance for a better future.

It would hurt, but I would do it. Because I had to do it.

For him.

The sun had been gone for at least two hours before I finally walked back through my front door. I hadn't even gotten fully inside before I noticed the simple but huge bouquet sitting on the kitchen counter, and its appearance locked me in place, stuck halfway between the apartment and the hall.

White calla lilies. I had mentioned them exactly once, and in passing at that. Somehow he had remembered, and now there was a gorgeous display of my favorite flowers sitting in my kitchen.

In fucking January, no less.

It was absolutely ridiculous.

When the door to Jen's room opened, I finished walking inside and shut the door hastily. By the time she had made it to the other side of the counter, I was standing in the fluorescent light of the kitchen, staring warily at the flowers.

"Those came for you around twelve. The other thing came at six-ish, I think." I hadn't even noticed the package, but my eyes scanned the counter and found it sitting underneath the spray of blooms, wrapped in plain brown paper and tied with a string. Tucked into the twine was another piece of paper, this one a heavyweight cream sheet that looked like it had been taken from a stationary set. It was folded in half with my name scrawled carefully across the front.

A baseball-sized ball of dread settled into my stomach. I tentatively reached out a hand toward the package before Jen's voice broke through yet again, causing me to drop my hand back to my side.

"He didn't stay last night, so I figured you ended it, but then..." Her eyes drifted down to the flowers thoughtfully and then flicked back up to mine. The thoughtful expression was gone, replaced by a look of irritation, served with a generous helping of disappointment. "I really hope you're not leading him on. He deserves better than that, and, honestly, Caro? So do you."

My jaw fell, and my fingers curled into indignant fists, but before I could summon a word in my defense, she was gone, back into her bedroom. Thankfully, there was no oppressive door slam, just a quiet click that was somehow much more ominous.

I tried to brush off the conversation and the way it made me feel like complete and absolute shit. Despite my best efforts, it clung to me like the smell of smoke after a night spent around a campfire, but I pushed it to the back of my mind to focus on the deliveries that had come while I was out.

The flowers were tucked into a tall bamboo vase I had never seen before, so I assumed it had been delivered with them. I considered them carefully, not quite sure what I wanted to do. The smartest choice would have been to trash them, but I didn't even treat that as an option. Part of me wanted to carry them straight into my room, but another, larger part of me worried about the effect they would have on my resolve. Between the bouquet's size and the crisp scent I could detect from a good three feet away, they would overpower the room, filling it with constant thoughts of Jimmy and his infuriatingly perfect wooing tactics.

Instead of carrying them to my room, I centered them on the counter and left them to brighten up the kitchen. My hands moved to the package, and I carefully lifted it into my arms. It was the right size and weight to be a book, but it felt strange, too malleable on one side.

Carrying it to my room, I settled onto the bed after grabbing the scissors from my desk drawer. I set them and the package down before pulling the paper carefully from under the string. My fingers carefully unfolded it, and I ran a thumb against the crease to flatten the thick paper, half-filled with black ink.

*If we were doing things my way, I would have taken you to dinner tonight. There's this great Italian place—amazing food, even better dessert. You're going to love it once we finally make it there.*

*Anyway, after dinner, instead of taking you to a movie, I would have brought you back to my place. I would have made you popcorn, and I would have had candy, so you got the full experience. And then we would have watched The Princess Bride together. But we both know we wouldn't have made it to the end because we never make it to the end of movies. Hell, we barely made it through the opening credits of Con Air. I'm still not convinced you didn't lie to me when I asked if you had a thing for Nic Cage. I won't judge, baby.*

*I'm getting off point. The point is, I wish I was with you. But, since I'm not, I'm giving you the movie we should be watching together right now. There's also a little something extra in there to go with it. It's not as great as the movie, but it's still a decent read.*

*I love you. I really, really love you.*

*Reason #3: I fucking love the way you say my name. Especially while you're coming. It's the sexiest fucking sound I've ever heard. Seriously, Caroline, if I wasn't worried about freaking you out, I'd tell you how much I want to record the sounds you make during sex just so you can begin to understand how absolutely magnificent you are.*

*…Whoops.*

My eyes skated over the last word, and I dropped the paper to the bed, utterly dumbstruck. It took a few minutes of vacant staring for me to regroup my emotional defenses enough to manage the scissors into my hand.

I carefully cut the string before unwrapping the paper, unveiling the movie and the novel underneath it. My eyes took in the cover of the hardback in my hand, and I quickly thumbed through the pages before setting it down. I couldn't help the tiny smile that curved my lips as my eyes slid over the DVD resting next to it. It was becoming glaringly obvious that Jimmy remembered everything, and I wished I was able to appreciate it. Instead, I wiped the smile from my face and re-fortified.

Unhelpfully, my eyes trailed back over the note, and I reread the words, my eyes catching on the number he'd assigned his list item. The letter earlier had contained Reason #1. If this was #3... My mind flashed to the flowers, to Jen saying they had been delivered first, and I sprang off the bed and out of my room.

I searched the bouquet as I closed the distance to the counter, but I didn't spot the card until I'd actually wrapped my hand around the vase to turn it for a thorough inspection. The white card was hard to spot amongst the white flowers, but I finally made out the square corners and rescued the small piece of cardstock from its holster.

*Reason #2: I love the way you smile first thing in the morning. It's the best possible way to start my day, seeing how incredibly happy you are to wake up in my arms.*

*I want that smile every morning for the rest of forever, Caro.*

I dazedly carried myself back to my room and headed straight for the bed. I scooped up both gifts, as well as the other note, and carried it all over to my dresser. Pulling open my top drawer, I shoved aside all my bras and underwear and pushed Jimmy's deliveries to the back of the wooden rectangle. Then, once I'd rearranged the clothing in order to fully hide the gifts, I shoved the drawer shut and collapsed onto the bed.

Once I'd pulled off my jeans and my leg, I slid under the covers and pulled them until I was completely hidden inside a cocoon of bedding.

For almost three hours, I whispered a near silent mantra. *It's for him. It's all for him.*

That simple message on repeat was the only way I was going to get through it all.

And so it began. Every day, three times a day, packages were dropped off at the door. There was always a note or card, but that was the only constant. I received candy, more movies, a few more books, loads of flowers, and tons of other odds and ends—things that, according to the notes that accompanied them, had made him think of me. And every single gift came with another reason. Each one different and uniquely beautiful, they all left a mark in the exact same way. In the exact same place.

The     not-quite-broken-but-definitely-bruised lump of tissue in the center of my chest was begging for respite from the endless onslaught, but I must have been a masochist because less than two weeks later, I'd started craving those deliveries like an addict in need of a fix. In the days before school started, I spent almost every waking moment inside my apartment, waiting for the knock on the door that signified another gift. There was never anyone with them, though. No matter how quickly I got the door open, I never caught even a glimpse of the person dropping them off. It was always a package on the floor by the door and an empty hallway.

By the time classes started, I was beginning to go a little crazy. Jen and I still weren't totally back to normal, mostly because I had barely seen her. Even before classes started, she was hardly ever at home, and I wasn't sure if she was just choosing to spend her time elsewhere or if she was actually trying to avoid me.

I decided I didn't particularly want to know.

Without Jen, though, and with Jimmy out of sight—if not out of mind—I was officially alone. I still hadn't heard a word from Nate, and it became really clear really quickly that I needed to find a way to keep myself busy or run the risk of going completely insane.

That need to keep busy was how I found myself standing in front of the wide glass doors that marked the entrance to the McCarthy family rink on a Thursday. It was almost one month after the night in my bedroom, which incidentally was also the last time I'd seen Jimmy. And I had been looking. I kept my eyes peeled around campus, hoping to catch just a glimpse of him. Once or twice I'd thought I'd seen him, but on second glance I always turned out to be wrong.

It took about five minutes to muster up the courage to walk inside. I wasn't even sure why I had shown up, except I knew that Jimmy wouldn't be there, so, in a way, it had seemed safe.

Standing at the door, though, it suddenly felt dangerous.

I swallowed the fear and pushed my way inside, scanning the empty front desk before walking past it to head toward the ice. There were a few people skating alone, as well as a couple small groups that filled the wide space with the muted echoes of conversations and laughter. Still, it was quiet, calm, and the cold sank into my bones in a way that I had been desperately missing.

Popping into the bleachers along the wall, I chose a bench a few feet off the floor and settled in to watch the skaters. I breathed in the crisp arena air, felt the chill of the ice, and for the first time in a month, my mind settled. I relaxed, practically melted into the bench in fact, and I stayed until closing time, just feeling the room and letting it fill me up.

And that's how I started going to Jimmy's rink twice a week, the two days that Jimmy was always off work for practice. The employees mostly left me alone, besides the few occasions when I zoned out enough to not realize it was closing time. Other than that, they seemed to have no problem with me sitting in the stands, watching the free skate sessions, and it quickly became my favorite place to spend time.

I finally ran into Chris during my third Thursday. He gave me a strange look but thankfully chose not to ask why I was spending my nights sitting in his rink. Instead, he told me about a league of guys that met for practices on Saturdays. He told me how they were all veterans and all amputees, at that. He told me he'd love to see me sit in on a practice, told me to come watch them instead of the teenagers and handful of stoned college kids who mostly populated free skate nights.

I didn't say yes, but I did agree that if he was willing to keep my visits to the rink from Jimmy, I would seriously consider it.

He agreed, so I did as well. And I did consider it, seriously. But I didn't go. Not the first Saturday, or the second.

Or a single Saturday after that.

Chapter Thirty Four

*Jimmy*

SO I HAD OBVIOUSLY UNDERESTIMATED her ability to freeze me out. I still waited every night to hear a knock at my door or even the ringing of my phone, but it had been almost a month and a half, and she showed not a single sign of wavering.

I had been utterly incessant. Gifts, letters, postcards... Hell, I'd had her favorite breakfast delivered one morning. I did everything I could to show her how much I cared about her and how good we could be together. How good I could be to her. Because she deserved nothing but the best, and I was ready and waiting to give it to her.

Apparently, she just wasn't ready to receive it.

My shock-and-awe campaign got harder the longer our estrangement went on. First, it was practice, then it was classes. Not long after that, my weekends were gone too, filled with games and even more practices. The team had a chance to make it into the playoffs, and as the regular season drew to a close, I worked my ass off along with every other guy on the team to see that we got there.

Thankfully, my shifts at the rink had been fewer and farther between. In Dad's words, I should have been focusing on school and hockey. All the rest was secondary.

But the rest didn't feel secondary. Because the rest was a whole lot of Caroline, and she was hands-down the most important thing I'd ever worked for. I wasn't about to give up, no matter what.

That said, I was well aware that I was starting to closely resemble the very definition of stupidity. I needed to change up my tactics because what I'd been doing clearly wasn't working. With that thought in mind, I set about deciding on a new plan of attack.

The new plan went into effect on Valentine's Day. In retrospect, that itself could have been a mistake, but at the time it had seemed like a foolproof idea. Because the new plan was a complete retreat.

The gifts, the letters, the hundreds of reasons scratched onto paper, they all stopped. It was the exact opposite of what I wanted to do, especially on Valentine's Day, but somehow my mind convinced itself that since it was the opposite of what I wanted, it would be the opposite of what Caroline wanted as well. And maybe it would be enough. Maybe the sudden absence of my pursuit would be enough to shock her into action.

All day I walked around with a spring in my step. Even an afternoon at work couldn't bring me down, although that also could have had to do with the fact that I was able to close up early. Ash had talked Dad into shutting down, so he could bring his girl to the rink, and Dad had agreed because Dad almost always agreed when Ash asked for a favor. Especially if it was a skating-related favor. Chris

McCarthy would do just about anything to get Ash on the ice, even if it meant missing out on a night's worth of income—on a holiday, no less.

I had just finished cleaning up when Ash and Parker walked through the front door. I met them at the edge of the ice, and we exchanged a few words. Mostly, I attempted to make up for the bullshit I'd pulled at Marco's party. I wasn't totally sure that it worked, but Parker's smile seemed genuine enough, so I hoped it was at least a start.

I'd been headed for the door when Ash's voice rang out behind me, bringing me down from cloud nine for the first time since I'd woken up committed to the new plan. "You talked to Maddie?"

I'd played off the question with a simple head shake that felt so much like a lie, it pissed me off. And then I'd headed out to my car, resigning myself to a talk with my best friend in the very near future. So much had changed in my life—so much was happening—and if I didn't clue him in soon, I worried it would be too late.

Pushing my impending conversation with Ash to the back of my mind, I headed for home, practically bouncing in my seat with anticipation. In my mind, there wasn't a chance that she wouldn't come. Wasn't a chance that she would make it through the night without showing up at my door, wondering why the gifts had stopped.

I was so convinced, I got home and sat my ass down on the top stair. I instigated the world's longest staring match with my front door, one that I eventually lost when I heaved myself off the floor with a frustrated sigh almost *five* hours later.

Relocating to the couch, I allowed myself two glasses of bourbon and finally passed out against the cushions, ears still straining for the sound of a knock at the door. Straining and hoping for a sound that never came.

That night, I dreamt I was in a room filled with doors. They completely covered the walls, leading to a hundred different paths and rooms. I stood in the room and heard the echoes of knocking all around me, but every door I ripped open revealed nothing but empty space. I ran in circles, opening door after door, desperately searching for the source of the knocking. Coming up empty every single time.

The new plan sucked, but I was committed to sticking to it. The way I saw it, I had three months to get Caro back into my life. Three months to break through the walls she'd constructed. After that, I'd be gone until the fall, and I didn't want to leave unless we were in a good place. That said, after a certain point, I wasn't going to have a choice in the matter.

It was hard, though. I was desperate to talk to her. I wanted to tell her about my plans, wanted to tell her about all the decisions I'd made since the last time we'd spoken. I wanted to see her eyes light up with the pride I knew she'd feel. I wanted to feel the joy she felt, just knowing someone she cared about was happy.

And I couldn't have any of it.

Yes, the new plan definitely sucked, but I was going to do whatever I needed to do to get her back into my life and into my arms. If that meant I needed to torture both of us a little, well, that was exactly what I was going to do.

About a month after the new plan went into effect, I realized that there were quite a few people besides Caro who needed to know my new plans for the future. First and foremost on that list was Dad. So one afternoon, I headed into work early and met him at the rink. The conversation took place in the office and lasted less than ten minutes. And although I'd never actually considered what my dad would say if I ever told him I was leaving Virginia (because I'd never actually *considered* leaving Virginia before), I can't say I was surprised by his reaction.

Really, it was more of a non-reaction. In fact, the sum total of his feelings on the matter had been, "Good. It's about damn time."

It further hit home a point that I'd already started to understand. As much as I had always felt trapped by this town, my family, and the role I felt I'd been assigned, I had never realized that I'd been the one to place myself in that cage entirely on my own. Dad's easy acceptance of my decision to leave town further proved that *I* was the only one who had ever held me back.

I had been scared. I'd been afraid of facing my potential, and I'd been afraid that my family would see it as a defection. I loved my family, and the last thing I ever wanted to do was hurt them, but Dad proved that they knew, probably even more than I did, that my leaving had nothing to do with them. It was entirely about me.

And, in fact, it may have been the first truly selfish thing I'd ever done, but it also somehow felt like the best decision I'd ever made.

With my future starting to look more appealing by the day, there was only one thing missing. Only one more thing that would complete my vision.

One funny, passionate, strong, beautiful, caring, and insanely stubborn thing that kept me from truly having everything I'd ever wanted.

But I'd never even *dreamed* of getting this close to the perfect life. I knew if I let this opportunity slip away, I would have to work twice as hard to ever get it back again, and that, frankly, was something I wasn't willing to do.

So, I stuck with the plan even as I started working on my next tactic, another idea to try out if this one failed to produce results. Because I wasn't going to accept anything less than what I wanted.

And all I wanted was Caroline.

Chapter Thirty Five

# Caroline

THE END OF THE GIFTS had signaled a change in me. I tried to feel good about the fact that he'd obviously given up. I tried to convince myself that he was doing exactly what I wanted him to do.

It all felt like a lie.

But I'd gotten through the hard part. Now that our contact had truly been reduced to nothing, I figured we would both begin to move on. I could finally get past him without having what we'd had endlessly being thrown in my face.

Easier said than done. I threw myself into classes and studying, and I kept up my visits to the rink to fill my days. Jen continued to spend most of her time somewhere that wasn't our place, and the rink had become somewhat of a second home in my attempts to avoid sitting in the empty apartment. Because of that, I wasn't all too happy when my visits ended right along with the men's hockey season.

The guys had had an impressive year overall, managing to make it to the finals, and even though they hadn't won, I knew it was still something to celebrate. It was the best showing the school's team had had in years, and I really wished I had been able to celebrate with both Jimmy and Nate. Hell, I wished I'd been brave enough to actually go to one of their playoff games.

When I let myself think about it, I hated that I hadn't gotten to experience that with Nate—absolutely hated that I hadn't gotten to be there as he came within touching distance of his first college title. But I also realized something in the moments that I let myself think about exactly why that was.

Since the accident, I'd refused to even *consider* a future that had anything to do with that world. But for all my insistence that I had left that life behind, I actually hadn't. Not at all. I'd thrown myself headfirst into becoming Nate's biggest supporter. The year that he took off before college, he'd played in two separate hockey leagues, and I'd gone to every game and almost every single practice. I'd relentlessly pushed him to skate faster and harder, to work on his passing, to do whatever it took to be the best he could be.

In truth, I pushed him to be everything I *couldn't* be.

And somehow I'd never realized I was doing it. Even more so, I'd never realized that watching him play and critiquing his game gave me more of a sense of contentment and fulfillment than anything else had since the day I'd lost my leg. Case in point, I'd spent weeks sitting on an uncomfortable wooden bench because the very *air* of a rink had the power to calm me.

And, suddenly, I wanted absolutely nothing to do with opening an art gallery. In fact, the entire idea seemed so incredibly insane—so magnificently asinine—I couldn't believe I had even managed to come up with it in the first place. I mean, sure, I enjoyed art. I'd gotten really into painting after the accident, and I'd taken an art class my second senior year that I'd really enjoyed, but I didn't want to devote my life to it.

I'd already devoted my life to hockey. Anything else would just be second best.

And even though I recognized that coaching would still be second best to playing, at least I would be back in the same game—back on the same playing field, so to speak. Maybe one day I'd have the courage to get on the ice again. Maybe one day I'd take up sled hockey or even go whole hog by investing in a bladed prosthesis. But until then, I could take the second best of helping other players reach their potential. In fact, if I was able to help even one person the way Coach Wade had helped me over the years, I was willing to bet that coaching would feel way better than second best.

Four weeks before finals, I sat down with my advisor, and we put together a plan for next year, which was surprisingly simple. Carrying it out was going to be a bit more complicated, but it was nothing I couldn't handle. Two hours later, I had a plan, and I had forward momentum. I felt great, better than I had since ending things with Jimmy, and I took that as a sign that I was doing the right thing. For once, I was making the right decision.

So, I decided to harness that forward momentum. The second I'd left my advisor's office, I pulled my phone from my pocket and sent a text to Jen, asking her to meet me at the apartment. I walked home, phone in hand, waiting for a response that never came.

Nonetheless, when I finally walked through the lot of the complex, I spied her car sitting a few spots away from the front door. My breath hitched over a nervous stutter, but I swallowed it down and steeled myself.

I was going to give Jen the best apology I had ever given. Once that was done, I was going to write Nate an apology letter that would one-up the apology I had given Jen. And then, if I had anything left, I was going to write one more letter, this one to Jimmy. Because even though it might have been a seriously bad idea, I felt like he deserved an apology as well. I still felt guilty for the way things had ended between us, and even though I was sure he didn't care anymore, I still did.

I still cared *way* more than I should have.

Pushing through the front door, I shuffled those thoughts away for later. I needed to focus on one thing at a time if I was going to make any progress toward getting my life back together. My footsteps echoed through the empty hallway as I closed the space to my door, and the sound of the key turning in the lock felt unnaturally loud.

Closing the door behind me, I turned back toward the common room and headed past the kitchen. It wasn't until I had cleared the counter that I spotted the head of short, brown hair that peeked over the back of the couch. Just as I started working to convince myself that I was seeing things, the head shifted forward and then turned, revealing Nate's profile in perfect detail.

"Oh my God," I mumbled, taking in the sight of him like he was the last sunset I'd ever see. I pored over every detail of his face, recommitting every feature to memory, as he twisted on the couch to face me.

*God, I'd fucking missed him.*

"Shit, Caro, don't cry," he urged, pushing off the couch to head toward me, and I dazedly reached a hand up to my cheek to find that he was right; a single, silent tear had escaped from one eye. I wiped it away with my fingers as he reached me. His arms slowly came up, and I didn't wait another second. I threw myself against his chest, tucked my head against his shoulder, and let loose a fountain of tears. My arms wound around his waist and held on like he was a lifeline as I drenched his shirt with the proof of just how much I'd missed him.

"You have...no idea," I choked out around the sobs that wracked my chest.

One of his hands slid to the back of my neck and gave a gentle squeeze, quieting me. "I know," he murmured. "I missed you too."

That set me off all over again. Five minutes later, once I'd finally calmed down and gotten myself under control, I reluctantly leaned back. Ducking my head, I wiped the remaining wetness from my face before I lifted my gaze back up to his.

"Come on," he urged, grabbing my hand gently, "let's sit. We should talk." I let him lead me around the couch, and then we both flopped down onto the cushions at either side. Pulling one leg up in front of him, Nate twisted to face me directly and then weaved his fingers together before placing his hands in his lap.

"So, first, I want to apologize. I wasn't very fair to you the last time we talked, and I'm sorry for that. I'm sorry for not actually giving you a chance to talk to me and for not really explaining myself. I just... It's not an excuse, but I was dealing with a whole bunch of shit, and then, when the whole situation with Sammi blew up in my face..." He sighed and leaned back against the arm of the couch. "I didn't handle it well."

"Nate, you don't need to apologize to me."

"I do, though. And not just for that. I'm also sorry for staying away as long as I did. Honestly, I didn't mean to, but life sort of got away from me, and then it had been so long... It just got scarier and scarier the longer I waited. But that wasn't fair to you, either, and I feel terrible that I haven't been around. And I absolutely hate that you've been absent from my life."

I swallowed down the tears that attempted to resurface and shook my head. "It's really okay. I mean, I've been pretty miserable without you, but I get that you needed to do what you needed to do."

I dropped my gaze, and my fingers began playing with a frayed string at the seam of my jeans. "Speaking of which..."

"Speaking of which," Nate echoed, and I glanced back up to find him watching me carefully.

I waited for him to continue, but he just stared at me until I opened my mouth. "Did you, um, manage to do what you needed to do?"

"If you mean did I manage to sort out my shit, then yes. Well, sort of. Life is a never-ending storm of shit, and I'm just trying to handle it the best I can. But, as far as you and I are concerned, consider it sorted."

"Seriously?" The question burst out so desperately hopeful that I winced. Nate just smirked.

"Seriously. I love you, Caro, I truly do. And, for a really long time, you were the literal archetype of my perfect woman. Tough, gorgeous, funny, and the only person I've ever met who loves hockey more than me. I clung to that for a really long time, hoping and praying that one day you'd wake up and see me as something more than a friend.

"But, at some point over the past few months, I realized a few things, the most important one being that, as incredible as you are, you're not really what I want. I realized that I'd been so fixated on you, I hadn't really let myself see anyone or anything else. So, in a way, the past few months were just me giving myself a chance to see the world."

"I'm glad you gave yourself that," I quietly intoned, gaze dropping back to the string I was wrapping around my fingertip.

"I am, too."

"I'm also glad I finally know the truth. And I wanted you to know that I'm so sorry for everything I've inadvertently put you through over the years. I love you, too, and I hate knowing that you got hurt because of me."

"Seriously, you don't have to apologize, Caroline," he argued but I shook my head to cut him off.

"No, Nate, I really do. I spent a lot of time thinking about what you said to me and, I'll admit, at first, I was angry. But I understand why you did what you did and I'll never stop being grateful for everything that you've done for me. And I'm not just talking about what you did after the accident."

He nodded, taking the moment I gave him to fight back the emotion pooling in his eyes.

"So," I finally supplied after a long minute of silence, "what else has happened in the life of the Great Nate Baker since November?"

I heard him quietly laugh, and then I jumped when his voice rang out across the apartment. "Babe! Get out here!"

Wide eyes flew to his as Jen's door swung open, and her voice rang out a moment later. "I told you not to yell at me like that, asshole."

Nate just chuckled and held my gaze. "I'm just going to put it out there. I'm giving it to your roommate regularly."

My mouth popped open just as Jen snapped, "Nate!" and my eyes swiveled to hers.

"Seriously?!"

She ignored me to glare at the back of Nate's head as she walked over and settled onto the arm of the couch at his back. "I told you I wanted to tell her!"

His head tilted back until he was able to meet the gaze leaning over him from above. "Sorry, Jenga. She asked what I've been doing, and I've been doing you."

My mouth burst open again, but this time it was to let out the laughter that exploded at his nickname. "Do you seriously call her Jenga?" I choked out as Jen playfully punched Nate's shoulder. He responded by grabbing onto her wrist and tugging her over his shoulder, pulling her head first across his body until he was able to turn her and settle her in his lap.

She immediately relaxed into him and settled her hands on his thighs as she focused on me. "He seriously calls me that when he's not in the mood to get laid," she answered with a smirk, and he pouted before pressing a kiss to her neck.

"You know you love me," he muttered against her skin, and the words scored across my heart like a thousand tiny papercuts. Worse than that, the way Jen just smiled in response to his words, making no attempt to argue, soaked the bleeding flesh in a torrent of lemon juice.

They both looked so happy, and obviously, completely into each other. And watching it play out in front of me made me realize just how much I wanted that for myself.

Worse than that, I didn't want it with just anyone. I wanted it with Jimmy. I wanted it with the guy I'd driven away. And even though I knew I'd done what was best for him, I couldn't help but wish I'd held onto it for just a bit longer. Even though I knew he was over me—over the month that we had spent together—I couldn't help but wish I could have it back.

I'd been happy. I'd been truly, blissfully happy. And, for the first time, I allowed myself to realize that I had truly loved him—that I still loved him. That even though I had been nothing more than a passing fantasy for him, he had been the most real thing I'd ever experienced. The way I felt for him, it had been pure and strong, so strong that I still felt it pulling at me painfully. Tugging at me and telling me to go to him. To tell him how I felt. To be honest and real for one more time before walking away forever.

But I couldn't do it. I *wouldn't* do it—not to him. And maybe that was my punishment for the way I'd treated him at the end, the way I'd pushed him away and frozen him out. Maybe suffering without him was what I deserved for every bad decision I'd ever made for us. And, when it came to James McCarthy, I had made a lot of bad decisions.

"You okay, Caro?" Nate's voice pulled me out of my head, and I looked up to find both him and Jen watching me.

"Yeah," I assured him brightly. Nodding, I pasted on a smile and continued. "I'm good. I'm really happy for you guys."

Nate gave me a small smile, but Jen just continued staring at me nervously. "Are you sure? Because I could totally understand if you're mad. I mean, he's your best friend, and-"

"Seriously, Jen," I interjected firmly. "It's all good. As long as you and I are good," I added hopefully, and she smiled in response.

"You and I are good. And I'm sorry that I've been absent so much."

"That's my fault," Nate added. "I have separation anxiety issues."

"So, what? You two have been hanging out with the yogi?" I smiled at the image of the three of them meditating together.

"God, no," Nate grumbled before chuckling. "Actually, the yogi went home for the holidays and never came back. And, since I was never assigned another roommate, my double became a single."

"That's fantastic," I pointed out, and he grinned.

"I know."

"Before I forget, Caro, what did you text me about?" Jen suddenly asked, and I smiled and sat up straighter. I hadn't planned on having this conversation, but now I was able to, and, even better, I was able to tell both of them at the same time.

"So," I started, "I went and talked to my academic advisor today, and I switched my major."

Jen looked confused, but Nate had leaned forward in his seat to stare at me with an intensity I had never seen. "To what?"

I gave him a small smile before answering his question. "Kinesiology."

He watched me for another long moment, as if he couldn't actually believe what I'd just said. Then, "No more art gallery?"

I shook my head. "No more art gallery. I was too late to start in the fall, so my new program starts the semester after, but I'm doing it. I'm going for my bachelor's, and then I'm going to get my master's in athletic training. In the meantime, I'm going to talk to Coach Miller, maybe get involved with the team next year if he's still willing to take me on."

The smile that slowly spread across Nate's face was absolutely glorious. Then, with an agile twist, he managed to unwrap himself from around Jen and was diving across the couch toward me to wrap me in a breathtaking hug.

"I'm so fucking proud of you, Caroline. So fucking proud." I heard the hitch in his voice and felt it against my chest as he held on tightly, rocking me slowly from side to side for a few long seconds before he finally leaned back.

Instead of letting me go, though, his hands settled onto my upper arms, and he squeezed me there gently. "This is going to be a good thing for you. I just know it."

I smiled weakly in the face of the emotion in his eyes, and nodded. "I think so too. I think it's the best decision I've made in a long time."

He watched me for another long moment and then pulled me back into his arms. I felt his breath brush against the shell of my ear, and his voice rumbled a quiet whisper into my hair. "I truly believe you could do anything you want and succeed. But I also think this is what you were meant to do. I think this is exactly where you're supposed to be. And I think if you work at it and give it your all, you're going to be amazing at it."

He sucked in a breath that had his chest lifting against me, and the exhale rustled my hair as his lungs expelled the air. "More than anything, I hope this makes you happy. You really, really deserve it."

I wasn't as sure as he sounded, but at the very least, for the first time in a long time, I was hopeful.

## Chapter Thirty Six

*Jimmy*

AS THE SEMESTER WOUND DOWN, time got away from me. There was just so much going on—so many things I needed to take care of and so little time to do it all. I didn't like it, but it meant I'd had to put off strategy number three, my final, grand-finale attempt at getting Caro to come around. At least, my final attempt until the fall.

As much as I hated it, I hadn't had much of a choice. Finals were only a week away. I was in the process of moving all my crap from the apartment into storage, as well as packing up what I'd be taking with me to Maine, and on top of that, I'd been trying to spend as much time as possible with Jack before I left. But I was almost out of time for strategy number three, and I needed to do something fast.

Unfortunately, as I headed out of the building that housed my last class of the day, I reluctantly admitted that it was going to have to wait another day. I had two papers I needed to wrap up before the end of the week, and I'd promised to swing by the rink. Dad had asked me to come in to pick up my last paycheck, and while I had no idea why he needed to make a production out of it, I'd agreed to humor him.

As genuinely happy as he seemed to be for me, I knew he was at least a little sad about my leaving. He hid his emotion better than Mom, though. She'd started crying a week ago, and I still had two weeks before I got in my car and made the drive up north. Granted, a lot of those tears were probably due to the fact that I'd decided not to walk at graduation. I could have, and maybe I should have, but in the grand scheme of things, with everything else going on, it just didn't seem important.

Didn't seem as important as leaving home for the first time. Didn't seem as important as my first real job. Didn't seem as important as convincing the girl of my dreams—the girl that I was still head over heels in love with—that I was *actually* in love with her.

In the face of all that, getting dressed up to receive my diploma just didn't seem worth it. They could mail it to me.

I brushed away thoughts of graduation and focused instead on the papers that I needed to finish as soon as I got home. Without those, there wouldn't be a diploma to receive, and all that worry would be for nothing.

My mind was creating a mental to-do list when I heard the voice calling my name. I spun around on the sidewalk until I spotted Baker weaving around co-eds to reach my side. I gave him a distracted smile and returned his part-handshake, part-backslap before stepping back to meet his gaze.

"How you been, man?"

"Eh, I've been alright," I answered truthfully. "Crazy busy, but that's senior year for you. How about you?"

"I've been good, really good. Trying to get ready for finals and all that bullshit, but otherwise everything's gravy." I smiled and nodded in acknowledgement as he opened his mouth again. "So, I'm glad I ran into you. I've been wanting to talk to you. Wanted to ask a favor, actually."

My eyebrows dipped, and I jerked my head up once. "What's up?"

"Well, I decided to stay here over the summer, and, long story short, I need an income. Caro and I were talking about it, and she suggested that I talk to you. I was kind of hoping that there was maybe a job available at the rink? And that you could maybe put in a good word for me with your dad?"

I grinned and shook my head. "I can't promise the good word, but you're in luck. I actually just worked my last shift two days ago, so I know for a fact Dad could use some help."

"You quit?"

"Yeah, I did. Or took a sabbatical, I guess? I'm leaving Virginia, and I'm going to be busy getting packed and ready to move since I'm out of here a couple days after finals wrap up."

"Wow. Well, I guess that's a good thing?" He phrased the question with so much hesitance that I couldn't help but laugh.

"Yeah, it's a good thing. I'm excited."

"Good," he responded with a wide smile.

It was quiet for a moment, and I tried to talk myself out of asking the question, but I just couldn't help myself. "So, you and Caro are talking again? You guys are good?"

"Yeah, we are."

"Good. I know she really missed you after your fight, so I'm glad you guys were able to work things out."

He nodded but didn't reply, just watched me carefully. That should have been enough to convince me to shut my mouth, but it was moving entirely on its own. "And is she okay? I mean, I'm sure she's okay, but she's good? Is she happy?"

He was quiet for a long moment, and I held myself still to avoid fidgeting under the intense way he watched me, like he was trying to see through the words to the intent underneath.

I didn't know what he was looking for because I thought my intent was pretty obvious.

"Yeah," he finally said with a short nod and a tight smile. "She's good. Great, actually. She's been working on herself a lot, really figuring out what she wants out of life."

His meaning couldn't have been more obvious if he'd just laid it out. *She's totally happy without you, asshole. Forget about her.*

Honestly, some days I wished that was an option. There were moments when I missed her so badly, when I was so desperate to hear her voice or to feel her skin against mine, I found myself wishing I didn't know exactly what I was missing out on.

But Caroline was completely unforgettable.

"That's good," I choked out roughly as I focused back on his face instead of the way my heart pounded painfully against my ribs. "I'm glad she's happy. And you too, man, but I should run. Maybe I'll see you around."

I heard his voice behind me as I turned on the sidewalk, but I didn't actually make out the words.

My pulse thumped loudly between my ears, blurring out the sounds around me as I finished the walk to my car. I didn't want to believe what he had said, didn't want to believe that Caroline really was doing great without me. Because, even though I knew it was massively fucked up, I didn't want her to be great. I wanted her to miss me. I wanted her to *want* me.

And, according to Nate, she didn't. Not at all.

I barely remember the drive home. I was torn between wanting to drive straight to her place and wanting to bury myself inside a bottle until it stopped hurting. Because everything hurt.

I knew that I'd fucked up, letting stage two of the plan go on for as long as it had, but I had never once thought that she would just move on. That she would just get over what we'd had. That she would get over *me*. I had honestly never considered it because, for me, getting over Caro wasn't an option. There was no moving on for me, and there wouldn't be—not for a long, *long* time.

It wasn't until I had walked in my front door that I realized I wasn't supposed to be home, but I couldn't summon the will to walk back out. The last place I wanted to be was the rink right now, so I sent

Dad a quick text letting him know that something had come up before I tossed my phone onto the dining room table. Heading for the kitchen, I pulled open the liquor cabinet and then stopped breathing when my eyes landed on the scotch that had been sitting there since January.

Besides those first two glasses we'd had together, the bottle hadn't been touched. I had refused to drink it without Caroline because despite what I'd told her, it had absolutely been a gift. Now, though, there was no chance she'd be back to finish it.

I quickly pulled the bottle from the cabinet and skipped getting a glass altogether to head for the couch. Propping my feet up on the coffee table, I pulled the cap from the bottle and froze, memories of New Year's Eve flashing through my mind.

You know how they say in the moment before death, your life flashes before your eyes? I experienced that, but it wasn't my body that was dying; it was my heart. It was my soul. It was the dreams I'd only just started having.

And God, did it fucking ache. So badly, I wanted to put my fist through a wall. Again and again and again until the pain in my hand was strong enough to make the rest feel a little less like my body was being ripped apart, limb by bloody limb.

I lifted the bottle to my mouth but gagged at the first bitter lash across my tongue. With an angry thump, I dropped the liquor to the table and then threw myself back against the couch, arms crossed over my face.

I couldn't believe this was the end. I couldn't believe that all that build-up—everything we'd been through to get to this exact moment—was all for nothing. It just seemed so...pointless. Pointless and wasteful. Because I knew that whether she had wanted to admit it or not, she had felt something for me as well. I knew there was no way the connection between us could possibly have been one-sided.

And that was the part that hurt the worst. That she had knowingly thrown away something that could have been truly amazing. Hell, it had *already* been truly amazing, and we had barely even gotten started.

I wasn't sure how long I'd been sitting on the couch when I heard the pounding. Long enough that the blood had all drained from my arms, leaving them numb and then cramped when I pulled them away from my face.

The sound echoed loudly through the apartment, and I groaned before heaving myself off the couch and stumbling toward the stairs. I tripped on the fourth step, managing to control my fall enough to remain standing when I finally slammed into the door. It rattled in its frame, and the pounding immediately cut out as my hand traveled to the knob. Then, without a glance out the window, I yanked the door open and froze.

*Holy shit, she's beautiful.*

Maybe it was because I hadn't seen her in four months, or maybe it was because I had missed her so much some days it hurt to breath. Maybe it was just because I'd spent every second since my conversation with Nate trying to come to terms with the fact that I needed to forget about her, but I just couldn't get over how fucking gorgeous she looked.

She'd gotten a haircut, and the normally dark brown looked lighter too. It was cut on a slant, with long bangs that fell into one eye and cascaded down to just below her shoulders. But, as I looked closer, I noticed that it wasn't just her hair that was different. Something else about her had changed.

It was as if she had gotten lighter. In some way, she looked happier, more at peace than I had ever seen her before, even though the one eye I could see around her hair was narrowed with concern.

"Hey."

That one word plowed into my chest with razor-edged sharpness and laser precision, scoring through the sinew and bone to rake across the frantically pumping muscle underneath.

"What are you doing here?"

I wanted to hit myself the second the words came out, fast and hot. I wanted to immediately apologize, wanted to explain that I wasn't angry, just shocked and scared and a thousand other things that meant I had officially lost all control. But when I needed it the most, my tongue refused to move, refused to relax enough to tell her all the things I needed to say.

She glanced from side to side uncomfortably, and then her eyes moved over my shoulder to scan the stairs. "Any chance we could talk for a minute? Maybe inside, where your family can't hear you yell at me, if that's what you need to do?"

I shook my head quickly to say no, that's not what I needed to do at all, but her head dropped, and I realized I'd fucked up again. Somehow, I managed to regain full control of my mouth just as she took a quick step backwards. "No! *Fuck*, I'm sorry. I didn't mean to yell at you; I don't *want* to yell at you."

She looked unconvinced, so I quickly shuffled back and pulled the door wide. "Please, come in. I promise not to be a dick."

The corner of her lip disappeared into her mouth for just a second before she released it and granted me a tiny smile. "Thanks," she mumbled before moving past me and up into the apartment.

I swung the door closed and then took the steps two at a time to find her at the landing, staring at the pile of boxes against the far wall. I hadn't gotten very far yet, so most of them were still empty, but seeing my life packed up, even in part, still felt surreal.

I glanced at Caro and realized she wasn't thinking about the strangeness of the proof of my decisions. I took a quick step toward her just as she turned and her glassy eyes met mine.

"Nate called me. He said you were leaving, but I..." Her gaze fell away, and she turned back toward the stairs. "I'm sorry. This was really stupid. I'm just going to-"

"Wait, stop!"

She had already reached the top, step but her foot faltered with the crack of my voice, and she stumbled. With a curse, I leapt toward her, managing to wrap a hand around her wrist just before she went headfirst down the stairs.

Once I knew she wasn't going to break her neck or any other valuable parts in yet another tragic accident, I acted without a single thought. My arm gave a firm tug, and I pulled her into my chest, arms wrapping tightly around her waist as I lifted her from the ground and buried my face in her neck. I stood motionless, feeling her warmth against my chest slowly soothing the rush of adrenaline and fear that had surged when she'd started to fall.

It had to have been a full five minutes later before I realized that she wasn't fighting to get away. In fact, I could feel her arms around my neck, gripping me just as tightly as I was holding her. And, as afraid as I was to get my hopes up, from the way she was hanging onto me, it *really* didn't feel like she had moved on.

Reluctantly, I set her on the ground and slowly unwrapped my arms from around her. We each took a slow step backwards, and I anxiously met her gaze.

"So, you're leaving?" The question didn't contain a trace of emotion, and it was asked completely casually, as if our embrace hadn't happened. As if I hadn't felt her clinging to me just as desperately as I'd been holding onto her. But I couldn't pretend that it hadn't happened, so I didn't answer her question.

"Why are you here?"

Her lip disappeared back into her mouth, and she just stared at me for a long moment. Then, with a slow shake of her head, she shrugged. "Honestly? I have no idea."

And that? That answer dashed every single hope that had sprouted since I'd felt her body against mine. Because it might have been the truth—hell, it probably *was* the truth—but it wasn't good enough. I dropped my eyes and turned toward the kitchen as I opened my mouth to tell her so, but a hand on my wrist stopped me.

"No, that's not true. I do know why I'm here. I'm here because finding out that you were leaving, even after four months without seeing you once, it... I just panicked. I know it's not fair, and I know that you've moved on, but I couldn't just let you go without seeing you. Without telling you-"

Her voice cut out, and I twisted my head back over my shoulder to meet her steady gaze. Her hand at my wrist gave a gentle squeeze to my pulse point, and I braced at the heavy expression on her face.

"I needed to tell you that I'm in love with you. And I know-"

That was all it took. Without giving her a single warning, I closed the space between us and swallowed her words with my mouth against hers. She was still for half a second, and then she was kissing me back, kissing me with all the angst, anger, pain, and love that my own mouth communicated. Her fingers wrapped around my neck and gripped me tightly, as if holding me to her, and if I hadn't been so distracted by the taste of her on my tongue and the painfully stiff erection I was trying not to maul her with, I would have celebrated the need that simple gesture communicated.

Before I realized it was happening, my palms had latched onto her sides, and then they were gliding down until I was able to wrap them under her ass, lifting her up into my arms. Her good leg wrapped around my back, and her hands slid up into my hair, using that grip to take control of the kiss as I stumbled across the floor toward the bedroom.

The door to my room was closed, and I reluctantly slid one hand from her ass to fumble for the doorknob. Just as I found the brass with my fingers, her lips curved, and she sucked my tongue into her mouth in a move that had my knees going weak. I stumbled forward, slamming her back into the door as my free hand went back to her thigh.

"Shit, I'm sorry."

A second later, my mouth was back on hers, and my hand was back at the door. Then it was open, and I was holding onto her carefully as I maneuvered us inside. We made it to the bed without further incident, and we both fell to the mattress. I managed to get my hands up to brace myself above her, and then we were horizontal on top of the sheets. Throughout it all, her mouth never once left mine.

Pulling one hand from the mattress, I suspended myself above her and brought my other hand to her hip, slowly working my fingers under the edge of her t-shirt teasingly. My fingertips lightly skated over the skin above the denim of her jeans, and I felt a shiver run through her body when my palm flattened against the warm skin at her stomach.

"Wait," she murmured between the kisses she continued to lave against my lips. "I think..." another kiss, "we should..." a little tongue, "probably talk..." a little more tongue, "before this gets out of hand."

She was half right. We should definitely be talking, but this was *already* out of hand.

I shook my head and worked my lips across her cheek and down her neck. "I like out of hand. Out of hand is fun. We can talk later."

I heard her quiet laughter, and, God, I'd fucking missed that sound. So much, it was unreal. Getting that back definitely eased the pain I felt when her hands landed on my chest and gently pushed against me. I tried to stifle my groan as I pushed off her and rolled to the side of the bed, collapsing onto my back and rubbing both hands along my face.

"Fuck. I'm sorry, Caro," I muttered from beneath my palms. "I didn't mean-" I stopped when she laid a finger against my lips.

The finger disappeared, and then she was pulling my hands from my face. I reluctantly opened my eyes and relaxed at the sight of her propped up on an elbow, head tilted down toward me and a smirk across her face. "Please don't apologize. That was the best thing to happen to me since New Year's."

My breath stuck in my lungs, and I felt the hope begin to resurface in earnest. Sure, she'd been all over me, but we had proved time and time again that our sexual chemistry was off the charts. Part of me had expected her to play it off, but she was doing the exact opposite. To be sure, though, I needed to talk to her.

"Did you mean it?"

I expected her to ask for clarification, but she just nodded. "Yes. I'm sorry it took so long to tell you, but it's the truth. I'm completely in love with you. Almost disgustingly so."

I couldn't help it; I laughed. "Is that so? You find your love for me disgusting?"

She smirked and then leaned down to press a closed-mouth kiss against my lips. "Only a little."

"Well, that's a relief, I guess."

Her smirk turned into a smile and then faded away completely as her finger began to run itself along the lines of my face. Down my nose, over my lips, and across my jaw. Her eyes watched the trail she traced carefully, as if she was recommitting my face to memory.

"I owe you an apology."

My eyes narrowed at her whispered declaration, and I grabbed her hand gently, twisting our fingers together. "No, you don't. You're here now. Nothing else matters."

"No, Jimmy, seriously. I'm so sorry for shutting you out, for trying to hide from what we had. I realized something on the way over here, actually. As much as I tried to pretend that I did what I did for you, I think that was just an excuse.

"Since the accident, I haven't allowed myself to want anything. Anything big, at least. Anything that mattered. It was like, if I didn't let myself want it, it wouldn't hurt when it inevitably got ripped away.

Because everything I'd ever wanted, all of my dreams, they'd all already been ripped away once before, and I didn't think I could go through that again. So, instead I told myself to live day to day. Because living like there was no tomorrow meant that I didn't need to worry about wanting anything past that.

"But living like that, it's not really living. And it's definitely not living like there's no tomorrow because that... Well, that's what I'm doing right now."

Her hand not held in mine came up to wrap around my neck, and she leaned down until our noses brushed. Until I could feel the gentle push and pull of air leaving her lungs. "If there really was no tomorrow, I'd want to spend today right here. I'd want to spend every second I had left with the person who makes me happier than anyone else ever has. I'd want to live out the rest of my life with the guy that I'm completely in love with."

I cleared my throat gently and gave the fingers against my palm a soft squeeze. "And what if there is a tomorrow?"

"Then that just means I get to wake up wearing a smile. It means I get one more day to spend with you."

Her head dropped down, slowly closing the last inch that separated us, and as much as I wanted to accept the kiss and get us back to what we'd been doing just a few minutes before, I forced my head to turn to dodge it. She was undeterred though, and her mouth worked over my cheek and down to my jaw as I smiled up at the ceiling.

"So, does that mean I'm allowed you call you my girlfriend now?" I expected a smile and an emphatic yes, easy acquiescence that meant we could move on to the more enjoyable part of the evening.

Instead, I got a gust of air against my neck as she sighed and then pulled back up to look at me. "You never answered my question earlier. Are you...? I mean, the boxes are a pretty obvious clue, but are you really leaving?"

I could hear the hesitation in her voice, could see the nervous vulnerability in her eyes, and I wanted to soothe away the worry. My free hand lifted up to her neck, and I rubbed my thumb over her jaw slowly.

"Yes, I'm really leaving. I got a job working as a coach at a hockey camp for middle-schoolers up in Maine, just north of Portland. It doesn't start for another month, but I was planning on heading up in about two weeks to get moved into the apartment I'm renting for the summer. But it's just for the summer. I'll be back in August."

"Wait," she said quickly and then paused to consider something. "You aren't..." She pulled her lip into her mouth and bit it gently for just a second before releasing it to mutter, "Shit. I have something I need to tell you."

I pulled in a fortifying breath at the guilt that coated her words and then waited for her to go on. After taking a breath of her own, she did exactly that. "I switched my major. I'm starting the kinesiology program next winter, and I'm going to talk to Coach Miller about working with the team next year. I want to coach. I want to help kids like the kid I was realize their dreams."

My smile was wider than it had been all night. Even just talking about it had her lighting up, and I couldn't imagine how happy she was going to be actually *doing* it. And, God, I wanted to be around to see that.

"That's amazing, Caro. I mean, *seriously* amazing."

She smiled shyly, and glanced down at our entwined hands resting against my chest. "Thanks. I think so too. But that's not all."

"Okay," I prompted when she failed to go on. "What else is there?"

"A couple weeks ago, I called your dad. We had a meeting, and he helped me find a summer coaching job, at a camp for middle-schoolers. Outside of Portland."

She ducked her eyes guiltily, and as I scrambled to figure out if she was *actually* saying what I was pretty fucking sure she was saying, she began to ramble. "I realize now that he was underhandedly trying to bring us together, and maybe that's a conversation for another day, but if you want me to, I can call and tell them I won't be able to do it.

"Wait a second," I finally managed to interject. "Are you telling me that we'll be working together? Did you seriously get a job at AHC?"

"Yeah," she said slowly, "but, like I said, I can-"

I interrupted her when I launched myself off the mattress and rolled her back onto the bed, pressing my mouth to hers in a kiss that was filled with all the emotion I was barely managing to contain in my chest. I wanted to scream or shout or cry or set off fireworks—something, anything, to celebrate the moment. The very moment when the girl of my dreams gave herself to me. The moment she handed over her future and told me I could weave and wind it into my own, creating a new one—one of our own—together.

The kiss had started to turn wild when I pulled away enough to rest my forehead against hers. Dazed eyes met mine, and even without seeing her entire face, I could perfectly picture the smile I knew she wore. The smile that I knew I matched.

"I'm so unbelievably proud of you. And, for what it's worth, I think you're going to be an amazing coach."

Her eyes crinkled, and I knew her smile had widened even further. "It's worth quite a bit, as a matter of fact. Are you sure you're okay with us working together?"

I gently shook my head, which turned hers as well. "I can't believe you even think you have to ask that. I'm more than okay with us working together. I'm absolutely thrilled."

I leaned in to press a quick, closed-mouth kiss to her smiling lips, and then I pulled away before she had a chance to deepen it. "I seriously fucking love you, Caroline Olsen."

She giggled quietly, and it was the most beautiful sound I'd ever heard. For about four seconds at least, before her next words left her mouth, changing my entire perception of beauty forever. "And I *seriously* love you, James McCarthy."

Chapter Thirty Seven

# Caroline

WITH ONE LAST LOOK AROUND the room where I had spent the last nine months, the place that had been my home through some of the biggest changes of my life, I picked up the final box and turned toward the door.

This was it. Jimmy's car was loaded with my stuff. Most of it had already been moved into his dining room, where he'd told me I could store it until we got back from Maine and found a new apartment. We'd just finished gathering up the last of my things, since I'd be spending the night at his place, and we wanted to leave bright and early in the morning. To go to Maine. *Together*.

Part of me still couldn't believe it. When I'd gone to Jimmy's that day, I hadn't been thinking rationally. I hadn't been thinking about the fact that I myself was preparing to leave Charlottesville for the summer. I hadn't been thinking about anything beyond needing to get to him. I hadn't been thinking beyond needing to know if he was really going to be gone.

The truth was, when I thought I was about to lose him forever, I had panicked. I had been forced to realize that despite the time we spent apart, my feelings for him hadn't faded in the least. And even if his had—even if he had gotten over what we'd had together—I couldn't let him go without seeing him one last time.

Luckily for me, he hadn't given up on me.

Even *luckier* for me, Jimmy's dad was sneaky as hell.

Back when I had originally spoken to him about looking for a summer job, I had been hesitant to apply at ACH. I had friends in Charlottesville. Jimmy was also in Charlottesville, and even though at that point I wasn't willing to let myself have him, I still wanted to be close—not twelve hours away, practically in Canada. But Chris had been insistent that it was hands-down the best opportunity for me.

And then, when I still said I wasn't sure, he'd brought out the big guns. "Caroline, look. I don't know what happened between you and my son. Frankly, it's none of my business, but looking at you is like staring him in the face. You're lost, and I know that because I see it in him every day. So take the job. Take the summer to sort out your head. It's a great organization, and they'd love to have you. Go, and when you get back... Well, you can figure that out then."

Sitting there, listening to what amounted to a near stranger laying it out for me, I got pissed. That was my go-to defense mechanism when shit got real. I got pissed, and I walked out.

And then I went home. And I thought about what he had said. And I slept on it.

Then I woke up and called him. I told him to give me the number, and I made the call.

He had been right about a few things, including the fact that ACH seriously wanted to take me on, even when I explained that I had never coached before and told them that I hadn't been on or even really been *around* the ice for years.

They still wanted me.

So, I'd taken the job and decided that Chris had been right. A summer away from this town and memories of all things Jimmy would do me good. I'd get away, breathe fresh air, and come back ready to take on next year.

Now, and not for the first time since we'd discovered what he'd done, I sent up a silent word of thanks for his underhanded matchmaking.

"You ready, baby?" Jimmy's baritone called from beyond the door.

Carrying my box, I left the bedroom for the last time. "I think so, but let me just do one last walkthrough."

He smirked, probably because this was my third *"last walkthrough,"* but he nodded and took the box from my arms as I walked to the bathroom. It was empty, I knew it, but I still checked all the cabinets before turning back to the living room. Also empty, but I peered under the couch and end tables before heading into the kitchen to give it one last check. Jimmy said nothing—just stood at the door, box in hand, watching me with a small smile on his face.

"Okay," I told him once I was sure there was absolutely nothing left. "I'm ready."

I moved toward him to pull open the door, but he stopped me with a hand on my wrist. It slid down, so he could slide his fingers between mine, giving them a gentle squeeze. "You okay?"

I considered it. I was about to embark on a totally new adventure, one I had no clue if I'd succeed at. I was also about to be working with my boyfriend, who hadn't really been my boyfriend for all that long, even though he also sort of had been. But, really, we'd only been technically together for two weeks, and now we were going to be living together and working together five days a week. So that was sure to be interesting. On top of all that, I was homeless—or I would be, just as soon as we got back from Maine. Jimmy had assured me that I could stay with him for as long as I needed to, but, as a worrier, I was a little worried.

Still, I knew that we were solid. I was excited about where my life seemed to be headed. And even though I knew better than anyone how quickly life could change from second to second, I was also content in the knowledge that I was happy and that I finally knew what I wanted. More than that, I was finally ready to let myself have it.

So I gave his fingers a squeeze back and then smiled and nodded.

"I'm great."

"Do you mind if we stop at the rink real quick?" Jimmy asked a few minutes after we'd pulled out of my apartment complex. "Dad said he had something for me and asked me to swing by to get it."

"No, that's fine."

He gave me a smile and steered us across town until we were pulling into the lot out front of the rink. Jimmy found an open spot near the door and turned the car off before we both climbed out. I met him in front of the car, and he grabbed my hand before leading us over the sidewalk and through the automatic doors.

Passing through the foyer, we set one foot into the open area where the ice was, and then...

"SURPRISE!"

I stopped short, pulling Jimmy backwards as I began to tilt back. Thankfully, his hand left mine, and he pulled me against his side with a strong grip at my waist. Once I was sure I wasn't going to fall on my ass, I looked up and took in the room full of people.

I saw Jimmy's parents first. They stood to the side, separate from the crowd, with a grinning Jack between them. My eyes continued to move, and I spotted Jen and Nate, standing close together and both smiling like crazy. I saw a few guys I knew from the hockey team as well, and then a bunch of people I'd never met before.

I let Jimmy pull me over to his parents first. While Jimmy reached out a hand toward his dad, his mom came forward and wrapped me up in a tight hug. I would have been surprised, but Jimmy had told me that his mom had been thrilled to hear we were "back together," as he put it. I returned her embrace and only loosened my arms when she pulled back to grab onto my forearms with both hands.

"Take care of my boy, okay?"

At the emotion in her voice, I felt my own throat grow hot, and I nodded, but she wasn't done. "He'll try to take care of you, and he'll give it everything he's got, always thinking it's his job, but he deserves to have someone looking out for him for a change, and, Caroline, as his mother, I'm absolutely thrilled that that person is you."

I couldn't find the words to tell her just how much that meant to me, so I just swallowed thickly and nodded again before saying, "I'll do my best."

She smiled and then stepped back to slide toward Jimmy as Chris approached me. "You ready?" he asked gruffly, and I smiled.

"I hope so."

He stared down at me for a moment and then slowly, and looking just like his son when he did it, he smiled. "You're ready." And, apparently, that was that because then he claimed his wife, pulling her away from Jimmy.

Jimmy gave Jack a fist bump, and I stepped forward to do the same. Then I lost my breath because Jack completely ignored my extended hand and stepped forward to wrap me in a tentative hug. I barely had time to lose the shock and wrap my arms around him in return before he scurried back to his mom's side. My gaze caught the open amazement on all the adult McCarthys faces, but they hid it relatively quickly, so I matched their casual expressions and let the moment go.

Jimmy led me toward Jen and Nate, and, once there, the team descended with congratulations and well wishes. I focused on my friends, who both wrapped me up in tight hugs. I returned the embraces and memorized them, not quite ready to let go, knowing I'd be gone soon. Even though I knew we would talk—knew I most likely wouldn't get through a single day without a text or call from at least one of them—I also knew I was going to miss the two of them like crazy.

We finally stopped hugging and crying, and Jimmy claimed my hand again, pulling me further across the floor to a guy and girl I didn't know.

"Caro, this is my friend Ash and his girlfriend Parker," Jimmy introduced us, and I shook both of their hands.

"It's nice to meet you," Parker told me.

"Yeah, finally," Ash added with a look at Jimmy that contradicted his easy smile.

"Shut up," Jimmy volleyed good-naturedly before asking, "Is Marco here?"

Ash's smile fell, and he shook his head. "I called, but I couldn't get ahold of him. And he never called me back…"

I could tell by Ash's voice that he didn't have a good feeling about this. Even if his body language wasn't radiating his concern, Jimmy had told me just a few days earlier that he was worried about Marco— that he'd been hard to get in touch with. I knew he was concerned about going away when he didn't know what was going on with his friend, but, according to Jimmy, Ash shared his concerns, and he'd promised to keep an eye on Marco while Jimmy was gone.

Clearly, it wasn't going all that well.

"I'm sure he's fine," Ash finally said. "And, anyway, tonight's about you guys. Don't worry about him."

Jimmy nodded, even though I knew he still would. Regardless, he pulled me back to his side and slid his hand around my waist to rest at the waistband of my jeans.

"You're right. It's our last night," he said as his mouth lowered until it was right at my ear, where he whispered, "Let's have some fun."

It was late. We had stayed longer at the party than either of us had intended, but it had been so much fun, we hadn't wanted to leave. After the tense but short conversation about Marco, the rest of the night went smoothly, except for one minor incident that was really only uncomfortable for me. That was when Ash proclaimed he'd finally realized why I looked so familiar to him. Something about the way he said it gave me a bad feeling, and that premonitory reaction was justified when he started telling everyone around how I used to spend hours sitting at the rink.

This, of course, was not missed by Jimmy, who, when he finally got the whole story from me, thought it was hilarious. I didn't appreciate his laughter, but he took the sting from it when his face dropped to mine, and he said quietly through his lingering smile, "You were *so* gone for me." His quiet voice and soft expression turned the teasing line into something else entirely.

Which is why I looked at him, and, without a trace of humor, replied, "I was. I still am."

Then, he kissed me. And it was not a kiss that should have been had in public, surrounded by our friends and his family. It was a kiss that stirred my blood and poured heat into my veins. By the time he'd pulled away, my hands were wrapped around his neck, holding him to me, and my body was pressed tightly to his.

And that was about when I decided I was ready to head home.

We made our rounds and said our goodbyes. And we made them count since this was it. After this, we were gone—on to the next adventure in our lives.

Once we'd given out hugs and handshakes to everyone, Jimmy led me to the door and took me home. His car was still filled with my stuff, so even though we were both anxious to get to bed, we unloaded the car so we wouldn't have to worry about it in the morning. It took a few trips to get the last of my boxes stacked inside.

When that was done, Jimmy grabbed my hand and, without another word, led me to his bedroom. Slowly, methodically, he undressed me, first pulling my shirt up and over my head until he was able to toss it away. After a slow kiss, his hands moved to the waistband of my jeans and those too were carefully pulled down over my hips. Dropping to his knees, Jimmy moved one of my hands to his shoulder and let me use him to balance as he carefully extricated my prosthesis from the denim. Slowly, he rose to standing again. When his hands landed just above the fabric of my underwear, I felt the heat there like a brand.

Gently, he pushed me back until I had no choice but to sit on the mattress. Once I was seated, his hands slowly moved to the prosthesis. One thumb pressed the button that released the suction, and then he was pulling the appendage away.

Maybe I was crazy, because if you had asked me ahead of time, I would have thought it'd be awkward as hell, but there was so much intimacy in the way Jimmy performed the simple act of helping me get ready for bed that I felt the tears hit my eyes before I could stop them.

If he noticed, he didn't say a word because as soon as he'd safely set my leg on the floor, his hands went back to my thigh, and he rolled away the liner and sock as well, baring the rippled flesh below.

I sat on the edge of the bed, expecting his hands to go to his own clothes, now that I was all but naked. Instead, he dropped to his knees in front of me and braced his palms on my thighs. His head was bowed, and I felt his gaze boring into the scars that ran across my flesh. I didn't say a word, too unsure of what exactly was happening—what he was thinking about.

We sat in silence for a few long minutes before he opened his mouth and clued me in. "When we were apart, I used to think about what your life would be like right now if the accident hadn't happened. And I thought about what my life would be like. And I know it makes me an asshole, but I'm grateful because I don't think I could have gotten here without you."

"You're not an asshole," I told him quietly, once I was able to find my voice. "I'm grateful too." I took a shallow breath and then went on, "I think a part of me will always wonder what could have been. But I'm glad I'm here, and I'm glad you're with me. I'm glad I found you."

His arms went around my waist, and his head landed on my chest as he wrapped me up in a tight embrace. My hands dropped to his head, and for a moment I just ran my fingers through his hair. Then, I used my grip there to lightly tug him back far enough that I could drop my mouth to his.

That was all it took.

Jimmy took over the kiss, and it went wild. His clothes disappeared, we moved up the bed, and then he was on top of me with nothing between us.

I held my breath and felt him do the same as he slowly slid inside. When he finally stopped, filling me completely, his forehead dropped to mine, lips just barely brushing my mouth, and his eyes met mine. And in them, I saw all his love for me. I saw peace and happiness and contentment. Like he had finally found what he had been searching for.

And I knew exactly how he felt because I felt exactly the same way. He had given me everything I wanted because he'd given me the strength and the belief in myself to go after what I needed and claim it for my own.

Just like I had claimed him.

"I love you," I told him, my lips brushing his in a feather-light kiss.

I felt his lips move, and his eyes tilted with his smile as he said, "I love you too."

"Good," I replied, and his grin widened as I continued, "Now, make love to me."

And then, just like he always did, Jimmy gave me *exactly* what I wanted.

## Author's Note

I have waited for this moment for over a year now. In truth, this was a hard book for me to write. Partly because, while working on it, I ended up pregnant with my third son, who has kept me on my toes since he first made his presence known. But it was also hard because I, like Caroline, at times can be my own worst enemy. I put so much pressure on myself to get this story *right* that it made it hard for me to function.

They call it a sophomore slump for a reason.

Really though, despite my stress and panic, I am ultimately so insanely proud of this story, and I can't describe how much I love it. And I hope you, the reader, love it as well. Because really, we all have things that can hold us back from chasing our dreams. Whether those hang ups and roadblocks are physical or mental, whether their of your own making or completely out of your control, I am proof, this *story* is proof, that if you persevere and you hold tight, you can accomplish anything you truly set your mind to.

Now, a note about artistic license.

I use it. I wouldn't say a lot, but I am not afraid of indulging in the reorganization of some facts when I deem it necessary.

The University of Virginia is a real place, with real people and a real ACCHL hockey team. I did my best to portray that all as accurately as possible, but if you happen to notice a discrepancy, know that it's probably there intentionally. And if it's not, then all I have to say is: No one's perfect. *Especially* me.

Lastly, if you enjoyed this book (or even if you didn't,) I'd ask you to consider leaving a review. They're so incredibly helpful, not just for authors but for readers as well.

Reviewers keep the book community alive. To anyone who takes a moment to share their thoughts: **thank you.**

## Acknowledgments

There is no way to possibly thank everyone that had an impact on this book. It would take days and days and honestly, half of the people responsible don't even know I exist. People like J.K. Rowling, Colleen Hoover, Jennifer Armentrout, Cora Carmack, Kristen Ashley, E.L. James, Kristen Callahan, Jamie McGuire, Sarah J. Maas, Megan Erickson… The list goes on and on, but the one thing they all have in common is that they opened up a whole new world to me. Hundreds of worlds, really, but the most important world they expanded was my own. They inspired me and set me on the course I'm currently following. To the superstars and the indie authors, to anyone who has ever written a book that transported me to another world, I thank you. You have changed my life in a way I will forever be grateful for.

To my husband, Jude, you are the best friend I've ever had and the best dream I've ever realized. Thank you for giving me the support and tools to make this my life. Some days I still can't believe it.

To my other boys, you drive me crazy but I wouldn't have it any other way. Thank you for loving me even when I lock myself away to play with people who don't actually exist.

To my biggest fan, Mom, your reviews will always be my favorite. Thank you thank you thank you.

To Melinda Clemmer, the greatest editor a girl could ask for. I am so grateful and so glad that you decided to take this journey with me and I sincerely hope we get to do it again and again.

To Jen, who didn't just inspire a name but who inspired an entire friendship. You are the Jen to my Caroline. You call me out, you keep my sane, you love my kids and you always have my back. What more could I possibly ask for?

To my writing group, and anyone and everyone who read this, either in pieces or its entirety, in its early stages, thank you for your excitement and your criticism. I wouldn't be the writer I am without you all.

Lastly, but maybe most importantly, I want to thank you. Whether this is the first book of mine you've read or not, thank you for your support. Thank you for your encouragement. Thank you for listening and giving even half a damn. Authors couldn't do what they do without readers and that makes you invaluable. I am eternally grateful.

K C O'Neill is a full-time Mom, a part-time editor, and a writer down to her soul. After spending too many years in a job that wasn't nearly creative enough for her liking, she left to spend the days writing about the people living in her head and chasing the two demon-toddlers who've invaded her home. It's hectic, it's loud, and it's messy, but it's life, and it's beautiful, and she wouldn't have it any other way.

If you want to drop a line or have a chat, you can reach her online at katrinaoneill.com; On Goodreads: K.C. O'Neill; On Facebook: KCOneillWrites; On Twitter: @TrinaMarieOh

Curious about Ash and Parker?
Check out their story in Just Parker, available now!

Stay tuned for news about book three in the series.
Title and cover to be revealed soon!